Acclaim

"One of the best books I have read in a very long time. I cannot recommend this book highly enough, but be warned, it is not for the faint-hearted and the haunting scenes faithfully reflect what could and did happen and is still happening in more than one country right now. *Hunting the Devil* might shock you and shake you out of your daily cotton wool cocoon, but it's true to life, and I applaud the author for bringing the horrendous subject of genocide to light." - Lucinda E. Clarke, author of *Amie: African Adventure*

"In vivid and deeply textured scenes, Suanne Schafer creates a compassionate and strong female physician who endures horror and becomes a witness in the UN genocide trials, bringing justice to Rwandan victims. *Hunting the Devil's* "eyewitness to history" approach is by turns enthralling, horrifying, and ultimately heartbreaking." - Alicia Rasley, author of *The Year She Fell*

"*Hunting the Devil* is a tightly-written, riveting novel layered with finely-crafted characters, the exploration of racism, and the horror of war's effects on individuals. Schafer has crafted an exciting tale that culminates with a daring climatic courtroom scene that will resonate and remain with readers long after the last page." - C. S. Fuqua, author of *Walking after Midnight* and *Alabama Musicians: Musical Heritage from the Heart of Dixie*

"Someone told me *Hunting the Devil* was a tour-de-force and while I agree, I think that summary needs a few more words. Gut-wrenching. Honest. Powerful. This is a story of a woman who claws her way back from the worst kind of adversity with no explanations and no apologies. Schafer pulled me in and kept me enthralled to the very end." - Dianne Freeman, author of *A Lady's Guide to Etiquette and Murder*

"This gripping novel travels the highs and lows of humanity and keeps readers on the edge of their seats. With powerful scenes and the ability to artistically weave the beautiful with the traumatizing, Ms. Schafer has written a novel that transcends time." - Holly Castillo, author of *The Texas Legacy* series

Praise for Suanne Schafer's debut novel,

A Different Kind of Fire:

Ruby Louise Schmidt is a splendid and fearless heroine you'll be rooting for every step of the way. - Wendy Tokunaga, author of *Postcards from Tokyo*

"I was amazed by Suanne Schafer's poetic and laconic turns of phrase. She has the gift of being simultaneously ornate and succinct, which is no easy task." - Joshua Mohr, author of *Sirens* and one of *O Magazine*'s *Top 10 Reads of 2009* and a *San Francisco Chronicle* best-selling author

Suanne Schafer's *A Different Kind of Fire* is a powerful story of a Gilded Age artist who brooks convention both in her art and her love. Read this book: It has both the depth of emotion of a modernist novel and the epic scope of a historical saga. - Alicia Rasley, author of *The Year She Fell*, Amazon bestseller

In Ruby Schmidt, Suanne Schafer has created a remarkable heroine, one who faces the challenges of time and convention with a vivid spirit and a sense of emotional adventure. It's a pleasure to follow her as she pursues her art, explores her loves and determines to live life on no terms but her own. - *Angela Pneuman*, author of *Lay It on My Heart* and *Home Remedies*

A sweeping portrait of forbidden passion, the talented and courageous Ruby Schmidt is torn between the Texas land and rancher that she loves and the art and the woman that give her life meaning. This belongs on every 'must read' list! - Emily Mims, author of *A Gift of Trust* and *For the Thrill of It*

Writer Suanne Schafer spins a unique tale of a turn of the 20th century Texas heroine and her way of artistic expression. Her paintings shock her contemporaries and the love she's drawn to shocks herself. *A Different Kind of Fire* depicts the journey of a determined woman to meet life on her own terms. - Pamela Morsi, USAToday Bestselling Author of *The Cotton Queen* and *Bitsy's Bait & BBQ*

Hunting the Devil

Suanne Schafer

Published by Waldorf Publishing
2140 Hall Johnson Road
#102-345
Grapevine, Texas 76051
www.WaldorfPublishing.com

Hunting the Devil

ISBN: 978-1-64316-597-4
Library of Congress Control Number: 2018943959

Copyright © 2019

All rights reserved. No part of this book may be reproduced or transmitted in any form or by any means whatsoever without express written permission from the author, except in the case of brief quotations embodied in critical articles and reviews. Please refer all pertinent questions to the publisher. All rights reserved. No part of this book may be reproduced or transmitted in any form or by any means, electronic or mechanical, including photocopying, recording, or by an information storage and retrieval system except by a reviewer who may quote brief passages in a review to be printed in a magazine or newspaper without permission in writing from the publisher.

DISCLAIMER: This is a work of fiction. Names, characters, businesses, places, events and incidents are either the products of the author's imagination or used in a fictitious manner. Any resemblance to actual persons, living or dead, or actual events is purely coincidental.

Disclaimer

Hunting the Devil was written after raising my adopted son in a white world and watching his efforts to integrate his two heritages. He admits to being an Oreo, black on the outside, but white on the inside. On a trip to Africa when he was a teenager, rather than connecting with his roots as he'd anticipated, he was startled to be considered a *mzungu,* a white person, which further exacerbated his identity issues.

That said, *Hunting the Devil* is a work of fiction. Names, characters, businesses, places, events, and incidents are either the products of the author's imagination or used in a fictitious manner. Any resemblance to actual persons, living or dead, or actual events is purely coincidental except where, for the sake of verisimilitude, certain historical figures have been incorporated. Their words, actions, and interactions with the characters in this book are derived purely from the author's imagination.

I tried to remain faithful to history but occasionally shift events around for dramatic license.

The Physicians Aid and Relief for Africa (PARFA) is a fictional foreign aid and humanitarian organization providing medical care throughout Africa. Dr. Hemings's clinic in Kirehe, a real town in southeastern Rwanda, is fictitious and predates the building of an actual hospital by a decade.

Angel of Mercy Hospital is a fictional hospital in the heart of Philadelphia within walking distance of Rittenhouse Square. Memorial Hospital also exists only in this author's imagination and is located somewhere in the Kensington area of Philadelphia. Hymie's Delicatessen and the Llanarch Diner are real and worth a visit.

Hunting the Devil
is dedicated to my son, Max,
with hopes that—within his lifetime—
racism will become as extinct as the dinosaurs.

****

In recognition of aid workers around the world
who fight disease and injustice against crazy odds
and under insufferable conditions.

Acknowledgements

Much appreciation to the kind souls listed below for their contributions to *Hunting the Devil*:

My editor, Alicia Rasley, who polished my words and helped me wrestle this devil into its final form.

San Antonio Romance Authors (SARA), the members of which critiqued many drafts.

Women's Fiction Writers Association (WFWA) members, LaDonna Ockinga and Martha Sessums, who also provided valuable insight.

Elizabeth Kracht of Kimberley Cameron Associates, who, after reading an early chapter, told me it needed to be darker. I think I succeeded.

My beta readers and reviewers, all of whom were most generous with their time and the quality of their assessments: Willa Blair, James Burnham, Holly Castillo, Lucinda E. Clarke, Camille DiMaio, Dianne Freeman, Christopher Fuqua, Michael Hardesty, Gail Hart, Kathleen Heer, Janalyn Knight, Kristine Mietzner, Alicia Rasley, Jeanne Schuster Tarrants, Tara West, and Guinotte Wise.

My sensitivity readers, Zandra Stothers and Joanne Godley, M.D.

My language coaches, Cynthia Bull, Céline Poligné, and Cathy Staats.

Kathleen Heer, D.O., who filled in the OB-GYN details I've forgotten since my residency.

*As soon as they [women] begin to speak, at the same time as they're taught their name,
they can be taught that their territory is black: because you are Africa, you are black. Your continent is dark.
Dark is dangerous. You can't see anything in the dark, you're afraid. Don't move, you might fall. Most of all, don't go into the forest. And so we have internalized this horror of the dark."*

Hélène Cixous,
French feminist writer and literary critic

Table of Contents

Part I
Rwanda and Tanzania

Chapter One
Dr. Jessica Hemings *3*

Chapter Two
Jessica *10*

Chapter Three
Michel Fournier *15*

Chapter Four
Dr. Thomas Powell *19*

Chapter Five
Jessica *22*

Chapter Six
Jessica *28*

Chapter Seven
Jessica *35*

Chapter Eight
Jessica *43*

Chapter Nine
Tom *49*

Chapter Ten
Jessica *52*

Chapter Eleven
Jessica *59*

Chapter Twelve
Jessica *66*

Chapter Thirteen
Jessica *74*

Chapter Fourteen
Michel *80*

Chapter Fifteen
Tom *84*

Chapter Sixteen
Jessica *87*

Chapter Seventeen
Jessica *94*

Chapter Eighteen
Jessica *102*

Chapter Nineteen
Jessica *110*

Chapter Twenty
Jessica *117*

Chapter Twenty-One
Michel *126*

Chapter Twenty-Two
Michel *129*

Chapter Twenty-Three
Michel *136*

Chapter Twenty-Four
Jessica *143*

Chapter Twenty-Five
Michel *146*

Chapter Twenty-Six
Tom *153*

Chapter Twenty-Seven
Jessica *158*

Chapter Twenty-Eight
Michel *165*

Chapter Twenty-Nine
Jessica *167*

Chapter Thirty
Jessica *172*

Chapter Thirty-One
Jessica *180*

Chapter Thirty-Two
Jessica *187*

Chapter Thirty-Three
Jessica *193*

Chapter Thirty-Four
Jessica *200*

Chapter Thirty-Five
Jessica *206*

Chapter Thirty-Six
Michel *212*

Chapter Thirty-Seven
Jessica *219*

Chapter Thirty-Eight
Jessica *225*

Chapter Thirty-Nine
Michel *235*

Part II
United States

Chapter Forty
Jessica *241*

Chapter Forty-One
Tom *247*

Chapter Forty-Two
Jessica *249*

Chapter Forty-Three
Jessica *257*

Chapter Forty-Four
Tom *263*

Chapter Forty-Five
Michel *270*

Chapter Forty-Six
Tom *277*

Chapter Forty-Seven
Jessica *279*

Chapter Forty-Eight
Michel *288*

Chapter Forty-Nine
Jessica *290*

Part III
Rwanda and Tanzania

Chapter Fifty
Jessica *303*

Chapter Fifty-One
Jessica *311*

Chapter Fifty-Two
Jessica *322*

Chapter Fifty-Three
Tom *328*

Chapter Fifty-Four
Jessica *335*

Chapter Fifty-Five
Jessica *340*

Chapter Fifty-Six
Jessica *350*

Chapter Fifty-Seven
Jessica *354*

Chapter Fifty-Eight
Jessica *361*

Chapter Fifty-Nine
Jessica *365*

Chapter Sixty
Jessica *373*

Chapter Sixty-One
Jessica *378*

Chapter Sixty-Two
Jessica *385*

Chapter Sixty-Three
Tom *395*

Chapter Sixty-Four
Jessica *398*

Chapter Sixty-Five
Tom *407*

Chapter Sixty-Six
Jessica *410*

Chapter Sixty-Seven
Tom *416*

Chapter Sixty-Eight
Jessica *423*

Chapter Sixty-Nine
Michel *429*

Chapter Seventy
Jessica *435*

Chapter Seventy-One
Michel *442*

Chapter Seventy-Two
Tom *444*

Chapter Seventy-Three
Michel *446*

Chapter Seventy-Four
Tom *448*

Chapter Seventy-Five
Tom *456*

Chapter Seventy-Six
Jessica *462*

Chapter Seventy-Seven
Michel *464*

Chapter Seventy-Eight
Tom *468*

Chapter Seventy-Nine
Jessica *475*

Chapter Eighty
Jessica *485*

Chapter Eighty-One
Tom *489*

Chapter Eighty-Two
Michel *494*

Chapter Eighty-Three
Michel *497*

Chapter Eighty-Four
Jessica *501*

Glossary 505

**Map of Jessica's Escape
through Rwanda and Tanzania** 508

**Book Club Questions for
Hunting the Devil** 510

Author Bio 512

Part I

Rwanda and Tanzania

Chapter One

Dr. Jessica Hemings

Kirehe, Rwanda, April 11, 1994

Powered by a potent mixture of hatred and fear, Jess raced up one hill, down the next in the pitch-black night. She couldn't stop. Branches sliced her arms and legs. Stones bruised her soles. With every gasp, a side stitch lanced through her right ribs.

Jess glanced back. With that distraction, her feet tangled. She stumbled down an embankment. Her feet fought for purchase on the water-slicked slope. Rocks rolled beneath her, their rumble audible above the rain. While sliding down the gully on her belly, she grabbed a tree trunk to break her fall. She pulled herself semi-upright and clutched her aching sides. As she caught her breath, she glanced around. The thick brush surrounding her provided good cover. She could rest a moment.

After making so much racket, she held her breath and listened. No sounds of pursuit. She wasn't sure when she'd last heard the baying of the dogs tracking her. Maybe her pursuers had given up and returned to her clinic. For the moment, she was safe.

She let her racing heart slow. Only then did she realize her right hand was empty. She'd lost the photograph of her children during her plunge. Darkness masked the surrounding landscape. She'd never find it now. Her search would have to wait 'til first light. She closed her hand, now as empty as her heart.

Two years ago, when Dr. Jessica Hemings had volunteered for a medical mission, she never dreamed she'd be fleeing for her life among the *mille collines*, the thousand hills of Rwanda. Now, to survive, she had to get as far as possible from her clinic in Kirehe. The *Interahamwe*, the Rwandan paramilitary group, lay behind her. To the east, the Rusumo Falls Bridge that spanned the Kagera River led to Tanzania—and safety.

Jess jerked awake, her extremities flailing. Her eyes snapped open. Shrill shrieks still pained her ears. Wisps of dream-images faded. Then came the awareness that she'd uttered the cries. After a moment's disorientation, she remembered where she was. And why. Exhausted from all the recent happenings, she wasn't surprised she'd slept.

During her respite, the eastern sky had lightened. Through tree branches, the rising sun made the fog resemble watery milk. Motionless, Jess remained hidden, listening intently, hoping no one had heard her. She caught only the whisper of the wind, scattered bird calls, and the sporadic drip of water from the leaves. No human sounds. She slumped with relief.

Her body ached—every bone, every muscle, every inch of skin—grim reminders of what she'd endured. She ventured a look downward. Thanks to Cyprien Gatera, a Hutu colonel, she wore only a brown scrub top and a polka-dot bra, both ripped down the center front. He'd confiscated her pants and shoes, believing nudity would prevent her escape. Her brown skin and dark scrub shirt had camouflaged her during the night, but after her tumble down the hillside, red mud stained her clothes. She tried to lift her bra, but dried blood glued it to her chest. Insect bites covered her body. Black and blue marks shadowed her skin. Flies circled inky scabs. She grimaced and flapped her hands in a vain effort to shoo them.

Next, she studied her feet. The muddy bottoms of her ladybug socks were shredded. Wincing, she peeled them off. Cuts and bruises covered her feet. Without shoes, the ladybugs were the only protection her feet had, so she turned them heel-side up and put them back on.

Suddenly Jess caught the distant sounds of men's voices and the underlying grumble of a straining motor. She wriggled through the brush and peeked over the top of the ravine. A farm truck, packed with men rather than vegetables, chugged over the hill. Clothed in bright *dashikis* and beating their machetes in a steady rhythm against the sides of the truck, they might have been local farmers heading to work in their fields, but their raucous chants "Hutu *pawa*" and "Exterminate the *iyenzi*," revealed their identity and their mission. *Iyenzi* or "cockroaches" was the Hutu derogatory term for Tutsis.

They were coming from the direction she needed to go. Damn! The militia stood both behind and ahead of her. She burrowed more deeply into the thicket and prayed for invisibility, remaining utterly still until their sounds faded.

For the first time since her escape, she had time to plan her next move. Her wilderness skills were minimal. Hell, she hadn't even been a Girl Scout. Somewhere she'd read that moss grew on the north side of trees. Was the reverse true in the southern hemisphere? Here in the forest, moss grew lavishly on both sides. She had nothing to gauge her direction besides sunrise and sunset.

She'd survive, though, damn it. She needed to use her brain and her knowledge of basic human essentials.

Her high-priced medical education was useless.

Oxygen. No problem. She was breathing.

Water. The rain had stopped, but water dribbled from branches overhead and trailed down her forehead and nose. She licked her dry lips and opened her mouth to receive the drops. In April, the height of the long rainy season, water was readily available, but she was concerned about its potability. Groundwater in Rwanda teemed with microorganisms guaranteed to give her dysentery. She preferred life-threatening diarrhea, though, to the fate she'd escaped.

Humans could live longer without food than water, but her last meal had been over twenty-four hours ago—her stomach grumbled in agreement—and being on the run burned calories at a rapid clip. Maxing out at 110 pounds, she didn't have much reserve left.

Shelter was of less concern than avoiding detection. The high altitude meant that at night she'd be uncomfortably cool in her scrub top but not cold enough to worry about hypothermia.

With a grimace, Jess fought down memories of Gatera and what he'd done to her two children, to her clinic staff, to her patients, to her. Her throat closed at the memory of the blood on the wall. Blood on the floor. Blood on her. She drew those thoughts into a tight ball of black-hot hate. No matter how long it took, she'd get the bastard. Even if she had to kill him herself. In visions incompatible with her role as a physician, yet disturbingly satisfying, she hacked him to bits with a machete.

Jess had been aware of growing unrest in Rwanda, but the US Embassy and PARFA, the relief agency she worked for, assured her she would be safe. When Hutu extremists began killing their political opponents,

Americans weren't being targeted. By the time the American Embassy called advising her to evacuate, it was too late. Gatera had already commandeered her clinic.

She crawled from her hiding place. Her tender body made every movement an effort. As she stood, a wave of pain made her wish she'd acted more slowly. With her first step, she winced. Her upside-down socks were no help.

Again conscious of how little she wore, Jess tugged the ragged edges of her scrub top together. Naked otherwise, she was vulnerable to the rampaging *Interahamwe*. For that matter, to any male who happened by. Mentally she added shoes and clothes, along with food and some sort of weapon, to her list of supplies to steal.

Before she did anything, though, she needed to find the photo of her kids. It was all that remained of them, her only proof of their existence. It had been in her hand before she fell, so she searched the trajectory of her fall. The flickering light through the trees glanced off the forest floor. Several times she investigated what turned out to be downed leaves. At last, a sunbeam reflected off the white paper, and she found the picture, limp and soggy from exposure to the overnight rain. She picked up the fragile photograph, trying to brand her babies' faces—their happy faces, not the horrific visions from the day before yesterday—into her memory before their image disintegrated. The paper melted in her hand.

Before she could drop the remnants of her boys, before she could release her own anguished cry, an animal-like wail resounded through the forest. She couldn't tell if the wind had carried a voice through nearby trees or if her imagination was working overtime.

Fearing Gatera's men might find her, she raced to

her prior hiding place. Her heart galloped. Her breathing escalated. Her fingers tingled. Her world blackened. She recognized the signs of an impending anxiety attack. She needed to rein in her terror and grief and remain calm. Panic would lead her straight into Gatera's hands.

Inhale. Hold. Exhale.

Slowly, her hysteria subsided. To survive, Jess had to be hyperaware of her surroundings. A sudden dearth of bird song might be the only clue her enemy approached. She allowed the sounds of birds chirping, animals scuttling in the brush, the scent of the wet earth and fallen leaves, the whispering of the trees themselves, to fill her senses so she'd be conscious of any changes. Defiantly, she straightened her shoulders. She'd endure—somehow—to beat her enemy at his own game and bring him to justice.

Again, a shriek disturbed the sounds of the forest. A wild animal? She shook her head. No lethal big game remained around here. Lions and other large predators were limited to the northeastern game preserves. She crouched behind several boulders. The sound grew nearer. Cautiously she peeked from behind the rocks.

Women dressed in colorful fabrics scurried by. Some carried babies on their backs, balanced toddlers on one hip, or dragged youngsters by the hand. Others balanced baskets of food on their heads or pushed handcarts loaded with household goods, produce, and chickens. A mother glanced hastily behind her before popping her nipple into her wailing child's mouth to hush it. Urged on by their mothers, older children tugged goats or carried jerry cans of water or bunches of bananas as big as they were. This wasn't the usual band of women carrying hoes and rakes and chatting merrily as they headed to work the fields. These were refugees, loaded with their worldly goods, fleeing the *Interahamwe*.

Jess thought of joining them, but they were moving away from the Tanzanian border. Where did they think they could go to escape the militia?

When the women passed, Jess slipped out of hiding. Gatera would expect her to head east. Limping, she turned north, remaining in the forest as much as possible. Later she'd circle back toward Tanzania. As she crested one *colline* and looked toward the next, a cloud of smoke stained the sky an oily black. Another burnt village. Maybe the women had fled from it. If the *Interahamwe* had already passed through, Jess could safely scavenge for the provisions she needed.

Her calves aching from climbing, Jess followed the smoke to the village. She dodged behind trees and bushes to remain out of sight as she approached. On the outskirts, she paused, doing a visual reconnaissance. Laundry, fluttering from tree branches, gave a sense of normalcy offset by an unnatural silence. Not a single human voice. Not even the twittering of birds. The humidity pressed the odor of burnt meat close to the ground. Only the crackling of flames from burning huts reached her ears. Oddly, not every house was aflame. The *Interahamwe*, guided by collaborators, only burned Tutsi homes.

Jess waited for several more minutes before slipping through the narrow space between two rough mud-brick houses and peeking into the main street. She stopped in shock.

Chapter Two

Jessica

Kirehe, Rwanda, April 12, 1994
Bodies—men, women, children, babies—were strewn haphazardly about, left where they'd been cut down by machetes. Those villagers who'd tried to run were mutilated. The *Interahamwe* cut the tendons in their victims' legs so they couldn't run, then amputated their extremities one at a time to inflict the most possible pain. Blood stained the rust-colored earth a darker red. Women, their clothing flung above their waists, had been raped and their breasts sliced off before being killed.

Jess couldn't understand the slaughter. Among her patients, as many Hutu looked Tutsi as Tutsi looked Hutu. Tutsis were as poor as Hutus. Their houses were identical. The terraced fields they farmed identical. The lack of health care and education identical. She often couldn't tell the two groups apart. Sometimes the locals couldn't either. Ethnicity was based on identity cards the Belgians issued in 1933 that classified every individual as Tutsi, Hutu, or Twa. Sixty years later, those same ID cards allowed *génocidaires* to readily identify their prey.

She closed her eyes, trying to shut out the sight. As she opened them, something moved in the periphery of her field of vision. She blinked and refocused.

A dog.

She breathed a sigh of relief until the canine approached a body, sniffed, then buried his teeth in the corpse's open wound. Unable to contain her horror, Jess shuddered at the ripping sound of flesh being torn from another human. She grabbed a large rock. Her first toss missed. Blindly, she hurled another stone. Again, she missed—barely. The dog raised his head, turned toward her, and snarled. Her third stone struck the animal on the flank. With a yelp and a menacing growl, he slunk into the forest.

Fists clenched, she forced herself to remain in place. She couldn't do any good if captured.

When nothing else moved, she ventured into the main street, immediately checking for survivors. With each corpse, she closed eyes frozen in horror.

Jess knelt beside body #23 and palpated a spread-eagled woman's carotid artery. A moan almost too low to hear snagged her attention. Quickly, she glanced around for the source. Nothing.

Again, the moan.

The sound came from a boy lying face down next to the corpse. Jess searched for his heartbeat. It was weak and thready. She tenderly turned him over.

Snakes writhed beneath his body.

Jess recoiled. Then shook her head. Not snakes. Worse. Far worse. His intestines spilled from a deep slash in his abdomen, and the boy's genitals had been amputated. He'd dragged himself to his mother's side, embedding dirt into his wounds and leaving a trail of blood.

Her guts clenched. He was only eight or nine years old. Who would do such vile things to a child? The militia killed simply because people were Tutsi or Hutu moderates who opposed the extremists. She understood the politics, the history between Hutu and Tutsi, but couldn't conceive of the mutilation of fellow human beings. Leaders who devised such atrocities should be shot.

Jess glanced at her filthy hands. No way to wash them. But it didn't matter. She had no treatment for the boy, no surgical instruments, no antibiotics. Life wasn't fair. Despite years of medical training, she couldn't save him. He was doomed to a painful death.

She ran her hands over the boy's head. His whimpers lessened at her touch. The Hippocratic Oath flashed though her mind. *Do no harm.* If she stayed to care for him, she risked recapture. He was too big for her to carry. Transporting him to safety would inflict more pain without improving his prognosis. Yet she couldn't abandon him. She shook her head. Though he had little time left to live, he shouldn't suffer. Only one option remained.

She wiped tear streaks from the boy's face then pulled his head into her lap. "I promise you'll join your family soon." Visions of her year-old twins flashed before her. They'd had the same smooth cheeks and innocent eyes as this boy. No! If she thought of them right now, she'd go insane. She shoved those memories into the deepest vault of her mind and slammed the door.

Jess closed her eyes, placed her hand over the boy's mouth and nose, and pressed firmly into his round face.

Go-away-go-away-go-away!

The raucous cry of a go-away bird jerked Jess back to the present. She opened her eyes. Looked down. Her hand remained clamped over the boy's face. With her other hand, she felt for his pulse. Nothing. She slumped in relief. A lifetime had passed—literally—in a moment. She lifted her hand and stared at her shaking fingers. Trained to save lives, she'd just—

Go-away-go-away-go-away!

Jess needed to follow the bird's advice. She had no time to mourn the life she'd just taken. She locked memories of this boy—and what she'd done—into the vault with those of her children.

Unsteady on her feet, Jess rose and studied the village. Heat waves danced in the humid air as flames enveloped thatched roofs. With the realization that the cooking odor came from the charred flesh of humans trapped inside burning homes, she gagged. She slammed her eyes tight, then forced herself to open them. No time to wallow in emotions. Focus on survival.

The intact structures belonged to Hutus, but they too had abandoned the village. Anyone who wasn't dead had evacuated, carrying everything they could. She'd be lucky to find a single item on her list.

Jess peered through the open door of a nearby hut. Bodies sprawled across the floor. The dead couldn't harm her, so she entered, tiptoeing around corpses. Pools of blood made life unlikely, but she checked to be sure they had truly expired. A rational woman, she didn't believe in spirits, yet as she scavenged for supplies, ghostly hands clawed her ankles, stroked her arms, and fluttered through her hair while ghostly lips kissed her face. Chills raced from her neck to the bottom of her spine.

Her search through the jettisoned belongings of strangers, their bodies surrounding her, was creepy, but her existence depended on it. Here, she found a tattered t-shirt several sizes too big. In the next hut, a dented pot, a wooden spoon, and a large knife. Wherever she found scraps of food, she stole it—sweet potatoes, bananas, plantains. Nearly every home stocked cassava roots, but she had no idea how to prepare them to get rid of the natural cyanide. She devoured a pot of *ubugali* on the spot, including the burnt parts, though the cold glutinous cornmeal mush stuck in her dry throat.

From the laundry she'd seen as she entered the village, she chose several rectangular strips of cloth—*kangas*—that could serve as anything from a shawl to a skirt to a backpack.

The eyes of the dead scrutinized Jess's every move, their gazes following her as she plundered their meager belongings. For a semblance of privacy, she hid between two buildings before removing her torn clothes, pulling on the t-shirt, and fashioning a skirt from a length of fabric.

If the *Interahamwe* found her clothes, they'd know a foreigner had been here, so she tossed her scrub top, bra, and ladybug socks into a flaming hut and watched them incinerate.

In the distance, a dog bayed. Then a second.

Gatera's men were catching up with her.

Hastily Jess returned to the corpses and removed sandals from anyone who remotely wore her size. By wearing shoes marked with other people's scents, she hoped to deceive the dogs. She shuddered as she wiggled her feet into sandals stripped from a dead woman.

Chapter Three

Michel Fournier

Two weeks earlier, Paris, March 25, 1994

Michel Fournier checked in at the head office of his employer, Global News Syndicate. By arriving at the lunch hour, he hoped to avoid being trapped by his boss's drawn-out reminiscences of his heyday as a reporter.

"Fournier!" his supervisor yelled.

Michel bit back a groan. No such luck. He wasn't escaping his chief after all. A war correspondent, Michel had been in and out of Yugoslavia since 1991, reporting on the Siege of Sarajevo and had returned to Paris only five days earlier. Usually glad to get a new posting, he preferred heading out after spending more time with his wife. Especially since they wanted to conceive.

Michel stuck his head into the office. Dense Gauloise cigarette smoke hung in the air. He coughed. "Yes?"

"I've got another assignment for you."

"Where?"

"Rwanda."

Michel blinked. "Where's that?"

"Somewhere in Africa," his boss replied. "You'll leave as soon as we secure your visa."

After accepting the assignment, Michel traversed the cobblestone streets of Paris between the newspaper office and his home. Another plum foreign mission to a place he'd never heard of. Michel's only reservation was that his wife was going to be unhappy he'd taken this job so soon after returning from the last.

Since she was working, he'd cook tonight to sweeten her response. He stopped at the gourmet grocery a few blocks from the apartment and picked up trout and asparagus. From the *boulangerie*, a baguette, and from the *patisserie* some macarons to eat while they watched television.

Michel let himself into their apartment on Avenue de Breteuil. He'd inherited the place when his *grand-mère* died. Most of her furnishings remained intact. He found their residence comforting while Manon thought it old-fashioned. Often, they talked of renovating, but until they'd decided to have children, he'd hesitated to change anything. Now the odor of fresh paint greeted his nostrils. He'd spent the past few days cleaning out a bedroom and painting it a buttery yellow, a color chosen from items Manon purchased to decorate the nursery.

He crossed the living room and opened the French doors. The view, as always, made his chest swell. To the left off the balcony, the Eiffel Tower stretched skyward. The Dôme des Invalides was across the Avenue de Tourville, the Rodin Museum to his right, the Rive Gauche further on. This—the heart of Paris—was the perfect place to live, to raise a family.

But his most recent assignment, where he dodged bullets and scooped interviews with Slobodan Milošević, Mate Boban, and Muhamed Filipović, had provided an adrenaline rush Paris couldn't provide.

Having spent years absorbing the socio-politico-economic history of Serbia, Michel was wholly ignorant of African affairs. He pulled out his world atlas and found Rwanda, a petite land-locked country near Lake Victoria. In fact, Rwanda was half the size of the lake.

Densely populated. No significant natural resources. Exported coffee and tea. The elevation diminished the equatorial heat. Two rainy and two dry seasons meant seasonal humidity. The atlas listed the three main population groups—Hutu, Tutsi, and Twa—but didn't distinguish between them.

Failing to find sufficient information at home, Michel went to the Bibliothèque Nationale where he removed the few books about Rwanda from the stacks and started taking notes. After World War I, Belgium controlled the area and perpetuated an anti-Hutu policy based on *physiognomy*, a system of racial classification based on a person's facial features. According to this methodology, the Tutsi were considered superior because their features more closely approximated the European ideal. He shook his head, wondering why the fuck White men contrived such false data to prove their supremacy.

Next, he researched current events. Rwanda became an independent republic in 1961. Since then, ill will between Tutsis and Hutu had erupted into sporadic violence. He copied a bunch of articles to read at home.

After cooking dinner and watching an American movie, *Pretty Woman*, Michel made love to his wife, slowly, with exquisite tenderness. They'd been trying for several months to get pregnant, so as often as possible, he scheduled his home visits with her ovulations. Her most fertile day had been March twenty-first. Four days later, her breasts were tender, so she was convinced she was pregnant. It was too soon to take a test. She was convinced her flat belly held a new curve, but he really didn't see any difference. All he knew was that his mouth on her nipples made her moan more loudly and draw his head more tightly to her.

They lay together afterwards, he stroking her shoulder. "Manon?"

"*Oui?*"

The dozy, post-sex quality of her voice told him he'd done a superlative job. He congratulated himself, then swallowed before he broke the news. "I have a new assignment."

"*Merde.*" She lifted her head to look at him, her mouth pinched in a moue. "You just got home."

"I know." He shrugged as best he could with her head occupying one shoulder. "But it's my job."

"Where?"

"Rwanda."

Manon suppressed a yawn. "Where's that?"

Michel laughed. "I asked the same thing. Somewhere in Africa. Apparently, trouble is brewing despite France's foreign aid."

"It's not dangerous, is it? You ought to stay home and be an *avocat*. After all, it's what you went to school for." Her tone implied *and-what-I-thought-I-married*.

He wrinkled his nose to tell her what he thought of lawyering.

"But remember …" she patted her stomach.

"I could never forget." Michel covered her hand with his. "Don't worry. Nothing's happening there." He didn't voice the *yet* at the end of his sentence. Manon needed to concentrate on being healthy and growing their baby, not worrying about him globetrotting to dangerous locales.

Chapter Four

Dr. Thomas Powell

Philadelphia, Pennsylvania, May 1994
A physician in a relatively new two-man interventional cardiology practice, Dr. Thomas Powell worked long hours. A last-minute cardiac catheterization at Angel of Mercy Hospital kept him well past his usual eight p.m. departure. Tired and grumpy, he returned to his studio apartment on Rittenhouse Square, stripped to his boxer briefs, and aimed the remote at the television to catch the news. There was the usual crap on WCAU ... same news, different faces. He surfed a few more channels. How could there be so many TV channels with nothing interesting? He pressed the off button. As the screen faded, an image registered in his brain. Jess's parents? Why on earth were they on the news?

Curious, Tom jabbed his finger on the button and waited for the picture to reappear. His eyes hadn't deceived him.

The camera caught a glint of tears in Regina's eyes. "Our daughter, Jessica Hemings, is a doctor volunteering in Rwanda. She and her two babies—"

Babies. Tom's mind hung up on the word and quit processing Regina's comments. Jess with children. She'd found someone else. They had kids. Little ones that should have been his. He staggered as a surge of emptiness swept over him.

At a sob from Regina, he returned his attention to

the TV.

"We've contacted the State Department. No one knows where they are." Regina's voice caught. "She's been missing since April eighth—nearly six weeks."

Greg, Jess's dad, handed Regina his handkerchief and picked up the story. "So far, our efforts to locate our daughter have been in vain. We're asking viewers join in our efforts to bring Jess and her children home. Please call your Congressmen, the White House, anyone who might help."

Tom muted the TV. Christ. He hadn't heard anything about Jess, even from her best friend, Susan, in over a year.

Somewhere in the basket of unread magazines by his recliner lay back issues of *Newsweek* and *Time*. He dug them out. The April eighteenth copies of both periodicals featured pieces on the "tribal war" in Rwanda. He'd glanced at the articles but set them aside to read later. He'd been so busy that later had never come.

Holding the two magazines, he returned to his desk. Memories interrupted his reading. For the past two and a half years, he'd tried to forget Jess. Really tried. The task proved beyond him. Their competitiveness had bound them together yet propelled each to be to the best physician possible. Compassion tempered her intelligence and drive. He missed her lithe body. Her little round bottom. The contrast of her skin against his when they made love. Her blue-green eyes, so startling in her face, revealed every emotion. In the years they'd been together, they'd learned each other's bodies and minds so well.

Tom shook off the recollections and sipped on his single-malt Scotch, a vice picked up from his ex-father-in-law, as he read *Time* and *Newsweek*. He glanced at his glass. Little waves danced across the surface of the Scotch. Waves caused by his shaking hand. Shit. If something happened to Jess, he'd never forgive himself. He needed to know her fate, the fate his actions had pushed her toward, the fate he'd give anything to reverse.

Tom finished the articles then picked up the remote and clicked to *Nightline*. Journalist Jim Wooten was tramping through refugee camps. In his tidy khaki shirt and clean slacks, he stood in stark contrast against the catastrophe behind him. "There are some stories that can never be told. This is one of them … it is all too much … the truth of it is far beyond journalism's reach."

The vivid imagery soured the whiskey in Tom's stomach.

If he called Jess's parents, he was guaranteed a cold reception, but, with Jess lost in Rwanda, Regina and Greg must be desperately afraid. Years ago, he and Jess played footsie while studying at the kitchen table, knowing they couldn't make out until her parents went to bed after *Nightline*.

Tom glanced at his watch. 11:27 p.m. They'd still be up.

Chapter Five

Jessica

Kigali, Rwanda, three years earlier, July 15, 1991

Jess scanned the people milling around the arrivals gate at Kigali International Airport then nervously glanced at her watch. Someone from PARFA, the Physicians Aid and Relief for Africa, was supposed to meet her. She surveyed the modern building which contrasted sharply with airport's single runway. On her third visual pass, she spied a compact man holding a sign reading DR. HEMINGS.

Relieved, Jess sighed. As she approached him, she wondered if the dour twist of the man's mouth was habitual or due to the poor surgical repair of his harelip.

The man gave a reluctant little bow. "Welcome, *Docteur* Hemings. Sylvestre Furaha at your service. I serve as the liaison between your agency, the Rwandan government, and the locals." When he spoke, he covered the scar with his hand which, rather than hiding it, caught her attention—and made his French-tinged English harder to understand. His shirt and suit were worn but spotless. His fragrant cologne, a strong blend of sandalwood, patchouli, and florals, immediately overwhelmed her senses.

She extended her hand. "Hello, I'm Jessica Hemings."

Furaha removed his hand from his face and shook hers. He grabbed her luggage himself rather than flag a skycap and led her to a beat-up Toyota Corolla, one older than the junker she'd driven through medical school.

The interior of the car soon filled with his fragrance, to the point she almost felt ill. She cracked a window, grateful for the balmy temperature. Her pre-assignment orientation had taught her that Rwandan custom dictated small talk about the weather and each other's family, so she tried to open a dialogue. "The weather's quite pleasant tonight."

Her escort yawned.

Jess looked at her watch. Maybe the current time—she adjusted her timepiece to three a.m.—explained Furaha's lack of conversational abilities. Jess, too, grew silent. She'd left Philadelphia thirty-two hours earlier and lacked the energy to keep up both ends of a dialogue.

A silent Furaha drove Jess to a three-story low-rise apartment building and hauled her bags up two flights of stairs. As he left, he said more than he'd said all night. "I'll give you the morning to catch up on your sleep. Tomorrow afternoon I'll escort you to register with the American Embassy. From there, we'll obtain your *visa d'etablissement*, your resident's visa. The next morning you will present your credentials to the Rwanda Medical Council and obtain your medical license. After that, your *permit de conduire*, your driver's license. The following day I'll introduce you to your colleagues at Sayashukah."

"Pardon?"

"Say. Ash. You. Kah. In English, you'd call it C-H-U-K. The Centre Hospitalier Universitaire de Kigali. You'll have three months of training there before being transferred to Butare Hospital."

After Furaha left, Jess opened the windows, letting a cool breeze in and his fragrance out. She shook down the mosquito netting tied to the ceiling and lay back on her mattress. The sheer mesh softened her Spartan room, making it almost romantic.

Despite her jet lag, she couldn't sleep. With a jolt, she bolted from the bed and double-checked her supplies. She'd brought enough drugs to stock a small pharmacy for malaria, traveler's diarrhea, vitamins. With one-third of pregnant women in Kigali and one-tenth in rural areas HIV positive, the odds of contracting the disease were high for an OB-GYN, so she'd brought anti-retrovirals just in case.

Jess put her meds into the apartment wall safe then unpacked her medical texts. She planned to work here a year before returning to the States to take Part Two of her Board Exams and needed to study. Next to them, she placed her field guides to East African birds and animals. She stopped to caress the cover of Albert Schweitzer's *Out of My Life and Thought* before adding it to her shelf. Since discovering his autobiography at age thirteen, she'd been determined to follow in his footprints. Knowing how much the book had influenced her, Tom gave her a signed 1933 first edition for Christmas. Until two months ago, she'd been certain they'd shared the dream of serving in Africa. Boy, had she been wrong. The final volume, her journal, she put on the nightstand.

Next she arranged her clothing in the closet, two dressy dresses bought for her honeymoon and never used, two everyday dresses, seven sets of dark brown scrubs, seven white lab coats, ten bra and panty sets still sporting Victoria's Secret tags—also bought for the honeymoon—and fourteen pairs of socks. She considered scrubs to be a uniform, and in a small act of rebellion, she wore bright, quirky socks. The fancy bras—well, she hadn't used them on her honeymoon, so she might as well be glamorous under her dowdy scrubs.

Once Jess tucked her suitcases under her bed, exhausting her meager to-do list, she paced her room. Her sense of isolation tempered her excitement about volunteering here. She'd never before been so far from her parents. From Susan, her best friend. From Tom, the man she'd loved and lived with since their first year of medical school. That loss felt like an amputation. Phantom pain invariably struck her just before she fell asleep. She still reached for him during the night, still had the urge to tell him every detail of her day, still hated him for betraying her.

The next few days passed in a whirlwind as Furaha hauled Jess around to get her paperwork done. In most places, they waited over an hour for a single signature, even when they were the only people in the waiting room. She couldn't help wondering if the local bureaucrats used inordinate delays to cut foreigners down to size. Despite their forced proximity in waiting rooms, Furaha proved no better at conversation, and they passed the time in silence. When they were in the car, though, Jess didn't mind the quiet. The sights of Kigali distracted her. Colorful markets. Tropical greens. Flowers everywhere. The air smelled different than Philadelphia, cleaner, yet around the markets, tinged with smells of roasting meats and exotic spices.

Everywhere they went Blacks were actually in charge. There were Black bank presidents not just Black tellers. In the crowds, every single person was Black. Many different shades, but all black. Jess shivered with excitement. Except when she'd hung out at the Swarthmore College Black Cultural Center, marched in Martin

Luther King Day parades, or attended her mom's family reunions, she'd been overshadowed by the eighty-eight percent of Americans that were something else. For the first time in her life, she wouldn't stick out. She hadn't seen a single blond to remind her of Tom.

On a Thursday evening, CHUK held a welcoming party for her with cocktails and canapés served around the pool of the Hotel des Mille Collines. A couple of boys, maybe six and ten, careened around the pool before approaching a stocky man. He knelt, demonstrated the breaststroke, then tousled their hair, and waved them away.

Before she could comment on the attentive father with his two cute kids, Furaha tugged her to the next group of hospital employees and introduced her. The hospital administrators, laughing and puffing on fat cigars, huddled by outdoor bar. Alcohol mixed with the cigar smoke on their collective breaths. She shook hands and murmured appropriate greetings.

Furaha pointed to another group and whispered, "You must meet Dr. Gatera, the only other obstetrician in the entire country. He's my uncle."

He waited a moment while Gatera finished a conversation before introducing Jess. She used that interval to study the father she'd seen earlier. Though short, he was massive—solid muscle on a broad body—and carried his chin thrust forward like a truculent boxer. An elaborate monogram *cGa* decorated the pocket of his suit jacket.

His high-pitched voice belied his broad chest. "*Docteur* Hemings."

As he took her hand in both of his, Jess glimpsed a huge monogrammed gold ring. Dr. Gatera was certainly enamored of his initials. His excessively-firm handshake was meant to intimidate her. After the briefest hello, he dropped her hand, turned, and resumed his prior conversation.

Chapter Six

Jessica

Monday, July 22, 1991

Jess paced the sidewalk outside her apartment, waiting for Furaha. Hospital rounds started at 7:30 a.m., and she was going to be late on her first day at CHUK. Built on a series of hills, Kigali's streets swirled around the terrain. The lack of sidewalks made hiking to the hospital challenging. She'd decided to make the trek anyway when Furaha arrived, silent and unapologetic.

She opened the car door and got in. "I was getting ready to walk." She allowed a bit of reproach into her voice.

"You must never go about without an escort. I'll find someone to accompany you once I return to my usual duties."

With three minutes to spare, he dropped her at CHUK's main gate.

Jess raced to join Dr. Gatera and his medical students on rounds on the porch of the obstetrical ward labeled *Maternité*.

"*Docteur* Hemings, you're late." Gatera glared at her. His starched white coat reflected the sunlight and blazed against his ebony skin.

Jess wanted to explain it wasn't her fault but decided it would be unwise to blame his nephew. "My apologies. It won't happen again."

Gatera looked down a broad nose at her. In a chilly

voice he said, "I pray your language skills are adequate. I'll translate for you today, but in the future, rounds will be conducted solely in French."

Jess gulped then responded in rusty college French. "*Très bien.*"

"Come along." Gatera marched briskly into the maternity ward with the others in tow.

Apparently, he had taken an immediate dislike to Jess at the cocktail party and carried that antipathy into the hospital. Her unease growing, she followed the medical students and residents who tagged behind Gatera.

"*Bienvenue à CHUK.*" A young man dropped to the rear and smiled at Jess. He was as slim as Gatera was broad. "I'm Benjamin Disi. We met at your welcoming party."

She smiled back, grateful at least one person was friendly and that he'd reminded her of his name. She'd met so many people recently that faces and names had run together, but she remembered Dr. Disi's wide smile and British accent. "*Merci, Docteur Disi.*"

He extended a warm brown hand, a bit darker than Jess's own. "Call me Ben."

She shook his hand. "I'm Jess."

As they entered the ward, she stopped and looked around. Narrow iron beds with chipped white paint lined its length. Green mold decorated yellow walls. Above each bed, mosquito netting hung like blue spider webs. Women in colorful dresses crowded around each patient. Again, every face—physician, nurse, orderly, or patient—was Black. The place seemed not dirty but well-worn and rather chaotic, nothing like a hospital ward at home.

"*Docteur* Hemings? Are you coming?" Gatera's

impatient voice sounded from the far end of the ward.

"*Oui*." Jess dodged a handful of children playing tag in the narrow aisle and caught up with Gatera. Why were kids running around a hospital ward?

At Gatera's side, a medical student reviewed the patient's history in rapid French.

Gatera turned to Jess and addressed her in English. "This is an eighteen-year-old female. One prior pregnancy. One live birth. HIV positive. Perhaps you'd enlighten us as to other conditions she might have?"

Caught off-guard, Jess appraised the patient. A huge pregnant belly contrasted with the woman's pencil-thin body. Flies buzzed around her listless eyes. In her mind, Jess ran through possible secondary infections that occurred with HIV and ruled most of them out. She placed her stethoscope on the woman's chest. After listening to her lungs, Jess pinched the woman's fingernail until it blanched and counted seconds before the color returned. "Tuberculosis. Malnutrition. Anemia."

Gatera seemed satisfied. At the next patient, he asked, "What's the primary cause of maternal demise in Rwanda?"

"Severe post-partum hemorrhage."

He raised an eyebrow, apparently surprised she'd known that particular tidbit. At each bedside, Gatera interrogated Jess, asking her three questions for every one he asked his students.

Jess, feeling like she'd been demoted to medical school, vowed she'd spend her evenings, after her Kinyarwanda language tutor departed, reviewing the old French medical texts a former resident had left in her apartment.

She couldn't figure out Gatera's attitude. A

Belgian-trained physician and—if Furaha had been correct—the only obstetrician in Rwanda, Gatera should be ecstatic she would share the load. Okay, perhaps that was the "ugly American" in her talking. Maybe he'd had poor experiences with foreign doctors. His reaction couldn't be bigotry; after all, they were both Black. Was he snubbing her because she was American? She raised an eyebrow. Or female? Through medical school and residency, she'd worked twice as hard a White woman and four times as hard as a White male to prove she was their equal. She gave an inward groan with the realization that, while she might not have to deal with racial intolerance, sexism was universal. She'd have to prove herself all over again.

After rounds, she accepted Ben's offer of a tour of the hospital campus. When she told him she adored his accent, he said "I was born here but raised in London. I went to medical school and did my residency there, before coming here, hoping to make a difference."

He led her to the front of the complex. "The campus wasn't always this extensive. It was built in 1918 as a health center. After independence, the government converted it to a hospital, and it now serves as the primary public health institution in Rwanda."

Jess glanced around. The one-story orange-brick buildings didn't look like any hospital she'd ever seen. Each ward, surrounded by lawn and hedges, was housed in its own building. Doors opened directly from a portico into the wards. Air-conditioning and heating systems didn't exist. Everything seemed too basic to be a country's main hospital.

Ben seemed to sense her skepticism. "King Faisal Hospital, funded by Saudi Arabia, is under construction a few kilometers away"—he pointed to the northeast—"and should be completed soon. It will be much more modern, but in the meantime, welcome to the Third World."

Before Jess could answer, a nurse ran toward them shouting, "Dr. Disi, you're needed in surgery."

Did the hospital paging system consist of a nurse running around looking for a physician?

Ben dashed toward the surgical unit. Jess followed. As they worked their way through folks milling on the veranda, she asked, "Who are all these people?"

"There's a critical shortage of trained nurses, so family members supply most non-medical patient care, like bathing, feeding, and obtaining medications from the pharmacy. Plus, Rwandans believe someone who knows you provides better care than a stranger."

The nurse led them to the patient's bed. "This woman has suffered from severe abdominal pain for several days."

At the bedside, Ben gestured to Jess. "Be my guest."

She examined the woman and found six shallow slashes across her belly. Curious about the significance, Jess hazarded a glance at Ben.

He shrugged. "She visited a traditional healer. That's the folk treatment for abdominal pain—they cut the skin to let the pain out."

Obviously, that hadn't worked. The woman, as Jess palpated her abdomen, groaned. Her pain in all four quadrants left the list of potential diagnoses wide open. "Why didn't she come in sooner?"

"Patients here simply can't afford health care. She must have been desperate to have even sought the folk healer."

Revolted by the idea of witch doctors, people without any real medical training, Jess scrunched her nose in an involuntary reaction. She quickly erased the expression from her face. "She needs exploratory surgery right now."

"I agree."

They strode off to write the woman's name on a chalkboard as Jess's first surgical case of the afternoon.

After eating lunch, Jess wandered around, getting acquainted with the campus, awaiting her operative time. One building smelled of strong soap and hot fabric. Outside, little blue-green flags lay on the hedge while others hung from lines strung across the porch. Seconds later, she realized those banners were surgical masks drying in the sun. She shook her head. She really wasn't in Kansas—rather Philadelphia—anymore. Impatient to start work, Jess returned to the OR. Her patient remained on the list. No surgical instruments were available, so the operation was postponed several hours.

Frustrated at the inefficiency, Jess raced to examine the patient and found Ben at the woman's bedside, pronouncing her dead.

"Damn it! This woman shouldn't have died. This would never have happened in the States, even in an inner-city hospital." Jess's voice carried her undisguised anger.

"I know." He lifted his shoulders and grimaced. "Things are different here, Jess. Better get used to it. You'll drive yourself crazy otherwise."

She forced herself to calm down. Though Ben was close enough to catch the brunt of her anger, the situation wasn't his fault. As he'd reminded her, she was now in the Third World.

Over the next few weeks, as she settled into a

routine, her resolve was frequently tested. When extra hands were needed for neurosurgery or orthopedics, despite her lack of training, she was expected to volunteer. Soon she'd treated gunshot wounds, animal bites, broken bones—maladies far outside her field of expertise.

She soon learned that she could accomplish a lot without a CT scanner or other technology—or more basic equipment. Ninety percent of what American hospitals threw away, CHUK recycled. She'd already seen how the hospital washed the cloth masks used by the surgical teams and hung them outside to dry. Surgical equipment was the old-fashioned kind that could be sterilized and reused. Nurses and physicians wore latex gloves only if essential. Simple laboratory tests often couldn't be performed because reagents were in short supply. A shortage of scrub techs meant medical students or residents handled the instruments in the OR.

The hospital required payment in advance for the most basic care. Although physicians went through the motions of ordering labs, patients couldn't afford them, so the tests were never performed. Thus, treatment decisions were based entirely on patient history and a physical exam just like in the Dark Ages.

Jess paused as she wrote up her findings on a patient's chart and thought over her first few weeks at CHUK. In the beginning, she'd felt completely out of her element. The technology she trained with didn't exist in Rwanda. Once she went to Butare University Hospital, she'd have even more archaic gear to work with. Despite these deficiencies, her clinical acumen was improving. So were her instincts. She could adapt—with effort. Tom, especially now that he was training in interventional cardiology, never could.

Chapter Seven

Jessica

Kigali, September 1991

Jess was pleased when Furaha found her an ancient Land Rover. She hoped she'd gain more independence, but since in Kigali, beggars, petty thieves, and out-and-out bandits abounded, he wouldn't let her drive alone. For her safety, he hired a *kigingi* who accompanied her everywhere. More than a bodyguard, Misago watched over the vehicle, loaded and unloaded packages, fixed flat tires, and kept the Land Rover serviced. He followed Jess like a shadow—which took some getting used to. Soon, she appreciated his expertise at finding bargains and providing company as she drove.

In Rwanda, the post office didn't deliver mail to people's homes, largely because street addresses didn't exist. Twice a week, Jess and Misago made a trip to the central market, the bank, and the main post office.

Most days she found a big depressing nothing in Post Office Box 903, but today it held a letter from her mother and, oddly, one from Angel of Mercy. The letter from the hospital could wait, though Jess wondered how they had tracked her down. Not wanting Tom to find her, she hadn't left a forwarding address.

Jess opened her mother's letter and smiled at the tight, precise handwriting:

A recent storm blew down the tree we planted when you were born. After thirty years, we should have expected such a thing, but the backyard seems empty. We're having to replant the flower beds with more sun-tolerant plants.

Her vision blurred at her father's postscript:

Please keep in better touch, Jessie. Your mother worries about you being so far away. Surely somewhere in that country, you can find a telephone so we can hear your voice.

After tucking her parents' letter into her satchel, Jess tossed the Angel of Mercy fund-raising junk mail into the nearest trash can. Mail from home was so rare, though, she retrieved it. Opening the envelope, she discovered not the form letter asking for donations she'd expected, but a newspaper clipping. She unfolded the newsprint to find a photo of a tuxedo-clad Tom standing beside a sultry woman in a wedding dress.

Dr. and Mrs. Colin Clooney announce the marriage of their daughter, Kimberley Marie Clooney, to Dr. Thomas Charles Powell. The couple, both of Philadelphia, was married August 4th at the Cathedral Basilica of Saints Peter and Paul...

The type blurred as she read *Chantilly lace* and *a reception was held at the Main Line mansion of Dr. and Mrs. Clooney.*

August fourth! He had married another woman on the very day he and Jess were to wed. And barely two months after she'd left him. She searched the article and the envelope but found no clues as to who'd sent it.

Jess would never forget the moment she learned of his secret life. She was at a conference in Chicago, taking an elevator with her mentor, when Dr. Giudice said, "Congratulate Tom on the interventional cardiology fellowship. It couldn't have gone to a more deserving physician."

"Thanks. I-I-I will."

The instant the elevator doors slid open, Jess bolted to her room. Dr. G. must have made a mistake. Tom would never have accepted a fellowship without telling her. She plopped on the bed and dialed home. Her own voice, flirty and happy, recited their phone message: *You've reached Tom and Jess. Leave a voice mail. We'll get back to you as soon as we can.* "Tom, call me back. I need to talk to you stat."

She paged him. No answer.

Hell. Something this important needed to be dealt with in person. Jess booked a red-eye and was in Philadelphia by four a.m.

Back home, after unlocking the front door, she turned on the lamp. The place reeked of cigarette smoke and designer perfume. Her nose curled in disgust. Two glasses, a bottle of bourbon, and Tom's pager sat on the coffee table. A tuxedo jacket and cummerbund lay on the floor beside a lacy shawl and one designer black stiletto.

Jess spit an expletive under her breath. Then, backbone ramrod straight to offset her dread, she followed a Hansel-and-Gretel trail—tuxedo shirt, pants, sparkly little dress, the other stiletto, hose, and garter belt—to the bedroom.

The door was open. So was the window. A sultry breeze parted the curtains and allowed a streetlight to illuminate the bed.

Her heart stopped.

Unable—unwilling—to comprehend what she saw, she stood transfixed in the doorway. Long blonde hair shimmered over white sheets. Blonde hair belonging to the woman wrapped in Tom's arms. A woman whose voluptuous body was everything Jess's wasn't. A woman whose fair skin matched his. Kimberley Clooney, the woman Tom would marry. A White woman.

Jess slipped out of the house, stopping long enough to drop her engagement ring in Tom's coffee cup, which sat on the counter awaiting his morning Joe. Maybe he'd choke on it.

That night in Kigali, dreams took her places she didn't allow herself to go during the day. The Napa Valley vacation with Tom. The fall crush with the rich scent of fermenting grapes flavoring the air, tantalizing their noses. Sitting in the hot tub at the bed and breakfast, listening to the gurgle of the Jacuzzi. Hot water below her breasts, cool air above. Her nipples taut, body eager. Tom hard beneath her fingers. His warm hand caressing her neck, his soft breath carrying whispered loves notes into her ear. Their laughter, their love, their plans for their life together, the cries of their lovemaking floated overhead to join the cosmos. Droplets of water freckled their bodies, repeating the motif of the Milky Way, a streak of glitter across a purple-grape sky and reflected in the new diamond on her finger. She'd stored that night in her heart, a snow globe she took out and shook to watch the stardust swirl. The best wine. The best sex. The best night she'd ever had.

In her Kigali apartment, Jess awakened with an odd mix of hostility, horniness, and homesickness but consoled herself with thoughts of her new adventures.

****

Jess asked Misago about the best place to shop, so he took her to Janmohamed, the Asian market, and Alirwanda Supermarche, the local supermarket. She walked the aisles, staring at goodies, wondering if she'd pay the equivalent of five American dollars for a king-sized Hershey bar. She hadn't had chocolate in ages, so five bucks it was. For weeks, she'd eaten at the same restaurant located near her apartment. Its food was adequate if boring. Frankly, she was tired of eating out, almost ready to cook herself.

While gathering her items, Jess ran into Ben who introduced her to his wife. Sabine was tall and thin with closely cropped hair, her skin considerably darker than Jess's. Ben trailed behind as the two women chatted and checked out the items in each aisle. The trip to Alirwanda became a social occasion.

Without consulting her husband, the effervescent Sabine said, "Come over for dinner tonight."

Jess glanced at Ben. When he responded with a reassuring nod, she accepted. A home-cooked dinner sounded great, though it wouldn't be American cuisine.

****

Jess and Misago drove to the address Sabine had given. Jess felt guilty leaving him outside while she partied inside. The action seemed so neocolonial, but she rationalized his job was to protect her vehicle.

Ben's place was a single-story brick home surrounded by flower beds and a small yard. The couple greeted her and showed her around. Even counting the maid's quarters tacked on the back, the place was definitely not the McMansion most young American physicians resided in.

During the meal, Jess probed an issue that had been bothering her since her arrival at CHUK. "Ben, I can't figure out what's going on. Maybe you can help me." Jess scrunched her eyebrows in thought. "Nurses are slow to follow my orders—and it's affecting patient care."

"It can't be the language barrier—your French and Kinyarwanda are improving daily."

"I know. But when you give an order, the staff carries it out like that"—Jess snapped her fingers—"I have to ask two or three times. Sometimes I get so frustrated I do it myself." She paused. "I keep hearing the nurses whisper two words. I know *dogiteri* means doctor, but what does *umuzungukazi* mean?"

Ben glanced at Sabine, then back at Jess. He grimaced. "It's the feminine form of *muzungu,* a White man. Literally, it means *one who wanders* but has come to mean a White person."

"But there aren't any White physicians at CHUK."

Ben's mouth twisted wryly. "You're the White doctor, Jess."

Startled, Jess recoiled. "But I'm Black."

Sabine shook her head. "Not Black like us. You're foreign. Your clothes are different. *Muzungu* can also mean a rich Black person who puts on airs. You seem wealthy compared to most Rwandans and have mannerisms they associate with Whites. Whites are still relatively uncommon in here. And sometimes not well thought of."

Ben added, "When we first moved to Kigali from London, we were 'White' too. It took us a while to learn that people don't necessarily mean anything disrespectful when they call you a *muzungu*, they're responding to you an oddity."

Jess frowned. "Does that explain why Gatera doesn't like me?"

Ben didn't bother to deny this. "I think he's threatened by you. Your medical acumen is superior, so you make him look bad."

Sabine raised her eyebrows. "I'd say he's reacting to your features. When the Belgians colonized Rwanda at the end of World War I, the theory of eugenics was popular in Europe—"

Jess blew out a small huff of air. "In the States, too."

Ben took over the Sabine's point. "So, based on craniometry and physiognomy, the Belgians decided that Tutsis, because they had bigger skulls and taller and thinner bodies, were superior to Hutus. Also, Tutsis had more European features with long thin noses, narrow lips, and straighter hair." He hesitated. "Your White blood makes you look Tutsi—and Gatera hates Tutsis even more than he hates Whites."

"So that's why he gives me a hard time?"

Ben nodded. "It seems counterintuitive, but Hutus have an odd love-hate relationship with Tutsis. Hutus, since colonial days, have been sort of"—he searched for words—"brainwashed, I guess, to believe Tutsis are superior. It's common for a Hutu man to marry a Tutsi woman but rare for a Tutsi man to marry a Hutu woman.

It's considered marrying down, like choosing a Honda when you can afford a Mercedes."

Jess sighed. There was no escape from racism, even when only one race was involved. "It's so complicated. Such animosity. Over nothing."

Sabine covered Jess's hand with her own. "Don't take this wrong but be careful. Don't go anywhere alone. Women are raped all the time here. Promise?"

"Okay. I'm used to being cautious, especially at night—I drove through some rough Philadelphia neighborhoods."

Chapter Eight

Jessica

Kigali, September 1991

On the drive home, Jess glanced at Misago, fully appreciating him for the first time. Over the last couple of months, he'd become a friend. Now she realized he protected her as well. The route took her past groups of young men hanging out on street corners, and an anxiety arose she hadn't felt before. Her thoughts ventured to what Ben and Sabine had told her about the racial tensions in Rwanda. Could they be any worse than in the States?

When Jess reviewed her life, she'd moved with ease between the worlds of her White father and her Black mother. Her parents raised her with the belief her skin tone didn't determine her future. With Tom, she thought she'd found a man who could accept her, regardless of color. Next, Jess remembered the blonde he'd married. Moira, Tom's bigoted Irish-Catholic mother, would have had no qualms about his marriage to a rich White Irish-Catholic woman, one who wouldn't bear "nappy-haired grandchildren." Somehow Tom's betrayal hurt more than any other discrimination she'd endured, sending her self-worth back to antebellum times. Here in Africa, she was learning that, even within groups of Blacks, "others" existed who were different enough to be discriminated against.

****

At CHUK, Jess saw pathology she hadn't encountered during her residency and soon realized how little she knew. Pregnant women—considered immune-compromised because of the fetuses they carried—were highly susceptible to malaria. To make sense of her patients' symptoms, she studied old textbooks for obscure tropical diseases. Though trained with the old medical adage "When you hear hoofbeats, think of horses, not zebras," she and Tom had developed a love of medical anomalies. Every night she wrote him to share the "zebras" she'd seen—leprosy, scrofula, schistosomiasis. The next morning, she tore up the notes. Sometimes she thought of writing him about his infidelity and his double life. In fact, she'd scrawled the single word *Why???* on a sheet of paper and stuffed it in an envelope. Not until she had addressed and stamped the envelope did she realize the futility of her actions. She ripped the letter to shreds. She knew why. Tom had worked hard to overcome his blue-collar background, but a Black wife, even one from Philadelphia's ritzy Main Line, couldn't offer him the prestige of the Clooney dynasty.

Nonetheless, she wished she could talk to him about Dr. Gatera. Tom had always been a good sounding board when she had problems with her fellow residents or medical staff. At CHUK, the difficulty of her practice tested her daily and was compounded by Gatera's behavior. He never wavered in his flagrant dislike of her, frequently questioning her medical knowledge and countermanding her orders. After talking to Ben, Jess realized Gatera was hard on all the Tutsis at the hospital.

One Monday morning, Jess's first patient was a woman curled in the fetal position, looking, as medical students would joke, like she was "circling the drain."

Jess checked the chart. The most recent blood pressure, taken over eight hours earlier, had been normal at 110/70. Jess moved her fingers over the woman's wrist, searching for a pulse. When found, it was faint and rapid indicating a dangerously low blood pressure.

She raced to the nurses' station. "I need a blood pressure cuff!"

The lone nurse looked puzzled but handed it to Jess. "Here you go, *Docteur*."

"The patient in bed four should have had vital signs every two hours. The last set was eight hours ago. How do you explain that?"

"The Emergency Room was busy, so they borrowed our blood pressure cuff."

Jess rolled her eyes, not believing the shortage of such basic instruments. "Take her vitals while I examine her." Jess's motions indicated what she was unable to convey in her poor—but rapidly improving—French.

She jerked on gloves, whisked back the rough, worn blanket, and gently positioned the woman for an exam. Beneath the covers, blood soaked the sheets. She shook her head. Another severe postpartum hemorrhage. Cautiously, she slid her fingers into the woman's vagina. She withdrew four pieces of gauze. Amazed so little was present, she again explored the area. No more gauze. Damn! The physician who delivered the woman's baby should have packed the *uterus* with a large amount of gauze, not placed an inadequate four pieces of gauze in the *vagina*.

Wondering if the physician had been lazy or inattentive, she checked the chart. Dr. Gatera, not a resident, had performed the delivery. He of all people should have been cognizant of the risks.

In an anxious voice, the nurse said, "Her blood pressure is 60/40. Pulse 140."

"She's bleeding out. We need to transfuse her stat. Get the lab to type and cross her blood. Turn up the IV to the max. And bring me gauze—a bunch!"

A few minutes later, the lab tech entered the ward. "*Docteur* Hemings, my apologies, but we can't test her blood. We used the last of the anti-A and anti-B antibodies yesterday. God willing, more is due in next week. Besides we don't have any blood in the blood bank."

Jess rolled her eyes at his words. Again, circumstances forced her to make decisions without data. Though at a clinical disadvantage, she knew from experience what to do. The woman had lost a lot of blood and needed intravenous fluids to make up the loss. Jess turned the IV flow to the maximum. "Take her blood pressure again."

The blood pressure cuff wheezed as the nurse pumped up it. "Forty systolic. I can't pick up the diastolic."

"Where's the crash cart?" Jess called for the red cart containing drugs to resuscitate a failing patient.

"What's that?"

"Never mind." Holy crap! Jess blew out a huff of hot air. No crash cart. Something else Third World countries lacked.

Fifteen minutes later, despite Jess's best efforts, her patient, with an almost-relieved sigh, expired.

The rest of the day, Jess alternated between grieving for the woman and being pissed off at what had happened. Working in a foreign country where doctors faced shortages of supplies like she'd never experienced didn't excuse Gatera's substandard care. Slipping the woman's chart beneath her lab coat, Jess spirited it away to look at later. Her action was less difficult than it would have been in the States as there were no real charts at CHUK, just occasional clipboards and piles of paper tossed on a table.

Over lunch, Jess met with Ben Disi. Together they reviewed the paperwork. Gatera had documented everything well. Nothing looked amiss—on paper.

She said, "In the States, the lack of proper packing would be malpractice."

"Things are different here, Jess." Ben lowered his voice. "Was your patient Tutsi or Hutu?"

Jess looked startled. "She looked Tutsi." She couldn't believe she was making such generalizations based on appearance. "What difference does that make?"

Ben's voice dropped so low Jess could barely hear him. "More than you might think."

Indignant, she raised her voice. "Surely you don't believe—"

He whisked a finger to his lips to silence her. "Sh-h-h."

She lowered her voice to a whisper. "—Gatera would allow personal prejudices to interfere with patient care?"

Ben shrugged. "Hard to say. Tension between Hutus and Tutsis has existed for years. Hutu extremists are now advocating the extermination of all Tutsis. Dr. Gatera is a powerful man—and, I suspect, a Hutu radical."

****

For days Jess agonized over the Gatera problem. In the States, she would have reported it to the hospital's quality control official, but things were less well-defined here. National accrediting organizations didn't exist. Malpractice claims, so common in the States, were unknown. Jess hesitated to start what Gatera would doubtlessly consider a witch-hunt. Due to his impeccable documentation, her accusations would be difficult to prove. All she had to go on was her gut instincts and the fact she'd found a miserly four pieces of gauze in the woman's vagina.

Jess had decided to let things go when a second episode occurred. A Tutsi mother and baby perished when left in prolonged labor instead of having a caesarian section. As Jess sat at the nurses' station writing on her own charts, she smuggled the chart of the newly-deceased mother into her own pile. After glancing around to ensure no nurses watched, she studied the woman's records. Gatera had written his usual squeaky-clean documentation. Once again, on paper, he appeared to be a superb physician. Based on Gatera's treatment of Tutsis in general—and herself by extension—Jess suspected he singled out Tutsi women.

With a third maternal death, she became convinced he was a serial killer who targeted Tutsi women and intentionally killed them via neglect.

Chapter Nine

Tom

Philadelphia, May 17, 1994

Tom picked up his desk phone and jabbed in the first few numbers of Jess's home phone number, still embedded in his memory from college. With a sigh, he replaced the receiver. Picked the phone up again. Lowered it. Savagely he yanked the hand-piece from its cradle. Hell, it'd be worth having Regina, Jess's mother, rip him a new asshole to know Jess was safe. He held his breath as he rapidly punched in the numbers.

On the fifth ring, Regina answered. "Hello?"

The hopeful tone in her voice hit him hard. He swallowed several times.

"Hello? Hello?" Her voice grew irritated. "Who is this?"

"Regina—"

She sucked in a breath. "Thomas Powell. What do you want?"

"How is she?"

"You have no right—"

"I know. I know. Just one question. Is she okay?"

A strangled sob confirmed Tom's fears. "Maybe ... no ... she and her babies have vanished—"

Babies again. Did they resemble Jess? With those curls? Those delicate lips?

"You still there, Thomas?"

The use of his full name brought Tom back to the

conversation. "Yeah, I'm still here. Have you heard anything?"

"The State Department is useless. On April ninth, the American Consulate in Rwanda advised her to evacuate. They drove Americans to Burundi by truck on the tenth. The State Department can only tell us she and her children weren't in their convoy or the one organized by the Red Cross."

"Christ." Tom swallowed hard.

"At first the Embassy thought Jess would be fine. She's American, and Rwanda was considered safe outside of Kigali. But the unrest has spread through the country." Regina's sniffles evolved into full-fledged tears. "The longer she's unaccounted for, the less reassurance the State Department can give us of her safety and the more worried we become. We imagine—we fear—the worst. We'd do anything to get our daughter and her children back. Even pay a ransom. But there's been no demand for money. Jess and her babies have disappeared. It's been thirty-eight days. The situation is so volatile we can't go look for her. All we can do is wait." She blew her nose. "We're helpless. Completely helpless. We can only pray she's safe."

Oh, shit. The situation was worse than Tom had imagined. "I'm so sorry, Regina. Can I do anything?"

"We call the State Department and our Congressmen every day, making a stink, urging them to use diplomatic means to save our daughter. Would you add your voice to ours?"

"Definitely. My prayers are with you and Greg. And Jess. Keep me posted if anything changes, please?" Tom slowly lowered the receiver. Jesus fucking Christ. The love of his life was lost, maybe dead, in the wilds of Africa.

They'd become lovers their last year at Swarthmore. They should have been studying for a physics test but were drawn together by Newton's Law of universal gravitation: two bodies attracting each other with equal and opposite forces. Now his life was governed by the Causality Principle: cause always precedes effect. Event A (the cause) influences Event B (the effect) which occurs later in time. Tom couldn't undo Event A—the moment he'd betrayed Jess. That caused Event B—Jess vanishing without a trace. What he needed was a new Event A, something to propel her back into his life and make him her knight in shining armor. He wished he could search for her, rescue her, anything that would convince her he still loved her. If not for his stupidity—and intervening marriage—he and Jess would have been married and had a child by now.

Chapter Ten

Jessica

Kigali, late September 1991

Furious about Dr. Gatera's deliberate neglect of Tutsis patients, Jess determined to do something about it. Disregarding Ben's advice to leave things alone, she approached the vice-president of personnel, the nearest thing to a morbidity-and-mortality officer she could find. Delicately she explained her concerns, trying to avoid overt accusations. Dr. Seromba, who appeared and sounded as oily as his coifed hair, assured her he would investigate.

Relieved, Jess headed home to spend an hour with her Kinyarwanda tutor, Mrs. Bikindi.

Halfway through the session, a heavy knock rattled her door. When Jess answered, Gatera shoved past her without waiting for a greeting. He spied the tutor sitting at Jess's kitchen table. "Get out."

The woman glanced at Jess.

Jess nodded and walked Mrs. Bikindi to the door.

Anger vibrated through Gatera as he awaited the tutor's departure, his lips clamped together as tightly as his fists.

Once her tutor was gone, Jess took her time closing the door. She guessed why Gatera had come, and her neighbors didn't need to hear the conversation. Somehow, she wasn't surprised that Dr. Seromba had betrayed her confidence, but she was amazed at how quickly

Gatera had taken offense.

The second Jess faced him, his fury erupted. He grabbed her and spun her across the room.

Jess rebounded off the wall. The expression on his face warned her of real danger. She ducked beneath his arm and sprinted for the door.

Before she was halfway across the room, Gatera caught her and shoved her against the wall. With his hand under her chin, he lifted her until her feet dangled off the ground and held her there.

Through clenched teeth he muttered, "Never question my clinical judgment again!"

Her airflow cut off, Jess couldn't speak. Couldn't breathe. Couldn't nod against the force of his fingers.

Stars formed before her eyes. Unless she did something, she'd pass out. She jammed a knee into Gatera's groin.

With a loud groan, he doubled over, releasing her.

She sucked in a breath and leaped for the door.

Faster than a man his size should be, Gatera dashed after her, tossed her on the bed, and threw himself over her. His left hand forced her arms above her head.

She opened her mouth to scream.

He clamped his right hand over her lips. "Don't—if you know what's good for you."

Eyes wide, she nodded.

His right hand left her face and returned with his handkerchief. He shoved it in her mouth.

With one finger, he caressed her from ear to chin then traced her eyebrows, her nose, her lips. "Your face is exquisite." He laughed. "Despite its Tutsi features."

His gentle touch terrified Jess more than his earlier brute strength.

Gatera maneuvered himself between her legs, his erection hard against her thigh.

My God! The bastard was going to rape her. Jess squirmed beneath his weight.

His hot breath drifted toward her nose. The sweet-sour odor of banana beer with its strong vodka-y tang assailed Jess's nose. Maybe intoxication explained his behavior.

He leaned forward and placed his mouth against her ear. Like an East African puff adder, he hissed, "Somewhere, somehow, you have Tutsi blood."

Beneath him, Jess struggled. Over her own rapid breaths came the *zzziiippp* of Gatera opening his pants. The whisper of skin on skin as he stroked himself. His rapid breathing. More banana beer breath, coupled with the aroma of his cigars. He jerked Jess's shirt above her breasts, ripped her bra apart, then pinched her nipples brutally.

With all her strength, Jess struggled to free herself.

"Be still." His hand closed around her neck. Tighter. Tighter.

Light-headed from lack of air, Jess couldn't sustain her efforts. Her muscles relaxed.

He fumbled for the ties at the waist of her scrub pants.

Before he could strip off her pants, he groaned. "*Merde!*"

Something warm and sticky splattered across her abdomen.

Abruptly he released her.

Gasping for air, Jess curled her fingers into claws to scratch his face.

Gatera grabbed her hands. "Careful, *Docteur*

Hemings. In Rwanda people disappear all the time. Especially Tutsis." He whirled and stormed from her apartment, slamming the door behind him.

Immediately Jess ran to her door and locked it. She removed the gag, noting the delicate embroidery of his *cGa* monogram, and stripped, throwing her scrubs, underwear, and his handkerchief into the garbage. In the shower, she attacked her body with a washcloth, then sat on the floor of the shower with the water running until the tank on the roof emptied and the water stopped flowing.

Neighbors pounded on the walls in protest.

Jess remained in the tub until driven out by her shivering.

****

The next morning, Jess considered calling in sick. Avoiding Gatera would signal his victory over her, so she wrapped a scarf around her neck and forced herself to go. A few minutes behind schedule, she stepped onto the maternity ward. At the sight of the man across the room, stomach acid burnt her throat. The hair on the back of her neck spiked. Goosebumps rippled down her arms. The events of the prior night had convinced her he was a monster. She no longer doubted he killed Tutsi patients through neglect. Her hatred coiled at the base of her spine, waiting for an opportunity to strike.

She received an icy reception from Gatera and his entourage. He addressed her only when necessary, with sibilant hostile words forced through clenched teeth. She'd expected him to be embarrassed at his inability to perform, but he'd converted his failure to increased hatred.

The bad vibes didn't come from him alone. Despite

her best efforts, Jess had never developed the bantering relationship here she'd enjoyed with hospital support staff in the States. The situation at CHUK became worse than anything she'd encountered. Gatera united the staff against her. Nurses carried out her orders in the slowest possible manner. No one addressed her except to carry out their duties.

Over lunch, Jess told Ben what had happened. At least part of it. "I talked to Dr. Seromba about the deaths of those three women yesterday afternoon. A very angry Gatera came to my apartment last night."

Ben smacked his forehead. "You should have known better. I warned you—"

"I couldn't let him get away with murder. Seromba must have called Gatera as soon as I left the hospital. Shortly thereafter, he arrived at my apartment, positively exploding with anger—" As she waved her hands to indicate a detonation, her scarf shifted.

Ben reached across the table, pulled aside the cloth, and touched her neck. "Are those bruises?" At her wince, alarm spread over Ben's face. "Gatera actually threatened you? He choked you?"

"Worse. He tried to rape—"

"Sabine and I warned you to be careful."

Jess burst out in inane giggles.

"Are you all right?"

Through her giggles, she said, "He couldn't do anything. He's a premature ejaculator."

"You mean? The manly Dr. Gatera couldn't—" Ben laughed. "I know it's not funny, Jess, but it is!"

Her merriment halted abruptly. "He said to never question his judgment again …." She trailed off, unable to tell Ben how powerless she'd felt crushed by Gatera's body. Or how filthy she'd felt afterward. Or how the smell of cigar smoke and banana beer had been embedded in her nostrils—and her memory. She sighed deeply before continuing. "He told me to be careful. In Rwanda, people disappear all the time."

Ben gave a low whistle. "He's right, Jess. People, especially Tutsis, vanish into thin air. Be careful. Make sure someone is with you at all times. Avoid walking anywhere alone. Keep your head down, Jess. Don't antagonize him. You'll be out of here in a few weeks."

Later in the afternoon, Jess made an appointment with Mr. Kabuga, the local head of PARFA, to discuss the situation. He heard her out, then said, "*Docteur* Gatera would never act in such a manner, Miss Hemings. You must have misunderstood his intentions. After all, you are a foreigner …."

"I didn't misinterpret anything. He threatened me." She sucked in a deep breath. As far as she was concerned, an erect penis was a damned good indicator of a man's intent. "He tried to rape me. Aside from the incident in my apartment, he is creating a hostile working situation and making it difficult for me to do my duties at the hospital."

"Do you wish to be reassigned? To a different country perhaps?"

Jess huffed in exasperation. "I've put in untold hours learning the language and getting settled here. I'd hate to start over somewhere else."

"You have somehow encouraged his attentions. I recommend you modify your attitude until you are transferred."

Grudgingly, Jess shook Mr. Kabuga's hand and, extremely unhappy with his response, left his office, slamming the door behind her.

Moments later she composed herself. She and other female residents had had similar conversations with Human Resources regarding American male physicians, but most had been regarding verbal sexual abuse or inappropriate groping, not quasi-rape. The difference was a matter of degree. If she bowed out, Gatera would win. She refused to give him that power. Besides, in a few weeks, she'd be in Butare.

Chapter Eleven

Jessica

Kirehe, October 21, 1991

Grateful she'd survived her orientation, Jess looked forward to her new assignment at Butare University Hospital. Instead, she was transferred to Kirehe, a small town located in southeast Rwanda, one of the poorest regions of an impoverished, overly-populated country, where a drought was causing large-scale starvation. Certain Gatera instigated the change, she was incensed. Once she calmed, she realized she would escape daily exposure to him, though he would still supervise her. She actually looked forward to establishing an obstetrical clinic. She'd train and supervise community health workers, attempt to lower neonatal mortality rate and maternal mortality, improve perinatal nutrition, increase the use of birth control, and advocate the use of condoms to help women avoid contracting HIV.

In her Land Rover, Jess and her *kigingi* followed Furaha's Corolla down the RN3 highway to southeastern Rwanda. Several hours later, Furaha pulled down a red-dirt road no wider than his car and parked before a group of three small buildings. Misago pulled behind Furaha's car.

When Jess got out of her vehicle, Furaha nodded toward a structure covered in a bilious-yellow stucco. "This is where you will live."

Her new home was definitely low-rent by American

standards, but, unlike many houses she'd seen in Rwanda, it had a real door, two front windows, and a yard with flower beds.

Furaha pointed at a house on the right. "Justine lives there. She will cook and keep house for you. Dorcas lives on the left." He pointed to a run-down house and after a pause, said, "She's my wife."

Knowing Furaha lived in Kigali, Jess wondered why his wife remained in Kirehe. His marital situation was none of her business, so she gave up that train of thought and looked around. She didn't see a building large enough to house a health center. "Where's my clinic?"

"A short walk past those trees." He pointed to the south.

While the *kigingi* unloaded Jess's luggage, she examined her new home, finding it Spartan but acceptable. Everything seemed new—a love seat and chair, a bed, mattress, and mosquito netting, desk, bookshelf, two sets of sheets, two sets of towels, four plates, along with a few pots and pans. In Rwanda, the modest contents of this home represented an embarrassment of riches.

Once everything was unloaded, Furaha drove her to the clinic. He waved a hand toward a building with peeling turquoise stucco. "There."

She wondered why he'd bothered driving. Her clinic stood less than twenty-five yards from her house and a few dozen feet from what Stateside would be called a strip shopping center, where a series of *dukas* or small stores held various occupants. First a hair stylist. Then, judging from the items displayed outside, the second *duka* was the equivalent of a dollar store, apparently selling everything from plastic chairs to plastic shoes to plastic gas cans—no, here they were called *jerry cans*. Last a *farumasi*. At least her patients wouldn't have to go far to fill their prescriptions.

She hopped out of Furaha's Corolla and walked toward a squatty building of rough adobe bricks with a paper-thin coating of stucco and a rusty corrugated-tin roof. Jess's heart sank to her toes.

Above the front door, a faded sign read *Restaurant & Cabaret*. Dismayed, Jess continued her inspection. Windowpanes were either cracked or missing. The front door hung askew. With a mental groan, she entered the building. Her nose itched at the overpowering stench of mildew. Streaks of green mold dripped from the walls. A large piece of corrugated tin dangled from the ceiling, allowing sunlight to streak through the roof. Puddles filled low spots in the uneven floor. The only evidence the place had been a restaurant was a few twisted chairs and a table tilting on three legs. She sighed. This building was worse than the cockroach-ridden row home where she'd counseled pregnant teens—and Gatera expected her to open a clinic here.

Now positive he'd set her up for failure, Jess stormed outside to talk to Furaha, who hadn't accompanied on her tour of the building. "This is unacceptable. Totally unacceptable."

"It's the only building around here big enough." He shrugged then looked at his watch. "Sorry, I must dash."

The coward whizzed off in his Corolla before Jess could list her complaints.

Fuming, she hiked back to her new home and let Misago drive her back to Kigali. She needed to chat with Mr. Kabuga. During the trip, she wrote down everything she needed and the repairs the clinic required. PARFA either had no idea what Furaha was doing or was in cahoots with him.

At Kabuga's office, Jess lodged her complaints.

"Surely you exaggerate, *Docteur*." Kabuga attempted to placate her. "Mr. Furaha assured us the building was in good repair—"

"The place is uninhabitable. Massive repairs are required before it can function as a clinic. A new roof. New windows. Paint." She counted her demands off on her fingers. "And that doesn't include furnishings. Gynecologic exam tables, autoclave, storage shelves, water purification system, generators, back-up generators. Here's everything I need to function." She handed him six sheets of paper.

He scanned the pages then tossed them on his desk in dismissive gesture. "I'll speak with PARFA's head office and see what they can do."

Weeks of frustration followed as Jess struggled to open her clinic. Misago quit without notice and returned to Kigali. She drove herself to the city to make her latest round of complaints to Mr. Kabuga. Fortunately, she wasn't alone on these trips. Local custom required vehicles be filled with anyone who needed a ride. She was amazed at how quickly word spread that she was driving to Kigali and how people magically showed up.

Every time she drove the RN3 highway, a new roadblock had been installed. She was always waved through after her papers were checked, but the routine took far longer than it had with Misago. He'd handled those situations better than she did.

Jess met with Mr. Kabuga and unabashedly shamed him into providing the necessary basic supplies. "I need a new construction foreman and a new *zamu*, a security guard, to watch the site."

"Why?"

"Construction materials disappear before they can be used. A new window was literally pried out of the wall. The current security guard—"

"Mr. Furaha has good connections in Kirehe. He can help you with anything you need." Kabuga waved a disdainful hand. "I'll speak with PARFA and see what they can do."

For a change, nobody needed a ride back to Kirehe, so Jess drove home alone in a dour mood. She recalled with nostalgia that Tom would order pizza when she'd had a bad day. An ice-cold Yuengling beer with a square of thick-crust tomato pie with extra Romano cheese always brightened her day. She shook her head, forcing away thoughts of him before her mood dipped further.

Instead, she plotted her next step. In theory, a *zamu* slept outside to guard a property. Jess had never been sure how a sleeping guard could ensure the safety of a building in the first place. Shouldn't they stay awake and patrol the premises? Not just the watchman, but everyone Furaha had recommended, other than Misago and Justine, was related to him—and equally ineffectual. She resolved to hire someone else, then fire the current *zamu*.

As soon Jess entered her house, Justine, her cook-housekeeper who lived next door came over to drop off Jess's dinner. Justine set a pot nestled in a cloth on the kitchen table.

Curious, Jess lifted the lid. It wasn't pizza, but it sure smelled good. "Thank you."

Justine lingered by the door. "*Madame Docteur*, you shouldn't go around alone. It's not safe for *une femme* to be alone. Especially one who is *très belle*. *Mon cousin*,

Jean-Baptiste Seminega, is a good driver. He is a religious man. You would be safe with him. He speaks English *très bien* and could translate for you."

Jess looked up from the pot. Justine had proven to be a superb cook and a reliable employee, so Jess was inclined to trust anyone she recommended. "Have him come by the clinic, and I'll talk with him."

The next afternoon, Jean-Baptiste appeared as Jess pried out a broken window with a crowbar. Hot and sweaty, she welcomed the break. Immediately, she liked the stocky man. His English was quite good, his French and Swahili were considerably better than her own, and, of course, he was a native speaker of Kinyarwanda. Kirehe was close enough to Tanzania that the local dialect contained a goodly amount of Swahili which complicated Jess's learning Kinyarwanda.

To her amusement, Jean-Baptiste had an aphorism for every occasion pulled from one of the four languages he spoke. The lines around his mouth, caused by his broad smile, boded well for an excellent relationship. Best of all, he lacked Gatera's arrogance and Furaha's ineptitude.

Nepotism was endemic in Rwanda. Anyone, qualified or not, who rose to the level of a minor bureaucrat, as Furaha had, was obligated to share the good fortune with family members. Thus, Jess's best bet was to establish her own contacts, beginning with Jean-Baptiste and Justine, with their solid work ethic.

Through Jean-Baptiste, Jess hired a new construction manager and *zamu*. Once she had good help, things moved smoothly, and she enjoyed rehabbing her clinic. Her dad, not wanting her to be a helpless female, had taught her home repair basics, but she'd never dreamed that after medical school and residency she'd put those skills to use. When the roof was replaced, Jess swabbed the walls and floors with bleach to kill the mold, then rolled on paint, a different bright color in every room. Jean-Baptiste kept telling her she shouldn't be working like a man, but it beat sitting around waiting for someone else to accomplish things.

Chapter Twelve

Jessica

Kirehe, late December 1991

After months of hard work, construction on the clinic was complete down to the finishing touches with a *Clinique Mère-Enfant* sign above the main entrance and over-sized silhouettes of pregnant women and children painted across the front facade. Jess lacked only the furnishings.

At last a large truck pulled in front of the clinic. Excited folks from nearby *dukas* came to watch it unload.

Jess was so thrilled she jumped up and down. "I only had to bitch forever, but we finally got the supplies we needed." She and her new nurse-midwife, Yvette Safi, a graduate midwife from Kirinda, unpacked exam tables, the equipment for the surgical suite, an autoclave, kerosene-powered refrigerators for the office and her home, and generators to augment the local electrical grid. With a grant from the US government, Jess purchased office furniture. She and Yvette spent several days placing drugs and supplies into new storage cabinets. Jess's pride and joy was the delivery room where she could birth babies and perform minor surgery.

Her clinic, the only "bush hospital" in the area, had its limitations. She was restricted in the scope of her practice because she couldn't provide full anesthesia. First, she didn't possess the appropriate equipment, and second, as Rwanda had a shortage of anesthesiologists, there was no one to administer it. She could use local anesthesia like lidocaine combined with ketamine and other IV sedation and spinals.

A new well was drilled—the first in the area—and plumbed directly to the building so water didn't have to be carried in by hand, but it still had to be boiled to be drinkable. The local electrical grid was iffy at best. In theory, the village's power was scheduled for six to eight a.m. and six to ten p.m., but sometimes the system kicked off for hours, necessitating multiple generators.

Another major problem: the clinic's only toilet was a long-drop loo, an outhouse located some fifty feet from the back door. Basically, a hole in the ground with a couple of oil barrels to reinforce the walls and two bricks to rest one's heels on, the toilet could only be described as primitive. Jess immediately set to expanding it. Another first for her—engineering a three-seater potty. Who knew a physician needed that particular skill? She installed a gravel path with a tin roof overhead, so staff and patients didn't get wet while walking to the bathroom or track mud into the clinic.

Together she and Yvette hired two young women, Didi and Elise, recent graduates of a medical assistant program. These two would alternate as receptionist and nurse's assistant.

Finally, with everything in place, they opened the clinic door.

Jess never expected her clinic would sit empty. For days, she either rearranged perfectly-stacked items on brand-new shelving or paced the floor. Finally, to drum up patients, she and Yvette, driven by Jean-Baptiste, went from village to village, examining women in a make-shift tent set up beneath a tree or in mud-brick huts of dubious cleanliness. They handed out condoms and prenatal vitamins while inviting women to come for Pap smears and birth control and to deliver their babies.

****

Kirehe, August 1992

"*Docteur* Jess!" Yvette called. "We have a patient!"

Jess dropped the letter she was slicing open with an unused scalpel and raced from her office.

"It's not obstetrics." Yvette shrugged apologetically. "He's a thirteen-year-old boy. His father brought him in because of abdominal pain. Can we see him?"

Jess never expected to encounter a teenaged boy in her mother-child clinic, but by now she was well-trained in ad-hoc medicine. "Let me examine him."

A few minutes later, she diagnosed the boy with appendicitis which was almost unheard of in Rwanda. Usually, only Kigali residents who ate like Europeans developed the disease. Surely her diagnosis was wrong.

Jess told the father, "You should take him to Kigali for treatment."

Yvette shook her head. "They can't afford it. The boy's been in pain for three days."

"Guess we don't have any choice. Get the operating room ready."

Jess had done countless operations for ovarian cysts. An appendectomy couldn't be much different. With a combination of local anesthesia and intravenous ketamine as anesthesia, she opened the boy's abdomen. Carefully she lifted overlying bowel, searching for his appendix.

"Shit!" Jess swore when she found it. Had she waited any longer to operate, the darn thing would have ruptured. The appendix was so tense—like a very swollen little finger—she hesitated to touch it. Gently she slid a stainless-steel sponge bowl beneath the organ in case it burst, then tied it off with two knots. She sliced between the two knots. The appendix separated from the bowel and dropped safely into the bowl. Relieved, she irrigated the stump and closed the wound.

When word of that surgery got around, Jess saw more farm injuries, kids with dehydration, and folks with malaria than she did deliveries. Eventually the maternity business picked up, and Jess built a dormitory behind her clinic where mothers from distant villages could stay while they waited to go into labor and recuperate afterwards.

****

Kirehe, December 1992

A sleek car pulled before Jess's clinic. A too-familiar monogram decorated the driver's door. The chauffeur opened the rear door, and Gatera stepped out. As usual, an unscheduled visit. Jess couldn't believe he refused to give her a courtesy phone call before dropping by. His visits unnerved her. His predatory gaze made her feel like she needed to shower. She made sure she and her female staff were never alone with him. Openly hostile, he constantly found fault. Though he never discovered anything significant to complain about—Jess and Yvette maintained the clinic in perfect order—he found countless imperfections.

He glowered at her. "Your pharmacy is understocked."

Jess smiled sweetly. "Everything that Furaha and PARFA send me is there. I'd be thrilled if you would send"—she counted on her fingers—"amoxicillin, doxycycline, quinine, powdered glucose, ketamine, microscope slides—"

Gatera flicked a dismissive hand. "Never mind."

Despite his nitpicking, Jess was proud of her statistics. Of the sixty-seven women she'd delivered, no babies or mothers had died.

****

Kirehe, February 14, 1993

Jess and Yvette dashed from their offices at Elise's panicky cry of "*Docteur* Jess! Help!" They found Elise bending over a pregnant woman on a makeshift stretcher on the waiting room floor.

Jess knelt to examine her. The woman was unconscious. Her facial features had been beaten into oblivion. Jess lifted the woman's eyelids. Both pupils were blown, meaning the injured brain couldn't tell the eye muscles to work. "Oh, shit."

She should have known that her successful delivery record couldn't last. Immediately she transferred the woman to the delivery room. On examination, she found a baby's foot jammed in the birth canal. "Quick. She needs a C-section."

Jess and Yvette scrubbed for surgery and prepped their patient. Jess didn't wait for anesthesia—the woman was brain-dead, after all—but sliced her open. Minutes later, she pulled out a baby and discovered a second. "Twins!" One at a time, she handed the babies off to Yvette.

Despite Jess's best efforts, the mother succumbed to her injuries.

After stripping off her gloves, Jess stepped into the waiting area and looked around for the patient's family. No one was there but Didi sitting behind the reception desk. "Who brought in our patient?"

"Two men." Didi gestured to the door. "They left."

"Did you get their names?"

"They dumped her on the floor and ran out of here. I chased them, but—"

Shaking her head, Jess returned to the delivery room where Yvette had placed both babies in the incubator. "We've just inherited two babies. The men who carried in our patient left without giving us her name—or theirs."

"Women who are raped or who have HIV are often abandoned by their families. She's lucky someone brought her here." Yvette shrugged. "Otherwise, we'd have had three casualties instead of one."

"Let's test the mother for HIV. If she's positive, we'll test the babies too." Jess filled out birth certificates, listing the weights of the infants. Together the twins made up a healthy full-term child, but individually they were small. With unwilling fingers, she wrote *Baby A* and *Baby B* into the blanks for the child's name and *Unknown* for their mother and father.

Yvette looked up from the incubator. "What are we going to do with them? We're not set up to handle abandoned children."

Jess paced the room, glancing back at the babies. "We're stuck with them for a while. Local orphanages can't handle underweight infants like these. We need to get them to decent weights before we can hand them off."

Because of the problems with their delivery, the boys remained in an incubator, bundled in their flannel blankets and knit caps.

Yvette shrugged. "In the meantime, let's check the local orphanage. Maybe they have room or can arrange a private adoption?"

The smaller baby uttered a weak cry. Gingerly, Jess

picked him up. He was so tiny. Swaddled in a soft flannel blanket with hair peeking from beneath a knit cap, he smelled of soap. She held a finger to his mouth, and he suckled readily. "What a sweetheart."

"It's a good thing we have all that donated infant formula." Yvette spoke as she mixed two bottles. "The mom was so beat up we couldn't determine her ethnicity. If she was Hutu, her ID card would be worth its weight in gold to someone who needed to pass as Hutu. If so, we'll never learn her true identity."

Jess replied, "And if she was rejected by her family, we're less likely to discover who she is."

"It's hard to tell at this age, but the babies look Tutsi." Yvette ran her fingers over the head of the one she held in her arms. "That could change as they mature."

"If the mom was Hutu, it's even more important to establish their ethnicity."

"Yes, but it may never happen, Jess. Be prepared for them to be labeled on the basis of their appearance."

Yvette fed one newborn, Jess the other. The soft sounds of babies sucking filled the room. Transfixed by the child in her arms, Jess's heart lurched. She drifted back to a memory. As she and Tom had discussed their upcoming wedding, she'd asked, "How many kids do you have in mind?"

He kissed her on the nose. "Let's not plan. Just dive in. We'll know when we have enough."

Not only had they not dived in, he'd betrayed her. They should have been married by now with a baby on the way, but he'd chosen a different life. Inadvertently, Jess had doomed her own hopes for a family by volunteering in Rwanda. She doubted she'd find a new love here and have a child before she turned thirty-five and became a high-risk pregnancy.

Jean-Baptiste arrived and, on learning of the mother's demise, came up with one of his now-famous axioms. "There is no pregnancy that isn't useful. *Docteur* Jess, I predict something good will come of her death."

Jess sighed. She couldn't think of a single way in which this pregnancy would be useful. Two motherless Tutsi children born into an overpopulated country that couldn't feed its people, a country in which Tutsis were threatened, a country in which women were all-too-casually beaten and raped.

The police came and hauled the body away. Once Jess filled out the death certificate, the detective apparently believed the case was closed. No one cared enough about a Black woman to investigate further.

Chapter Thirteen

Jessica

Kirehe, late April 1993

Jess vowed she wasn't going to get attached to those babies. They'd be sent to an orphanage, and she'd never see them again. In the meantime, everyone in the clinic, beguiled by the little ones, shared in their care.

Later in the week, the mother's test came back negative for HIV. Jess offered up a silent prayer of gratitude. HIV-negative children would be easier to place.

The boys soon weighed enough to safely leave the clinic, but the orphanage was jammed with children whose mothers had died from HIV. The nearest church-run home for children, already overwhelmed, wouldn't take the boys.

Jess and Yvette struggled to find the twins a suitable home. Unlike her staff, Jess had no familial responsibilities, so she took the twins home most nights. Caring for them exhausted her, especially as the little ones took an ounce and a half of formula every hour and a half. With each passing day, she grew closer to the infants. She warned them as she fed them, "I'm not falling for your cute little faces. We'll find you a real mom." Jess couldn't take them—she was a single, career woman with no man in sight. A doctor with immense responsibilities at the clinic and basically on-call every night. She couldn't give them the stability, the love, the everything her folks had given her.

"You need some rest, *Docteur* Jess. Let me take the babies for the night." Yvette volunteered her services the next day.

Jess agreed, but rather than sleeping, every time she dozed off, she dreamed one of the twins cried and jerked awake. Clearly shipping them off to Yvette's hadn't been restful. Okay. Jess admitted she missed the little ones.

One evening, while a fatigued Jess fed the smaller, the larger began to squall. She placed both babies on her kitchen table, and with a bottle in each hand, fed them. Her eyelids drooped. Her head crashed to the table between the two boys, and she jerked to alertness. How did mothers handle the constant feedings and diaper changes? Especially moms who worked full-time? Tired and cranky, she pushed back the tears threatening to dribble down her cheeks. Her hope of bearing children was a pipe dream—she couldn't handle two newborns. Realistically she could never be a mother.

Minutes later, as she nestled them into the basket they slept in, she stroked their little heads. Damn, these little guys even looked like her. As their mouths suckled phantom breasts, Jess realized the babies had finagled their way into her heart.

****

A month later, when no one stepped forward to claim the children, Jess made an appointment with the U.S. Embassy in Kigali to learn about adopting Rwandan children. The drive to Kigali took forever. The number of roadblocks on the RN3 highway had risen to six. The radio daily announced increasing unrest. The capital city felt like an armed camp. An occasional soldier from UNAMIR, the United Nations group, kept the peace.

Jess and Jean-Baptiste, having arrived far too

early for her embassy appointment, did a little shopping. Goods filled the shops. People crowded the streets. No one seemed worried by the soldiers or the tension in the air.

She popped into the main post office. The week before she'd read in the local English language newspaper that a bomb exploded in the central post office of Kigali, wounding fifteen people. Now she was surprised at how much damage had been done. Rubble still littered the area. Post Office Box 903 had literally disappeared. She had to stand in line at the main counter to collect her mail.

Afterwards, Jess stopped at the PARFA office to call her parents. For some reason, overseas calls were easier to accomplish from Kigali rather than her office. "Mom, Dad. You're going to be grandparents." Silence greeted her announcement. She giggled as she realized what they were thinking. "I'm not pregnant. I'm adopting twin boys whose mother died in my clinic."

After a pause, her mother managed to say, "That's lovely, dear."

Her practical father asked, "When are you coming home? Will you bring the kids with you?"

"I can't leave until the adoption is complete. Since I don't have the official paperwork, I can't take the boys with me, and if I leave them behind, the Rwandan government will assume I abandoned them. I'll take a longer leave next year to make up for skipping this year." She'd made the decision to adopt the boys and didn't want to jeopardize their future.

"We miss you, dear."

"I miss you too, Mom." Jess did miss her parents and had looked forward to her home leave but wrestled with turning her new clinic over to someone else for an entire month.

From the PARFA office, Jess drove to the US Embassy to discuss adoption. Her appointment there wasn't as successful as she'd hoped. The bureaucrat she spoke to didn't encourage her but handed her a pile of American forms to fill out. "Next, visit your local branch of the Rwandan Ministry to obtain the appropriate papers."

Paperwork in hand, Jess dutifully trooped there once she returned to Kirehe. An obsequious young bureaucrat told her, "You must present a release from the child's parents in order to adopt."

Jess struggled to control her exasperation. "The mother was dying when she was dumped—literally—at my clinic. The men who left her took off straight away. She died during childbirth. I didn't have an opportunity to get her name. I have tried everything to find them homes. The orphanages won't take them."

"You must also provide"—the official read from a paper—"a legal or administrative certificate that proves date of birth and identity."

"I can neither supply the mother's name for the birth certificate nor the release to adopt. I can show you notarized statements from the receptionist who admitted the woman to my clinic and from the woman who assisted with the delivery. Both confirm the situation."

"Leave the papers with me. We will contact you when we've made a decision."

Jess swallowed her anger and, as politely as possible, muttered, "Thank you." She shook his hand and left a handful of folded Rwandan franc bills in his palm as *baksheeshi* to grease the governmental workings. She left her paperwork with him, but despite the bribe, thought her efforts in vain. After that, she returned to the ministry office weekly and paid increasing inducements, yet each time the bureaucrats told her they were unable to make a decision due to her lack of appropriate paperwork.

Jess placed an advertisement in the local newspaper and taped signs to the windows of the *dukas* next door asking for information related to the births. No one responded.

The babies needed a stable family. As she was filling that role, she might as well name them. She completed the boys' birth certificates, calling the bigger boy *Theo* and the smaller one *Matthieu* and still listing the parents as *unknown*.

Jean-Baptiste gave her a hug. "I told you something good would come from that woman's pregnancy."

Jess's own family, however, wasn't so supportive. A letter from her mother awaited Jess on her next trip to the post office.

> *Jessica, dear, are you certain you understand what you're getting into? Children are such a big responsibility, and—unlike here at home—you have no support system there. Are you sure they are healthy? No hidden diseases or anything?*
>
> *And when are you coming home for a visit?*

Annoyed, Jess wrote to her mother to again explain that if she left the country at this time, the children would go to an orphanage since their adoption wasn't final.

The twins, now that they didn't sleep most of the time, needed a babysitter. She hired a woman to watch them in the clinic. Between patients, Jess would interact with them. After a time, she couldn't imagine not having her children at work. Back in the States, eyebrows would be raised, but here, her system worked.

****

The phone rang as Jess scribbled on charts in her office. She answered and scrunched it against one ear while continuing to write.

"*Docteur* Jess," Didi, her medical assistant, said, "the American Embassy is on the line."

"Thanks." Jess took the call. She crossed the fingers of her left hand hoping they had good news regarding the adoption.

"Dr. Jessica Hemings? This is the American Embassy. We're calling to check on you and find out exactly where you are and if any other Americans are with you."

"I'm in Kirehe. The sole American here. But I have twin boys."

The sound of papers being flipped carried to Jess's ear. "We have no record of you having any children …."

"I'm adopting them, but the paperwork hasn't been finalized yet."

"Keep us posted in the event we order an evacuation."

"Can I bring my sons even if their paperwork is incompl—"

The phone clicked in her ear.

Chapter Fourteen

Michel

Kigali, April 8, 1994

When Michel's plane touched down at Kigali Airport, he gave a prayer of thanks. He'd been luckier than Rwandan President Juvénal Habyarimana, a Hutu, whose airplane had been shot down two days earlier. Michel grabbed his camera bag, his laptop, his knapsack with his clothing and his "war bag"—a duffle filled with extra socks, candy for any children he might meet, playing cards for moments of boredom, and his flak jacket and helmet.

Once in Kigali, Michel learned the ambush of the president's plane had triggered a Hutu uprising on April seventh. The Rwandan Armed Forces, the Hutu *gendarmerie*, and the *Interahamwe* set up roadblocks throughout the city and went from house to house, killing every Tutsi they found as well as those Hutu politicians they considered traitors.

Ten Belgian soldiers who guarded the Prime Minister were slaughtered on the day Michel arrived. He accompanied Roméo Dallaire, the commander of UNAMIR, the United Nations Assistance Mission for Rwanda, to retrieve their bodies. In response to these soldiers being tortured and killed, Belgium pulled out their troops on April fifteenth. UNAMIR had been sorely understaffed with 2500 troops, yet on April twenty-first, after the Belgian deaths, the UN withdrew all but 270 men. Without a substantial military presence, Kigali became increasingly dangerous. Dallaire estimated 5,000 troops might have stopped the violence in Kigali and prevented its spread. He sent an urgent message to the UN asking for these additional men. To his dismay, UN officials advised him to not intervene.

On April ninth, Michel's second day in Rwanda, Belgium and France evacuated their embassy personnel and other citizens. A truck convoy transported Americans to Burundi on the tenth. Only Whites were rescued. Michel snapped photographs of Blacks being tossed off trucks carrying evacuees to the airport. Apparently, none of the Rwandans who'd worked for the embassies were to be saved.

Michel arrived so early in the game that the big news agencies hadn't gotten their satellite technology set up yet. In Serbia, he hadn't liked being embedded with UN forces—reporters only got the UN's point of view. He preferred taking off on his own and building his own contact list. Here he was dependent on Dallaire to forward his stories to Global News Syndicate in Paris.

Desperate for the world to understand what was happening in Rwanda, Dallaire took foreign journalists under his wing. He provided transportation, even guaranteed their safety by providing bulletproof vests and other protective gear. Using UNAMIR resources, he ensured their stories reached Nairobi, the nearest city capable of transmitting images. He even fed them—the same MREs, or Meals Ready to Eat, his troops ate. Though packed with calories and nutrients, MREs were low on flavor—anathema to a Frenchman. As far as Michel could tell, their sole redeeming quality was that they didn't require cooking.

As Michel established connections, he learned most reporters in the country were local stringers, many of them Hutu sympathizers, who passed on biased stories to any foreign press who'd pick them up. Their spread of propaganda grew easier as most international reporters fled the country.

Worldwide, the media either ignored the Rwanda situation or mistakenly reported it as tribal uprisings. Within Rwanda, the media, Radio Mille Collines in particular, fueled the killings with anti-Tutsi propaganda. Michel reported that Dallaire had asked the UN to jam the hate transmissions of RTML. That request was denied due to the cost, and the radio station continued to flame the fires of the mass killings.

Like most people, Michel didn't know much about Rwanda beyond what he'd gleaned at the Bibliothèque Nationale. He depended on UN soldiers to fill him in. The relationship was reciprocal. The United Nations had denied UNAMIR the equipment to surveil appropriately, so Dallaire relied on information garnered from reporters to update the map boards in his war room.

After a week spent accompanying the *Interahamwe* on a killing spree, Michel entered the war room and pulled off his flak jacket and helmet. He smelled awful, a rank mixture of blood, gunpowder, and body odor. At least there was no vomit. Rather than show weakness, he'd re-swallowed the MRE that forced its way up his throat as he watched the *Interahamwe* butcher an old man. Michel wasn't sure he'd be able to suppress that memory long enough to get his job done. He needed to report to Dallaire's office first, then clean up and sleep—if he could even get to sleep. He'd started having nightmares again. They'd dropped off once he left Serbia, but the killing here far surpassed what he'd seen there.

"Anything new?" Dallaire asked.

Michel pointed to a map of Kigali. "There are roadblocks here, here, and here." He pointed to three areas on the map. "Piles of ten or twenty bodies at each." His stomach flip-flopped as he switched to a large map of Rwanda. "A mass of bodies about here."

"How many?"

"Hard to tell. At least fifty, maybe seventy-five."

Dallaire frowned. "Better than some, worse than others."

Michel asked, "Any hope for peace?"

"I doubt it. The Hutu are hard-liners. Radio Mille Collines is whipping people into a frenzy," Dallaire said bitterly. "I can't do a thing. The Americans haven't paid their UN dues, so there's no budget. This mission has to be run cheaply. No one's really interested in Rwanda to start out with."

The body count soon rose to astronomical levels.

As a result of the killings, most foreign aid workers evacuated, which meant local hospitals virtually shut down. Only *Médecins Sans Frontières* and the International Committee of the Red Cross (ICRC) kept the main hospitals in the city operational.

At a press conference Michel attended, MSF-France begged for military assistance. He scribbled their take-home point to include in his article, "One cannot stop a genocide with doctors."

Chapter Fifteen

Tom

Philadelphia, May 1994

From his office, Tom called Susan Clarke, Jess's best friend, and explained that he and Jess's parents had formed a "Bring Jessica Home" movement, sending petitions to the government, writing and calling their congressmen and the State Department, appearing on TV and radio, trying to keep her alive in the public's eye. The words "Will you help out?" caught in his throat.

"Sure." Susan paused. "Just curious, but why'd you volunteer?"

He hesitated.

"Don't tell me you still love Jess? After all this time?"

"Yeah." Tom's eyes started watering. He closed them. Must be allergies.

"You burnt those bridges three years ago." She sighed. "She's my best friend. I'll help any way I can. So will Kevin. Keep me posted."

Tom had never paid much attention to foreign affairs, but now he followed the news avidly, even taking issues of *Time* and *Newsweek* from his office waiting room. He finished the April nineteenth *Newsweek* magazine and pitched it into his outbox, then picked up *Time*. Both contained articles he'd read multiple times. Jess was in Rwanda in the midst of the violence. He knew she'd gone there to get away from him. He wasn't sure he'd forgive himself if something happened to her. He had to know her fate.

In Washington, D.C., while attending a conference, Tom made an appointment with the State Department. They made empty promises about "doing everything possible" to find Jess. He took their business cards, promising to call them every day until they brought Jess home.

As time passed, the tension between Tom and Jess's parents thawed a bit. They called him "Tom" like in the old days.

He phoned them from his office. "Any word?"

"No."

The restrained emotion in Greg's voice twisted Tom's heart. Not knowing what else to say, he blurted, "I'll start calling right away." He disconnected, then punched numbers that were in speed-dial on every phone he owned. Marjorie Margolies-Mezvinsky, the House representative for Gladwyne where Greg and Regina lived. Lucien Blackwell, the member for Tom's own district on the Main Line. Senators Arlen Specter and Harris Wofford. The State Department. The White House.

After making his calls, Tom picked up the cover of the new *Time* magazine, released May sixteenth. The words *"There are No Devils Left in Hell," the Missionary Said, "They are All in Rwanda."* were printed in red across a photo of two children. Tom flung the periodical across his living room. "Fuck, yeah, and they've done something with Jess." Obsessed with the killings, he retrieved the periodical and studied images of piles of dead bodies with morbid fascination. Jess might be buried somewhere in those heaps.

He called Susan. "If Clinton and the State

Department had sent aid to Rwanda early on, events might have played out differently. Jess would never have disappeared."

"Tom, cultural issues are involved. Money wouldn't help."

"Bullshit. The United States had lots of excuses for not getting involved. Africa is far away. Rwanda's population is Black. The country has no natural resources for us to covet. And, after those eighteen American soldiers were killed in Mogadishu back in 1993, the government decided more American deaths would be too high a price for saving another nation."

"You're searching for someone to blame for this situation, Tom, but you're really angry with yourself—"

Tom snorted. "She wouldn't have gone there if we'd—"

Susan's voice softened. "Jess made her own decisions. You're not to blame. What happened, happened."

Tom didn't want to consider his own role in Jess's decision. It was easier to focus on the inadequate response to the genocide. "We Americans need an attitude adjustment. Christ, Nancy Kerrigan and Tonya Harding get more coverage than the hundreds of thousands of deaths in Rwanda. In fact, the whole genocide thing just isn't a big deal here."

Chapter Sixteen

Jessica

Kirehe, a year later, February 14, 1994

Jess couldn't believe how fast the twins were growing. Chronologically a year old, their gestational age was a month less. Both babbled away in their secret twin language. They'd be slow to speak real words because they were processing three languages. They heard English from her, French from the office staff, and Kinyarwanda from everyone else.

She laid Matthieu on the floor while she changed Theo. She'd finished swathing him and was reaching for a clean shirt when she felt Matthieu's hand at her knee. She glanced down. He'd grabbed her pants, pulled himself up, and was toddling around her. By gosh, the little dude was cruising. He took another two steps before landing on his bottom with a wail.

Jess put them down for their nap and checked her chart of developmental milestones for infants. She thought she knew the list by heart. Surely year-old babies weren't supposed to cruise, but, yes, it was right there. Weren't they were supposed to crawl first? She was so not ready for this. Handling two stationary kids was bad enough. What would her life be like with two walkers?

****

Kirihe, March 21, 1994

Six weeks later, leaving the boys in Yvette's capable hands, Jess and Jean-Baptiste drove to Kigali to shop at Alirwanda. Stories about *shiftas* or bandits circulated constantly, so she feared driving at night. As a result, these little jaunts took a full two days. Soldiers stopped them and searched the Land Rover at two new checkpoints on the RN3 highway.

"Pretty soon there'll be a roadblock every mile, and it will take days to get anywhere," Jess said.

Kigali seemed normal, despite newspaper accounts of Tutsis being killed. Jess arranged to meet Ben and Sabine for dinner. They reported most people had developed a war-zone mentality and planned on staying put, but the Disis were leaving.

"We're Tutsi," Sabine said. "Things are getting bad. I worry constantly about our children."

Ben rubbed his chin. "My parents immigrated to Britain in 1961 after Hutus carried out a coup with the tacit approval of the Belgian colonial authorities. Against my father's wishes, I came back. Now Sabine and I can't take a chance on something happening to our children. I accepted a position in London. We depart next week."

Stunned, Jess took a second to reply. "You're leaving? But—"

"We no longer have a choice." Ben glanced at Sabine. "We fear for our lives. Any Tutsi who can afford it is emigrating. There's no future for our children and potential danger if we stay. Quotas exist on admissions to schools, jobs, everything, and Tutsis are the last to be accepted. We must leave the country before the situation gets worse—or pay for it with our lives."

"I understand." Jess hugged them both and wondered if she'd ever see them again.

On the way home, Jean-Baptiste got them through all the roadblocks without her perishable foods, packed under ice in coolers, being opened and allowed to thaw in the heat. He had a natural talent for getting on people's good side.

When Jess arrived at the clinic, Yvette, who'd proven to be another invaluable employee, caught Jess between patients. Worry etched her face. "*Docteur* Jess, do you listen to the radio?"

Jess shook her head. Her Kinyarwanda wasn't good enough to follow the Radio Mille Colline's broadcasts. The station broadcast in street slang to best communicate with the young men they were radicalizing.

"You should," Yvette warned.

Jean Baptiste intervened. "RTML is a Hutu-power station. It broadcasts racist propaganda against Tutsis, moderate Hutus, Belgians, even UNAMIR."

"Surely the government will shut them down."

"The various factions of the government squabble constantly. They can't come together to sign the Arusha Accord, much less handle these radicals. Most government officials are Hutu militants. Few people dare oppose them." He paused. "Have you considered leaving Rwanda?"

"I should be safe. PARFA assures me Americans aren't being targeted. I'm in no real danger."

Jean-Baptiste shook his head. "Still, I'd be careful if I were you." He paused again. "Like it or not, your features brand you as Tutsi. Your American passport may be all that saves you someday. Carry it with you at all times."

She patted her hip. "It's in my pocket."

Jean-Baptiste regarded her with a stern eye. "Make sure you don't go to the villages or go shopping alone. People here disappear all the time, especially *une belle femme* like you."

Jess gave him a snappy salute. "Yes, sir!"

Yvette reminded her, "Remember, Jess, you must think about your sons now."

Chastened by their seriousness, she replied, "I'll be careful. I promise."

****

After work, Jess cuddled her babies, now fourteen months old, while worrying about what Jean-Baptiste and Yvette had said. Matthieu sucked on his fist while Theo made cute little gurgles as he blew spit-bubbles. She couldn't believe that anyone would hurt such adorable boys, but she had to be realistic. For the last few months, she'd been lax about harassing the ministry. She no longer had that luxury. Their adoption must be finalized to ensure their safety. Once they were American citizens, no one would dare harm them.

The next day, Jess carried the twins to the Ministry, hoping the powers-that-be would be more sympathetic if she showed them her healthy, happy kids. Her plan failed. A new official—she never encountered the same one twice—took her into his drab cubicle. She shook his hand, sliding Rwandan francs into his palm. For what felt like the zillionth time, she recited the complete story. She'd told the tale so often it was becoming rote. She struggled to keep it fresh and appealing, but it was difficult in another language. Though her French had improved, by no means could she be considered a native speaker.

After a brief show of patience, the official interrupted her, "I am sorry, *Madame Docteur*, but you must produce a release from the children's parents or nearest relative before the adoption process can proceed."

"If you read the documentation I brought on my first visit, you will understand. The mother was abandoned at my clinic and died before we learned her name." She pulled the covering from the babies' basket. "Take a look at these adorable children."

The official looked down his broad nose at the two babies.

Jess continued, "I'm removing two orphans from the system and providing them with a good home. Under those circumstances, the Rwandan government should allow a little leeway."

The bureaucrat shrugged. "If we allow one person to bend the rules, everyone will want special treatment. Chaos would ensue." He flicked his fingers in a sign of dismissal. "You may go."

At first Jess was stunned into speechlessness. Then, pissed, she bit her tongue to keep from telling him off. Chaos ensued when a government wouldn't care for its people, when bureaucrats performed their jobs only when bribed, and when government-sponsored discrimination prevented children from finding homes.

Back at the clinic, Jess spoke to her staff about her predicament. "I can't figure out how to finalize the boys' adoption. The ministry is completely uncooperative."

"Can you forge their birth certificates?" Yvette asked.

"That's illegal. I might get in big trouble for falsifying government documents."

"You may not have a choice. I'd be willing to be their 'father.'" Jean-Baptiste winked. "I'd need to explain things to my wife, though."

Jess nodded, her lips pursed in thought. After her staff went home, she stayed late in the clinic. Her chores complete, she returned to her desk. From a locked drawer, she took blank birth certificates and filled them out, listing herself as mother and Jean-Baptiste as father. Lying went against her ethics, but illegal or not, she couldn't think of another solution. The papers still needed the official stamp, though. She couldn't figure out how to forge that.

****

On a beautiful Saturday afternoon, Jess invited her entire staff and their families for a potluck dinner. Everyone brought their specialty, and, after a trip to Alirwanda supermarket, Jess made fried chicken and potato salad. The dishes didn't quite taste American but were well received.

She mingled with the picnicking group, snapping photographs of everyone. Her parents would enjoy seeing pictures of the people she worked with.

Memories bubbled up of the day she'd bought the camera. While still in college, she and Tom had taken the train to New York City. On a crisp fall day, they'd wandered through Midtown and Chelsea checking every discount store for the best price. Then they'd hiked through Central Park as she tried out the Leica. How many times over the years had she asked him to say *cheese* before its lens?

She forced thoughts of Tom out of her head. Now she had someone else to dote on—two someones, in fact.

Folks filled their plates, then sat on the ground. Jess placed the camera behind her to protect it from grubby little boy hands. She held her wiggly sons in her lap, laughing as she fed them bits from her plate.

Jean-Baptiste picked up the camera. "If I may? You've taken pictures of everyone here but yourself. Let me take one of the three of you."

"That'd be lovely." Jess had taken photos of the boys but didn't own a single photograph of the three of them together. Theo was grinning and drooling, and Matthieu's mouth was pursed in a sour look after eating a bit of pineapple. Laughing, Jess pressed them close to her face and smiled as Jean-Baptiste clicked the shutter. He took another one, "just in case," but Jess knew the first was perfect.

Jess glanced around at her friends. The relaxed atmosphere at the picnic belied the political unrest in Rwanda. President Habyarimana, before his assassination, had acknowledged that political leaders lacked confidence in the government and didn't have the will to press forward on the peace process. Voice of America Radio reported that radical Hutus insisted on being included in the transitional government, and the RPF had refused. Thus, the installation ceremony for the new government stalled for the umpteenth time. Jess grew mildly concerned, but PARFA still insisted that Americans were safe.

A week later, when Jess picked the pictures up from the photo lab in Kigali, she'd been right. Jean-Baptiste's first photo was perfect. She framed the image, putting one on her desk at work, one on her bedside table at home, and set aside one to mail to her parents.

While in Kigali, Jess and Jean-Baptiste searched for powdered glucose to mix in IV fluids. None was available. In addition, Furaha had shorted her supply order and hadn't included any blood administration kits. She now lacked two vital items for treating patients. If only the country would resolve its political differences and resume something approaching normality.

Chapter Seventeen

Jessica

Kirihe, April 6, 1994

After putting the twins to bed, Jess sat outside in a plastic chair enjoying the air. Though April tended to be the rainiest month, the sky was clear. She listened to birds chirping from nearby trees. Some, like the go-away bird, she'd learned to identify.

From next door, Justine came and sat beside Jess to chat for a few minutes. Further down, Furaha's wife Dorcas, stood on her front step and glanced around.

Jess waved at her.

Dorcas didn't wave in return. In fact, once she spied Jess, she stalked inside.

Justine said, "Don't mind her. Dorcas views you as an enemy. This house"—she jerked her head towards Jess's home—"used to be hers. Furaha moved her into that shabby one in order to rent this nicer one to you. When someone rents to a *muzungu*, he gets three times the rent he'd get from a Rwandan."

As Justine said goodnight, the electrical grid in the area shut down again for some unknown reason, so there was no ambient light from neighboring houses. Kirehe lacked streetlights. The night was pitch black except for small yellow dots of cooking fires sprinkled like stars across the hill in front of her. A breeze carried the smell of cooking and wood smoke. In the quiet, nearby transistor radios played, all tuned to the same station, Radio

Mille Collines.

Suddenly the timbre of the broadcast shifted as the disc jockey read what sounded like a list. Jess tuned it out. She never listened to RTML because she couldn't understand the idioms lacing the broadcasts. Voice of America, the English-language broadcast, gave a more balanced view of world news and kept her informed on American affairs.

Usually Jess didn't need to look at her watch to know her bedtime had arrived. When RTML went off the air at ten, she went inside. Oddly, tonight RTML remained on the air but switched to classical music.

The night was peaceful, and the music added to the sense of calm. Jess remembered one of Jean-Baptiste's sayings, "There isn't a place where peace reigns at night. Peace exists nowhere." Jess shook her head at his pessimism.

****

Kirihe, April 7, 1994

In the clinic the next morning, tension filled the air. Patients and staff alike pressed transistor radios against their ears.

"Dr. Jess, have you heard the news?" Yvette asked.

"Why? What's going on?"

"Last night, President Habyarimana's airplane was shot down by a surface-to-air missile as it circled to land at the Kigali airport. No one survived the crash. The perpetrators are unknown. RTML—Radio Mille Collines—blames Tutsi rebels and is calling for a 'final war' to exterminate the Tutsi with the code words 'cut down the tall trees' and 'exterminate the *iyenzi.*'"

"You should take Theo and Matthieu and evacuate," Jean-Baptiste advised.

"I'm American. PARFA says I should be safe. Besides, southeast Rwanda is more moderate than the north." Jess wrinkled her nose in thought. "Plus, I have a mother in labor."

Jean-Baptiste shook his head. "I've told you before the *Interahamwe* won't bother looking at your passport, *Docteur* Jess. I'll drive you to Kigali, and you can take the first plane out of here."

"What about the boys? I still don't have paperwork for them."

"Try one more time. Under these troublesome circumstances, they might help you."

"All right. One last attempt."

On the way to the local branch of the ministry, Jess stopped at her bank to empty her account in the event she had to flee. An inordinate number of people filled the small lobby. She jiggled her foot as she waited. Minutes ticked by. Thirty. Forty-five. An hour and forty minutes. At last Jess's turn arrived. She huddled over the counter to disguise how much cash she withdrew. Once in her vehicle, she tucked most of her francs deep into her underwear.

As she headed to the ministry, Jess passed several young men, garbed in bright *dashikis* or worn t-shirts, setting up roadblocks. She wasn't concerned until she noticed their machetes. The *Interahamwe*. These disaffected young men, unemployed, uneducated, and futureless, fell prey to the Hutu-centric propaganda spewed by RTML. Jess felt uneasy approaching them, but, to her surprise, she was waved through, though whistles and obscene gestures followed her.

At the ministry, Jess met with another minor official. Thank God, it was someone she hadn't already seen, someone who hadn't already heard her story. She could lie to him and perhaps get away with it. Giving a perky smile, she brought out the birth certificates she'd faked and passed them to him. "I need these to be certified."

The bureaucrat scanned the paperwork. "*Madame Docteur*, surely you don't expect me to sign such blatantly fraudulent forms? I reviewed your file. Despite many visits here, you have yet to provide us satisfactory documentation."

Jess jerked the papers from his hand and forced a smile. "The records you want don't exist. The infants' mother died before we learned her name. I cannot provide you with what you wish. It's simply unobtainable."

The official glanced at the paperwork. "The gentleman you met with last time recorded that the boys in question are Tutsis."

"Just because they look Tutsi doesn't mean they are. You know as well as I do that you can't tell by looking. As they're infants, we can't be certain of their ethnicity." She struck her fist on the desk. "Sign the papers, and I will get these so-called Tutsi children out of your country."

The official thumped a rubber stamp with giant red letters against her file. "I regret we must permanently deny your request."

Furious, Jess played her final card. Clearly, her prior *baksheeshi* hadn't been enough. She reached into her pocket, counted out 30,000 Rwandan francs and placed them on his desk. The stack of bills, totaling roughly a hundred dollars, was more than most Rwandan civil servants made in months. "Perhaps now you can find a way to help two innocent orphans?"

The official's eyes opened wide.

She separated the money and shoved half toward him. The rest she returned to her pocket. "You'll get the remainder when the adoption documents are complete."

He bowed slightly as he stuffed the money in his pocket. "Your credentials will be ready next week."

With an obsequious smile, Jess said, "Thank you. I appreciate your hard work."

Praying he wasn't lying, Jess left the ministry. Each frustrating encounter with the bureaucracy increased her awareness that she needed an alternative plan. Somehow, she'd escape with the boys. Somehow, she'd get them over the border to safety in Tanzania. Somehow, she'd get them home to America.

As she drove back toward the clinic, the roadblocks, manned by those machete-toting young men she'd seen earlier, were fully operational and effectively closed the main roads. For so many blockades to have been placed so fast, plans must have been underway for weeks. Behind the makeshift stopping point, a line of vehicles, alternating with people carrying everything they owned, waited to pass.

A handful of bloody bodies had been tossed haphazardly at the side of the road. She swallowed her dread in one large gulp. The extermination of the Tutsis—the "cockroaches"—had begun.

Jess shuddered. She'd thought this would be a quick trip. She should have brought Jean-Baptiste. Anxiously, she looked for a route around the roadblock but didn't see any way to avoid it. With no other choice, she joined the queue waiting to present their ID cards.

An obnoxious young man snatched at her arm through her open window and demanded she get out of her vehicle.

On seeing the blood-stained machete stuck in his belt, Jess suppressed a shudder and, with a suddenly-dry throat, presented her passport.

"Tutsi woman!" A second man sneered as he frisked her, examining her breasts more thoroughly than required.

"No, I'm American." Jess held her breath. Trying to control her shaking, she wiggled out of the grasp of the second man and moved beside the one perusing her passport. The man was most likely illiterate, but she pointed to each word on the page as if he could read and exaggerated the foreignness of her accent. "See? I was born in Gladwyne, Pennsylvania in the United States. I came here to volunteer in a medical clinic."

He stared at her for a long moment before returning her passport. "You may pass."

****

Kirihe, April 8, 1994

At the clinic the following morning, Jess spoke to Jean-Baptiste. "I paid a huge bribe, but the ministry promises my paperwork will be ready next week. After all the disappointments, I'm not sure I believe them."

"You can't have meat from the cow that gives you milk." He laughed. "If they solve your problem, there'll be no more *baksheeshi* for them. Seriously, *Docteur* Jess, I fear you may have run out of time."

"You're right. At this point, the ministry may not approve the adoption only because they think the boys are Tutsis." Words poured nonstop. "Roadblocks, manned by the *Interahamwe,* are already in place." She started shaking. "The killing has already started with bodies being stacked beside the roadblock. They stopped me. I was petrified they'd think I was Tutsi, but they looked at my passport and let me go."

Jean-Baptiste exhaled audibly. "You were lucky."

Yvette glanced up in alarm. "Evacuate. Maybe you can get the Matthieu and Theo out in the confusion at the Tanzanian border rather than the airport in Kigali."

Jess nodded. Overnight the situation had become deadly. Not only for her but for her staff, all of whom were moderate Hutus. "Gas up the Land Rover, Jean-Baptiste. While you do that, I'll pack a couple of suitcases and bring the twins to the clinic. We'll leave as soon as this woman delivers."

Yvette wrung her hands. "You should leave right now."

"I can't. I'd endanger my patient. She's nearly completely dilated. The baby should arrive any minute."

Two hours later, Jean-Baptiste returned.

Jess welcomed him with relief. "What took so long?"

"I waited forever to fill the tank, but the Land Rover is ready. I parked behind the clinic so I wouldn't arouse undue suspicion. For the last few weeks, I've bought up cases of beer and hard liquor, thinking we might use alcohol to bribe men at roadblocks. I loaded it into the vehicle with your suitcases." He handed her the Leica. "I thought you might like to take a few last-minute photos."

"Thanks. What would I do without you?" Jess patted him on the shoulder. "And the boys? Where are they?"

"Asleep in their baskets in your office."

Jess took photos of her clinic and all her staff before then handing the camera to Jean-Baptiste who took photos of her with Yvette, Didi, and Elise.

"Hang on to my camera in case I want to take a few more pictures." She passed her camera to Jean-Baptiste, checked on her babies, then went to examine her patient. The mother had delivered multiple children, so this delivery should proceed quickly. Afterwards Jess could safely turn her over to Yvette and evacuate.

Jess had just placed her hand up the woman's vagina to feel the cervix when loud voices and trampling feet interrupted her train of thought.

Chapter Eighteen

Jessica

Kirihe, April 8, 1994

The door behind Jess burst open. Someone stomped into the delivery room.

"Get out of here. You're contaminating a—" Her face flaring hot with anger, Jess whirled to see who was interrupting her.

A familiar figure, now wearing a stiffly starched military uniform with gold clusters on the shoulders, strode through the door.

Holy shit. Acid churned in Jess's stomach. Cyprien Gatera. In person. Now an uppity-up officer in the Hutu army.

The image of a martinet with his uniform stiff with starch and a baton in his right hand, Gatera motioned to two soldiers standing behind him. "Get that woman out of here." He pointed to the patient.

"She's in labor. You can't take her." Jess draped herself over the woman.

Gatera flung Jess against the wall and held her there.

She squirmed beneath his grasp like a pithed frog. "What are you doing?"

He backhanded her into shocked silence.

Ignoring the woman's screams, the soldiers lifted her by her arms and dragged her out the clinic's back door.

"You have no right—" Jess spat the words at Gatera

as she struggled to escape his grasp. He drew his pistol and shoved it beneath her chin with enough force to bruise the bone. Outside, the woman screamed a prolonged agonized shriek. Seconds later, a shot rang out. Followed by another.

Jess's "No-o-o-o!" dissolved into a wail. She jerked free and ran to the door.

The soldiers pitched the disemboweled woman into the drainage ditch twenty yards from the clinic. They'd torn her child from her and mutilated it before tossing it on top.

Glancing toward the dormitory, Jess prayed the men didn't discover the women and their newborns recovering from childbirth there. They should be okay. Unlike the woman in the delivery room, those two were Hutu.

Jess wheeled to face Gatera. "What the hell are you doing?"

"Commandeering your clinic." He dragged Jess from the delivery room. He motioned to indicate the entire clinic, then ordered his soldiers, "Round up the clinic staff."

Furaha entered through the front door. He stood erect and saluted. "Colonel Gatera."

Jess was shocked to find her nemesis and junior nemesis together, but she should have expected Furaha to be wherever his uncle was.

As her employees filed into the reception area, Furaha held a rifle on them.

Gatera continued, "No one is permitted to leave. A troop transport will arrive within the hour. You will treat wounded government forces."

"No." Jess crossed her arms over her chest.

He waved his pistol toward her staff. "You will—if

you and your employees plan on staying alive."

A deep exhale marked Jess's resignation. "How many can we expect?" Why the hell wasn't Gatera treating them himself?

He shrugged. "As many as arrive."

Jess shook her head, her mind whirling with possibilities and potential solutions. It had been years since she'd participated in a disaster drill. Surely, a single truck couldn't hold that many wounded. She hated to admit it, but her Hippocratic Oath wouldn't let her deny care—even to the bad guys.

Screams filled the air, coming from the rear of the clinic.

Jess's heart jumped into her throat. Oh, shit! The soldiers had found the occupants of the dormitory. She whirled and ran toward the back door, hoping to stop the slaughter.

The guard there blocked her exit. To peer around him, Jess shifted back and forth on her feet. The women's wailing stopped, only to be replaced by infants' squeals. Then silence. A silence so powerful it hurt Jess's ears. The guard made an about-face to observe the activities behind him, giving Jess a clear view around his torso. The soldiers dragged the two women to the drainage ditch and pitched their limp newborns on the growing pile.

Jess opened her mouth, but the shriek died in her throat. Her stomach heaved. She swallowed the bile and raced toward Gatera. "Why in God's name has the army resorted to killing mothers and babies?"

"They were in the way." He shrugged. "Prepare your clinic to treat my men." He whirled and stomped off.

Furaha waved his rifle toward her and her staff. "Get

busy."

Jess growled at the suddenly-authoritative man. The usually-uncommunicative Furaha was downright cocky with a gun in his hand. She scrutinized the men guarding the doors. She was certain their weapons could wipe out her entire staff in seconds.

Grudgingly, Jess nodded to Furaha, then motioned to her personnel. "Let's get organized. Make sure all our instruments are sterilized." She and her staff started pulling bandages and antibiotics off shelves, readying IV fluids, filling basins with water.

Occasionally, she slipped into the back storage room. Mercifully, Theo and Matthieu still slept. She prayed they would remain quiet until she figured out how to sneak them to safety. She returned to the reception area of her clinic. The loud motor of a truck chugged into the front parking area.

The front door banged open.

Jess, who was stacking bandages on a table, lifted her head at the noise. She began walking to the back.

"Where are you going?" Gatera seized her arm in a tight grip.

She remembered that grasp all too well. "I need to check supplies—"

"Send someone else." Gatera tightened his hold. "I can't restrain you because of your medical duties. Rest assured, I'll shoot you or your workers at any sign of resistance."

Jess gave a reluctant nod. "*Très bien.*" She gave a silent entreaty to God for her children then nodded toward Yvette. "Can you please bring any extra antibiotics from the storage room and check on our other … uh … supplies?" Hopefully Yvette, who was less essential than Gatera considered Jess, would have more freedom of movement.

Yvette bobbed her head. "Certainly, *Docteur*."

Gatera addressed Furaha, "The clinic staff, especially *Docteur* Hemings, are to be under constant surveillance."

Furaha forced Jean-Baptist to help unload the wounded. Men were dumped helter-skelter directly on the floor with no attempt at triage.

Jess began checking her patients, fearing most were beyond her OB/GYN expertise. A young man of about twenty was first. Jess unwrapped his bandaged arm to reveal a long gash. With only skin and muscle involved, his laceration could be sutured later. Though not seriously injured, he appeared petrified. They all did. Despite her aversion to Gatera, Jess's attitude softened. She patted the soldier on his uninjured shoulder and said in Kinyarwanda, "You'll be all right in a few weeks. Don't worry."

At her next patient, Jess removed dressings from a mangled hand. Parts of fingers were missing, but he wasn't bleeding badly so, again, this trooper could wait. She'd need to amputate and reconstruct what remained. That sort of sub-specialist orthopedic work was beyond her expertise, but she suspected Gatera didn't give a damn.

Jess turned to Yvette. "Start IV's on these two. Give them both some ibuprofen for pain."

Yvette asked, "Only ibuprofen?"

"We need to save our narcotics for the more seriously injured. Re-bandage these men. They're non-urgent and can wait. While you do that, I'll figure out who are the worst and start treating them."

Anxiously, Jess glanced at her watch. Less than thirty minutes had passed since Furaha and Gatera had arrived. The twins were still asleep but wouldn't be for much longer. She had to come up with a way to carry them to safety.

After inspecting the tenth patient while kneeling on the floor, Jess's back tensed under the strain. She stood and stretched before waving a hand at Didi. "Get some paper and write the numbers one through four on each page, one for every bed. Big numbers, easy to read from across the room. A number one needs immediate care, two is less, three can wait, four is for minor injuries we can treat and street."

Didi seemed puzzled. "Treat and street?"

"Once they're treated, we can get them out of our hair. Yvette and Jean-Baptiste will help you." Jess paused. "The number five will be for hopeless cases—comfort measures only. As you triage patients, tape a label above each bed. Write the same number on the chart and put it at their feet. The first patient is a three. The next is a two."

Jean-Baptist sidled over next to Jess. "We've unloaded all the wounded. We ran out of space in the clinic, so the minor injuries are in the dormitory."

"What's the grand total?"

"Twenty-eight."

Jess grimaced. More than she'd expected.

Jean-Baptiste lowered his voice to a whisper. "I moved the babies under your desk where no one can see them."

With a tight smile, Jess said, "Thanks. How are they?"

"Still asleep."

Jess breathed out in relief. "That won't last long."

"Any idea of how to get them out?"

She shook her head.

Jean-Baptiste touched her shoulder. "*Docteur* Jess, the radio says most of Rwanda's politicians have been assassinated and an interim government formed of Hutu extremists. The country is in turmoil. You should have left when I told you to."

"I'm aware of that!" Her voice was terse. She hated herself for delaying her evacuation. She'd endangered herself and her children to help a woman who'd been killed anyway.

Abruptly Jess changed the subject. "Which of our patients need to be treated first? I should work on the most serious cases while you and Yvette do triage."

"I put the worst—an abdominal wound—directly in the delivery room."

Yvette approached Jess and Jean-Baptiste. "I checked on the boys. Matthieu is awake but still quiet."

Jess groaned. If Matthieu was awake, it wouldn't be long before Theo was, and he'd scream for food. Though bigger than Matthieu, Theo was always starving when he woke. Hopefully, the groans of the wounded would drown out his squalls.

Jess whispered to Yvette and Jean-Baptiste, "If you two have a chance to slip away, for God's sake, get out of here. Gatera will hold us prisoner until we're no longer useful, then he'll kill us."

Yvette whispered, "You, too, *Docteur* Jess. Gatera bears a tremendous dislike for you. He'll keep a close eye on you. The first chance you get, take the babies and run."

"What about you?" Jess asked.

"You refuse to run, and there goes your fall." Jean-Baptiste smiled. "Nothing is gained without risk."

Jess smiled grimly. Despite the seriousness of their situation, Jean-Baptiste had a witty saying.

"Jean-Baptiste and I are Hutu," Yvette whispered. "We have a better chance of getting through this alive than you do."

Suddenly Gatera reappeared and made his way to Jess's side. "What are you doing?" The wave of his baton indicated the three friends.

Jess gave an irritated toss of her head. "We're setting up triage criteria and devising a system to easily communicate each patient's status."

Gatera turned to Furaha. "Make sure these three are never together to plot an escape."

Jess snapped. "You've got to be kidding! How the hell can we ensure the safety of your patients if we can't communicate?"

At that moment, a wail sounded from the rear of the clinic.

Jess blanched. Theo! She glanced at Gatera.

The colonel was already striding toward the sound.

Chapter Nineteen

Jessica

Kirehe, April 10, 1994

Jess raced after Gatera. She grabbed his arm.

With a shove, he pitched her backwards so hard she toppled. He continued down the hall.

Theo's wails grew louder.

Jess lifted herself from the floor.

As Gatera entered her office, Matthieu joined Theo in crying.

Jess dashed to her little ones.

The colonel snatched the babies' baskets, dumped Jess's sons on her desk, and inspected them. "Tutsi brats. I heard you were adopting vermin, little *iyenzi* that need extermination." With both hands, Gatera grabbed Theo's tiny feet.

Startled, Theo momentarily grew quiet. Gatera raised the child into the air, winding up like a discus thrower. Theo then wailed louder.

"No!" Jess rushed forward.

Gatera swung Theo. The baby's little head crashed against the wall.

A sickening thud reverberated through Jess's ears. Through her heart. Through her soul. Blood and brains splattered the wall.

With an expression of disgust, like he'd been holding a bag of shit, Gatera dropped the boy to the floor.

Terror raw in her throat, Jess screamed as she

stretched toward her desk, grabbing Matthieu just as Gatera did.

He jerked the baby from her grasp and flung the screaming child head first against the wall.

In the sudden silence, Jess howled in despair then raced around her desk, pummeling Gatera with her fists.

"Two fewer little cockroaches." He laughed as he seized her arm and twisted it behind her, then placed his mouth against her ear. "*Docteur* Hemings, if you wish to remain alive, you will control your emotions and care for my men."

Wearing a sinister smile, he marched her from the room, calling, "Get those bodies out of here."

Still not believing what had just transpired, certain her children had survived somehow, Jess twisted in an effort to get one last glimpse at her family but couldn't overpower Gatera's brute strength.

Roughly, he shoved her into the reception area. "Get to work."

Jess glanced around. Yvette and Jean-Baptiste had been diligent. To facilitate Jess's efforts, they'd posted every soldier's status on the wall.

Her staff, each more friend than colleague, glanced at Jess, acknowledging what had happened. The dampness of their eyes revealed their sympathy and concern.

Jean-Baptiste gave her a commiserative pat on the arm. "Don't fret, *Docteur* Jess. You never know who will make the spade that will avenge you."

"Thanks." Jess's throat constricted on the word as she nodded for Yvette to accompany her.

A guard attempted to stop Yvette.

Jess turned and, in a snippy voice, said, "I need her as a surgical assistant."

"But my orders are—"

"I can't operate and give anesthesia at the same time. Ask Gatera."

The soldier stepped back. "Very well."

Followed by Yvette and their armed guard, Jess walked with wooden steps to the delivery suite where Jean-Baptiste had placed the most serious patient.

The soldier waved his rifle at her. "Get busy."

"All right." Jess couldn't keep her anger and grief from her voice. Now that she knew exactly what these monsters were capable of, she didn't bother reassuring the soldier that he'd be all right. Gatera might force her to treat his men, but he couldn't make her care about them.

With trembling hands, she examined the soldier.

He moaned at her touch.

She didn't hear him. The sounds of her babies' cries and the sound of their heads hitting the wall still echoed through her mind. She shoved her grief aside. To keep herself and her staff from being killed, she must perform her duties. She'd mourn later.

Jean-Baptiste had been right. This case was serious. A belly wound. Her little bush hospital didn't have the general anesthesia the man needed. She had only the most primitive anesthetic agents, and when that was gone, she might as well be doctoring in the Dark Ages. She asked Yvette to give the patient ketamine while Jess injected the local. Once he was under, she flushed his wound, ran the bowel to check for perforations, closed the wound, then ordered IV antibiotics. Performing the surgical procedures, ingrained in her by years of study, calmed her and gave her something to focus on besides her children.

She hoped her supplies held out. For several months, Furaha had been delivering half of what she ordered, though the PARFA shipping label showed a full case had been sent. He short-changed her on anesthesia, narcotics, and antibiotics. The clinic only received entire cases of birth control pills and baby formula. He assured her the theft occurred on the shipping end, but now, she suspected he "appropriated" supplies for the Hutu army. Graft and corruption were so commonplace, she could never prove where in the supply chain the medications vanished.

****

Kirihe, April 9, 1994

Twenty-eight hours later, an exhausted Jess sat on the waiting room floor for a moment's break.

Didi approached Jess. "The U.S. Consulate called half an hour ago. Your embassy is suspending operations and evacuating its personnel. They're staying long enough to destroy important documents and turn things over to a caretaker staff. Outside Kigali, Rwanda is relatively safe, but they recommend you evacuate. Americans are being transported tomorrow in overland convoys to Burundi. They said to bring only one bag."

"Call them back."

"When Gatera heard me on the phone, he ordered the phone lines cut."

"We're too late. So much for the embassy's assurances I'd be safe." Jess blew out an aggravated breath. "It'd easier for me to get to Tanzania than Burundi, but I can't imagine Gatera allowing us to evacuate."

Hours later, Jess had exhausted her IV fluids, pain medications, and antibiotics. Fortunately, she'd operated on most of the serious cases before she ran out of anesthesia. Eyes closed, she sat on the floor, feeling herself slide into sleep, then jerking awake, trying to summon the energy to go on. As tired as she was, she should go check on the babies. If Matthieu and Theo weren't crying, though, they were all right. She could take a break and catch her breath.

Someone nudged her right shoulder. Unwillingly she pried her eyelids open.

"*Khat*?" One of Gatera's men held a handful of green leaves toward her.

She shook her head, restraining her derisive snort. No wonder Gatera's men appeared wide awake and alert. They were jacked-up on the amphetamine-like substance contained in *khat*. The chewed leaves served as a stimulant, increasing violent behavior and causing a heightened sense of invincibility, side-effects obviously valued by the Hutu military.

Jess's fatigue pushed her into sleep.

Furaha's rough shake awakened her to resume her duties.

She began post-op checks on the wounded. She wondered where Gatera had disappeared to. Other than making sure that she performed her duties, he'd shown no concern about his men. Just as he'd also shown no remorse when killing her babies. The suppressed thought sank in. He'd killed her babies. That son-of-a-bitch had murdered her children. Grief postponed for hours surfaced. Jess staggered, nearly collapsing.

Furaha grabbed her elbow, preventing her fall. "*Docteur* Hemings, are you all right?"

Jess glanced at him, surprised to find his eyes showed genuine concern.

"I'm sorry—"

"Don't say it." Jess held up a warning hand. "I'll cry, and I need to be numb until this is over."

When Furaha released her arm, Jess looked around for Jean-Baptiste. He was re-bandaging a wound. Yvette, Didi, and Elise were in a corner, bound hand and foot, asleep. At least they were still alive.

****

Kirihe, April 10, 1994

Thirty-four straight hours of work made Jess numb—and dumb—with fatigue. Though she couldn't think straight, she made rounds on the handful of worst patients. With a sigh, she sank to her haunches in a corner. She instructed the guard, "Wake me in four hours."

He approached her, rope in hand, to restrain her. Too tired to argue, too tired to resist, she dutifully held out her wrists.

Gatera strode in. "Wait. Take her to her office." With his baton, he motioned to a second guard. They jerked Jess to her feet and dragged her down the hallway.

She dug her heels into the concrete floor. There was no way she was going back into her office, no way she could endure the sight of that blood-stained wall, no way could she bear the thought of her babies' bodies falling behind her desk. She jerked free and flew toward the reception area.

Two soldiers blocked her escape.

Gatera struck the back of her neck with his baton.

She screeched with the sudden pain and doubled over.

He recaptured her, threw her over his shoulder, and hauled her into her office. He flipped the light switch. The two guards followed him. With a swipe, Gatera sent everything on Jess's desk to the floor, including her mail and the scalpel she used to open the envelopes. The closest thing she had to a weapon now lay at his feet.

He flung her on her desk, his baton pressed against her chest. He spoke to the guards. "Hold her down."

They jerked her arms above her head and pressed the baton against her airway.

Chapter Twenty

Jessica

Kirehe, April 10, 1994

Pinned in place by Gatera's thugs, Jess gasped for air.

"You've been a thorn in my side since your arrival." Gatera grasped the neck of her scrub top and ripped it down the center. Then did the same with her bra. Next, he jerked off her pants. With a growl of pleasure, he resumed where he'd left off months before.

Unable to endure the sight of the broad streaks of blood swathed across the walls, Jess closed her eyes. She counted Gatera's thrusts. Her hatred rose every time he shoved inside her.

With a satisfied grunt, he finished and adjusted his clothing.

He spoke to a soldier. "This woman is mine." He thought a moment. "I'll guarantee no one else uses her." He picked up the scalpel and held it to her left breast. "If you wish to live, you will remain completely still."

Jess froze. The scalpel bit into her flesh. The blade was so sharp she almost didn't feel the cut. With the second cut, she screamed.

Gatera laughed.

By the third, her world darkened. The pain from each cut merged into the next. She prayed she'd black out but didn't.

Minutes later he laughed. "My personal Tutsi whore.

Take her shoes and pants so she can't escape. No one but me is allowed in here. *Docteur* Hemings is not to leave this room without my consent." He turned to Jess. "Get some rest." Then he slammed the door behind him.

Motherfucker! He'd left her in the office where he'd killed her sons and ordered her to rest—like sleep would ever come.

Seconds later, the generator outside chugged and shut off. The room darkened.

Still sitting on her desk, Jess wrapped her arms around herself. Gatera wouldn't kill her right away. He needed her medical skills. Without qualms, he would use her body whenever he desired—and turn her over to his men when he tired of her. Once her shakes stopped, she fished in the top drawer of her desk and pulled out the box of tissues. She wiped away Gatera's fluids. He hadn't used a condom. Rwandan HIV statistics played in her head. God, please let him be clean. She pressed the last of the tissues against her chest to stop the bleeding from his cuts and sorted out her options.

Matthieu and Theo were dead. Their soft little heads couldn't have sustained the blows. Jess wandered into a morass of despair. Unsure of how much time had passed, she forced herself to think. She studied her surroundings—except for the stained wall—for some way to escape. Three small windows lined one wall of her office. The waning moon outside wasn't much help. The near-total darkness left her virtually blind. Anything she did would have to be done by feel.

She was petite, but could she squeeze through a window roughly fifteen inches square? She had to try; it was her only hope.

Millimeter by millimeter she shoved the file cabinet

over the concrete floor, stopping if she made too much noise. At last, the cabinet obstructed several inches of the door, enough to slow anyone who entered.

She'd stashed the clinic toolbox in the cabinet's bottom drawer. Silently, she retrieved the hammer. Fortunately, since she'd installed these windows herself, she could un-install them with ease. While standing on her desk, she inserted the claw of the hammer into the window frame and began prying it loose. Every few seconds, she stopped to be sure no one had heard the wood creak under the stress. She loosened the window from the wall and laid it on her desk. She leveraged herself to the sill and stuck one leg through.

Damn. Forgot something. She pulled her leg back in and lowered herself to the floor, unable to leave without the picture of her sons. Without it, she had no proof that her babies ever existed.

She ran her fingers over the floor until she found the photo. The frame was bent and its glass broken. She pulled the image from its setting. Holding between her teeth, she slid one leg through the frame.

Her hips got stuck.

She silently cursed her butt—her widest part—then twisted her torso diagonally in the window. Exhaling every drop of air, she wiggled through the opening. The framework scraped long raw abrasions on her skin.

Her ass was free. The rest of her body should be easy.

Jess grabbed the frame of the window and squeezed through. Her upper arms strained uncomfortably as she lowered herself. When both feet touched the ground, she took the picture from her mouth, stretched her aching jaw, dropped into a crouch, and listened acutely.

Nothing. She crept to the corner of the building and peered at the back of the clinic. Jess hoped the *zamu* slept in his usual cubbyhole under the front porch. He, at least, didn't constitute a threat. Unable to make out the position of the guard Gatera had stationed, she remained in place.

Her Land Rover was still parked at the back of the clinic beneath a bank of windows in full view of Gatera's soldiers. Her fanny pack—holding her passport and the birth certificates she'd faked for her sons—was tucked beneath the passenger seat. The money she'd withdrawn from the bank was hidden in a secret compartment under the spare tire. Too bad she couldn't retrieve them without being seen. Too bad she couldn't drive out of here. Too bad her children were dead. Too bad she was still alive. Jess tightened her grip on the picture, the only remaining trace of her family.

For a minute, she waited to be sure no one was on the far side of her vehicle. Afraid she'd see her babies, she avoided looking at the drainage ditch. Only ghosts remained there.

Ten feet separated Jess from the back of the dormitory. She prayed she'd make it without anyone seeing her.

She tensed to dash that short distance.

The clinic door slammed. Someone clattered along the gravel walkway following a bobbing circle of brightness from a flashlight.

Startled, Jess ducked back into the shadows. A soldier opened the back of the Land Rover and lifted out a crate of Primus beer. Maybe Jean-Baptiste was deliberately getting Gatera's men drunk. The stones crunched beneath the soldier's feet as he carried the box inside.

A loud cheer greeted his arrival. The soldiers already sounded inebriated. Were they drinking to reward themselves for killing Tutsis or to forget their part in the slaughter? Either way, they wouldn't be paying much attention to her.

Jess wondered how her staff was holding up. She should try to save them but couldn't figure out how. Hell, she hadn't been able to save her own children. Alone, she had no way of handling the soldiers. A silent prayer was the best she could do. Jean-Baptiste and Yvette were right. Being Hutus, they stood a better chance of surviving than she did.

A last glance showed that she remained undiscovered, so Jess flew to the shadows behind the dorm. Cautiously, she worked her way to the corner of the building, then dashed to the rear of the outhouse. Jess moved past the loo toward the drainage ditch. She didn't dare glance back toward the pile of bodies behind her—she'd scream.

Her toes sank into the soft wet soil of the ditch. Another step brought muddy water to her ankles—it was deep enough to hide her footprints. She huffed in relief.

Gatera would expect her to turn east toward Tanzania; instead, she'd head north into Rwanda's interior and turn east later.

Clouds obscured the weak moonlight. Drizzle started and moved into a downpour. Jess tiptoed until the clinic was out of sight, then ran.

****

Benaco, Tanzania, April 29, 1994

After eleven days of living in the forest, Jess joined thousands upon thousands of refugees on the road making their way to Rusumo Falls. For the next ten days, she hid among those gathered at the gate between Rwanda and Tanzania, seeking asylum in the neighboring country. On April twenty-ninth, the portal finally opened. Jess and over 250,000 others crossed the Kagera River and made their way to refugee camps.

So weak she was staggering, Jess moved toward Benaco where she joined a procession of refugees five miles long, all waiting to be registered. Afraid to sit down, afraid to sleep, afraid she'd lose her place in line, she propped herself up with a branch she used as a walking stick. Like everyone else, she sought the white card permitting her a daily allotment of food. Hours later, her feet achy and her ankles swollen, her turn finally arrived.

In a monotone, a bored clerk asked, "Surname?"

Before the interpreter could translate, Jess said, "Hemings. I speak English."

The clerk moaned her gratitude. Without the interpreter, they zipped through the form quickly.

White card in hand, Jess went to the next tent and joined the queue for a medical examination. For the first time in weeks, certain she was safe, Jess dozed off while squatted against a tent pole. No one would attack her with all these aid workers around.

"Hemings? Hemings?"

The sound of her name woke Jess. After a few seconds, she realized where she was. "Here." She raised her hand. "Right here."

Her vital signs were normal, except her blood pressure was low from dehydration. Her weight, though, scared her. She'd dropped sixteen pounds in three weeks. She studied her wrists and hands with new interest. So little fat remained on them that they could be used for an anatomy lesson.

At last a nurse directed her to a cubicle. Once inside, Jess waved the interpreter away.

A red-haired man said, "I'm Dr. Chuck Bernard. Do you have any health problems that require treatment while you're here?"

"I need to be tested for syphilis, Hepatitis C, and HIV. I've had the hepatitis B shots."

He exhaled loudly. "When were you raped?"

Astonished at his perceptiveness, Jess blinked.

"I don't have ESP." The clinician gave a rueful laugh. "I swear half the women here have been raped. Apparently, Hutu leaders released men with AIDS from hospitals with instructions to rape any Tutsi female they found. They considered Tutsi women to be a fifth column of sexually-seductive warriors."

Jess lowered her gaze. "Somehow, I'm not surprised."

"So?"

"So what?"

"So when were you raped?"

Jess clenched her fingers until her knuckles whitened. "Three weeks ago."

"The date of your last period?"

She counted backwards. "Five weeks ago." The significance of the dates hit her. "I need a pregnancy test too." God, she couldn't bear the thought of carrying Gatera's child.

As Dr. Bernard checked her out, he said, "You sound like Katherine Hepburn. Take a deep breath."

"I'm American. A physician." She inhaled and exhaled. "Hepburn and I were raised in the same town in Connecticut—at least until I started junior high. We also attended college in the same part of Pennsylvania."

"What are you doing here? Another deep breath."

"I worked in a mother-child clinic near Kirehe." Inhale. Exhale. "When FAR soldiers arrived, I escaped. Unfortunately, I left everything behind. I have no ID, no money. Nothing."

"We can arrange for you to get home somehow."

"I'd rather stay."

"You sure?"

She nodded.

"We need all the help we can get. I can't let you do surgery since you can't prove you're a licensed physician, but I'm sure we can find plenty for you to do. Now lie down." He examined her belly. "Everything seems fine. You're quite thin, but no more so than many who've come through here. Have a seat. When I'm through, we'll get you some dinner at the mess tent and find a place for you to sleep." He wrinkled his nose. "And you'll want to shower."

****

Benaco, May 3, 1994

For two days Jess slept, only getting up to eat. On the third day, she walked to the medical tent looking for something to do.

Dr. Bernard waved at her. "Jess, you look better. You've been through a lot. Are you sure you don't want to return to the States?"

She shook her head.

"Not even for a few weeks to recuperate?"

"I'm fine. Really."

He raised an eyebrow. "If you're certain, I'll observe you for a few patients, then turn you loose."

With a borrowed stethoscope, Jess examined her first patient. When she released the man, Dr. Bernard said,

"Nicely done." After he'd shadowed her several hours, he said, "As far as I'm concerned, you can do anything except surgery. You speak Kinyarwanda pretty well."

"I do all right in medical situations. Beyond that, my vocabulary drops off sharply."

Later, she checked on her own labs. The pregnancy test was negative, but she'd repeat it in a week or two just to be sure. The other labs wouldn't be back for days. After Dr. Bernard's comments about men from the AIDS hospitals spreading the disease, her worry about Gatera's HIV status intensified. She only hoped that as a physician Gatera was fully cognizant of the risks. She wouldn't be able to perform surgery if she was positive. On top of ruining her sanity, he'd destroy her career—and end her life.

Chapter Twenty-One

Michel

Benaco Refugee Camp, Tanzania, May 10, 1994

Relief bubbled through Michel as he boarded a plane, leaving Rwanda and its miasma of death behind. As he said goodbye to the UN soldiers, Dallaire's aide-de-camp passed Michel a fax saying, "Congratulations."

Michel read it and groaned. *Merde*. A UN soldier was the first to learn of Manon's positive pregnancy test. At least Michel was going somewhere safer—Benaco Refugee Camp.

As the plane circled Ngara airport, a man chased a herd of impala off the dirt landing field so the plane could touch down safely. Michel laughed. He immediately felt more secure after observing that the runway lacked the craters from artillery fire Kigali's had. The plane taxied to a stop, and Michel stepped off carrying his war bag, his camera equipment, a duffel bag jammed with clothes, and a hard case holding his laptop. He headed toward the two one-story white buildings set in a bare field of red dirt. The control tower consisted of an air sock dangling from a pole. A row of UNHCR planes lined up like soldiers on one side of the airfield.

A man approached him. "*Bwana* Fournier?"

"Yes?"

"I'm your driver, Enoch Jonguo."

After they shook hands, Enoch led Michel to a beat-up Toyota Land Cruiser, a safari vehicle he hired out at the astronomical price of two hundred US dollars a day to reporters and relief personnel pouring into western Tanzania.

On the six-kilometer drive from the airport to Ngara, the smell of *merde* mixed with cooking odors and wood smoke assailed Michel's nose. Where was that scent coming from? Then, Enoch drove over a rise. Below, the green savannah gave way to a sea of blue. A buzzing noise joined the stench. A low, smoky fog from thousands of cooking fires floated above the sea, intensifying the fetor Michel had noticed earlier. He choked and coughed.

He'd heard estimates 250,000 people crossed the border between Rwanda and Tanzania on April twenty-eighth and twenty-ninth in the largest mass exodus in the history of the world. The sheer magnitude exceeded anything he'd seen in Serbia. He couldn't imagine how the non-governmental agencies, the NGOs, handled such large numbers. He needed to write about the chaos but also bring personal elements into his stories to humanize the situation.

As Michel and Enoch approached Benaco, the buzzing grew louder before coalescing into the voices of thousands upon thousands of people. The sea separated into individual blue plastic tents emblazoned with the UNHCR logo. Here and there, a few "real" houses, made of tree limbs plastered with red mud, sported a tin roof, but most were plastic tarps propped up by branches with the edges of the tarp pinned down by rocks.

Along the dirt roads, Michel's vehicle warred with men driving long-horned cattle to graze on the savannah. At least the vehicle offered its occupants some protection from the livestock's lethal-looking horns.

People swarmed like insects everywhere Michel looked. Their faces all held a common look—despair.

Chapter Twenty-Two

Michel

Benaco, May 11, 1994

Michel interviewed UNHCR workers the day after his arrival. In Bosnia, he'd learned when camps are serviced by a number of NGOs, there could be gaps—or overlaps—in their services as well as inter-agency squabbles and clashes with local leaders. With fifteen organizations managing Benaco, he took his time getting a sense of who did what and to whom he should speak first.

Surprisingly, things seemed well-delineated here. Doctors without Borders or *Médecins Sans Frontières*—Netherlands supervised the construction of latrines. Tanganyika Christian Refugee Services supplied transportation. MSF—France provided both hospital and outpatient health services, epidemic control, sanitation, and special care to pregnant and breast-feeding women and their infants. The UNHCR oversaw them all as well as the refugees in the second largest city in Tanzania. Benaco had been set up in record time. An Italian contracting firm, Cogefar, had already been in the area building roads. Their machinery proved invaluable in upgrading the road to Ngara Airport, clearing termite mounds from the airstrip, preparing food storage sites, and providing water tankers.

Michel and Enoch joined a steady stream of people moving toward a series of large white tents. Each person held a white ticket. Enoch didn't speak Kinyarwanda but had located a Rwandan who spoke Swahili. Michel asked a question in English which Enoch translated to Swahili, and the Rwandan translated to Kinyarwanda to the actual interviewee. They repeated the process in reverse. The four-way interviews tried Michel's patience. Eventually, he learned the tickets allowed refugees to receive a food allotment based on the size of their families, but the population of Benaco had increased so much that everyone needed to reapply for food supplies.

Michel and Enoch randomly explored streets named after well-known activists like Julius Nyerere, the first Prime Minister of Tanzania. Throngs of people had worn red dirt paths crisscrossing the camp. Invariably, whether plowed by Cogefar's vehicles or worn by feet, these unpaved routes turned muddy with the afternoon rains of the *masika*, the long rainy season.

The two men followed a crowd of women and children carrying buckets, jerry cans, plastic bottles, anything with the capacity to hold fluid, to a gully filled with runoff from the rains. They filled their containers with water guaranteed to make them ill.

Michel passed a man and a woman sleeping on the ground, their child between them. Their rude shelter consisted of an undersized piece of torn plastic and an umbrella. Michel snapped a picture, then moved on before his emotions overwhelmed him. He'd thought things in Rwanda atrocious, but conditions here appeared worse. He shook his head. No one was more bereft than innocent civilians trapped in the throes of war.

Michel interviewed members of Doctors Without Borders who pointed him toward the women and children's clinic. He motioned for Enoch to wait outside, then Michel wormed his way past an endless stream of listless, big-bellied women and silent, potbellied children.

Inside, he glanced around. Those old-fashioned privacy barriers, the kind with fabric stretched across a frame of metal tubing, divided the tent into a series of exam rooms. He located an official-looking woman in scrubs and introduced himself. "With your permission, I'd like to interview the staff here."

She pointed to a stool. "Have a seat. Dr. Jess is in that cubicle. She'll be with you when she has a chance."

Glad to rest his feet, Michel sat where he could keep an eye on that exam room. A screen partially blocked his view, but if he cocked his head, he could see a petite woman examining a pregnant patient's abdomen. She appeared competent and reassuring as she handled the mother-to-be. Not just thin, this *docteur* was *maigre*, that under-nourished kind of skinny, with hollows beneath her cheekbones, no flesh to soften her collarbones, wrists of pure bone, all covered with too-big clothing. Michel wondered if she'd make a good story. With his telephoto lens, he snapped a couple of shots.

At the click of his camera, she raised her head and glared at him.

She had the most phenomenal eyes he'd ever seen. The blue-green of the Mediterranean Sea in Cannes, his childhood home. He stared at her until she tugged the screen closed, blocking his view.

Unable to take pictures, Michel pulled a spiral notebook from his pocket and scribbled the first lines of a story.

"*Excusez-moi.*"

Startled by the female voice, Michel looked up.

The *docteur* stood at his elbow. "*Si vous attendez quelqu'un, veuillez patienter à l'extérieur. Ces femmes ont le droit à la vie privée pendant que je les examine.*"

Her voice revealed her irritation, and her French carried an odd accent, American tinged with Rwandan.

"Michel Fournier." He extended his hand as he switched to English.

She shook his hand. "Dr. Jessica Hemings."

"I'm a reporter—" Michel switched to English.

"No kidding." Like a little kid, she rolled her eyes. "And you work for Global News Syndicate."

He nodded. "How'd you know?"

She eyed him like he was *l'idiot du village* before pointing to the logo on his backpack, a bright green-and-blue earth emblazoned with the initials GNS. Then her voice sharpened to a rapier point. "I don't mind if you photograph or interview my patients, but you need to get a release from them first."

"A release?" Intrigued by her accent in English, he decided she sounded like that film star, not Audrey Hepburn, the other Hepburn. The one in love with Spencer Tracy. The star of *The African Queen*. What was her name? Ah, Katherine Hepburn.

"They may be refugees, but they have rights, especially here where we examine their most intimate parts." *Docteur* Hemings shook her head. "You're a professional. You know the rules. Follow them."

Michel shrugged. She was correct, but no one else had made him get releases. "*Très bien.*"

"Let me introduce you, and we'll see what my lady says." She returned to her patient and, in Kinyarwanda, introduced Michel.

This interview went much more quickly with

Docteur Hemings translating—English to Kinyarwanda and back—than with Enoch and his Swahili. Michel was surprised the woman he interviewed was Hutu. He'd thought he'd find mostly Tutsi in this camp, but so far ninety percent of those he'd spoken to claimed to be Hutus. This woman had evacuated, carrying as much of her household goods as possible, because Radio Mille Collines had broadcast that Tutsis would kill all Hutus in a retaliatory reverse genocide. Michel shook his head. *Merde.* That damned radio station had stirred up all of Rwanda with its hate-filled broadcasts.

He fished in his backpack for an official release, had the patient sign it with an *X*, slipped her some Tanzanian shillings, and thanked her for her time.

He and the *docteur* stepped out of the fabric-enclosed exam room. "You speak Kinyarwanda pretty well."

Docteur Hemings laughed. "I can get through a medical exam, but don't ask me about the weather."

Michel wondered why she downplayed her linguistic skills. As far as he could tell she communicated quite well in three languages. For another hour, he worked in the women's health clinic, snapping pictures, chatting with the personnel. Intermittently he studied *Docteur* Jess, as her staff called her. She moved with quick, self-assured actions. Her voice soft and calm.

Eavesdropping on her conversations, Michel picked up a few words he understood. She asked each patient if they came from Kigali, Kirehe, or Rusumo. If they replied *yes*, she queried them about a list of names. The French part of the names was easy—Michel scribbled *Jean-Baptiste*, *Yvette*, and the others in his trusty notebook—but the Kinyarwanda last names were impossible to spell, so he skipped those. If he wanted to do a story on her, he needed to know who those people were and a lot more about her than the few sentences he'd written earlier.

About five p.m. the clinic wound down. Patients departed one by one, leaving the waiting area empty. Only the staff remained, cleaning up.

Michel sought out *Docteur* Hemings as she washed her hands and loosened her curls from her *queue de cheval*, her ponytail. He cocked his head in a winning look. "May I interview you?"

"No." The look accompanying that single word made it very clear no meant no. She took two steps from him.

Ah, playing hard to get. "What if I took you to dinner? We could find a restaurant in Ngara."

She halted. Half-turned toward him. "Okay." She held up a hand. "This isn't permission for an interview." Her lips pursed. "I'm tired, hungry, and sick of camp food." A second later she added, "And you have to pay. I'm flat broke."

Michel struggled to contain his smile. "Understood."

As they walked toward his vehicle, *Docteur* Hemings studied the face of every person they passed. Michel wondered if she was looking for people on his list.

Amid the chaos of Benaco, shops had opened almost immediately, siting themselves along the camp's main roads. Michel stored the locations of the *dukas* they passed in his memory, places to return to photograph and interview refugees. At several big markets, refugees traded part of their rations for fresh vegetables. Butcher shops sold meat from poached animals alongside the usual goat meat. Bars, hairdressers, tailors had set up stores fashioned from UN tents. Tanzanians sold cloth, cigarettes, or vegetables. The local nightclub charged an entry fee, the equivalent of thirty-seven American cents for men, seventeen for women. Beer from Zaire and Tanzania flowed freely. Thus, a tent city was born.

Just before sunset, Michel and the *docteur* reached Ngara. In the evening light, it had the air of a gilded boomtown. Everywhere buildings were being constructed to hold United Nations and NGO offices. Some companies did business beneath UNHCR plastic tents. The place bustled with activity. Men loaded bananas into a truck. The newspaper kiosk consisted of papers and magazines displayed on the ground and weighed down with rocks.

Vehicles with logos of various NGOs lined the front of the restaurant. They dodged a woman roasting fresh corn on what passed as a sidewalk before entering. Inside, the place was hopping. Michel slipped a tip to the waitress and claimed the last table. He guided the *docteur* there, determined to get her story.

Chapter Twenty-Three

Michel

Benaco, May 11, 1994

Once seated in the restaurant, Michel noted that *Docteur* Hemings again studied the faces of everyone in the restaurant. "Are you searching for someone in particular?"

"No, just looking around." She gave a careless laugh, one that sounded forced. "Call me Jess."

"*Jess* sounds like that cowboy who robbed banks." Michel held his hands like pistols and fired at her.

"You must mean Jesse James." She laughed. "Don't you dare call me *Jesse*."

"How about *Jessica*?" Jess was too harsh; he preferred Jessica. It seemed more feminine for someone so delicate.

An eye-roll as she testily said, "Fine."

"So, husband? Kids?"

She lifted the beer bottle, swirled it a few times, took a long drink, then shook her head. "You?"

"Married three years. A baby on the way."

Jessica smiled. "How nice. Congratulations."

She picked up his camera from where he'd laid it on the table. "A Nikon F4." She patted it fondly. "I had a Leica. An M4."

"Had? What happened to it?"

"Disappeared in Rwanda." She shrugged. "How'd you become a photojournalist?"

"When I started out, I used a throwaway camera to take pictures to jog my memory. GNS liked the images so much they made me a *photojournaliste*." He laughed. "Reporting wars is expensive, so I think they promoted me to save money. They can send one person to do a two-person job."

"So, what have you been shooting today?"

"A few cute kids—every one of them undernourished. A lot of dispirited mothers and fathers. Long-horned cattle. Goats. Tents. Overviews of the camp. This whole place is depressing, one *énorme* fucking mess." He decided to take another stab at drawing her out. "What made you come here?"

She took another long swill. "Albert Schweitzer."

"Explain, *s'il vous plaît*?"

"As a teenager, I read his *Out of my Life and Thought* and decided to become the next Schweitzer." She whirled the bottle, watching the liquid spin, then lifted the bottle to her mouth, and swallowed several times.

Merde. She was hiding behind the beer bottle, taking a drink while she thought about her replies to his questions. She never ventured into her emotions, never revealed anything personal, stuck to generic chit-chat. After three Uhuru Peak Lagers at nearly six percent alcohol, the scrawny Jessica should have been *rond comme une queue de pelle*—drunk as a skunk—and more susceptible to questioning.

Michel's stomach was stuffed with East Africa's ubiquitous cornmeal mush *ugali*, flatbread chapattis, and *nyama choma*, grilled goat on skewers. He left several pieces of meat on his plate.

Jessica, a tiny little thing, ate like she was starving. With her fork, she pointed at his meat. "You finished?

Can I have that?"

Michel chuckled. "Sure." He scooted his plate toward her.

Once Michel and Jessica returned to Benaco, she stumbled getting out of the vehicle. Using the door handle, she pulled herself upright but wobbled unsteadily. "Would you mind walking me to my tent?"

Michel smiled. Ah, the beers were hitting her hard at last. He took her arm. "Not at all."

She leaned into him. "Most of the people here are Hutu. It's not safe for anyone who appears to be Tutsi, especially a woman alone."

Ça y est! At last, she'd slipped up and revealed something. He glanced down at her. Tutsis generally were tall, and she was quite petite. Otherwise her appearance was that of a classic Tutsi. No wonder she seemed uncomfortable. But when she spoke, her accent defined her as American.

The main street of Benaco was congested, almost impassable. Michel turned sideways to shove through and pulled Jessica behind him. It was slow going. Apparently, the simple task of placing one foot in front of the other required her utter focus. When they arrived at her tent, she pulled aside the flap and peeped in. "I share this with five nurses, but no one's here, so come in."

Inside she slumped to her cot.

Michel sat on one across the tent. Since she'd opened up a bit, he probed. He'd get her story out of her yet. *Mon Dieu*! With a flash of insight, he realized why she was so concerned about appearing Tutsi. "Your clinic was in Rwanda, wasn't it?"

Jessica recoiled.

"You were forced to evacuate, *n'est-ce pas?*"

Emotions darted across her face. She slid lower on her bed and pulled her pillow over her head.

Almost afraid to push the issue, Michel lifted the pillow. "Tell me about being a refugee, Jessica."

Tears hung on her eyelashes. He figured she kept her emotions in such tight control the drops were afraid to fall.

In a voice fraught with tension, she asked, "What do you want to know?"

"*Tout.* Everything."

She pulled a rubber band from her pocket and gathered her hair into a ponytail. Her fingers moved to the left side of her neck and scratched.

Michel glimpsed a patch of red, angry-looking skin.

She must have become aware he'd fixated on her neck, because she removed the rubber band and loosened her hair to hide the area. "The Forces Armées Rwandaises commandeered my clinic. A FAR colonel murdered my patients, mothers and their newborns, and …" She scrutinized a button on her shirt, twisting it as she chewed her lower lip. She shuttered something deep inside before continuing, "… forced me and my staff to treat their wounded."

Jessica stood, swayed, then began an agitated pacing. "I escaped. Like a coward, I left my employees—my friends—behind."

Pauvre femme. She carried enormous guilt. "You can't blame yourself."

Her pacing halted abruptly when she tripped over her own feet. She seemed surprised at her lack of coordination.

Michel reached out to steady her but too late.

She fell on her cot, struggled to sit erect, failed, and lay where she'd landed. "I was stupid. Just plain stupid. I should have gotten out earlier. Made them come with me." Her fingers moved to her neck again. She caught herself before she scratched and jerked her hand away.

Ah, the irritated skin was the *manifestation physique* of her emotional state.

"I escaped with nothing. No passport. No food. No money. Nothing. For eleven days, I lived in the swamps—"

Michel jerked his head in astonishment. Jessica didn't appear capable of sustaining herself in the wild. "How'd you survive?"

She watched her fingers writhe in her lap. After a long pause, she spoke. "I stole." Her voice dropped to a whisper. "I stole from people who had nothing. I stole from the dead. Clothing, shoes, food, everything, anything …" She shrank into herself. Her silence grew prolonged.

He stored those words in his memory. For now, as he watched her, he speculated as to where her memories had taken her. When she focused on him again, her blue-green eyes revealed only the ashes of whatever hopes she'd had. He asked, "Then what?"

"I ended up on the Rusumo Falls Bridge, hoping FAR soldiers couldn't find me in the sea of refugees. FAR used us as human hostages to hold off the Front Patriotique Rwandais. Finally, the RPF arrived on April twenty-ninth, and the FAR troops withdrew. But Radio Mille Collines—"

Michel snorted.

"—broadcast propaganda that the Tutsis were massacring Hutus in retaliation for Tutsi deaths, so thousands of Hutus crossed into Tanzania." Her face grew guarded.

Michel decided he'd inflicted enough pain for the night. He stood. "Good night, Jessica."

Already asleep, she lay slumped to one side on her camp bed. For a moment, he watched her face relax. Without the perpetual strain in her face and with a few more pounds on her, she'd be a striking woman. He straightened her out, covered her with a blanket, and pulled mosquito netting around her before he tiptoed out.

The main road was still busy. Young men were waving machetes, harassing women on the road, laughing, and showing off. With them around, Michel wasn't comfortable leaving Jessica alone. He wasn't sexually attracted to her. She was too *décharnée*, too emaciated, to arouse his lust—besides, he was married. He smiled. With a baby on the way. Young Hutu studs wouldn't be as particular. He returned to her tent and sat on a cot.

In his trusty notepad, he jotted down what little he knew about this female physican. He'd peeled off the outer layer of onion skin, yet additional layers of her psyche remained to be explored, revealing more of the story he couldn't wait to write.

Jessica was in her mid-thirties. Michel had been the same age when he blithely traipsed off to Bosnia for the first time. Though old enough to know better, in the beginning, he'd viewed incidents through the lens of naiveté. As he saw more death, anger replaced his sense of shock, of sadness, of horror. In turn, numbness replaced anger. Despite his desensitization, some images refused to fade. A mental video loop frequently played through his head in a cycle of infinite reruns. Images of dead children, women, old men, comrades—alive and dead—were now seen through a filter of sorrow and nostalgia.

Jessica was in the same situation. Her eyes held a shadow, her hands a tremor, and that spot on her neck—he'd bet none of those had been present before Rwanda. Her ideals, her *joie de vivre,* her life itself had changed forever.

In Serbia—hell, even in Paris—he'd hung out with his fellow correspondents, rehashing the shit that had happened, unable to release the memories. Just as he had, Jessica needed a friend. He doubted there was another person in all of Benaco who could understand her better than himself. And the account of a beautiful American *docteur* swept up into the tribal uprisings in Rwanda—*Mon Dieu,* that'd be a great story to fax back to Paris.

Chapter Twenty-Four

Jessica

Benaco, May 31, 1994

As Jess escorted her last patient from the tent and said goodbye, she gently touched the woman's badly-bruised face. In Kinyarwanda, Jess advised her, "Uwimana, men are more likely to attack a woman alone. I know you women band together for protection and carry sticks and knives for weapons. Somehow, though, men still manage to harass women. Maybe together we can figure out how to defend ourselves more effectively."

The woman's eyes widened. "How?"

"Come by here tomorrow night. Bring your friends. We'll figure something out."

Uwimana left, and after rounds of good nights, the nursing staff followed.

A lanky man uncoiled from a chair. That reporter, Michel Fournier, again. Silver strands ran through his temples and the scruff on his face. He was tall, at least six-three, with a looseness of limb that was somehow elegant. Perhaps being French gave him the sartorial grace to pull off the slouch hat and lumpy safari-type vest filled with camera lenses and filters. His long narrow nose appeared to have been broken. He had such an exotic look, Jess envisioned him in a burnoose, waving a scimitar and riding a horse across the desert.

"Jessica." His mouth quirked in a crooked smile.

No one ever called her *Jessica*, but Michel not only

called her that, but pronounced it *Zhesseeca*. If she'd had any idea her name could sound so romantic, she'd never have insisted on being called Jess.

She was attracted to him, not in a sexual sense, but as a comrade-in-arms. A few weeks ago, they'd met at the clinic, and now he came by every evening to walk her home, take her to dinner, or just talk. Having witnessed the same atrocities in Rwanda, they shared similar views about the politics of the country and the futility of war.

"*Bonsoir*, Michel." She pursed her lips in thought, not paying much attention to him, but more focused on her current predicament.

"Why such a long face?" Michel followed her outside.

Jess gave an aggravated growl. "I opened my big mouth. Now I have twenty-four hours to come up with a self-defense class for women, and I'm clueless."

"What brought this on?"

"My last patient, Uwimana, was attacked and gang-raped"—Jess shuddered—"in front of her children. I want women like her to be able to defend themselves."

"Many women are programmed to be passive. The most important thing is for them to be willing to fight back. Aggression can make up for lack of technical proficiency."

Jess nodded, thinking of her first run-in with Gatera—where she'd kneed him in the balls—and how at the second one she'd been too stunned by her children's deaths to resist.

Michel touched her arm. "You okay?"

She shook her head. "Sorry. What'd you say?"

"We can give them four or five basic moves that might save their lives."

"We?"

"When I became a war correspondent, I realized I might need to defend myself, so I took up Krav Maga."

With a laugh, Jess high-fived him. "Consider yourself drafted."

They left the clinic together. Jess said, "I'm concerned about what is going on here at Benaco. The powers-that-be are putting the *bourgmestres*—the guys who were in Rwanda's local government—in charge of the camp."

"So?"

"Those are the same men who implemented the killings. They were low enough on the governmental totem pole to know the location of every Tutsi in the villages in their communes. But because the *bourgmestres* had the most experience governing, the UN put them in charge. They've organized Benaco along the same lines as communes in Rwanda."

Michel's voice raised in disbelief. "The bad guys are in charge of the people they tried to slaughter? Any proof?"

"Any evidence I had, I left behind when I fled. I hate to be a prophetess of doom, but things will go to hell really quickly around here."

Chapter Twenty-Five

Michel

Benaco, June 1, 1994

The next afternoon, Michel arrived at Jessica's clinic to teach the self-defense class. He brought Enoch as his assistant. To Michel's surprise, Uwimana and two dozen women waited, each carrying a big stick.

Jessica stepped out of the clinic and looked around.

Michel said, "Are you ready for this, Jessica?"

"I guess." She looked around, apparently amazed at the crowd. "Wow. I didn't expect so many."

She translated as Michel spoke. "How many of you want to protect yourself and your family?"

Every woman, Jess included, raised their hands.

"Okay, raise your hand if you know the story of David and Goliath."

Most raised their hands.

"Good. These techniques are designed with David and Goliath in mind. Speed and well-placed blows are more important than size, strength, fitness, or age. You'll use quick, easy-to-repeat movements that can break an arm, perforate an eardrum, or knock someone out. The techniques are easy to learn." Michel paced a bit as he talked. "One of the best ways to protect yourself is to be aware of where you are and who's around you at all times. When you encounter a potential conflict, escape if you can."

Michel pulled Enoch to the forefront to use as a

teaching tool. "Once a confrontation is unavoidable, there are no rules. Do whatever you can to defend yourself, disarm your assailant, and escape the situation. Gouge your opponent's eyes, elbow him in the face, and systematically attack his groin."

The women gasped at the idea of assaulting a male.

Michel paused to let them get used to the idea. Patriarchal societies conditioned females to be passive. To protect themselves, these women needed to project authority, which must be hard when you've been deprived of home and livelihood. He wanted to ask how many had been raped but refrained. That tactic hadn't worked with Jessica. These women would respond negatively as well. While he considered how to inspire these women, he said, "I'll demonstrate on Enoch before giving you a chance to practice."

"You're the bad guy." Michel stepped a few feet away from Enoch and whispered, "Act like you're going to attack me, but do it in slow motion." As Enoch moved toward him in exaggerated motions, Michel narrated the steps to self-defense. "Don't wait for him to hit you. Attack first. Go for the eyes, then the groin." Michel let out a loud roar as he pretended to gouge Enoch's eyes.

Without conscious thought, Enoch covered his eyes.

"See? His hands move to protect his face, so he leaves his balls vulnerable to attack."

The colloquialism had the effect Michel wanted. The women giggled and began to relax.

With another loud cry, Michel took advantage of the opening, kicking toward Enoch's genitals. "Keep attacking until you disable him."

With a loud groan, Enoch obediently dropped to the red dirt.

After the demonstration, Michel paired the women up. Their first efforts produced more giggling than action. Even Jessica came closer to hugging than attacking her partner.

"Yell at your opponent."

More titters.

Michel rolled his eyes. "Jessica, tell them physical aggression is the most important component in a fight. They may be fighting for their lives. Shouting heightens their hostile feelings, which makes them feel stronger, thus more likely to succeed. They need to be avenging lionesses."

Another round of practice ended with somewhat better results, but Michel demanded more. "Don't be passive. Yell. Get angry!"

He partnered with Jess. "You want to help these women? Show them how it's done. Be fierce, damn it."

"Really?"

"Really."

Before he could prepare himself, she stiffened her fingers into claws. With a loud scream, she rushed toward him, her arm stretching for his eyes.

Startled at her ferocity, Michel's hands flew to protect his face. Instinctively, he fell back.

Jess advanced and kicked at his groin—and succeeded in hitting his upper thigh so hard he yelped.

Immediately she backed down. "Sorry."

"Don't be sorry. Get mad. Stay mad."

The last technique Michel demonstrated was using a cudgel to best advantage. He looked around, nodding in approval. "I'm glad you all brought weapons. Remember, ladies, if possible always travel in a group. A man might attack one woman, but he's less likely to attack a bunch of women carrying big sticks."

After running through several moves, he dismissed the women. Chattering and waving their cudgels, they left.

The initial pain from Jessica's kick subsided, leaving Michel with a dull throb and a slight limp.

Jessica, the consummate *docteur*, noticed his discomfort at once. She patted him on the arm. "I'm sorry I got so carried away."

"I'm glad you did. It was a turning point for Uwimana and her friends." He ruffled her curls. "They watched a tiny woman take down a much larger guy."

"Do I need to examine you?"

Heat rushed over Michel's cheeks. For the first time, the intimacy of her looking at his thigh—so close to his privates—left him flustered. He swallowed hard. "That won't be necessary. I'm not seriously injured."

She patted his arm. "Some ibuprofen from the clinic?"

"That'd be great."

She whirled, popped into the clinic, and brought out four tablets and a bottle of water.

"You up for dinner tonight?" Michel asked after he'd gulped the pills.

Jess shook her head. "It's been a long day."

"Where'd you get the balls for your attack?"

She tossed her head. "I pretended you were Gatera."

Ça y est! She'd slipped up again. For some reason, Jessica hated this Gatera. Michel had had that name for weeks but no context. He was putting together her story a word or sentence at a time. Once complete, it would be explosive. Maybe good enough to win the Albert Londres Prize, the French equivalent of the American Pulitzer

Prize, awarded each year to two journalists under forty, the best reporter in the written press and the best audio-visual reporter. He was thirty-seven now. As a dual print and photojournalist, he had twice the chance—but only three years left—to achieve his goal.

Reining in his ambition, Michel escorted Jessica to her tent. She again studied the faces of everyone she passed. Despite weeks of intense surveillance, she apparently hadn't encountered whoever she was looking for. Whatever had happened to her, *elle était trop choquée et traumatisée,* she was still shell-shocked. Her constant state of apprehension struck a chord. Her breakdown might not be imminent, but it would come. He reminded himself that he wasn't her keeper. He still hated to leave her, but he needed to take his film to Kilimanjaro Airport to be flown to Paris.

"I'm going to Arusha tomorrow. Can I bring anything back for you?" He didn't know why he hadn't offered before. Surely, she needed something.

Her face brightened. "Could you mail a letter to my parents? And wait a minute while I write it?"

"*Certainement.*"

****

Arusha, June 6, 1994

Michel picked up his mail at the business center of the Arusha Hotel. A note from his parents who were looking forward to their holidays in Antibes and another from Manon. He smiled as he read details about her pregnancy. He called her despite the expense just to hear her voice. "How's my little *maman*?"

"*Très bien.* My morning sickness is almost gone." She paused.

Michel chuckled at the mental image that fleeted

through his head. A pregnant pause from a pregnant woman.

In an excited voice, she continued, "Guess what?"

"What?"

"I heard the baby's heartbeat at my obstetrician's. When are you coming home? You should be here when I have the ultrasound to determine the baby's sex."

"I'll be home in time for your next visit. Just another week or two here."

"Promise?"

"*Mais oui, bien sûr.*"

With the call to his wife out of the way, Michel turned Jessica's envelope over and over in his hand. Even *par avion*, the letter could take days to reach her parents. If she were his daughter, he'd want news of her right away. He pulled his pocketknife from his pants. For a few seconds, he hesitated, knowing he was invading her privacy. But he hadn't become a good journalist by avoiding risk, so with a shrug, he slid the blade under the seal.

Feeling only slightly guilty, he read the letter. *Mon Dieu*. He shook his head. Jessica was no more communicative with her parents than she was with him. He removed his notepad from his vest pocket and wrote *Children—Matthieu and Theo*. He added *Parents—Greg Endicott and Regina Hemings* and their address in Gladwyne, Pennsylvania. These names joined the list that included *Cyprien Gatera, Furaha, Jean-Baptiste, Yvette, Didi,* and *Elise*.

Michel started to fax Jessica's letter to the American Embassy in Dar Es Salaam but hesitated. She'd said she was in Tanzania illegally. He'd bet she hadn't done anything about her status because Dar was all the way across the country, and having found shelter at Benaco, she was too traumatized to venture out. He wasn't sure how intimate a relationship Americans had with Tanzanian immigration, but he didn't want to get her in trouble. Instead, he tracked down the fax number of the American Embassy in Paris. Quickly, he typed a cover letter explaining Jessica's situation, then faxed both pages to France, asking them to send it to her parents posthaste.

Michel resealed the envelope and dropped it in the outgoing mail basket.

Chapter Twenty-Six

Tom

Philadelphia, June 20, 1994

Already on his second drink, Tom nuked a potato then tossed a steak on a preheated grill. His stomach growled as the smell of charred meat filled his apartment. With luck, the smoke alarm wouldn't go off. In the aftermath of his divorce from Kimberley, he'd mostly eaten at restaurants or at the hospital. In self-defense, as his cholesterol and weight ballooned, he learned to cook a few basics.

He sat down and sliced the steak. Blood oozed out, mixing with steak sauce and staining his white plate. Perfectly done. He groaned in appreciation on his first bite.

His cell phone rang.

Shit! He'd kill his office if they were disturbing him. He wasn't on call tonight. He grabbed the phone, cursed again, wiped his mouth, and muttered around his steak, "Dr. Powell."

"Tom, guess what?" A childlike glee permeated Regina's voice.

From her tone, Tom figured she had news of Jess but played the game anyway. "What?"

"The State Department just hand-delivered a fax from the American embassy in Paris. Jessica wrote us a letter. Won't you come share our joy?"

"Be right there." Tom left his dinner on the table.

Twenty minutes later, he pulled in front of the gray

stone house with white marble steps and a slate roof. He compared this spacious upper-middle-class home in Gladwyne with the tiny red-brick blue-collar Philadelphia row house of his childhood. The sole common feature was the white marble steps where he stood. He knocked on the red front door.

His first glimpse of Regina took his breath away. Except for her eyes, she bore an uncanny resemblance to her daughter. Regina's hazel eyes matched her amber skin while Jess's aquamarine eyes glowed like jewels against the same skin. In medical school, Tom and Jess worked out the dihybrid-cross chart for hazel eyes and learned she stood a one-in-eight chance of inheriting the blue-green eyes she hated and he adored.

Regina smiled, her relief about her daughter showing on her face. "Come in, Tommy."

Tommy. He smiled. Regina hadn't called him that in years. Her use of the diminutive must mean a full detente in their hostilities.

"Drink?"

He nodded.

"Whiskey okay?"

"Perfect. Thanks."

While she poured, Tom studied a now-unfamiliar room, one redecorated since he'd last been here. Jess's swim team trophies had been banished. Cool, restful ocean colors and elegant furniture replaced the family-friendly earth tones and the dual Barcaloungers.

Regina disappeared for a few minutes. She returned, bringing Greg with her. She opened a file folder and handed a paper to Tom.

He took the page, a bad photocopy of a fax. The sight of the familiar chicken-scratches made him choke up. His handwriting was bad but legible. Nurses had complained that reading Jess's was like deciphering hieroglyphics and frequently asked him to decode it.

Dear Mom and Dad,

I finally met someone who can get a letter out via a reliable mail system. I'm too exhausted for more than a short note. I survived the turmoil in Rwanda. Unfortunately, Theo and Matthieu did not. I can't bring myself to tell you—or anyone—about their deaths. Work here keeps me from thinking beyond the next moment.

I'm now in western Tanzania at the Benaco refugee camp working a million hours a day. You can't imagine the chaos. This cesspool of humanity is so deep Dante's ninth circle of Hell looks like Heaven from here. Disease is rampant—cholera, dysentery, and malaria—and death rates are astronomical.

I am safe. Will write or call when I can.

Love, J.

"I'm glad Jess is all right. You two must be relieved." With shaky hands, Tom returned the page to Regina. The last sip of his whiskey didn't begin to clear the frog in his throat. "I didn't realize she'd married and had kids." She must have hustled to have produced two children in two and a half years.

"Oh, she never married. She is—was—adopting

twins whose mother died in childbirth. They'd be fifteen or sixteen months old by now."

She'd never married. Maybe there was hope. "She must be shattered."

Greg said, "At least Jess is all right. We'd been so worried. I guess our harassment of our public servants worked, Tom."

"I'll notify everyone on my list that we've heard from her."

Regina pulled a photograph from the drawer of an end table and handed it to Tom. "As you can tell, they are—were—adorable." She shrugged. "It's hard to mourn for someone you've only met in a photo. Jess was so excited. Those babies stole her heart."

Tom examined the picture and smiled. Christ, the kids even looked like her. The same loose curls, endearing noses. Jess must be really torn up if she couldn't tell anyone what happened. "You're right. Cute kids."

"We deserve another drink, don't you think, Tom?" Tears glinted in Greg's eyes as he poured a couple fingers of whiskey into Tom's glass. "We're holding a wake and a celebration at the same time." He raised his glass. "To Jess, may she come home soon. To Matthieu and Theo, may they rest in peace."

Tom lifted his glass. "To Jess and her babies." The mood in the room was somber but with an underlying sense of reprieve. Despite the odd tenor, he relaxed for the first time in ages. He'd missed Regina and Greg. Once he'd gotten to know them, he'd grown closer to them than he'd been to his own parents.

When Tom and Jess had applied for medical school, his parents pooh-poohed his decision, telling him he couldn't afford the additional education. He needed to get a real job right away. Jess's parents, though, encouraged him. Greg pulled Tom aside and said, "We can't pay your tuition, but we can help with rent, groceries, things like that." Regina sent him care packages, boxes filled with homemade snickerdoodles, cans of soup, Ramen noodles, Spam, and a twenty-dollar bill in the bottom of every box. Even when he and Jess moved in together, the boxes continued.

On the drive home, Tom grew thoughtful. Jess was safe somewhere in Tanzania. He should take a few vacation days and go find her. He shook his head. That would mean leaving his partner alone and would cost Tom a lot of money. He and Chuck started their practice right after residency with no clue how much setting up a cardiology office would cost. The equipment was pricey and malpractice insurance astronomical. Now they were saddled with practice debt on top of student loans. Some months, Tom barely made the mortgage payment on his studio apartment on Rittenhouse Square.

Besides, he reflected, when she found him in bed with Kimberley, Jess slammed the door on their life together. He sighed. Would knowing he was divorced make any difference to her? Now that he knew she was safe, maybe he could let her go. After a moment's reflection, he realized he'd have to see her, talk to her, hold her to know she was all right. She needed to come home, then—maybe—he could let her go.

Chapter Twenty-Seven

Jessica

Benaco, June 19, 1994

Jess's past few days had been exhausting, lots of births, long hours at the clinic treating women for cholera and dysentery. After a solid eight hours sleep, though, she felt human again. Well, at least like a low-level primate. Her roommates had already departed for their shifts, so she was blissfully alone. In this rare moment of solitude, she considered going back to sleep, but the noise level at Benaco—the perpetual roar of thousands of voices—made that impossible.

No Michel to distract her either—he was still in Arusha. He'd asked if she needed anything. She could think of about a million things, but she wasn't comfortable asking him to buy bras and underwear and having him pay for them.

Jess drug herself out of bed. With a brush, she impatiently swatted at her hair, gave up, and piled it into a messy topknot. She frowned as she dressed—in someone else's clothes—and headed to the registration tent.

Months after her escape from Gatera, Jess still worried about her staff. She hadn't been able to locate them or even determine if they'd survived. Whenever she had free time, she checked Benaco's inventory of inhabitants, hoping to find them on the roster. Furaha and Gatera were unlikely to register under their real names, but her friends might. Searching through the names of the

250,000 Rwandans was a gargantuan, frustrating job. The administration complicated her chore by periodically requiring a new registration campaign before she finished the current list, thus her task began anew. Adding to the impossibility of her task, people flowed freely between several nearby refugee camps. Her sense that she'd abandoned her friends grew as did her guilt.

The clerks flipped the lights off and on to signal closing time. Jess looked up from her research. Her neck ached from being hunched over a desk, and her eyes no longer focused. She'd skimmed thousands of records, finding she often lost track of her friends' names, but somehow always retained those of Gatera and Furaha. Her desire for revenge eclipsed the search for her friends.

Exhausted, she skipped dinner, returned to her tent, and slipped into one of Dr. Bernard's t-shirts. It was too big to wear except as a nightgown. She shook her head. Her whole wardrobe was a hodge-podge of other people's clothes. One of these days she needed to do something about that. And her illegal immigrant status.

****

Benaco, June 23, 1994

Jess was getting out of bed when someone knocked on the tent pole at her front door.

"*Bonjour*? You awake?"

She smiled. Michel. "Just a sec." She hurriedly threw on a set of oversized scrubs. "Come in."

"Good morning." Michel carried two cups of coffee. He handed one to her before settling on her cot.

"Good morning yourself." She lifted her cup of coffee in a salute. "Thanks, I needed this. What are your plans for the day?"

"I'm shadowing Uwimana and some of her friends,

looking at life in a refugee camp from a woman's point of view. I can't imagine the obstacles they face on a daily basis."

She shook her head. "I know. My predicament can't compare to theirs."

He sat up. "What problems are you having? Other than too much work and too little time?"

Jess sipped her coffee, thinking. She wasn't ready to reveal everything, but since she'd opened her big mouth, she should say something. "I've been here for weeks without money, without a passport. When I arrived, I was wearing clothing I'd worn for three weeks. Things I stole." She set her coffee on a wooden crate, stood, and paced. "Nurses from the NGO's loaned me some things." Ashamed, she tugged at her scrubs. "The doctors were so desperate for help, once I proved myself, they accepted me. I can't operate because I don't have a medical license. And you've fed me about a million meals."

"And well worth the results." Michel patted her cheek. "You're no longer as skinny as *un haricot vert*."

Jess leaned into his hand. The affectionate gesture felt good. She hadn't been touched in ages, not since—she repressed thoughts of Gatera. Then she addressed the cause of her foul mood. "I've literally been living off the proverbial kindness of strangers. I need to go to the American embassy, get a new passport, and have my parents wire me some money."

"The nearest US Embassy is in Dar Es Salaam, literally all the way across the country." Michel blew out a breath. "Once you get there, with no ID, you'll have a hard time"—he hesitated—"proving you're not a refugee sneaking into the country."

"Yeah, because I'm Black."

"*Oui*." He stood. "Let's look at a map. I've got one in my tent."

Jess, as they walked toward Michel's tent, continued her visual scanning of faces. Suddenly she recognized a face and darted away.

Michel chased her. "Jessica, where are you going?"

After a dozen yards, Jess halted.

He caught up to her. "What's wrong?"

"I thought I saw someone I know."

"Where'd he go?"

Jess, her back toward Michel, kept peering into the mass of people. "He disappeared."

"Who?"

With a shake of her head, Jess said, "He's long gone. And I can't be certain."

"Was he ..." Michel paused.

"Was he who?"

"The man who raped you."

Her head whipped around to confront him. "Who said I was raped?"

"You do. With every action. You avoid most men. You search every face. You jump if someone touches you."

Jess whirled and stalked away.

Michel grabbed her by the arm. "So, you're not going to talk about it?"

"I will neither confirm nor deny your hypothesis." She gave one hard nod to indicate nothing else would be forthcoming.

They walked in tense silence to Michel's tent. Inside, Enoch lay stretched out across his cot but rose as soon as Michel and Jess entered.

"Grab our maps, Enoch. Jessica needs to get to Dar Es Salaam."

Enoch spread a map of Tanzania across his cot and followed the route of the B3 highway with his finger. "Ngara lies 1300 kilometers from Dar."

"Yikes." Jess grimaced. "With no ID, I can't fly. I'm left with trains or buses."

Enoch frowned. "By those methods, you'll take you a week or more to get there."

"Shit. Allowing time for the Embassy to do its duty …" Dismayed, she shook her head. "I could be in Dar forever."

Enoch traced the B1 highway. "It's only 600 kilometers from Arusha to Dar."

"You can ride with us to Arusha if you can wait a week." Michel said, "That'll save you some time."

Jess stared at Michel. "You were there only a week or two ago, weren't you?"

"Yes. Normally I ship my film off to Paris, but I'm hand-carrying it this time."

"You're going home?" An instant sense of loss overwhelmed her.

Michel grinned. "My wife is lonely. She thinks I should be present for every minute of her pregnancy. And she's having the ultrasound that will tell us the sex of the baby." His smile deepened. "So, I'm returning to Paris for a bit."

****

Arusha, June 27, 1994

Jess, in the company of Michel and Enoch, pulled into the Arusha Hotel and took the last rooms available. Arusha was crowded, partly from the influx of NGOs heading toward Benaco and the other refugee camps, and partly because tourists scheduled southern hemisphere winter safaris during their northern hemisphere summer vacations.

After weeks of camp food supplemented by an occasional meal in Ngara, Jess eagerly anticipated a European meal. Michel humored her by taking her to the hotel restaurant.

"I haven't had non-African food for three years." She buttered her fifth dinner roll. "This is delicious."

Michel shrugged. "Food in Paris is better."

"This bread is wonderful."

"Good." He laughed. "Not great, like in a Parisian *boulangerie*."

"You're a French-food snob, Michel."

For dessert, Jess polished off a banana milkshake. Without asking, Michel ordered another. Between slurps, she said, "I hate that you're paying for everything."

"Thank Global News Syndicate. Everything goes on my expense account." Michel winked.

The three woke at four a.m. to get Jess to the bus station early enough to get a seat. Michel paid for her ticket and handed her a wad of bills as they left the kiosk.

Jess shoved it back. "You've done enough. I can't take your money."

He grinned and shook his head. "You'll need to pay for food, your room, your passport, minor things like that."

Her hand wavered. "I don't know when I can pay you back."

"*Ça ne fait rien.*"

"It might not matter to you, but it does to me. I keep my word. I pay my debts—"

"You're too independent for your own good." He

pulled her into a hug then they kissed each other's cheeks in farewell.

With a deep breath, Jess boarded the bus and looked out the window to see the two men waving farewell. She'd miss Michel. He'd been a good friend, helping her retain her sanity at Benaco.

Chapter Twenty-Eight

Michel

Paris, June 28, 1994

As a war correspondent, when Michel flew to an assignment, he wondered if he was courting death. On the flight home, he wondered why he'd survived. He viewed airports and flights as neutral zones, using the hours in transit to decompress, to shift gears. He didn't even like for Manon to meet him. He needed those precious moments in the airport and the taxi ride home to shed his last assignment and become a Parisian and a husband again.

With only his carry-on luggage and nothing to declare, Michel should have whizzed through *la douane*, but customs always checked his "war bag" thoroughly.

Only seconds after he stepped into the baggage claim, he saw Manon striding toward him, elegant in a loose-fitting dress and high heels that click-clacked on the hard floor.

He enfolded her in his arms, hiding his face in her hair. With a deep breath, he compressed weeks of refugees and bloodshed into a box in his mind. He kissed her forehead, pulled back, and forced a smile. "How's my wife?"

"*Très bien.*"

Her adoring gaze tugged at his heart. Another kiss, this time a hungry one on her lips. Surreptitiously, he rubbed her belly. "How's my little son?"

She giggled. "We won't know if we have a boy until the day after tomorrow. I hope you're not going to be disappointed if it's a girl."

"I don't care—as long as she's as beautiful as her mother."

At their apartment, he dropped his luggage on the floor and gathered Manon into his arms for a round of quick get-reacquainted sex followed by a slow rediscovery of her changing body. The curve to her abdomen was more pronounced. He definitely saw the difference since he'd last been home. And her nipples, *Mon Dieu*, were bigger, darker, more sensitive, more delightful. "*J'adore*." He kissed her nose.

"I love you, too." Manon exhaled in contentment.

Michel stretched. "It's great to be home. To sleep in a real bed. At Benaco, my feet dangle over the end of my cot like this." He scooted to the end of the bed and lay with his feet suspended in the air.

She laughed. "You could sleep here all the time …."

"This story is a really big deal." Without being overly graphic, Michel described what Rwanda was going through. "The world needs to understand what's going on."

"You're going back?" Disappointment shaded her voice.

Michel nuzzled her neck. "I've done enough damage in Africa. I'll stick around Paris for a while."

Chapter Twenty-Nine

Jessica

Dar Es Salaam, June 28, 1994

Despite Jess's early arrival, the bus was packed when she boarded. She claimed the last available seat. Kind of like a local train, an "ordinary bus" stopped at every wide spot in the road and only vaguely kept to its published schedule. Unlike American buses, no toilet was on board, so when she used the squatty potty, as she'd started to call them, at one of the stops, someone took her seat. She stood in the aisle until someone got off.

Jess arrived in Dar Es Salaam well after dark, too late to do anything but take a taxi to the hotel Enoch recommended. After she'd paid for a couple of nights, she realized Michel was right. She'd need every cent of the money he'd loaned her to survive until she got a new passport.

Early the next morning, Jess stood outside the U.S. Embassy, waiting for the doors to open. Once inside, she waited an hour and a half and talked to multiple people before being shown to the office of a bureaucrat.

"You don't understand, sir. I escaped Rwanda with only my life. I have no ID. Nothing—no passport, no birth certificate, no driver's license."

The official, a Mr. Gillespie, raised a doubtful eyebrow. "How have you been surviving?"

"Benaco refugee camp took me in."

The Embassy official sputtered. "H-How are we supposed—"

Jess stood and flapped her too-big clothes at her sides. "Do I look like anything but a refugee? I've lost sixteen pounds since the Forces Armées Rwandaises took over my clinic. I'm wearing someone else's clothes and shoes. Doctors Without Borders would hire me if I could prove my identity and show them my medical credentials. I'd get a salary and per diem pay. I'd no longer be dependent on charity."

Mr. Gillespie's face remained unsympathetic.

"Can I talk to someone else? Your supervisor, perhaps?"

Mr. Gillespie steepled his index fingers and remained silent.

Jess stood as her voice crept up in volume. "Can you at least call my parents and tell them I'm alive?"

The official remained silent.

"I want my mommy." Dejected, Jess dropped back into her seat. Had she actually said that? She was thirty-four, too old to be wailing for her mother. She tried to stop the tears, not wanting the embassy guy to think she was a basket case. Once the blubbering started, though, she couldn't control her tears.

"There. There." The embassy guy patted her shoulder and handed her a box of tissues.

Jess gave a few shuddering breaths. She wiped her eyes and blew her nose. Inhale. Hold. Exhale. She forced her tears back into hibernation.

"Sorry." She sniffed loudly, pulled out another tissue, and blotted her eyes. She'd never cried like this in her life. Not even when she and Tom—

Why was she apologizing for her breakdown? More

embarrassed than anything, she covered her chagrin with anger. "You're treating me badly because I'm Black, damn you. I'm an American citizen. My dad teaches at Wharton School of Business and is an advisor to the World Bank. My mom teaches chemistry at Swarthmore College in Pennsylvania. Their names are Greg Endicott and Regina Hemings."

Mr. Gillespie sat upright. "What did you say your name was again?"

"Dr. Jessica Endicott Hemings."

"I'll be right back." Mr. Gillespie returned moments later. He held a page in the air next to her face, looked at it, at her, then back at it. "This Jessica Hemings?" He handed her a fax.

Jessica studied the page. Beneath a photo of herself, she read:

Bring our daughter home!
Dr. Jessica Hemings disappeared while
working on a medical mission in Kirehe,
Rwanda. She hasn't been seen or heard from
since April 8th.
Please call the numbers below if you have any
information on her whereabouts.

Immediately Jess recognized her parents' phone number. The second number was Susan's. The third unfamiliar. "Yes. That's me."

"The State Department is being inundated by phone calls—"

His intercom beeped and a nasal voice said, "Mr. Gillespie, the parties you requested are on the line."

He pressed a button. "Thanks." He picked up the

phone. "Hello?" A pause. "Wonderful." He handed the phone to Jess. "Miss, uh, Dr. Hemings. Your parents are on the phone."

Jess put the receiver to her ear. "Mom? Dad?"

"Jessie, baby, is that really you?"

Her parents' voices in her ear were enough to restart Jess's waterworks. Eventually, she calmed enough to give her folks an expurgated version of what had happened.

"Oh, baby. You've been through so much. We had no idea." Her mother sniffled. "We're glad you're all right. We got your letter. The State department hand-delivered it. We're so sorry about your little ones. Can we do anything to help?"

"No, Mom. I need to handle it myself."

Her ever-practical father chimed in. "Come home. We'll send you a plane ticket."

"I want to continue at Benaco."

Her dad again. "But—"

Then her mother. "Come home, Jessie. Won't you at least consider it? Please?"

"It's important work, Mom. Doctors Without Borders really needs help." Her parents didn't need to know her true mission—the destruction of Cyprien Gatera. Her entire body clenched at the thought of that man. She willed herself to relax before she conveyed her feelings to her folks. Inhale. Hold. Exhale. "Can you wire me some money? I lost everything when I fled Rwanda."

"How much do you need?"

Thank goodness, her parents were financially stable enough to help her out. She shrugged then realized her parents couldn't see her body language. "I don't know. I need to buy clothes, shoes, pay the fees to replace my passport, and get back across the country to Benaco."

And pay back Michel.

"Is five grand enough?"

"Sure."

"Should you need anything else, baby girl, let us know."

"Yes, Daddy."

When she hung up, Jess turned to Mr. Gillespie. "Do you have a library? I need to do some research."

Mr. Gillespie led Jess to a small book-lined room and left her alone.

She borrowed sheets of dot-matrix paper from the library's computer printer and started her investigation of Gatera.

Chapter Thirty

Jessica

Dar Es Salaam, July 1, 1994

Over the next few days, Jess went to every major library in Dar Es Salaam. At last, in the Muhimbili University College of Health Sciences, she discovered a photograph of Gatera attending a pan-Africa conference on obstetrics five years ago.

"May I use your copy machine?" Jess asked.

After an affirmative reply, she blew up Gatera's image picture to wallet size and made grainy copies. At least now she could ask people if they'd seen him. Unfortunately, she found nothing on Furaha. Such a minor bureaucrat probably would be completely off the grid. Somehow, though, she'd find these two and exact her revenge.

Three weeks later, with her new passport and enough money changed to make it to Benaco, Jess hopped on a westbound train. From Dar Es Salaam, she rode west toward Dodoma and Tabora, then north to Shinyanga and Mwanza. On secondary routes like the one to Ngara, trains kept no perceivable schedule.

Once in Mwanza, transportation grew more complicated. She boarded rickety buses with windshields too cracked to see through and with brakes that vocalized in agonizing squeals. Drivers raced over wash-boarded roads with potholes the size of elephants. Jess muttered constant prayers that she'd survive the trip—no wonder so many vehicles had *Mungu Atubariki* or "God Bless Us" emblazoned on them.

In Ngara, Jess convinced the driver of a UN vehicle to give her a lift to Benaco. As they approached the camp, the smells of shit and wood smoke made her shudder.

After eight days on the road, Jess entered her tent, nearly as tired, filthy, and stinky as she'd been after days on the Rusumo Falls Bridge.

Her parents had faxed copies of her medical license and diploma, so Jess resumed her work at Benaco, this time as a full-fledged physician. She found solace in the routine work in the mother-child clinic. Though she shared a tent with five women, she missed Michel. He never flaunted the role, but he'd become her friend and self-appointed protector.

Over the next several weeks, Jess recognized several *génocidaires* in the crowds. One even accompanied his pregnant wife to the clinic. On seeing him, Jess's heart rate ratcheted up. He acted like nothing had happened, like he hadn't organized the *Interahamwe* and sent them on killing sprees. He was blasé enough to light up a cigarette in the clinic tent.

Jess spread her arms and raised her voice. "You can't smoke in here. It's a fire hazard. You have to go outside."

He blew a stream of smoke into her face, then slunk outside, trailing fumes behind him.

After checking to be sure he was truly out of sight, Jess pulled her photo of Gatera from her pocket and asked his wife, "Do you recognize this man?"

The woman's eyes widened. She glanced quickly in the direction in which her husband had vanished then back at Jess. "He's a big man in the FAR army."

Jess's knees weakened. "Do you know where he is?"

Fear in her eyes, the mother shook her head desperately. "No more questions."

As Jess poked and prodded *Madame Génocidaire*, she was disappointed the woman wouldn't provide more information. Jess wanted to report this *génocidaire* but doubted it would do any good. He was small potatoes compared to Gatera. Only two men rated her vengeance, and neither appeared to be at Benaco.

****

With the *génocidaires* in charge, as Jess predicted, Benaco became an armed camp. The death rate, at times in the thousands, once included only diseases like cholera and malaria as causes of death. Now it listed five or six homicides a day as the *Interahamwe* or ex-FAR soldiers continued killing Tutsis and moderate fellow Hutus. She and other doctors took turns handling the medicolegal issues, so Jess again became accustomed to determining causes of death, most often garrotings, gunshot wounds, or machete slashings.

Some days Jess spent more time in meetings than treating patients. Benaco's health unit met twice a week plus meetings with the various NGOs. Good communication was key to providing care to a city of refugees, so she endured.

The problems brought on by the *génocidaires* prompted Jess to speak out at MSF's general camp meeting where all departments sent representatives. "As the RPF, the good guys"—she made air quotes with her fingers—"moved toward Rusumo, many FAR soldiers, the bad guys"—air quotes again—"fled, fearing retribution. They joined the refugees already at the bridge and escaped into Tanzania. They're turning Benaco into a mini-Rwanda with all its racial problems."

"Do you have any proof?"

"I recognize men who were heads of communities around mine." Jess's voice turned desperate. "For years, Rwanda remained a tightly-controlled society. The government sat at the top of a pyramid, then districts, then communes governed by the *bourgmestres*. The MRND, the governing party, had a youth wing the *Interahamwe*, akin to the Hitlerjugend, they trained as a free-form militia. The *bourgmestres,* the most powerful men in the communes, claimed an authority far exceeding what the law allowed. They commanded the gendarmerie and passed out weapons and hit-lists to local gangs. Haven't you noticed we now include homicide among our causes of death?"

"Can you prove your allegations?"

"I witnessed it first-hand."

Arguments rose and fell around her. Eventually, in typical committee fashion, the group decided to do nothing.

Jess's warnings fell on deaf ears. In disgust, she threw her hands in the air. "Jesus Christ! You can't put the bad guys in charge of the very people they tried to slaughter. How many people need to die before you guys wake up?"

In the aftermath of the various committees deciding to do nothing, she became accustomed to gunfire disturbing her sleep and to a vague sense of threat from men carrying automatic weapons. Her powerlessness fueled her anger at Gatera and her desire for revenge.

She organized more self-defense classes but lacked Michel's command of the subject. Women resigned themselves to sexual exploitation. They also continued to get pregnant and give birth, increasing the already-staggering population of Benaco.

Graft and corruption were rampant. Medical supplies disappeared before making their way to her clinic, or worse, afterwards. Antibiotics disappeared from shelves overnight. Antivirals she needed to treat HIV-positive mothers and babies—gone. Prenatal vitamins—gone. And who, other than pregnant women, needed prenatal vitamins?

The food supply reached a state of terminal chaos. People in the supply tents reported food crates vanished without a trace. She'd heard estimates one-third of the food that arrived in camp was resold to Tanzanian markets, thus lowering prices and devastating local farmers.

If refugees couldn't gather materials they required for food or shelter, they scavenged local farms, damaging the crop yields. Nearby subsistence farmers could no longer count on selling or consuming their full complement of crops. With no cushion to fall back on, they were particularly hard hit.

Many days the UN couldn't supply the minimum nutritional needs of Benaco's inhabitants. Most of the patients Jess saw were malnourished. Every rib stood out in relief against children's little potbellies. *Génocidaires*, chubby in comparison, stood out from the rest of the population.

The lack of meat in refugee rations and their inadequate caloric levels created a huge black market for *mchicha wa usiku* or "night spinach." Refugees earned money and improved their diet by dealing in poached animals. They hunted wildlife with AK-47s. Soon the lions and leopards Jess had heard coughing when she first arrived moved on in search of prey.

Even the landscape changed beneath the weight of 250,000 people. Trees disappeared. In their constant search for firewood, women trekked six to eight kilometers from Benaco and were thus more vulnerable to attack. So, more patients who had been raped and mutilated by thugs appeared at her clinic.

And Tanzania's good deed of accepting all these refugees wasn't going unpunished.

****

Benaco, July 1994

To catch up on current events Stateside, Jess read her roommates' month-old newspapers and learned O.J. Simpson had allegedly killed Nicole Brown Simpson and Ronald Goldman. South Africa inaugurated its first Black president, Nelson Mandela, so perhaps there was hope the world might eradicate racial intolerance. On July Fourth, Voice of America provided good news: the Rwandan Patriotic Front had captured Kigali. Jess prayed it meant an end to the genocide.

As RPF soldiers moved further into Rwanda, FAR troops fled in disarray. Undoubtedly including those cowards, Gatera and Furaha. Furaha most likely didn't have the financial resources to leave Africa, but Gatera would definitely escape to some safe place. He had the wealth to have plastic surgery too. Jess removed his photo from her pocket and clenched her jaw as she imagined how he might disguise himself. Losing weight wouldn't help. Even at a normal weight, he had a broad frame with bulky muscles. He could gain weight, though. She studied his features. A plastic surgeon could change his face. How would Gatera look if his nose was more tapered? His thick lips thinner? His cheekbones more prominent?

Hell, he'd look Tutsi. Would he want to avoid capture enough to turn himself into the very thing he hated most?

Jess's prediction Benaco would become a mini-Rwanda proved true. At a July staff meeting, the coordinator announced that an MSF worker had seen a man killed by a crowd. The leader of the mob said he was an RPF spy. The coordinator urged, "Don't go out alone. We'll have policemen escort personnel to and from their assignments."

On August twenty-second, Jess and another doctor determined causes of death of nineteen refugees killed because they were suspected of wanting to return to Rwanda. Hutu extremists in the camps intimidated the refugee population to keep them from returning home. *Bourgmestres*, local leaders who were part of the previous political structure, stockpiled items stolen from the NGOs to supply future attempts to topple the current government. Gangs controlled distribution of food and other supplies. These groups had lives of their own, not needing support from outside the camp. The only thing sustaining them was humanitarian aid. The relief operation was accused of "feeding the killers," causing a *crisis of conscience* among MSF physicians.

Jess developed a deep paranoia, a natural response to the chaos and increasing violence directed toward relief workers and refugees. Her feelings intensified when word came from another camp that CARE-Canada's expatriate staff was on the militia's hit list. Relief agencies couldn't do much to protect themselves or others. Security in refugee camps was supposed to be the duty of the host country, but sometimes those countries didn't accept that responsibility. Tanzanian authorities promised to remove the ringleaders, but their policemen were unarmed and unaccustomed to dealing with hardened warriors. In fact, their attempts led to an uprising which forced relief workers to leave the camp for seven days.

She attended another MSF meeting to discuss the deplorable situation in which the administration presented two options—stay and continue providing aid or withdraw from the camps. The debate raged for weeks. No one could decide what to do. Only big bucks and armed troops would cure the problem. But the West was no more interested in policing refugee camps than they'd been in interfering in Rwanda.

Jess's hatred of Gatera assumed a laser-like focus, increasing in direct proportion to her frustrations with camp life. Though stymied by the politics at Benaco, the inability of anyone to take military control, and her lack of control in her life, she held one thought constant: revenge.

Chapter Thirty-One

Jessica

Benaco, November 1994

One of the nurses in Jess's tent read aloud from an October 1994 *Reader's Digest*. An article, "Escape from Terror," described the horrors in Kigali with Hutu extremists killing Tutsis in a veritable bloodbath. Soldiers and the *Interahamwe* broke into homes, shooting people, tossing grenades. They'd ambushed ten Belgian UN peacekeepers.

Jess clapped her hands over her ears. She didn't need to hear about the genocide. She'd lived through it.

The next day, *Médecins Sans Frontières* announced its decision to pull out, stating, "This operation is a total ethical disaster."

Hutu militants had a vested interest in preserving the status quo rather than repatriating the refugees. The camps provided protection and resources for their military activities. In effect, they the refugees became semi-hostages and humanitarian aid a resource to manipulate.

Jess herself was torn. Women and children comprised roughly half the camp. Though being female didn't preclude participation in genocidal activities, those women had truly innocent children who needed food and healthcare. She hoped the agencies' actions would force the international community to disarm the camps. Those thoughts didn't assuage her sense of guilt.

Jessica called her parents. "We're pulling out of Benaco." She explained the tense situation to her mother and father. "Doctors Without Borders can't work under such untenable conditions."

"So, you're coming home?"

"Once we get everything packed up." Jess hadn't given up her need for revenge, but she needed rest and money to finance a new plan.

****

Benaco, November 25, 1995

Someone knocked at Jess's tent as she stuffed her belongings into her duffle bag. Before she could answer, Michel poked his head in. "*Bonjour*."

She pulled him in the rest of the way and gave him a hug. "What are you doing here? I thought you were staying in Paris until the baby is born."

With an expression simultaneously guilty and glad, he said, "I have a new assignment—to go back into Rwanda."

"What does your wife think of this new assignment?"

"She's not happy, but she understands—I think. Frankly, I was going crazy covering the French political scene. I could only write so much about François Mitterrand's secret daughter."

"The ultrasound results?" At his proud-papa look, she said, "You're having a boy! Congratulations." She gave him another hug.

"I wouldn't mind if the baby is a girl as long as she is healthy. Manon made me promise to be home in time for the birth. She's due December thirteenth." Michel changed the subject. "What about you? *Médecins Sans Frontières* is pulling out. I guess that means you're heading home?"

"Yes, I called my parents a few days ago." Jess looked directly at Michel. "What are you doing back at Benaco?"

"Looking for a guide-translator. Someone who wants to return to Kigali." He paused then said, "On November eighth, the UN Security Council established the ICTR, the International Criminal Tribunal for Rwanda, to conduct trials in Arusha."

"Think it will do any good? They can hardly try every Hutu male above the age of sixteen." Sarcasm made Jess's voice brittle.

"I'm sure they'll concentrate on the ringleaders, the hardcore Hutu *pawa* guys, and those assholes who blasted hate rhetoric on the radio."

"What are you going to be doing in Rwanda?"

"I'll be documenting the aftermath of the war, mass graves, burial sites, the effects on those who remained in the country. The world finally woke up. This conflict is now officially a genocide."

Jess pursed her lips before saying, "Anyone who lived through it would agree."

After Michel left, Jess sank to her cot. On one hand, going home sounded wonderful. But here at Benaco, despite showing Gatera's photo to everyone she met, only one person admitted knowing him, and that lead had amounted to nothing. Maybe people in Kigali would know more, especially the doctors and nurses she'd worked with. Surely, they'd have some idea as to his whereabouts. The thought raced through her head—maybe he'd even *be* in the capital. And any information she picked up she could pass to this newly-formed tribunal.

Jess dashed out of her tent. When she caught up with Michel, she grabbed his shirt sleeve. "I'm going with you."

"You need a break from all this." Michel waved a hand in the air to indicate Benaco.

She countered, "You could use some company."

"Jessica, don't you think you've been through enough? Besides, I'll have the interpreter for companionship."

"You said you wanted to talk to survivors." Jess turned her best puppy-dog eyes on him. "Women might open up better to another woman. Please?"

He shook his head. "Don't lie to me."

"I'm not—"

"Do you think I didn't notice you asking everyone you met to look at that photo? Do you think I really believe you've stayed here out of charity? I know what you've been doing, and you want to return to Rwanda for the same reason."

"What exactly do you think that is?"

"You're looking for the *génocidaire* who killed your children and raped you."

"Know-it-all." Stretching to her full five-feet, two-inches, Jess put her hands on her hips. "Can I come with you or not?"

With a resigned nod, Michel said, "*Je suppose que oui*." Under his breath, he muttered, "At least then I can keep an eye on you."

Eager to prove herself useful, Jess helped Michel hire a driver-guide before they left Benaco. Protais Ngeze was a Kigali native. A Hutu moderate, he'd fled the country when the massacre started. With his family scattered, he seemed eager to find those who'd survived.

In anticipation of a ten-to-fourteen-day road trip, Jess packed everything she owned, including the knife she'd stolen during her escape from Gatera. She also appropriated drugs and equipment from Doctors Without Borders, rationalizing that she wasn't *stealing*, she was simply continuing their work in a new area. MSF was pulling out anyway.

On the day of their departure, Jess shoved her luggage at the driver. Then she raced ahead and grabbed the front passenger door of the green Toyota Land Cruiser. "I call shotgun."

Right behind her, Michel said, "I get the front seat."

"But I called shotgun." Her lower lip stuck out in a pout.

"What's this *shotgun*?"

"Kids in the States say that when they claim the front seat."

Michel drew himself up to his full height and peered down at her. "I haven't fit in the back seat since I was twelve."

Jess glanced at the backseat and then up at him. His six-three body would never fit. Not only that, once he scooted the front seat backward for comfortable leg room, even her petite self wouldn't fit in the rear passenger side. She resigned herself to spending the whole trip staring at the back of Protais's head and sharing the back seat with Michel's camera gear, but at least she was pushing forward in her search for Gatera and Furaha.

On Rusumo Falls Bridge, Jess scrunched her eyes shut, assaulted by memories of crossing into Tanzania in the company of 250,000 people, of seeing blobs tumble over the waterfall and realizing they were bodies. The Hutus, in their promise to "send the cockroaches back where they came from" dumped thousands of bodies into the rivers which flowed north to Ethiopia, the reputed homeland of the Tutsis.

"You all right?" Michel twisted around from the front seat.

Jess shivered. "Yes." To her ears, her voice sounded weak and frightened.

Michel's long arm traversed the space between them and touched her knee. His hand shook. The unflappable Michel was showing fear. No. Her own trembling caused his tremor. Through a big sniffle, she said, "Sorry. I'm okay, really. Thanks." She took a deep breath. Inhale. Hold. Exhale.

"What do you know about Rusumo, Jess?" Michel asked.

"When I was stuck on the bridge, rumors circulated that the mayor of the *commune* had provided the weapons for Hutus to massacre the Tutsi *iyenzi*. He also refused to allow us refugees to cross into Tanzania."

Michel blew out an explosive breath. "Fuck. I wouldn't want to meet him in a dark alley."

"The mayor headed a military-type convoy transporting communal police and *Interahamwe*, armed with spears, machetes, rifles, and grenades. The *Interahamwe* also used *nta mpongano y'umwanzi*—"

Michel shot a questioning glance in the rearview mirror.

"Clubs studded with nails." Jess's voice dropped to a whisper. "It means *no mercy to the enemy*. Anyway, he took these men to the parish of Nyarubuye where Tutsis and Hutu had gathered for sanctuary. Earlier, the *génocidaires* herded people there, concentrating their victims in one spot for mass killings."

Just west of Rusumo, Jess pointed to a battered roadside stand and asked Protais to pull over. Smoke and the odors of roasting food rose from a grill made of the top of an oil barrel. A woman with streaks of white running like lightning bolts through her hair.

Jess nudged Protais. "Get out and ask her what she knows."

He hopped out.

The woman, with machete slashes on her arms, greeted him and indicated her roast vegetables and chapatis.

He refused with a shake of his head and asked her a question.

Wielding a large kitchen knife, the woman shrieked and chased him away.

Protais barely slammed the door before her knife hit the window, leaving a zigzagged crack in it. Immediately, he cranked the engine.

Michel asked. "What'd you say to set her off?"

"You wanted me to find massacre areas. So, I asked if she knew of any killing sites or mass burials."

"Nothing like being subtle." Michel grimaced. "I figured getting information from survivors would be tough, but I never thought we'd get off to such a bumpy start."

"Let me try." Jess opened the door.

Chapter Thirty-Two

Jessica

Road trip to Kigali, November 1994

Michel tried to pull Jess back into the vehicle, saying, "She's got a knife. Get back in here."

Jess dodged his grasp. With both hands in the air, she approached the woman. Then, she moved her hands into the prayer position. In Kinyarwanda, she asked, "Mother, do you have any brochette?"

The woman shook her head. "No meat. Not for a long time."

"Then may I have three chapattis with vegetables?"

The woman's toothless mouth smiled. "Certainly, *Docteur* Jess."

Jess was astounded. "You know me?"

"Everyone around here has heard of the White lady *docteur*."

Jess beat down a cringe. After all this time, she hadn't gotten used to being called White. But this was her chance to get information—at least the woman wasn't threatening Jess with a knife. "Maybe you can help me." She pulled the photo of Gatera from her pocket and showed the woman. "Have you seen this man?"

Reluctantly, the woman took the picture, studied it, then, with no evidence of recognition, she returned it. "Why?"

Jess swallowed hard and blinked back tears. "H-he killed my children. I don't even know where their bodies are."

The woman put an arm around Jess and towed her behind the little shack. "I haven't seen your man." She pointed dead ahead with her index finger. "Up there is a bunch of bodies."

"How far?"

"Go past two villages. You'll know when you've found the right place."

The two returned to the front of the hovel, in sight of the vehicle, where the woman placed roasted vegetables into chapattis and wrapped them in paper.

"Thank you." Jess paid the woman too much, then took the food to the vehicle. Once inside, she passed out the chapattis. Around her first bite, she said, "A killing field lies to the north." Jess jerked her head toward the shopkeeper. "She said to pass two villages and we'd know when we got there."

Michel grimaced. "That sounds ominous."

Protais made a U-turn on the RN3 and drove as Jess gave directions. She remembered the hamlets from visits she and Yvette made to drum up business for the clinic. After a hundred yards or so, Jess directed him down a one-lane, red dirt road pockmarked with potholes.

Off the main highway, things changed quickly. No vehicular traffic competed with the Land Cruiser for road space. The threesome drove into the first village. Not a person stirred. In fact, nothing moved. The silence was creepy.

With the November rains, vegetation flourished. Grasses danced over the road. Their seed heads swished against the vehicle like the fingers of the dead. Terraced fields, with no one to cultivate them, had gone from pristine to neglected. Cold tremors chased each other across

Jess's shoulders.

They drove past empty homes. A ghost town lay before them. No one ran to greet them eager for gossip. With the wet weather, the red adobe houses were slowly disintegrating, a mud-to-mud variant of dust-to-dust. The stuccoed houses fared little better. Boards supporting porches slid downhill, and thatched roofs decayed from lack of care. In small orchards, birds—too fat to fly—feasted on unpicked fruit.

Jess remembered Rwanda as a vibrant country in constant motion. People gathered wood, cooked outdoors, strolled to town, hauled water, walked to carefully tended plots thick with cassava, beans, corn, and sweet potatoes. The absence of people was eerie.

Some of the abandoned houses had belonged to Tutsis who'd been killed by their Hutu neighbors. The rest belonged to Hutus who'd participated in the genocide. Jess couldn't tell the difference. With so many refugees and so many dead, would this village ever be repopulated? Or would the forest absorb the homes?

Again, chills raced down Jess's spine. She looked at her companions. Michel and Protais both looked uncomfortable.

"Stop the car." Jess grabbed Protais's shoulder.

He braked. "What's going on?"

"Roll down the windows." She cranked the handle of her window. "Now listen."

The wind shimmered through leaves and flattened grasses. There was no other sound. The hush hurt their ears.

"This *colline* is too quiet," Jess said. "It used to be filled with children singing, men laughing, women calling to each other across the fields." Her voice quavered as she waved her hand outside. "*That* is the silence of death."

At the second village, as deserted as the first, Michel got out to take pictures. Jess and Protais stayed in the Toyota.

Michel returned to the vehicle and shook his head. "This is really depressing."

Jess agreed. "Spooky's more like it."

"Where do we go from here?" Protais asked.

She pointed out the window at the sky where vultures rode air thermals like airplanes awaiting permission to land. "Follow them."

Half a mile from the second village, the fetor of rotting flesh reached their noses long before the killing field came into view. Moments later, an annoying hum filled the air. The sound grew louder. Flies. The trio rolled up their windows.

"Turn here." Jess indicated an overgrown road, barely visible beneath the vegetation.

Protais followed the rugged track. The stench and the buzz intensified. Tree growth stopped abruptly. They entered a clearing. He slammed on the brakes.

Disturbed by the vehicle, vultures ascended from a mountain of bodies. Snarling dogs retreated. A thick dark blanket of flies rose en masse. An odor, so strong Jess tasted it, seeped through the closed windows of the Toyota and shrouded its occupants. She gagged.

Michel took a deep breath, held it, then opened the door. He raised the camera to his eye and began taking photographs. He seemed totally unaffected by the horror before him. How did he maintain that control?

Hesitantly, Jess and Protais got out.

Immediately she dropped to her knees, throwing up

every bite of her chapatti-wrapped vegetables.

Protais was right beside her.

When her stomach was empty of everything she'd eaten in her lifetime, Jess got back in the vehicle. She opened a bottle of water, rinsed her mouth several times and spat out the open door. The smell of decay overpowered the taste of residual vomit in her mouth. Nothing short of cinnamon schnapps would rid her mouth of the sickly flavor the odor laid on her tongue.

She studied the stack of humans. Bones, clothing, and partially decomposed bodies were tossed like garbage into a pile as tall as a house. Parts of the bodies had blackened. Dogs had pulled limbs from the pile and randomly strewn them.

It'd been months since Gatera had killed her babies. If their bodies had been cast aside like that, she'd never identify them.

The thought fortified her intent to pursue Gatera.

"Hurry up!" Jess yelled at Michel. She leaned her head against the seat in front of her, pinching her nose together with her fingers to forestall her sense of smell and breathed through her mouth. Inhale. Hold. Exhale. Nothing reduced the fetor of decay. How could Michel stand being near enough the bodies to shoot close-ups?

An eternity later, he put his camera gear in the back. Then he fished around in his backpack and brought out a small bottle. He liberally sprinkled its contents on his hands and swiped it across his upper lip. He handed the bottle to Jess. "Cologne?"

She splashed herself. The scents of citrus, spices, and musk helped, but by the time she passed the bottle to Protais, the effect faded.

Sobered, they drove in silence to the RN3.

The group moved on to Nyarubuye itself to look at the church, convent, and school. The red brick house of worship would have been called austere under the best of circumstances. The only signs of its religious life were a two-story steeple topped with a cross and a white statue of Jesus guarding the front door.

Months after the killing, corpses still rotted in the church and courtyard. Some, the ones not thrown into large piles, had dried out, their teeth bared in grotesque rictus grins. Oddly, a banana plant, fertilized by the decaying bodies, thrived in the space between a woman and her child. Inside, where babies' heads had been shattered, a dull red stained the church walls. Jess's finger traced an aimless pattern on the stucco, connecting dots of brain matter, wondering if this method of killing was unique to Gatera, if he had been here, or if it was a common way to end a little one's life.

Quickly she escaped the claustrophobic confines of the church. Outside was no better. To the east, the stand of trees where she'd hidden remained vigilant, guarded memories. She swallowed her nausea and returned to the vehicle. Inside she breathed rhythmically. Inhale. Hold. Exhale.

After Michel had taken enough photographs, he and Protais knocked on doors in the little community, talking to survivors about the genocide. Jess tagged along, hanging back and watching.

Chapter Thirty-Three

Jessica

Road trip to Kigali, late November 1994

Back on the RN3, Jess poked Protais in the shoulder. "Turn left at the next road." After a bit she said, "Veer to the left." Seconds later. "Stop here."

Jess threw open her door and got out. "Oh God oh God oh God."

Her little house was no longer pristine. The front porch roof sagged to the right as if it had suffered a stroke. The door stood ajar. Shattered glass from the windows sparkled on the ground. Bits of clothing and household goods littered the front yard. Weeds had conquered the previously manicured yard. Next door, the houses belonging to Justine and Dorcas, never as well-cared for as Jess's, had fared no better.

Willing her emotions to disconnect from her vision, Jess steeled herself to open the door.

The inside had been utterly trashed. Graffiti painted on the walls. Furniture was missing or destroyed. Mildew and mold dripped down the walls. Her pots and pans, kitchen utensils, and dinnerware had vanished. In her bedroom, her clothes and shoes were gone. Photos of her boys—what she'd most hoped to find intact—had disintegrated in broken frames. Her medical texts had been dumped onto the floor, and through a broken window, rain had soaked them. She flipped the books over with her toe, bent, and picked one up. Schweitzer's pages had merged into a solid mass, his inspirational words and Tom's sweet dedication locked inside.

Jess entered the boys' bedroom hoping to salvage something—anything—as a keepsake. Everything had been stolen. Nothing remained. No toys. No baby clothes. No pictures. Her entire life had been stolen.

Shaken, she stepped out of her house to find Michel standing on her front porch.

"Are you okay?" He tilted his head, a questioning expression on his face. "This isn't a random house. You lived here, *n'est-ce pas?*"

Too overcome for words, Jess nodded.

Michel put his arms around her.

Jess tore away. "I need to check on my clinic." She ran, Michel right behind her, past the trees that separated her house from her office—and came to a dead halt. Only his arms kept her from falling to her knees. Her clinic was in worse shape than her house. The *Clinique Mère-Enfant* sign dangled by one nail. The silhouettes of children and pregnant women had been used for target practice. The windows Jess had hammered in place were broken. All the hard work and blisters had come to naught.

Inside, any furniture that hadn't been stolen was broken. More graffiti—giant penises, Hutu *pawa* slogans, obscenities. All the medical equipment had disappeared and, she supposed, appropriated by the FAR army.

Drawn against her will to her office, Jess leaned against the wall to support her wobbly knees and made her way with faltering steps toward the closed door. Fearful of ghosts, she hesitated before venturing in. The file cabinet, its drawers sticking out like broken fingers, was empty. The desk Gatera had raped her on had vanished.

The window she escaped through was still missing its glass. Now the hardest part. Jess turned her gaze to the far wall and lurched across the room. Blood stains, like rusty Rorschach tests, covered the floor and walls. Two little lives—and hers—reduced to those spots on the wall. Jess banged her forehead against the plaster in time with her finger, rubbing little circles in the discoloration. Hate welled up inside her and burned her heart to ash.

Jess knew Michel was behind her before he touched her shoulder. The smell of death permeated his clothes, lingering since their visit to the killing field.

"Are you all right, Jessica?"

"I don't know." She shrugged before facing him. "I need to check one more thing, then we can go."

"I've been taking photographs." He looked at her intently. "If you want me to stop, I will."

With a shake of her head, she said, "No, people need to see how bad it was back then."

She walked out the back door. The only thing intact behind the clinic was the loo. The bodies discarded in the drainage ditch were gone, dumped, along with those of her sons, in some mass grave or burned in a massive pyre. She'd never find her little ones now.

With an anguished scream, she sank to her knees, rocking back and forth. "Damn you. When I find you, I'll kill you!"

Michel knelt behind Jess. He took her in his arms and rocked with her until she calmed. "I've never seen you like this. Do you want to talk?"

"No." She shook her head. "It hurts too much."

When they returned to the vehicle, Protais wasn't around. They wandered the area calling his name, but he was truly gone. They checked the back of the vehicle.

Food and several bottles of water were missing.

"I guess what we experienced earlier was too much for him." Michel kicked the dirt, sending a stone skimming across the road.

"It was pretty gruesome. I don't know how you managed to take photographs without throwing up."

"Back in April, I photographed similar sites in Kigali. Before that, Serbia." He swallowed before continuing. "I don't think you ever get used to that kind of brutality, but maybe it gets easier to divorce yourself from the sights, to let your mind go elsewhere while your body does the job you're supposed to. The human mind places those things into boxes rather than deal with them. You know what I mean?"

"Yes. The medical term is *compartmentalization*."

"If we bury these horrible deaths in mental coffins, we don't have to deal with the dissonance between *thou shalt not kill* and all this." The wave of his hand indicated the vast discordance he'd buried.

"Exactly." She peered around. "The sun will set soon. We shouldn't be on the road in the dark. There used to be a hotel in Kirehe. Shall we see if it still exists?"

****

Jess directed Michel to an old colonial home that had seen better days, now converted to a hotel. He pulled up before a sign that read *Guest House*.

Inside, she rang the bell at the front desk. Down a hallway, loud voices and raucous laughter overpowered the tinkle of glass and silverware.

Soon a woman appeared, her scalp marked with shiny red scars from machete slashes. "I have one room left. Soldiers fill the rest."

Jess glanced at Michel. "One of us could sleep in the

back of the truck."

"I won't fit back there." He nodded toward the dining room. "And I don't like the idea of you being alone outside—or inside, for that matter. Those soldiers have already had too much to drink. Are you comfortable sharing?"

Jess shrugged. "Sure." She couldn't bear the thought of letting Michel out of her sight, much less being alone. In the months she'd known Michel, he'd never demonstrated an iota of sexual interest in her. He was married to a pregnant wife. She'd be safe with him.

Jess talked to the receptionist before they went to their room. "I ran a clinic just down the road. During the"—she stopped to find a neutral word as the woman appeared Hutu—"conflict, my colleagues disappeared. Have you heard anything about them?" Jess listed Jean-Baptiste, Yvette, the others. "How about Sylvestre Furaha or this guy?" She brought out the photocopy of Gatera.

The lady lowered her voice. "I heard Dorcas followed Sylvestre to Zaire. The rest …" She shrugged then led Jess and Michel to their room and opened the door, revealing an old-fashioned double bed dating from times when people were shorter. She pointed down a long hallway. "The water closet is down there. The generators run from six until ten in the evenings and from six until eight in the morning."

Michel said, "I'll move the Land Cruiser under our window and bring in our luggage and the flashlight."

"Good idea," Jess agreed. "You never know when the power will go out." After Michel strode away, Jess asked the receptionist, "Can you bring us a meal, please?"

"Of course."

When the headlights of the vehicle danced against the wall, Jess pulled back the curtains and watched Michel unload most of the stuff from the rear then replace all but a few items.

He returned with their backpacks and dropped everything on the bed. Their garments landed with a hard plop.

Jess looked at the bed, then him. "What was that sound?"

"I had a gun hidden under all the stuff in the back. I brought it in—just in case."

"Where on earth—?"

He carefully unwrapped a pistol and laid it on the bedside table. "Benaco's black market. Only paid twenty American dollars."

"That's a small fortune to most refugees." Jess grabbed her backpack, pulled out her knife, and held it aloft. "I'm armed and deadly too."

A knock announced the receptionist carrying a tray of food.

He slid the pistol under his clothing, then opened the door, took the tray, and slipped their hostess some francs. After he closed the door, he turned to Jess. "Good idea to eat in the room. The dining room, with all those soldiers, seems too risky." He set the tray on a table. "I don't want to alarm you, but my intuition is in high gear."

"I have the same sensation."

Michel nodded. "All this death and destruction is messing with our minds."

"Not just the smell of death but the scent of violence hangs over the country." Jess sniffed her sleeve. "We reek. Let's get the stink off before we do anything. You go first."

Michel shook his head. "No, you. I'll keep watch in the hall. The combination of alcohol and rowdy soldiers makes me nervous."

Chapter Thirty-Four

Jessica

Road trip to Kigali, late November 1994

After an uneventful shower, with a clean body and fresh clothing, Jessica returned to their room.

Michel gathered his belongings. "Lock the door. Don't let anyone in but me." After he returned, they made quick work of the meal and placed the tray outside their door.

He made sure the gun and flashlight were within easy reach, then jerked the bed-covers down and dropped onto the bed. It creaked as he sank onto the mattress. "At least they're RPF, not FAR soldiers, but we should sleep in our clothes, just in case."

Jess lay next to Michel. Though both were slender, the bed was a tight fit. She kept tangling with his legs. He finally rolled to his side and slept with his knees bent. She turned so they lay back-to-back. Years had passed since she'd shared a bed with a man. And never with anyone except Tom. She closed her eyes and prayed for sleep while rehashing the past, revisiting old what-ifs.

A blow hit Jess hard enough to rattle her teeth. At first, she thought her bad dreams had made their nightly visit; instead, Michel flailed against the sheets beside her. She shook him. "Wake up. Wake up." He didn't respond to her English. She switched to French. "*Réveille-toi.*"

His combativeness eased, though he didn't fully wake. He muttered to himself as he thrashed.

Jess pinned his left arm between their bodies to prevent another blow, then stroked his hair, tracing the white streaks that curved from his widow's peak like angel wings. "Sh-h-h. Go back to sleep."

Tension in his body eased.

She held him until a snore indicated he'd drifted off. At some point she fell asleep too.

Through a series of violent shakes, Jess fought her way to consciousness.

"*Réveille-toi*, Jessica. *Tu as fait un cauchemar.*"

Just above her, Michel's face swam into focus. "Oh, it's you." She blinked several times. "I must have been having a bad dream. You had one too."

"*Moi*? I slept like a baby."

"Yeah, a baby that nearly knocked me unconscious." She rubbed her chin.

"You were crying in your sleep." Michel brushed away her tears. "Want to talk?"

Jess shook her head.

"What if I hold you 'til you go back to sleep?"

"Perfect." She spooned into him. Michel's fingers combing through her hair, gently tugging out every tangle, soothed her. A hard rod formed between her butt cheeks. Oh shit. He had a hard-on. A big one. Startled, Jess wasn't sure what to do. She hadn't even masturbated since—she shut her mind to that experience—and had never had a man other than Tom—she shut out that experience too.

Michel lay flat and pulled her on top of him.

She lay on his chest, listening to his heartbeat. She began to rock on him to its slow, comforting rhythm.

Fully clothed, they ground against each other. No kissing. No intimacy. Just two people desperately trying to forget what they'd witnessed.

Their rutting over, Michel said, "*Mon Dieu*. Jessica, I'm sorry. I—"

"Don't be. I wanted it too."

"This can't happen again. My wife …"

"Sh-h-h. I understand." She placed a finger on his lips. "Dry humps don't really count. Do they?"

Clothing readjusted, they lay beside each other as far apart as the bed would allow. Sometime during the night, they rolled into each other's arms.

The next morning, Jess and Michel drove further north on the RN3 highway. They made slow progress toward Kigali. Almost every bend in the road held a memorial with a handmade wooden cross. He seemed compelled to document every one.

In areas where he suspected mass graves, Michel hired a guide. With either the guide or Jess translating into Kinyarwanda, Michel interviewed survivors. The stories he obtained were horrific.

Jess's interactions were no less daunting. A woman approached Jess and motioned for her to follow. When Jess complied, a foul odor hit her nose. She turned to Michel. "Can you bring my doctor's bag?"

When he returned, Jess gloved up and positioned the woman for a pelvic exam. Jess spread the woman's legs and immediately jerked back. The stench came from the woman's vagina. Holding a flashlight between her teeth, Jess performed a bimanual exam.

Something sharp snagged her glove. Shit. She jerked her hand out. Her glove was torn but not her skin. With a sigh of relief, she applied a second set of gloves over the first and tried again.

Oh shit. Literally. The woman had been tortured by

having bamboo slivers shoved into her vagina which caused the formation of a passage between the woman's vagina and rectum, resulting in a constant leakage of feces. Even in her little clinic, Jess would have had no way to fix the woman's problem. Here and now, she was limited to pulling out as many slivers as she could find—without anesthesia—effectively torturing the woman a second time.

When she finished, Jess shook with anger. The *Interahamwe* might as well have killed the woman. The miasma that followed her meant she was ostracized from her village, doomed to a solitary life until she died. How could any human do such vile things to another human? Fuck, fuck, fuck.

That night they stayed at another guest house. While Michel showered, Jess delayed dressing, lounging on the bed, her robe wide open. She jumped when Michel, clad only in unbuttoned slacks with a towel draped over his shoulders, returned sooner than she'd anticipated.

She jerked on a t-shirt and pulled up her scrub bottoms, tying their drawstring in a tight knot.

He laid the pistol and the flashlight within easy reach.

Their room had two beds, but bound by nightmares, they shared one. They started out spooned together, but she turned toward him, rubbing between his thighs with her hand.

With the last shudder of another dry hump, Jess said, "Michel, this can't happen again."

"You started it."

She pulled away, moved to the other side of the bed. "I know. But Manon. Your baby."

"I know. We'll stop." He moved as far from her as

possible. "This is the last time."

****

Jess and Michel zigzagged through southeastern Rwanda, heading vaguely toward Kigali, their path determined by the location of the next killing field. At a second church massacre in Nyamata, what resembled flattened dolls strewn about were actually bodies so decayed only bones remained to support the fabric of their clothing. Blood stained the altar. Bullet holes and scars from grenade shrapnel adorned the walls. Holes from explosions dotted the tin roof, letting through star-like specks of light.

Ntarama, a small parish an hour from Kigali, was the third church massacre Jess and Michel encountered. Here, again, FAR soldiers had collected all the children in one room and killed them by smashing their skulls against the wall.

Jess's knees wobbled at the now-familiar sight of blood-stained walls.

Michel caught her before she fell. "You need a break from all this." He carried her to their vehicle and forced a bottled water into her hand.

She dropped her head. "I'm sorry. I'll be okay. Finish what you need to do."

"Are you sure?" He rubbed between her shoulder blades, soothing her.

"Please hurry." She tilted her head and sucked down a long drink before splashing the tepid water on her face. Inhale. Hold. Exhale.

After that, she didn't bother getting out of the Toyota. In her mind, she saw the aftermath of the killings all too well.

On the third night, clean but still reeking of death,

they fell into bed and spooned. His bottom hand, the one she lay on, found her nipple. His top arm pulled her close then snaked down her abdomen and into her pants.

She tightened her legs against his hand.

Michel nudged his erection tighter into her crack. His fingers slid beneath her underwear, his fingers poised over her clitoris. "Jessica? *Oui ou non?*"

All day the ghosts of the dead had encroached on Jess's body and soul. Now Michel offered her something that would make her feel alive again. "*Oui.*"

She wanted this. Wanted him. She faced him, her hand finding his cock.

He touched her in slow gentle circles before his long thin fingers sought their way inside. She tilted her pelvis to allow access.

Afterwards, they lay together panting.

Jess said, "Mutual masturbation is kind of like dry humping, so it shouldn't count either."

She lay awake long after Michel had drifted off. What she was doing with Michel was far worse than what Tom had done to her. He'd at least loved Kimberley enough to marry her. Between Michel and Jess, there was no kissing. No sensuality. No touchy-feely connection. Just fucking to feel they were still alive. Despite her misgivings, she was incapable of not doing *it* again, and Michel's mental state was no better—and maybe worse—than her own.

Chapter Thirty-Five

Jessica

Kigali, December 9, 1994

Jess couldn't believe her eyes when she and Michel arrived in Kigali. Nearly-empty streets greeted them. Most of the city's inhabitants were either gone or dead. Michel pulled into the Hôtel des Mille Collines, one of the best-preserved buildings. After they checked in, Jess cleaned up while Michel, finally having phone access, contacted the UN and Major-General Guy Tousignant, Roméo Dallaire's replacement.

Later, as he talked to Jess over dinner, he glanced at his notes. "The UN believes some 800,000 Rwandans were killed in the genocide."

"Unbelievable." Jess commandeered his pen and notepad and scribbled some numbers. "Wow. Six people a minute—around the clock—for the hundred days the war lasted. Killing with machetes requires a lot of energy, so I don't know how they killed so many so fast in such a low-tech way."

The next day, as he investigated at mass killings in Kigali, Michel took her to places he'd visited back in April. At some sites, the bodies were still present; at others, evidenced by piles of freshly-turned soil, they'd been dumped into a mass grave.

On the grounds of Kigali's École Technique Officielle, where Belgian soldiers sheltered two thousand Tutsis, Michel reminisced. "When UNAMIR started evacuating, the Belgians were ordered to abandon their posts to help clear out foreign nationals and UN soldiers, but not those Tutsi. The poor souls fell into the hands of the *génocidaires* who massacred everyone inside."

After lunch, they drove to Amahoro Stadium.

Jessica said, "You realize *amahoro* means *peace*, don't you?"

"A bit ironic, I agree." He laughed, harsh and mirthless. "I was here early on. The genocide had just started. Twelve thousand people gathered here under United Nations protection. The UN didn't have the manpower to protect them or the resources to feed them. People were starving. UN soldiers shared what little they had, in effect, starving themselves to feed an impossible number of people. Once the UN pulled out, the Hutu moved in and slaughtered the refugees." He swallowed hard. "Jessica, bodies were everywhere. Too many to count. In the stands. On the field. Everywhere." His throat tightened until his voice grew garbled.

Jessica wrapped an arm around his waist and pulled him against her. "I know. Walking through piles of bodies, you sense their cold forms rising, their ghosts clinging to your legs, begging for justice."

"*Exactement*. You understand completely."

Michel dropped into a seat in the stands, his shoulders slumped, his head hang-dogged down. He looked beaten. Nothing she could say would fix the situation. Despite his outward sangfroid, this trip had worn on him, maybe even more than on herself. She stood in front of him, blocking his view of bodies that existed only in his memory. His body convulsed with heart-wrenching sobs. She patted him like a child until he calmed.

She could think of one thing to make him feel better.

"Let's go back to Mille Collines."

Immediately after their showers, she led him to bed. They tangled in oral sex. No kissing. No penetration. So, it didn't count either, did it?

The next morning, Jess asked Michel to drive with her to CHUK. She couldn't believe how different the place appeared. The pharmacy and dispensary were gone—literally. Potholes from artillery shells dotted the earth and walls of buildings. Few people wandered the campus.

In the maternity ward, most beds were empty, and a stranger sat at the nurses' station. Jess asked for a doctor.

"No doctors left." The woman shrugged. "No nurses either."

Damn! No one was left to tell her where Gatera and Furaha had gone.

Jess and Michel next stopped at King Faisal Hospital.

When she hopped out of their vehicle, Michel asked, "Want me to come with you?"

She shook her head. "I shouldn't be long."

What seemed like a million years ago, she'd attended the grand opening ceremony here. More modern than CHUK, King Faisal possessed up-to-date technology like CT scanners and real operating rooms physicians at CHUK envied. Now, like everything else in the country, the electrical grid had failed. Without a consistent power supply, that technology was useless.

Jess asked for a doctor and learned only two physicians manned the entire place, Dr. Rugero, a Rwandan, and Dr. Bergeron, a Frenchman.

After introducing herself, Jess asked if either knew Furaha. At their negative responses, she pulled out the picture of Gatera. "Have you seen him?"

Rugero shook his head. "Cyprien? Haven't seen him in ages."

Dr. Bergeron added, "Almost every *docteur* in Kigali—whether Hutu or Tutsi—has fled. Zaire seems to be a popular place for lesser Hutus, Europe for the elite."

Jess shrugged. "Guess I've been looking for him in the wrong spot. He probably fled the continent. Any idea where he might go?"

"France maybe?" Rugero pursed his lips in thought. "I vaguely remember hearing that asshole went to Paris."

"Thanks."

Bergeron looked at Jess. "And what are you doing here?"

Jess explained her trip from Benaco to Kigali documenting mass graves.

"Sounds brutal. We're no longer seeing people who've been chopped up by machetes, but every day we get people who've stepped on mines." He jerked his head toward a large city map taped to the wall. "Our map shows the most current locations. We try to get people to avoid them."

Jess turned her gaze to the map and was stunned by the number of red dots highlighting nearly every main street in Kigali. "Wow."

With a sigh, Bergeron said, "No kidding. Can we persuade you to stay and help out? We could use another set of hands."

"I'm heading back to the States in the next few days." Jess shook her head. "I'm burnt out."

On her way back to the Land Cruiser, Jess studied the worn picture of Gatera. She'd carried it for months, shown it to thousands of people, and hadn't gotten a single solid lead. With a fierce growl, she started to rip it to shreds. The phantoms of her children curled around her heart, demanding justice, stopped her.

Glumly, she got into the vehicle.

Michel asked. "Something wrong?"

"A doctor here says Gatera went to France. Other than that, I haven't turned up a single clue. Except for a vague story that Furaha went to Zaire, I've got nothing on him either. I need more time—"

Michel's jaw tightened. "I have to leave, Jessica. Manon's due on the thirteenth. I'm already cutting it close." He gave her an intense look. "I'm not leaving you here alone. You're obsessed with those two men. Forget them and move on."

He was right. She knew that but didn't answer, just closed her eyes, leaned back against the headrest, and plotted her next move as they drove back to the hotel.

Inside, Jess pointed to the payphone. "I'll meet you upstairs in a minute. I'm going to call my parents."

She'd placed her hand on the phone but removed it once Michel was out of sight. She really just needed a minute of privacy to finish formulating her plan. If he had any inkling what she wanted to do, he'd talk her out of it. Then she changed some of the money her parents had wired her.

The sight of her bony fingers reminded her she was nearing the limit of her endurance. For eight months, she'd been under constant stress. She'd regained only half the weight she'd lost. Her periods were still screwed up. Nightmares wreaked havoc on her sleep.

When she'd spoken to her parents from Ngara, she'd promised to be home by Christmas. She'd go to Paris with Michel, search for Gatera and Furaha until the last possible moment, then head home for the holidays to rest, gain weight, and earn enough money to finance a fresh search.

Chapter Thirty-Six

Michel

Kigali, December 9, 1994

Michel, while Jessica was downstairs, consulted his trusty notepad. Exasperated, he tossed it across the room. Despite months of hanging out with her, the notes he'd taken on her story amounted to nothing. He set up his tape recorder. Tonight, he'd pin her down and wrestle her story from her, one way or another. With it, the Albert Londres Prize lay within his grasp.

The doorknob clicked. He glanced up.

Jessica walked in looking morose.

He asked, "Did you tell your parents were heading home?"

She nodded.

"Will you do something for me?"

"Sure. What?"

"You promised to tell me your story. Our plane leaves tomorrow. We're out of time."

"I don't know if I can—"

"Shower first. You'll feel better. Then share your burden. That'll make you feel better, too."

Half an hour later, she came out of the bathroom, fully dressed, stars of water sparkling in her hair, her clothing stuck to still-damp skin. Even after her shower, she looked exhausted, almost haggard, yet she projected an inner strength he found both enchanting and frightening.

"Come here, Jessica." He motioned her toward him where he sat on the bed.

She approached him hesitantly. "Why?"

"You swore you'd tell me everything." He tugged her shirt. "This is our last chance. Come on. You'll be safe in my arms the whole time."

With a sigh, Jessica sank on the bed.

Michel spread his legs wider. "Come closer." He wrapped his arms around her, pulling her back against his chest. With the microphone in one hand, he dictated, "This is Michel Fournier interviewing Dr. Jessica Hemings on December 9, 1994, in Kigali, Rwanda." He waited a couple of seconds. "How did you end up in Rwanda?"

Jessica told him everything. Tom. CHUK. Her difficulties adapting to life in Rwanda. "In the States, I wasn't white enough to be White. In Rwanda, I was a *muzungukazi,* a White. I wasn't black enough to be Black. I'm apparently a chameleon that changes color depending on my surroundings."

She moved on, describing how she built her clinic and became friends, as well as colleagues, with Jean-Baptiste, Yvette, Elise, and Didi. How happy she'd been in her little house with her sons. How pleased she'd made a life for herself without Tom. How Furaha and Gatera had destroyed that.

When she related the deaths of her children and Gatera's sadistic rape in the same room, Michel's tears melted into her hair, that glorious pile of wild curls that couldn't decide which way to go.

Jess described her escape. The child she'd killed. She stopped and stared at her hands as if she finally realized they were instruments of death.

Michel wasn't sure how Jessica got through her narrative without breaking down. Her flat voice showed she'd distanced herself from her emotions, detached herself from the horrors she'd survived—*compartmentalizing* as she called it. While controlling the quaver in his own voice, he probed, forcing her to dig deeper. He expected her to react like he'd twisted a knife into an open wound, but she continued in the same toneless voice describing the time she'd spent alone in the wild. After hiding in the forest, she'd planned to seek shelter at the Nyarubuye church. The huge crowds of Tutsis made her realize there was no point in joining them. That many people would have overloaded the village's capacity to provide care—if the Hutus even offered aid.

Michel looked at her in surprise. She hadn't said a word about this when they'd been at Nyarubuye.

She asked, "Remember the statue of Jesus above the front door?"

Michel nodded.

"When I first saw Him, He was intact. Hidden in a stand of trees, I watched the militia descend on the church and hack everyone to death. Some trigger-happy Hutu amputated Jesus's left hand. It's odd that I remember the exact moment Christ's hand was shot off like it's a still photograph, but other details of the massacre run together like a slow-motion movie. I couldn't offer aid without being sacrificing myself. I turned and walked away. My cowardice saved my life."

"You'd have been killed if you'd interfered." Michel patted her reassuringly.

Jessica's shoulders lifted in a helpless shrug. "I still feel guilty." She continued her story with the weeks hiding among the refugees at Rusumo Falls Bridge at the

Tanzanian border. Constantly looking down so her aquamarine eyes wouldn't give her away. Always standing near a family, holding babies when the parents' arms grew tired, helping an old person walk, anything to look like she belonged.

How the bridge quivered from the falls themselves and from the thousands of feet shuffling across it. Driven by fear, people staggered under the weight of their worldly belongings, staggered with grief, staggered from machete or gunshot wounds. All in shock. Their faces vacant. Their eyes haunted by the atrocities they'd witnessed. She stopped and tilted her head to look up at him. "You already know about Benaco and the rest."

"Tell me again anyway so I have your whole story in one place."

After two and a half hours, Jessica's voice dwindled then stopped. "Say something."

Michel's throat was tight from reining in his emotions. "*J'ai un chat dans la gorge*." He cleared his throat.

She laughed, a real laugh. "In America, we say you have a frog in your throat, not a cat." All too soon, she turned serious again. "My story is hardly unique. What happened to me happened to hundreds of thousands of Rwandans."

She rose to her knees from where she'd been nestled between his legs. Her hands sought the fly of his pants. The *z-z-zip* roared lion-like into the silence of the room. She bent and closed her lips around his cock.

Michel moaned and dropped the microphone. He lifted her until she faced him. "Jessica, I want this to count."

She stared at him a long moment before saying, "Me, too." Then she touched his wet cheeks, kissed each eyelid. "You're a big softie." A finger traced his nose. "I love your nose."

"It's too big."

"It's perfect." She ran her tongue down its length. "So are your ears. Your lips." Her tongue followed the outline of his mouth. "But you need a mustache and a little goatee to be truly dashing."

His retort dissolved in his laughter.

Her breath kissed his lips first. Her mouth hovered a centimeter away as if she was uncertain whether to actually kiss him on the mouth. When her tongue traced his lips, he opened to let her in. *Mon Dieu*. He wrapped his fingers in her curls and pulled her against him in a bruising kiss. He nuzzled her neck, kissed it, even that nasty patch of skin. Then their lips and tongues explored new worlds.

He didn't know how he'd explain this to Manon, but tonight, he needed solace only Jessica could provide.

As they made out like teenagers, the generator chugged, then died. The lights went out. Darkness covered them like a cloak. He unbuttoned Jessica's shirt, undid her brassiere, and ran his hands over her breasts. Manon's breasts were champagne-coupe size, but Jessica's were mere mouthfuls. Ironically, he'd never seen her breasts. During their dry humps as she called them, she'd seemed ill-at-ease when he tried to remove her upper clothing, so he hadn't pressed her. Now total darkness precluded his looking. Without sight, Michel's other senses assumed super-power proportions. Her nipples puckered under his touch. She retreated when he tried to touch the upper part of her left breast. He moved his hands to her back. Her shoulder blades remained sharp despite regular meals at Benaco. She had no more meat on her bones than a little quail. "*Ma petite caille.*"

Michel explored her body as she explored his. Slowly. Patiently. Intimately. For the first time, they undressed completely and made love, not rushing half-dressed through sex to scratch an emotional itch. He loved her, in some weird undefinable way, but would never see her again. To cram a lifetime of loving into one night, they made love, dozed, woke, and loved again, the cycle repeating for hours.

Dawn was breaking when Michel woke. Jessica lay on her stomach. He stroked her back. With a languid stretch, she rolled toward him. For the first time, he saw her breasts in the light. In all his memories, even those from Serbia, he couldn't remember seeing anything like the scars on her left breast. *cGa.* Anger surged through him as he realized whose monogram that was. Last night she hadn't mentioned her disfigurement. "Jessica—"

"What?" She rolled away, hiding her chest from his view. "Where's my shirt?"

He stretched for her t-shirt at the bottom of the bed.

She twisted, jerked it from his grasp, and hastily pulled it over her head. "What did you want?"

"*Rien du tout.* Nothing at all." Michel pulled her against him.

She buried her face against his chest.

He ran his fingers through her hair, untangling her curls for a bit, then changed the subject. "Jessica, what do we call this?"

Her answer was muffled. "Hair."

He chuckled and tugged on a curl. "Not your hair. This … this thing between us."

"What do you mean?"

"It's more than sex—"

She raised her head. "But less than love."

"I wasn't going to say that."

"What were you going to say?"

"I love you." He traced her lower lip with his thumb. "From the moment you ordered me to get a model release from your patient, I knew you were extraordinary." He tilted her head and kissed her.

She pulled away abruptly. "No, you can't love me." The air vibrated as she shook a threatening finger at him. "You have a wife. A baby on the way. You love them. You're going back to Paris, to your life, your family."

"But—"

"At Benaco, I wondered why women kept having babies in that miasma of despair. Once we started this … this … whatever we have, I understood why. In the midst of all the death and despair at the refugee camp, people found a way to affirm life, to prove they still had hope. That's all we're doing"—her voice caught in her throat—"we're proving we're still alive, that we can still feel … something."

Chapter Thirty-Seven

Jessica

Paris, December 10, 1994

On their flight to Paris, Jessica sat by the window so Michel could stretch his long legs into the aisle from their bulkhead seats.

Uncomfortable with his declaration of love the night before, Jessica emotionally distanced herself—all right, she was compartmentalizing again—by reminding him of his wife. "Tell me about Manon. How did you meet? When did you fall in love?"

"My best friend, Gaspard, set me up on a … how do you say … a blind date? For me, it was *un coup de foudre*."

"Ah, love at first sight? So romantic." Rather than being instantly attracted to each other, she and Michel, much like she and Tom, had progressed from friends to lovers.

"*Oui*, she was so beautiful. Very tall, svelte, with such gaiety about her. She brought out the best in me. Still does. *Mon Dieu*, how can I tell her of my infidelity?"

"Keep this—us—to yourself. You love her. You're going to love your son. You'll only harm your marriage if you confess."

"What about you and me?"

"We were two people trying to save our sanity in an insane world. Nothing more."

"What if we made a child?"

"We didn't." She looked at her lap. "I've lost so much weight my cycles stopped."

Regret shaded his voice. "We would have created a beautiful baby."

"It's better we didn't. I'm not ready to replace my sons." Tears threatened to overwhelm her.

"I understand. They can't be replaced. But you still need a child to love."

Michel wiped the dampness from her eyes with his thumb before taking her hand. "Let me write their story—your story. I can refer to the tape for details."

She shook her head.

"Don't refuse so quickly. Think about it. Your narrative will make the genocide and plight of the refugees more accessible to Westerners. If one of their own was involved, they'll have a harder time putting on blinders."

Her answer was slow to come. "All right." She pursed her lips then fixed him with an intent stare. "Keep my identity hidden. I don't want Gatera to know I survived."

"Done!"

The plane touched down.

Jessica stood, joining the mêlée as people forced their way into the queue to exit. "We shouldn't be seen together. I'll get off first. You wait a few minutes, then follow."

"Why you first?"

"You'll look back to say good-bye. I won't."

"*Très bien.*" He glanced at her. "We should exchange addresses—"

Jess shook her head. "It's better we don't." While she kissed him quickly on both cheeks, she slipped the money she owed him into his coat pocket, then quickly merged into the throng.

In the jetway, cold air assaulted her. It had been summer in Rwanda. Hoping to forget the country and all it stood for, she'd left everything behind except the clothes she wore. She needed a winter coat and—she lifted her sleeve to her nose, sniffed, then recoiled—clothes without the sickly-sweet perfume of death.

At customs, the *douanière* checked Jess's passport. With raised eyebrows, she asked, "No baggage?" Her suspicious tone implied Jess was a criminal.

Jess shook her head. "Everything was stolen in Rwanda."

"*C'est la vie.*" The *douanière* replied cheerfully as if being the victim of a crime mitigated any criminality. With a forceful *thump*, she stamped Jess's passport.

Beyond customs, a beautiful woman waited. Manon. Tall, with chestnut hair twisted in a chignon, even in maternity clothes, she carried herself with an innate elegance that matched Michel's. No wonder he loved her.

Jess had promised herself she wouldn't look back, but she hid behind a column for a final glimpse of Michel, to be certain he followed their plan.

Going through customs delayed him a bit, but when he spied his wife, he waved. The kiss he gave her moments later was long and heartfelt.

Unsure if she was hurt or relieved, Jess forced down a teary sniffle. With determined steps, she walked away to reschedule her flight to the Philadelphia.

The agent scanned her computer screen and *tsked*. "The holidays are a bad time to travel. One seat remains. On the twenty-first, eleven p.m."

Jess frowned. "I'll take it." She had only eleven

days to get everything done. But she'd promised to be home for Christmas.

At the curb, she hailed a taxi. "I need a safe but cheap hotel."

Soon the driver let her out before a five-story building. "I think you'll find this suitable."

Immediately Jess liked the place. The top floor had those cute little mansard windows, and wrought iron railings decorated the balconies. Inside, the place was run-down but spotless. A grandfatherly man worked the reception desk.

She nodded at him. "*Je voudrais une chambre pour deux nuits.*"

"Two nights? Certainly. Fill in this form, *s'il vous plaît.*" He chatted as she completed her paperwork. "I'm *Monsieur* Desmarais. This is a family-run hotel. We're located on the border between the tenth and nineteenth arrondissements. All our rooms have televisions. Breakfast is served from seven until nine. The Jaurès metro is nearby"—he pointed to his left—"and can take you all over the city." He gave a quick glance at her feet. "Any baggage?"

"No. My luggage disappeared at the airport."

"*Quel dommage.*" He shrugged.

"I noticed the clothing store next door. Is there an office supply store near here?"

He pointed to his right. "Around the corner and down two blocks."

After a whirlwind shopping trip, Jess checked in at the reception desk to get her key. "May I borrow your phone book?"

"*Absolument.*" He reached under the desk, brought out a thick volume, and handed it to her.

"I'll return it shortly."

Upstairs, Jess unpacked her newly-purchased items: a basic black business dress and a multicolored silk scarf. A camel-colored winter coat. Two of everything: pleated slacks, blouses, nightgowns. Plus, French underwear. She spent a fortune on mere scraps of fabric, but once she saw herself in the dressing room mirror, she couldn't deny herself. Stylish ankle boots. A spiral notebook and mechanical pencils.

Jess sat on her bed, notebook in hand, and drew up a list of things to do.

1. *Write letters to various governments*
2. *Make copies of Gatera's photo*
3. *Check phone books*
4. *Check medical schools*
5. *Call hospitals for new doctors on staff ...*

Since she had no evidence Furaha had actually gone to Zaire, she decided to search for him and Gatera simultaneously. Though she doubted they'd used their real names, she checked the phone book. Neither was listed. While she was in the *F*'s looking for Furaha, she studiously avoided looking up Michel Fournier. She needed to steer clear of him—for both their sakes.

Gatera and Furaha spoke French much better than English. If they immigrated, they'd choose a large city in a Francophone nation, a city with a diverse population where Black men wouldn't stand out. Jess listed all countries she could think of, then crossed off the least likely:

1. *France*
2. *Belgium*
3. *The Netherlands*
4. ~~*Luxembourg*~~
5. ~~*Monaco*~~
6. *Switzerland*
7. ~~*Andorra*~~
8. *Northern Italy*

Next, she drafted letters to various European Departments of State, detailing the men's war crimes and warning them to be on the lookout for Cyprien Gatera and Sylvestre Furaha.

Chapter Thirty-Eight

Jessica

Paris, December 11, 1994

After several false attempts because she didn't know what the French equivalent of the US State Department was called, Jessica found the number for the *Ministre des Affaires étrangères et du Développement international*. She dialed and asked for their highest-ranking person. She wanted to make an appointment with Charles des Jardins but was referred to his underling.

Later, at a computer-rental café, she typed her letters and duplicated Gatera's picture.

An hour early for her appointment at the *Ministre des Affaires*, she tapped her foot and flipped through old magazines. *L'histoire* had stories about historical events. The Rwandan genocide wasn't one of them. *Le Magazine Littéraire* discussed literary topics. She scanned pages absently, too nervous about her meeting to struggle with reading in French.

At last she was shown to the office of Paul-Henri Broussard. After the formalities, she passed Gatera's picture to him. "I'm looking for this man. We were colleagues in Rwanda, and I haven't been able to contact him since. I'm concerned something may have happened to him."

He handed the image back. "I'm afraid I cannot help you."

"But it's urgent I find him."

"You're on your own in that regard."

"Then I would like to report two war criminals who may have immigrated here from Rwanda. This man is Cyprien Gatera. I don't have a photograph of Sylvestre Furaha, but he has a scar from the surgical repair of a hare lip." Jess drew a line down the filtrum of her upper lip. "This is a description of their crimes." She handed all the paperwork to him.

Monsieur Broussard blinked in astonishment. "You can't just walk in and accuse someone of war crimes. You need proof."

"I witnessed their actions."

"Nonetheless …"

"France supported the Forces Armées Rwandaises, so you must bear some of the responsibility for the genocide—"

"*Mademoiselle*, you are making serious allegations against France. I must ask you to leave." He reached under his desk.

Hearing a faint buzz, Jess looked up in alarm, then realized he had pressed an alarm.

The door opened. Two uniformed men unceremoniously grasped her by the elbows and lifted her bodily from her chair.

"At least read my report," she yelled as they escorted her away. "Gatera massacred innocent mothers with their newborns. He killed my sons!"

At every step, she fought the guard detail as they carried her, one at her feet, the other with his hands under her arms into the main lobby.

"Let her go." A Black woman spoke from the reception desk. "I'll escort her from here." She gazed sternly at Jess. "Calm down before they send for the *gendarmes*."

Grudgingly Jess complied, forcing herself to go limp and to remain calm and quiet.

One guard dropped her feet to the floor. The second, at her arms, waited to be certain she would control herself before releasing her.

Jess took a deep breath and straightened her coat.

"Come," the woman said. "I'll walk you outside." She took Jess's arm and led her into the cold and damp. She peered around before she moving closer and sliding a hand into Jess's coat pocket. "Be careful what you say in places like this. You might wind up in jail." The woman released Jess and returned to the *Ministre des Affaires*.

Like an undercover agent, Jess walked down the street, turned the corner, then reached into her pocket. A business card had a note scribbled on the back: *Meet me at Café Le Rotonde at nine p.m.*

By eight thirty, Jess was at the café. Feeling all cloak-and-daggery, she took a seat in the back and ordered *un café décaféiné*.

The woman from the ministry arrived right on time. She sat and ordered a café before introducing herself in English. "I'm Anne-Marie Bwakira. I was born in Burundi. My parents immigrated here when I was a teenager after most of our family was slaughtered by Hutus. I'm a French citizen, but that doesn't matter. Even here, there is bigotry against us Blacks."

"I thought I escaped all that once I left the United States, but in Rwanda"—Jess sipped her coffee—"racially-motivated hostilities were everywhere."

"You would experience problems." Anne-Marie took a long look at Jess. "Except for your stature, you look like a typical Tutsi. My mother is Tutsi, my father Hutu. They left Burundi because of those arbitrary divisions."

"I found it disconcerting that, in the States, I was too black to be White, but in Rwanda, I was too white to be Black. I hated being called a *muzungukazi*."

"There are worse insults." Anne-Marie gave a rueful smile. "You were there during the genocide?"

"It was awful." Jess shook her head as she mentally replayed the horrors she'd experienced. "The worst thing is that it was preventable. A friend spent time with the UN troops in Kigali. According to him, Roméo Dallaire might have forestalled the genocide with 5,000 soldiers. Roughly 800,000 people were slaughtered because the UN wouldn't approve 5,000 men to keep the peace."

"Tell me your story."

Jess quickly related how Gatera and Furaha had commandeered her clinic and how they'd murdered her patients—mothers and their newborns. Unready to speak of her sons, unready for Anne-Marie's sympathy, Jess finished bitterly, "But no one believes me. Or maybe they simply don't think the deaths of a few Black women and children are important."

"My parents told me of similar horrors in Burundi. No matter where we live, Black women are not deemed worthy of protection. And when we tell such tales, we are never believed." After a long pause, during which Anne-Marie searched Jess's face, she said, "I sense there's more to your story?"

Jess stared at her index finger circling the rim of her coffee cup. Her throat tightened. She swallowed repeatedly. When she could get words out, her voice sounded as bitter as her *café décafféiné*. "He killed my sons, my two babies."

Anne-Marie patted Jess's hand. "You have good

reason to hate these men."

"I want to bring these monsters to justice. I'm trying to give French government a heads-up that these two war criminals may attempt to emigrate here—if they haven't already. If only I had access to names and addresses of recent immigrants from Rwanda, especially physicians …"

Anne-Marie hesitated. "I could be fired for this …." Though she lowered her voice, she gave a defiant lift to her chin. "You're American, but you've suffered the way only women from Rwanda and Burundi have, the way only Black women have. Maybe I can assist you. I can't access complete lists, but because I must verify that an *émigré* has all the appropriate documents before I make their appointments, I have limited access to some immigration records. Give me your information, and I'll keep an eye out for those two."

Jess pulled out her spiral notebook and a pencil then passed a copy of Gatera's photo to Anne-Marie. "This is Cyprien Gatera." Jess wrote as she spoke. "He's a physician. Trained in Belgium. He's about forty-five, short, stocky." She wrinkled her nose. "I can't believe I'm saying this, but he's a typical Hutu. His nephew is Sylvestre Furaha. I don't have a photo or additional information, but he served as liaison between PARFA, my aid organization, and various governmental bodies. He's about thirty-five, slimmer than Gatera, but just as short."

Jess tore the page from her notebook and added another line. "This is my parents' address." She passed the page to the other woman. "Please, keep in touch? I need all the help I can get."

Anne-Marie glanced at her watch. "It's getting late. I can't stay longer." She opened her purse and pulled out her business card. "Here's my post office box. I'll do what I can to facilitate your search for those butchers."

"*Merci. Merci beaucoup.*"

The two women embraced and departed separately.

Back at her hotel, Jess planned a circular tour through Europe—Bern, Amsterdam, the Hague, Brussels—that would get her home by Christmas.

The next morning, en route to the Gare du Nord and her train to Bern, Paris whizzed by her taxi window. At the train station, she bought a strip of postcards—separated by perforations—of Parisian sights. She had no intention of mailing them. They were a promise to herself she'd return. All the places she wanted to see—the Eiffel Tower, the Arc de Triomphe, the Champs-Élysées, the Louvre—she put on hold until she found Gatera and Furaha.

In Bern and The Hague, Jess encountered identical idiotic bureaucracies that wouldn't listen to her. No one was interested in helping her. No one was interested in justice.

By the time Jess hit Brussels, she was running out of time and money. To stretch her Belgian francs, she stayed in a youth hostel. Amidst thumping rock and roll and gyrating twenty-somethings, she pored over the phone book. Gatera had studied medicine in Belgium. Jess's gut told her he wouldn't have left "civilization" for Rwanda unless he saw the potential for getting rich there, and he wouldn't emigrate to anywhere "uncivilized."

Jess didn't know any family appellations associated with Gatera other than those of his nephew. She looked up every combination of their names before giving up. Next, she discovered several options for obtaining information about her nemeses: the Belgian Immigration office, the Federal Public Service, and the *Veiligheid van de Staat*, the Belgian federal intelligence agency. She wasn't sure who she should talk to and decided to go with whoever could see her first.

The Belgian Immigration Office scheduled Jess that afternoon. When admitted to the office of Marie Ambroos, another low-level bureaucrat, Jess first asked if a physician might be able to immigrate more quickly than the average person.

"Yes, it's possible a physician might get an expedited visa. Are you interested? What is your specialty?"

Jess wasted several minutes explaining she personally didn't want to immigrate. Once that issue was settled, she focused on getting through her spiel without becoming hyper-emotional. Too often recently she'd been branded a kook. Calmly, she reiterated she was searching for a colleague she'd lost track of in Rwanda, one who might have returned to Belgium. She slid Gatera's photograph across the desk.

Ms. Ambroos's eyes widened when she glanced at it. "I'm sorry. Even if I had seen him, I couldn't reveal such information to you." With trembling fingers, she returned the image to Jess.

Jess noticed the quivering hand. "Are you sure?"

"Positively."

"Do you have children?"

Ms. Ambroos nodded.

Jess played what she hoped was her trump card. "At my clinic in Rwanda, Gatera killed my patients—mothers and their newborns—plus my own babies." Jess sighed dramatically. "Surely you can understand a mother's anguish?"

"I am sorry, but I can't help you."

Jess left convinced Ms. Ambroos knew more than she admitted, but Jess had no idea how to weasel the information out of the woman. At best she knew Gatera might be here and his nephew Furaha might be in Zaire. After months of searching, all she had was a couple of maybes.

The VSSE should be a good place to start reporting war criminals, especially since Rwanda had once been a Belgian colony. She set up an appointment for three p.m. with someone supposedly knowledgeable about Rwanda, one Hugo Lambert.

Back at her hotel, Jess combed the phone book for other leads. She found Le Centre Hospitalier Universitaire Brugmann. A major hospital was bound to have a medical library. As Gatera had trained in Belgium, she might find something on him there. After calling to verify that non-personnel could access the library, she hopped on public transport.

The bus let her out before a red brick building with white trim and arched windows. Once inside, she sniffed. Hospitals everywhere had the same distinctive smell. All the antiseptic and bleach in the world couldn't obliterate the odors of sickness and death.

She wandered to the library where the librarian informed Jess that Belgium had five medical schools and pointed her in the direction of their yearbooks. She groaned. The dust-covered editions stretched back so far for each educational institution that she half-expected to see an illuminated manuscript. Sighing, she estimated Gatera's age, then searched each school and each year he might have been in attendance. She kept checking her watch—she had to be on time for her meeting with the VSSE.

She was about to give up when she stumbled upon her monster in the 1972 yearbook for Ghent University. Cyprien Alphonse—so that's what the *A* stood for—Gatera. Jess touched her chest. Through her winter coat, she couldn't feel the initials he'd carved into her chest, but the skin beneath her fingers burnt at the thought of him.

With a shiver of revulsion, she studied his photograph. The only Black man in his class, his features hadn't changed much in the intervening years, his face as arrogant then as now. Nothing in his countenance revealed a genocidal monster.

Jess glanced around. No librarian in sight. She tore out the pages with his photograph and biographical data, those listing his classmates, and images of him with his soccer team. Old colleagues or teammates might know his whereabouts.

A few minutes late, Jess arrived for her meeting with Hugo Lambert. Rather than seeing him, she was directed to the office of an underling. As Jess told this man her story, she could tell from his expression he too considered her a crackpot.

She spent her last afternoon in Brussels at the Royal Library of Belgium on Boulevard de l'Empereur, which kept copies of every publication produced in Belgium, reading microfilmed newspapers from Ghent. She was surprised when she found Gatera's wedding announcement followed by a birth announcement a few years later. She jotted down that information. Once again, she found nothing on Furaha.

Her watch said it was time to catch the train to Paris. Just as well, she was out of money, and her library approach wasn't working. If those two were hiding under false names, she had to change her game plan and recruit allies like Anne-Marie in embassies and consulates around the world.

Chapter Thirty-Nine

Michel

Paris, December 22, 1994

Despite Manon's concern that Michel had waited to the last possible moment to return home, little Serge didn't appear for another week.

Amidst the whirlwind of a new baby, a new routine, breast feedings, and breast pumps, Michel worked on his article about Jessica at night while Manon slept. Periodically, in response to his son's wail, he'd bottle feed the boy with Manon's breast milk. After hearing Jessica's story about the loss of her boys, he resolved to cherish the infant in his arms.

Once Serge fell back asleep, Michel resumed work, wrestling with how to best describe the diminutive powerhouse that was Jess. Sometimes photographs actually proved to be worth the proverbial thousand words, but because he'd promised to conceal her identity, he couldn't use the ones he'd taken at Benaco. Images couldn't reveal her inner torment or the revenge driving her every action. Words alone had to capture her essence.

With painstaking care, he transcribed the tapes so he could edit her words on paper. He completed the last tape and, just before he stopped the recording, a thud reverberated in his ears. His heart stopped. The sound, the moment the microphone hit the floor in Kigali, marked the end of his interview and the beginning of … something else. The *whiz-z-z* of his zipper as she loosened his pants. His own moan. The sounds, more erotic than any porn movie, re-awakened memories—the texture of Jessica's skin, her scent, the taste of her sex, the feel of each orifice. His sudden hard-on didn't surprise him. Manon's physician had ordered her to avoid sex for six weeks. Michel didn't mind too much—they found ways to pleasure each other—but he'd been celibate, except for Jessica, for months while in Bosnia and Rwanda. He needed an outlet. He slapped on earphones. Unzipped his pants. Listened to his own guttural utterances—captured on tape—while Jess sucked his cock. Then her sweet cries as he went down on her and grazed her watercress.

Mon Dieu. In moments, he came.

Michel should have erased the recording but was loath to erase the memories. Perhaps it was knowing he might never see Jessica again. Perhaps it was knowing no one else could understand what they'd been through. Perhaps it was nothing more than the most phenomenal sex, the most intense twenty-four hours he'd ever experienced. But the sounds of their lovemaking aroused him countless times, especially as Manon became obsessed with the new baby.

Part II

United States

Chapter Forty

Jessica

Philadelphia, December 22, 1994

Well after noon, the aroma of waffles, bacon, and coffee wafted up the stairs to Jess's childhood room. Her parents must have slept in too, after they'd spent hours catching up the night before. She crawled out of bed. Damn, the house was cold. After digging through her chest of drawers, she dressed in layers with long-handled underwear beneath her jeans and sweatshirt before following her nose downstairs.

Her mom handed her a cup of coffee. "I forgot to mention it last night but—"

Jess cringed. Her mother's too-perky tone meant she was about to deliver bad news.

"—we planned our annual Christmas get-together for the twenty-third. We'll turn it into a 'Welcome home' party, too."

"That's tomorrow." Jess wasn't entirely successful in suppressing a groan. "Do I have to be there?"

"This party is a family tradition, started well before you were born. People expect invitations. Many of our guests, including your doctor friends, pitched in to help us locate you. They joined us in calling and writing Congress and the State Department. It's only polite to thank them."

With a sigh, Jess agreed though she mostly wanted to go back to bed, pull the covers over her head, and sleep for several years.

"Baby, I know working in the refugee camp was no piece of cake, but it's Christmas. We're sorry Theo and Matthieu didn't survive, but we're grateful you're home. What better reason for celebrating?" With glistening eyes, her mother scanned Jess. "Try on a few dresses. I don't think anything you own still fits." She patted Jess's cheek. "How'd you get so thin?" Two more waffles landed on her daughter's plate. "Put plenty of butter on those. You need the calories."

Jess bit her tongue before *you should have seen me at ninety-four pounds* popped out.

Unwilling to fight frantic Christmas shoppers to buy a stupid outfit, Jess poked around in her closet, removing outfits helter-skelter. In the rear, she spied her wedding dress. Shit. After fuming a moment, she hid the white confection behind a too-big winter coat and slammed the door on that compartment in her mind. At last a wine-colored dress caught her eye. She tried it on over a thin long-sleeved undershirt. The dress draped loosely on her frame, but a belt cinched the excess fabric.

She ran to the drugstore on Lancaster Avenue in Ardmore for new cosmetics where she waited in an endless line of last-minute shoppers. Back home, she looked in the mirror and wondered if her new extra-strength cover-up would hide the circles under her eyes. After she applied make-up, she stared at her reflection. It had been so long since she'd seen herself with lipstick and mascara, she looked odd. And stressed. And *old*.

Jess trudged downstairs to ask if her mother needed help. The house sparkled and smelled like pine trees, cinnamon, and sugar cookies. In the background, Bing Crosby's "White Christmas" floated like snowflakes through the air. The annual holiday party was catered, except for desserts. Her mom made the sweets, including fruitcake, English trifle, and a vast variety of cookies, and her dad made the eggnog. Fresh bottles of booze glittered before the bartender. Two tables groaned beneath loads of food. Faces of the starving people at Benaco flitted in and out of Jess's mind.

A homemade banner hung over one window. The words *Welcome home, Jessica* were printed on continuous paper with giant dot-matrix letters hand-colored with bright fluorescent highlighters. Ah, shit. Her artsy-fartsy mom.

Guests arrived. The noise level increased. Her parents circulated, dragging her with them, introducing her to folks they'd met during her three-and-a-half years in Africa.

Jess's tolerance for crowds was limited. She felt overwhelmed. Names and faces ran together. She hadn't recovered from jet lag or weeks of working to exhaustion at Benaco, so her brain no longer functioned. Her feet hurt from wearing pumps. Her first eggnog—her dad always had a heavy hand with the whiskey—made her flushed and *mzunguzungu*. Dizziness sounded like so much more fun in Swahili. Too bad it wasn't.

She excused herself and sat on the stairs, sipping her second eggnog. Maybe she'd sleep better if she drank enough alcohol. She slid out of her shoes and discreetly tucked her panty-hosed feet under her dress. The stockings made the bottoms of her feet slick and rubbing the smooth tread with her toes soothed her. Eyes closed, she leaned against the railing, half dozing, listening to the commotion around her, wondering how soon she could gracefully escape.

A familiar voice said, "Hello, Jess."

Her heart banged against her teeth. Tom Powell, the person she was least prepared to encounter, had shown up at her parents' party. With so many people around, she couldn't make a stink and tell him what she thought of him.

With deliberate slowness, she took a good-sized slug of eggnog before she opened her eyes. She eyeballed her glass. Hell, might as well polish it off. Finally, she looked at him. "Hello, Tom." She tried to make her voice stern, but the eggnog anesthetized her tongue.

"Jess, can we talk? Please?"

"I don't think so." At this point, she didn't have the energy to deal with him. "I'm going upstairs." She picked up her shoes and whirled. Three steps up, she slipped, hitting each tread on the way down and bouncing her head off the wall.

Jess woke up disoriented. She peeked under the covers. Someone had removed her dress and hose, though her fancy French bra and panties remained. A vague memory of Tom carrying her up the stairs floated through her mind. Had she passed out? No, she hadn't had that much to drink. Oh God, who had undressed her? Having her former lover or even her parents see her half-naked—ugh!

She glanced at the window. The angle of the light said it was late afternoon. She'd slept forever. Still groggy, she threw on old jeans and her favorite t-shirt, wishing Michel had slept with her. In the few months they'd known each other, they'd been through so much. In her dreams, his voice, from the other side of the world, reassured her, tender expressions that reached her on a level she'd never experienced. He alone grasped what she'd been through. If that wasn't love, what was? But he was married. Unavailable. God, she'd committed adultery. She was no better than Tom. Seeing him last night awakened memories of old love—and old hurts. Unable to reconcile her feelings, she shoved them back into the vault and went downstairs.

Her mother stood in the kitchen, storing leftover cookies in tins.

Jess's back burned from the heat of her mother's glare. To postpone the coming confrontation, Jess poured a cup of coffee, opened the refrigerator, glugged in a healthy dose of eggnog, grabbed a handful of snickerdoodles, and dropped into a kitchen chair.

Her mother glared at Jess. "You made an utter fool of yourself last night. You embarrassed your father and me."

"Mom—"

"You were falling-down drunk."

"I was not drunk." Jess resented her mother's words. "I only had two of Dad's eggnogs. I slipped on the stairs." She dropped into a chair at the kitchen table. "Mom, for months I've lived in a state of constant tension. I'm exhausted—physically, mentally, emotionally. Before I adjusted to being home, you hijacked me—"

"I'd never do that."

"—when you didn't tell me that Tom would be here."

"He organized a bunch of physicians in a campaign to bring you home." Her mother dried her hands, sat across the table from Jess, and patted her daughter's hand. "You and Tom had your differences, but he's come back into our lives. Since his mother died and his brother moved to Silicon Valley, he doesn't have family here. I think he's lonely. We have dinner together once or twice a month before going to the symphony. Your dad and I enjoy having a young person around. You forget, Jess, he's a charming young man."

"Fine. Just tell me when he's coming so I can disappear." Jess shook her head. Obviously, her mother had forgotten Tom's infidelity. Forgotten he'd changed the course of their life together without informing Jess. Forgotten he'd essentially left Jess at the altar.

"Don't be so snippy." Her mother's sharp tone cut the air between them.

"Mom, he left me for another woman. How can I forget?"

Jess left her eggnog-laced coffee and cookies on the table and ran upstairs. After slamming the door, she broke into tears. The very man she'd gone to Rwanda to escape had replaced her in her family's affections.

Chapter Forty-One

Tom

Philadelphia, January 3, 1995

Tom tried to see Jess between Christmas and New Year's. Whenever he called, Regina always said Jess was sleeping. He wasn't sure if Regina was covering for her daughter or if Jess remained exhausted from her ordeal.

His true love had changed profoundly since their breakup. Looked emaciated. Seemed distant. No, more absent. Her eyes held an impenetrable sorrow. Whatever had happened to her, she'd trapped it inside. That couldn't be good for her.

Despite her reticence, Tom determined to find out what had happened. With enough clues, he could piece together her history—then hopefully piece her back together. His investigation started on the internet where he found scholarly articles she'd written on family planning, antenatal risks in Third World countries, and the incidence and treatment of HIV in Rwandan women. He checked her out through the State Board of Medical Examiners. They showed no records on her. He should have expected that since she'd been out of the country for three years.

Unable to gather more information on his own, Tom pulled up the contact list on his phone and speed-dialed Jake Brennan.

Their history went back to high school. While Tom went to college to escape his blue-collar life, Jake followed his father's footsteps and became a cop. After fifteen years on the force, a herniated disc forced him into retirement. He supplemented his disability check by becoming a cyber-sleuth, a private investigator specializing in electronic surveillance. Jake was expensive but worth every penny—he'd obtained enough evidence of Kimberley's affairs to minimize her settlement in the divorce.

"Yo, Doc, what's up?"

"Not much, Jake. I need your expertise again."

Chapter Forty-Two

Jessica

Philadelphia, January 15, 1995

Jess crawled out of bed. She'd slept long and hard. Her family usually had a Sunday brunch of bagels and cream cheese in the family room. She headed downstairs and sleepily poured herself a coffee and slathered cream cheese with smoked salmon on an everything bagel from Hymie's delicatessen.

The house already smelled of her mother's pot roast, being prepared for the late afternoon combination of lunch and dinner.

Her mother waved a section of the paper toward her daughter. "Jess, you should read the *Sunday Inquirer*. There's a story about a doctor in Rwanda. Her experiences sound worse than yours." Her mother flapped the newspaper toward her daughter. "Here."

Curious, Jess took the paper and skimmed the first of a three-part series.

> **RWANDA: VIEW FROM WITHIN**
> By MICHEL FOURNIER
> Special Correspondent,
> Global News Syndicate
> **Kigali, Rwanda —** In April 1994, an American physician became entrapped in the racial conflict

> in Rwanda. The United Nations
> has only recently labeled this
> conflict a genocide rather than
> simple tribal warfare. Dr. X (her
> name has been redacted to protect
> her identity) …

"Count your blessings, Jess. Though you lost your babies, you survived when a lot of women wouldn't have."

Absently Jess nodded her agreement then read the article more closely. The good news: Michel had changed enough things to hide her identity but kept the basic story. The bad news: his story had been picked up by international presses. Her own mother didn't recognize her, so he'd done a good job. The thought popped into Jess's head that maybe her mother didn't *want* to know what her daughter had endured.

Jess shuddered. Maybe it had been a mistake to let Michel write about her. What if Gatera figured out she'd survived? A frigid wave of fear slithered down her spine. Surely, he wouldn't track her to Gladwyne, Pennsylvania.

After breakfast, still exhausted and in culture-shock, she yawned. "I'm going to take a nap."

Her mother stood and smoothed her apron. "I need some help putting dishes away."

Jess dutifully followed her mother into the kitchen. She gave a soft snort. Her mother had everything under control. Jess tied an apron around her waist anyway. "What needs to be done?"

Her mother handed her a serving platter. "You're sleeping too much. I understand you're mourning your children, but sorrow doesn't mean you can't visit your friends or have some fun."

"Mom! I just got home. Give me some time—"

"Take all the time you need. Your dad and I love you, baby. You'll always have a home with us." Her mother patted her on the shoulder. "Would you like to have a memorial service for Matthieu and Theo? I'm sure Gladwyne Presbyterian would let us have it there."

Jess considered her mother's idea. No one here other than her parents even knew about her children. And if someone asked how they died, Jess wasn't emotionally equipped to either lie or tell the truth. Sadly, she shook her head. "I don't think so, Mom. But it was a nice idea. Thanks."

****

Philadelphia, January 21, 1995

In self-defense Jess called Susan Clarke, her best friend and fellow obstetrician. "You've got to help me! Mom is driving me crazy. I've been here a month, and I might as well be back in high school."

"She's just worried. Your parents took your disappearance hard. They were beside themselves with fear, with grief. They did everything possible to get you back." Susan gave a little snort. "They even took Tom back into the fold—that's how desperate they were."

"I guess." Jess's agreement was halfhearted. "I can't talk to them anymore. I can't tell them what really happened."

"I bet they just want things to go back to normal. Now that you've returned, they're probably afraid you'll disappear again." She paused. "And learning exactly what happened to you would freak them out."

"I guess." Jess felt the same way. She'd shared her

story with Michel, but the emotional cost of doing that again—even for her parents—was more than she could bear. They wanted things to be normal, not realizing she would never be normal again.

After a bit, Susan asked, "What are your plans?"

"Get a job so I can get out of this house." Jess groaned. "And I need to take my oral boards. I have to start all over. The medical records for any patient care I provided in Rwanda are gone."

"You sound like that Dr. X that's been in the papers. Look, I've got more patients than I can handle. Maybe we can work something out. Let's chat next week."

Tucked into a booth at Hymie's delicatessen in Merion Station, a bored Jess waited for Susan. She should have had better sense than to arrive early. Susan was invariably ten minutes late.

Susan entered the deli, and Jess waved her over to the Formica table.

Jess inhaled her whitefish sandwich and two pieces of Jewish apple cake. "I'd forgotten how good this place is."

"Still think we can work together?" Susan sucked diet soda through her straw.

"It would be fun. What kind of deal are you talking about?"

"You're too late for this year's—or even next year's—oral boards. Better plan on two years to collect the thirty cases they'll test you on. You're stuck taking the exam in March or April of '97 and won't get results for another sixty to ninety days."

Jess sighed. Two-plus years was a long time for her life to be on hold. But if she lived like a miser during that time, her savings would finance an international search for her demons.

Susan continued, "I'm in private practice and have admitting privileges at Memorial Hospital. Work for me until you get your results. We can share call a week on, a week off."

"Okay." Jess nodded. "Any apartments near there?"

"Kevin and I are rehabbing our carriage house. Live there for free while it's being renovated, and once repairs are complete, pay nominal rent. Okay?" Susan sounded ecstatic. "For the first time in ages, we'll be close enough to visit any time we want."

Jess extended her hand. "Great. Draw up a contract. This comes none too soon. My parents are driving me insane."

****

Philadelphia, March 6, 1995

Memorial Hospital took nearly two months to grant Jess privileges, and her first day on the job, she'd twisted her ankle running to a Code Blue, a cardiac arrest. No good deed goes unpunished, she thought as she limped outside to her little patio. Though the day was relatively warm, she'd bundled up. Surely Philadelphia hadn't been this cold when she'd last lived here. Maybe the old wives' tale was true: your blood thinned in warm environments.

She placed her coffee, legal pad, and new laptop on the table. A narrow umbilical cord tied her to the phone outlet in her kitchen, allowing internet connection on her computer. One of those new cellular phones might be more convenient, but the plans remained too expensive. While working with Susan, Jess was determined to save every cent possible, gathering enough capital to track down war criminals.

With a sigh, she logged onto the internet and took a quick glance at her personal mailbox before tackling emails from Anne-Marie. It had been a blessing when they both got computers and their correspondence became almost instant—and free, except for the phone line charges for their dial-up connections.

Jess's phone chimed. She glanced at her watch. Right on time. Her mother's Sunday morning call. On one hand, Jess wanted to avoid a reprimand for not visiting her folks more often. On the other, she understood her parents' over-protectiveness. Her index finger wavered over the button. What the hell. With a savage jab, she took the call.

"Hi, Mom." Jess forced cheer into her voice.

"Are you avoiding us? You're finally home, but we never see you."

"Don't guilt trip me. I stayed with you for weeks before I started work, and all you did was complain. Anyway, I've been studying for my boards."

"That's no excuse. You only live half an hour away." Her mother changed the subject. "Don't go overboard with your studies. You need balance in your life. Time to meet people—"

"Mom!"

"We want you to settle down. Get married—"

"Mom, I know—"

"—and have kids. Getting on with your life doesn't mean forgetting the babies you lost." Her mom's voice held concern. "You can't replace them, but a family will bring you joy and comfort." After a long pause, she added, "And Tom is such a sweet young man. You should give him another chance."

"Mom!"

Her mother gave a weighty exhalation. Jess tensed at the sound.

"Some grief therapy might help."

"Mom, you don't understand what it's like to lose a child—"

Her mother sniffled. "I know exactly what it feels like. When you disappeared, we feared you were dead. Every day your dad and I prayed for some sign you remained alive. I kept thinking parents weren't supposed to bury their children. I worried that we wouldn't even have a body, that we'd never know your fate, and that a dark cloud would always hang over our hearts. With all those awful pictures in *Time* and *Newsweek*, we prayed you'd escaped somehow. Please, baby, get some help."

Her mother's sniffling sparked Jess's own tears. "All right, I'll think about it. I need to go. Give Dad a hug for me." Blindly she disconnected.

Her mom was right. Jess should move on. If only she could. With the back of her hand, she swiped a tear from her cheek. She was exhausted. Depressed. She closed her computer and pounded her head against the table hard enough to slosh her coffee.

When her head started hurting, she returned her attention to her laptop. Since getting back to the States, she'd researched every possible lead and compiled her own databank by scouring the internet, magazine and newspaper archives, interviewing as many people as she could, searching every possible atrocity in and around her village, looking for proof against the bastard who'd slaughtered her children, something beyond her own eyewitness account.

She'd even cornered her dad and—subtly, she hoped—quizzed him about his contacts in the World

Bank and those officials her parents had contacted in their search for her. She told him she was going to write thank-you notes to everyone who'd helped her folks in their search, so he willingly turned over the files he accumulated. Jess had no qualms about using her parents. All's fair in love and war, and she was definitely going to war. She'd use any technique, any information, any person in her quest to build rock-solid cases against Gatera and Furaha, not only for homicide but for crimes against humanity.

Slowly, with the help of Anne-Marie from Paris, Jess was building a network of contacts. She kept in constant communication with reporters, government administrators, members of the US Foreign Service in Rwanda and embassies in surrounding countries. Every week since leaving Rwanda, she'd emailed the immigration office of Zaire to check on Furaha. In Paris, Anne-Marie periodically searched her archives for both men. So far nothing concrete had turned up on either.

Jess was lost in her research when a *screeeeech* from the wrought iron gate announced a visitor. She jumped at the unexpected shriek. Her heart jammed so tightly into her windpipe she couldn't scream.

Chapter Forty-Three

Jessica

Philadelphia, January 15, 1995

Jessica glanced around wildly before recognizing the intruder. Tom Powell. Carrying a pizza box and a six-pack of Yuengling and wearing a smile he knew would get him to third base—if not all the way home.

She willed her light-speed heart rate to return to normal. If she passed out, she didn't want him touching her, taking her pulse. A cardiologist, he'd understand nothing major was wrong and would assume her heart raced for all the wrong reasons.

"I didn't mean to scare you." He peered over her shoulder at the computer screen. "Gruesome. Why are you looking at that shit?"

Without answering, she slammed her laptop closed.

"Susan said you'd taken a tumble." He sounded worried. "How's your ankle?"

Jess snorted. "No bruising. Moderate swelling. Grade 1 sprain. I'll live." She winced as she stood. "I was just going inside."

His eyes held concern that looked genuine. "Jess, can't we talk? Please?"

"I don't think so."

He stood before her chair, blocking her exit, and spoke in his authoritative doctor's voice. "Sit back down."

She couldn't move past him without touching him,

so she complied.

He knelt before her, lifted her foot, and with accomplished hands, unwound her Ace wrap.

As he palpated her injury, she flinched. Less from pain than from the memory of the last time he'd knelt before her, holding the blue velvet box with her engagement ring.

"Sorry." His touch grew more restrained. "Grade 1 sprain," he pronounced as he rewrapped her ankle.

"Told you." She stuck out her tongue. "We took the same orthopedics rotation, remember?" They'd had fun together then. Tom had practiced casting, wrapping her arms and legs in plaster, immobilizing her, while he found other things to touch. Heat flared on her cheeks as she recalled the intensity of her orgasm.

"I remember." The thickening of his voice said the same memory occurred to him. He stood. "Jess—"

She ducked her head, hoping to hide the color rushing to her face, and put both hands on the arms of her chair. "I need to go inside."

Tom opened the pizza box before she could escape. "I brought your favorite—Gino's tomato pie with extra Romano cheese." With a grandiose flourish, he opened two beers and handed one to her. He clinked his against hers. "To us."

She shook her head. "No way." Somehow the shake of her head met her shiver of revulsion, and her whole body vibrated.

With a cheeky grin, he said, "I can still make you tremble."

Jess stood so quickly the napkin tumbled from her lap.

"Sorry." Tom reached for her, his touch, tentative,

somehow awkward, his eyes pleading. "You're too thin, Jess. You have to eat."

Her stomach had the gall to agree with him and released an untimely grumble.

"See?" He chuckled. "It won't hurt to share a meal."

Damn. The moment her gaze met those tanzanite-blue eyes, she was lost. She'd loved him once upon a time. It was hard to let go of those feelings even after all this time.

He took advantage of her hesitation and opened the pizza box.

The smell hit her in the gut. She was starving. He was right, she rationalized, she needed to eat. She sat back down. With a reluctant nod, she conceded. "One meal. No more."

His smile made him look as boyish as when they'd been in love. Jess closed her eyes to shut out the sight but couldn't shut out the memories. Don't go there, she warned herself. Slowly she opened her eyes, resolved to get through one meal without falling apart.

Tom scrubbed a hand through his hair, lifting the curl off his forehead, leaving it stranded in mid-air. "About that night at your parents' party, I didn't mean to spring myself on you like that. I thought your parents would have mentioned inviting me."

"No, they knew better than to warn me. And that was weeks ago anyway. What are you doing here now? I thought you had some la-di-da Center City practice and didn't come to the old neighborhood anymore." In fact, she'd taken the job with Susan because Memorial Hospital was outside his orbit.

"You're enough to bring me here." He wrapped his hand around hers. In a familiar gesture, his thumb strummed her palm.

She jerked her hand away, pissed that he still thought he had a right to touch her. She needed to resist his advances. Her plans for revenge didn't include Tom Powell. "What a bunch of bull."

He cleared his throat. "How are you holding up, Jess? It's got to be hard, coming home and starting over after … after what you went through over there."

She closed her eyes, letting memories overtake her. Different memories. Ones without Tom. Tears swam onto her lashes. "Hard is an understatement."

"Too hard to talk about?"

"Oh, yeah." Her throat was so tight she couldn't swallow.

"I read that article in the *Inquirer*. The one about some Dr. X in the Rwanda genocide." He shot her a quizzical look. "You're not her, are you?"

Surprised, Jess blinked. How had he guessed when her own mother hadn't? After a pause, she said, "I never thanked you for everything you did to get me back." Her mouth twisted in a smile. "You and my parents tilting at windmills."

"You're welcome. You know I'd do anything—" He peered at her intently. "What Dr. X experienced sounds like what I imagine you went through. You don't get over that sort of trauma quickly—if at all. Christ, Jess, when I heard that you were missing in that hellhole, I knew my actions drove you there. And the little help I gave your parents wasn't enough. Not nearly enough." He paused, then said, "If you need to talk, I'm here." He paused again, "If you don't want to talk, at least not to me, I can track down a good shrink. Whatever it takes."

"I don't need a shrink." She glared at him. "I know

what I need to do."

"Fine. God, you're hard-headed." Swiftly, he changed subjects. "I had an odd case last week"—he dropped pizza slices on napkins and passed one to her—"This is a real *fascinoma*, a medical oddity. A grad student from Penn developed an inflammation of the heart muscle. Turns out she'd been to Alaska to study the Inuit and contracted trichinosis from eating undercooked walrus meat. You ever seen a case?"

"Walrus meat isn't real common in sub-Saharan Africa." She took a sip of Yuengling, languidly rolling it over her tongue. She and Tom had always shared a quirky sense of humor, the same interests. It was good to trade stories, to share their lives again, even if briefly.

Somehow, by tacit agreement, they talked about everything but the big breakup—and Rwanda. The past hung between them, a dark ghost howling in pain with neither of them willing to say words they should have said three years and nine months before.

It wasn't fair that Tom had reappeared and opened doors she'd sworn to keep shut. Just two beers later, though, she was having trouble remembering her vow. As he told another medical anecdote, she studied him covertly. He was as boyishly handsome as ever. A few new crinkles in the corners of his eyes. Signs of strain on his face, but every surgeon developed those from long hours and high stress. She had similar lines herself—worse than his. She snorted.

"What?" he asked.

"Nothing." She shook her head and continued her mental inventory. He obviously still worked out. Needed a haircut. To keep from fingering those blond curls, she clenched her fingers.

He gazed at her with *the* look. The one that said she was sexy and he wanted her. Not just pain, but pure electricity arced between them. High voltage. Even after all these years.

As if it would do any good, she scooted her chair further from him. She couldn't afford to feel the voltage right now, not if she was going to find Gatera. She needed the human equivalent of a ground fault circuit interrupter, like the one installed in the kitchen, that would shut off the passion if she got overloaded.

Chapter Forty-Four

Tom

Philadelphia, January 15, 1995

After they finished the pizza, Tom followed Jess into her kitchen. She hadn't invited him in, but he tagged along anyway, carrying their picnic mess. She rinsed their beer bottles in the sink while he put the leftover pizza in her refrigerator. He shook his head. The only things in her fridge were a half-empty jar of mayonnaise and a yogurt. Christ, nothing said *lonely workaholic* like an empty refrigerator. Maybe as long as those items remained, she could pretend she was meeting basic human needs like nutrition. He glanced at the use-by date on the yogurt. "Jeez, Jess, dinosaurs were still alive when this expired." He tossed the container into her garbage can. "Don't you keep any real food on hand?"

She threw him a dirty glance. "I mostly eat at the hospital." She put the beer bottles in the recycling, then washed her hands.

Feeling dismissed, Tom wandered into her living area. The size of a three-car garage, her place was small. A nest for one. No room for a rooster or little chicks. The furnishings, stylish but sparse, appeared to have come from the new IKEA store in Plymouth Meeting. No personal items indicated she actually lived here.

The back door opened and closed. Tom turned to see what was going on.

Jess had stepped outside. Within seconds, she closed

the door and walked in with her laptop. Apparently bewildered by his presence, she blinked before remembering her manners. "Thanks for the pizza."

"You're welcome. Gino's always was your favorite." Tom hoped she'd offer him a drink, something, anything to prolong his time with her. With a laugh, he indicated her meager furnishings. "You've done wonders with the place."

She examined her home, as if seeing the emptiness for the first time, but didn't respond.

While she was lost in thought, he focused on her. The young woman who'd been emotionally translucent, whose emotions had once danced across her face, seemed distant and anxious. Exhausted. Thin to the point of fragility. Her joints bony. Her cuticles chewed. Even during the most stressful months of her residency, she'd never appeared so worn out. Something troubled her deeply. Loving this woman wasn't going to be easy.

Her hand compulsively stroked a spot on the left side of her neck.

He moved close enough to inspect the thick, leathery area, rubbed so often the skin had thickened and lichenified. As long as he'd known her, she'd had that stress-induced tic, but this level of abrasion indicated her habit had reached the point of neurosis. He thought she was going to cry and reached to comfort her.

She avoided him with a quick sidestep and gave a tremulous breath. "Would you mind leaving? I've got work to do."

Despite her brush-off, he refused to take her rejection personally. They were still getting reacquainted. "Promise me we'll get together soon."

She rubbed her neck again.

As he pulled her hand from her neck, he winced. "You've got to stop that." He started to kiss her neck, but the skin was so raw, he kissed the top of her head instead.

She pulled away and turned a venomous gaze on him. "You're worse than my mother, Tom."

She'd called him Tom, but the expression on her face told him not to get his hopes up. She wasn't ready to resume their relationship.

He pulled a business card from his wallet, flipped it over, and scribbled his home, cell, and beeper numbers on the back. "Here's my card. If you change your mind—Christ, if you need me—if you need anything, Jess—call me."

She took the card but stuffed it into her pocket without looking at it. Then she gestured toward the door. As if on cue, her phone rang. "Hello? *Oui*, Anne-Marie … *bien … pas encore …*" More conversation followed that Tom couldn't understand. He and Jess had both studied high school French, but neither became very proficient. At Swarthmore, she'd added to her two years of French. He'd switched to French from Latin—talk about a useless class—and couldn't remember a word of either. Now Jess seemed pretty fluent, way beyond college level. When had that happened? Oh, right, they spoke French in Rwanda, didn't they?

She put her hand over the receiver and said to him, "Can you let yourself out, Tom? I need to take this call. It's long-distance."

****

In the Llanerch Diner on City Line Avenue, Tom sat in a booth where he could keep an eye on the front door while he waited for Jake Brennan. Outside, rain dribbled down the window, streaking the headlights of cars pulling into the parking lot. Tom glanced at his watch. The PI was late. To pass the time, Tom studied the menu, mentally totaling the cholesterol in the Tuscany Omelet. Loaded with eggs, Genoa salami, capicola, pepperoni, provolone—plus onions and peppers—the egg dish should be anathema to any self-respecting cardiologist. He ordered it anyway, feeling his arteries clog long before his food arrived.

Finally, Jake materialized at the front of the diner. He peered around, and sighting Tom, waved and hollered, "Yo, Doc." After a few words to the waitress, the detective slid into the seat across the booth.

The waitress appeared with a cup of coffee and a piece of Boston cream pie and placed them in front of Jake.

The PI said, "Put them on the doc's tab."

The waitress raised an eyebrow toward Tom.

He nodded, then turned his attention to the detective.

"What's up, Doc?" Jake snickered as he laid a fat manila envelope next to Tom's coffee.

"You find anything?"

"Nothing. Nada. Zip. Zilch. Your Dr. Hemings lady friend is as clean as a whistle. 'Course, she's been out of the country for several years. Since she got back, nothing. No scandals. No financial misdealings. Not even a fucking unpaid parking ticket. She's well-liked by her colleagues, though they refer to her as *intense*." He waggled his eyebrows. "She doesn't have many close friends, but she is tight with Susan Clarke, the gynecologist she works with. My teenage daughter would say they're BFFs and have been since junior high. Way before Dr. Hemings met you."

Tom made a gesture of dismissal. "Tell me something

I don't know. Any ... uh ... love interests?"

"Nope. Not a hint of anyone since—"

"Enough about the past." Tom held up a hand to stop Jake in mid-sentence. He got it. No one since himself. "Any clues as to what happened to her children?"

"Why?" Jake consulted his notes. "There's no evidence she had any."

Tom exhaled. Another mystery involving the woman he'd once known so well. "What's she up to now?"

"The only unusual thing is that little woman has better connections"—he wiggled his fingers in air quotation marks—"within the diplomatic corps of some of those African nations than the CIA. She's pretty well-traveled too. Rwanda. Tanzania. And just before coming home, she hit a bunch of European countries." He glanced down and rattled countries off his list. "France, Holland, Switzerland, Belgium. Only a day or two in each."

Tom raised an eyebrow. "Any idea why?"

"I couldn't discover exactly what she was doing in those places." The PI leaned conspiratorially toward Tom and dropped his voice to a whisper. "Her phone here is tapped. Someone besides me is monitoring her e-mail. She's either a spook or a terrorist. Any idea which?"

Tom sat back and shook his head. None of this sounded like his Jess, the earnest med student who worked her ass off and still found time to volunteer with center-city teenagers. He had no clue what she was up to now. "She's not the terrorist kind, nor is she technologically capable of being a spy. When they installed computers in the hospital, she never remembered her password or how to log in."

"Explains her stupid-ass password. *Mutter Museum*. Can you imagine? Anyway, she's now computer savvy enough to handle e-mail, recently started online banking, shit like that. Of course, I can't fully check out her overseas activities without making a trip abroad. Always wanted to visit gay Paree. I don't suppose ..." The PI gave a hopeful grin.

Tom snorted and shook his head. "That won't be necessary. Keep me posted if anything changes." He wrote Jake a hefty check and handed it over. He waited until the PI left before sorting through the contents of the envelope, flipping pages while he chewed his omelet. Nothing explained what Jess was up to or who might be tracking her.

For a physician, Jess wasn't terribly flush. She put everything she made into savings while maintaining a shockingly low balance in her checking account—which might explain the lack of personal possessions in her home. She still drove the ancient Corolla she'd had through college and medical school. It must be a rust bucket by now. Nothing unusual in her life except the whole Rwanda episode. In the meantime, something had prompted her to become technologically astute.

Tom smiled. Jake was right. *Mutter Museum* was a stupid password, but one she would remember. They'd gone there when they were in medical school. He'd always hated the place, its exhibits too off-kilter for him. She wasn't into horror movies, but for some reason she liked the Mutter's macabre things.

From the information in the file, she led a monastic life. She didn't do anything but go to work and come home. No visitors except Susan and her husband, Kevin. No men hanging around. Tom nodded. That was good.

No, not good. He shook his head. He was being selfish. After what happened, he had no right to begrudge her building a life with someone, preferably somewhere else, somewhere he wouldn't run into her with a new man. Deep down, he'd accepted, sometimes hoped, she'd found happiness. But, from her reticence to talk about Rwanda, coupled with what he'd read in *Time* and *Newsweek*, her reality must have been quite different from what he'd imagined. And she'd gone through it alone. That thought stabbed a near-mortal wound through his heart.

Chapter Forty-Five

Michel

Paris, February 1995

During his tenure at Global News Syndicate, Michel had been sent to political hotspots around the world. Life as a foreign correspondent, despite its supposed sex appeal, was the diametric opposite of a nine-to-five job. The unpredictability of a reporter's life entranced him. In essence, like his friend Jessica the *docteur*, he was on call twenty-four hours a day, always available if a news story broke.

Now that Michel had completed her story, a lengthy three-part series, he was at loose ends. He hadn't turned up much on the role of France in arming and training FAR and the *Interahamwe*. He knew the story behind the French support of the Hutu and the absurdity of *Operation Turquoise* was somewhere, but he couldn't find the thread that untangled the behind-the-scenes machinations. Other things bothered him besides his failure to dig out that story. He felt off, distracted, inattentive. His *joie de vivre* had disappeared. When he spent time with Manon and his new son, he felt absent. No, not merely absent. More like his soul was so dirty he risked contaminating his family.

Though guilt-ridden for neglecting his family, he hung out with fellow reporters more frequently, drinking too much, rehashing the war. Remember this? Remember that? Remember when? They, like him, were constantly *rouvrant des plaies*, reopening old wounds, picking at the scabs, rather than allowing healing to occur.

One night at dinner, Manon regarded him with concern. "You're not yourself anymore, Michel. You're nervous and edgy." His wife hesitated, then patted his arm. "I don't worry about you hurting me—"

Remembering the events of the night before, he stretched over the table and stroked the bruise on her cheek. "I'm so sorry. I didn't mean to hit you."

"I know. You were having a nightmare. It wasn't your fault. I don't worry about myself, but I do worry about the baby. What if you inadvertently—"

He exclaimed, "I'd never hurt Serge."

"I'm sure you wouldn't injure him on purpose." Manon stood and moved away from Michel, glancing toward the bedroom where the baby slept. "Listen to me. You don't want to admit it, but you—we—have a problem. You're showing signs of *syndrome de stress post-traumatique*."

He opened his mouth to protest.

She wagged a finger at him. "Don't argue. My words make perfect sense. In Serbia and Rwanda, you were exposed things usually encountered only soldiers in combat. *Vous avez besoin d'un psychiatre*."

He became so angry he came close to hitting her. Again. He stared at his clenched fist several seconds before lowering it. "I do not need a psychiatrist."

She held up her hands in surrender. "*Très bien*. I'm moving to the other bedroom."

After several nights alone in their bed, Michel reluctantly admitted Manon was right. PTSD symptoms had followed him from Rwanda and revealed themselves in a host of ways. Some days, restlessness overwhelmed him to the point he couldn't sit still. Others days, feeling powerless, he remained immobile, lying in bed all day. Constantly on guard, he was startled by the slightest noise. *Merde*. Last night while he fed the baby, the refrigerator clicking on made him jump. Now his behavior was so pervasive Manon had left their bed. He feared it was the prelude to her moving out, to him losing her and little Serge forever. He needed help. Badly. And now.

He remembered the brutal journey with Jessica, moving from one killing field to the next. They'd both grown more silent as the trip progressed, shuttering their emotions, only communicating through desperate couplings. He prayed she sought therapy as well.

Once he had a plan, Michel grew more hopeful and contacted a psychiatrist a reporter buddy recommended. Michel's first two appointments with *Docteur* Ambrose Apollinaire went well, so well, Michel became convinced he could breeze through these consultations.

On the third visit, Apollinaire said, "Your assignment for our next session is to write down your experiences in Bosnia and Rwanda."

"I already did. That's my job. To write about war."

"Michel, that's reporting *facts*. I want you to write your *feelings*."

On the fourth visit, Michel read his writing aloud. Somehow his experiences seemed more real when his words rang in his ears rather than when he read them on his computer screen. At the end of the first page, he sniffed back tears.

In silence, the *psychiatre* watched and listened.

By the fifth page, Michel was blubbering. With the last page, he fell apart, and sobs wracked his frame.

Docteur Apollinaire handed Michel tissues before

rendering his impressions.

In a subdued mood, Michel finally accepted that photographing and reporting on two genocides impacted his innermost self. Before now, instead of dealing with his problems, he'd shoved them further into his subconscious, sealed in tidy little boxes. It'd been easy to do when a new assignment distracted him. Jessica was even better at what she called *compartmentalizing* than he was.

"You understandably are drawn to this work," Apollinaire said. "War provides a rather addictive adrenaline high."

After a long exhalation, Michel said, "So, hypothetically speaking, I might seek out friends who've had similar experiences to recreate that high?"

"*Précisément.*" The *psychiatre* steepled his index fingers and peered at Michel. "Frankly, I don't think you can survive emotionally if you report another war. You're experiencing flashbacks, particularly of Rwanda. Severe anxiety. Uncontrollable thoughts about the events. Hyper-alertness. All those reactions can be triggered when words, objects, or situations remind you of what happened. You often detach yourself from family and friends."

Michel gave a vehement shake to his head. "No, I don't."

"When was the last time you had sex with your wife? Played with your son?"

Michel stood and paced the office. He stopped and ran his hand through his hair. "It's been awhile."

"Have you been unfaithful to her?"

Memories of Jessica slammed against Michel's heart. He'd only been unfaithful with her. She'd thought they could go their separate ways. She might have, but he was having a hard time giving her up. "There was this one woman …." He told Apollinaire about her and her theory that *frottage*, dry humping as she called it, and *soixante-neuf* weren't really infidelity.

Apollinaire snickered. "Do you believe that?"

"I think we both wanted—maybe even needed—to believe it at the time." He didn't tell his *psychiatre* that his marriage nearly ended when Manon, thinking she'd listen to the music on his portable cassette player, heard his tape of Jessica reliving her experiences in Rwanda—and the robust sex they'd enjoyed afterward. She confronted him and erased the tape before his eyes. He'd had to *manger son chapeau*, to eat his hat for months. "I think Jessica and I were in denial about the sex, about our feelings for each other—and about how we were continually bombarded by horrific examples of man's inhumanity to his fellow man."

"Denial doesn't make you more resilient," Dr. Apollinaire observed. "Denial entrenches those bad memories in your mind. Trauma affects you until it forms a scar on your soul."

Michel tapped his fingers against his thigh, taking care to hide his actions from the psychiatrist.

After a pause, the *docteur* resumed his explanation. "Untreated PSTD has long-term adverse effects like depression, anxiety, decreased ability to have successful interpersonal relationships, separation or divorce, even self-harm including suicide."

Michel thumped his fingers harder. "I'd never kill myself," he said as forcefully as he could. Though the idea had occurred to him. The lowest he'd ever been was the day Jessica pulled him from Amahoro Stadium and took him back to the Milles Collines. If she hadn't distracted him with sex, he might have used the gun …. He didn't tell Apollinaire about that episode either.

"Those words are easy to say now, but PTSD can alter your beliefs, perceptions, and behaviors." Dr. Apollinaire mimicked Michel's posture and finger tapping. "Your body is giving away the intensity of your emotions. You worry Manon might leave you because she's concerned about the safety of herself and your child. Are you willing to give up your family?"

Michel shook his head. "They're my life."

"People who've had to be strong for too long in absurd conditions develop PTSD. If you bend a piece of steel over and over, it'll snap. You don't want to"—he made a clicking sound with his mouth as his hands broke an invisible rod—"shatter, do you?"

"I-I-I—"

"We'll work together to teach you to evaluate these bad thoughts and provide the skills to change the upsetting ideas about your trauma. You'll come to realize there are more helpful ways to think about your war-weariness. With time, you'll learn to examine the facts and whether or not they support your thoughts. Ultimately, you can decide whether or not you need a new perspective. In essence, by changing your thinking, you change your feelings."

Michel protested, "But what about my job?"

Docteur Apolliaire replied, "You have options, Michel, something few people have. You can remain a reporter but avoid conflicts or become the lawyer your wife thought she married."

Michel wended his way down the stairs from Apollinaire's office. Lawyering. He'd worked in his father's law firm a few years after he finished school. He shook his head. It had been so fucking dull.

Chapter Forty-Six

Tom

Philadelphia, June 1995

Tom continued his attempts to reconnect with Jess, despite her turning him down multiple times. He'd asked her out time after time and tried everything to get her attention—flowers, offers of movies, dinner at any restaurant she chose, even jogging together through Fairmount Park. She politely declined every overture. Though he'd done his best, he hadn't put a dent in the titanium armor she wore around her heart.

Tom couldn't believe he was still trying. At times, he thought he should give up. Somehow, he was convinced she still loved him but wasn't letting herself acknowledge her feelings. One afternoon, he called her again. "Let's go to the Philadelphia Orchestra. Their Centennial Season features music written during the twentieth century." He put on his most persuasive voice. "This conductor, Sawallisch, isn't as sexy as Muti, but he's still great." She'd once told Tom she'd love to run her fingers through Ricardo Muti's long, dark hair—then teased Tom about being jealous.

"No, thanks," she replied, her tone terse. "Besides, you go to the symphony with my parents."

"Maybe we could visit the Mütter instead?"

She gave a sharp, unladylike humph. "You hate that place."

That was true. He'd never understood her fascination

with the odd exhibits there, the sorts of things Edgar Allen Poe would have written about. "I'll go anywhere you want."

"Yeah. Anywhere but our wedding." Another humph followed by a long pause. "This has to stop. You're married to someone else. I'm not going to commit adultery—"

"Kimberley and I divorced a year ago. And separated long before that."

Her silence was prolonged, deafening.

"Jess, you know I'd never—"

"Never what? Be unfaithful? Live a lie?" Her voice snagged in her throat. "I'm not the booby prize, Tom. We're adults. This isn't some childhood game where you get do-overs when you fuck up."

A large wet sniffle with a little vibrato tacked on the end sounded in his ear. He pictured her on the other end, tears sliding down her cheeks, her mouth and eyes scrunched up as she held everything inside.

"Christ, Jess, don't cry. Tell me what's going on. You can tell me anything. No judgments. I'll just listen—"

"I am not crying." Her voice became strong and decisive. "Stop harassing me, or I'll block your calls."

Chapter Forty-Seven

Jessica

Philadelphia, March 1996

Jess found the OB-GYN board certifying process to be arcane and complicated. She'd worked with physicians who'd survived their boards, so she knew how the system worked. The orals consisted of three hours split between six examiners with an hour devoted to each of three categories: Obstetrics, Gynecology, and Office Practice. The first half of the examination was based on questions from her submitted cases and the second half on case scenarios. She started collecting case information the moment she began working with Susan and was creeping toward the thirty required cases.

She'd already taken Part I, but like all OB/GYN residents, she needed to practice a couple of years before she could take Part II. To be sure the Board understood her rather unique situation, she wrote them a letter explaining that, due to the outbreak of war in Rwanda, she was unable to submit a letter from a senior responsible officer in the hospital where she'd practiced. The medical records no longer existed, and her supervising physician had vanished. She snorted to herself as she drafted the letter. Even without the intervening war, she doubted Gatera would have verified her independent, unsupervised care of patients.

She placed the list of deadlines on her refrigerator and ticked off every trifling accomplishment.

1. ~~Return application and application fee~~
2. ~~Hospital Privileges Verification Form~~
3. ~~Letter of explanation~~
4. Get photographs made
5. Return case lists and examination fee

Now Jess had to study ... and wait. Her career depended on her scores. Hospitals found a board-certified physician infinitely more marketable than one merely board-eligible. With her credentials up-to-date, she'd have more options in the future.

****

Philadelphia, July 1996

At Memorial Hospital, as Jess scribbled on patient charts, she found herself longing for the simplicity of her obstetrics practice in Rwanda. She decided the lack of paperwork there more than offset the dearth of modern equipment. Here, charts, labs, and trade journals formed a literal mountain on her desk, and a backlog of charts in the Medical Records department awaited her signature.

With a huff of exasperation, she signed a set of discharge orders, then glanced at her list of patients. She'd crossed off everyone except Amanda Vogel. Technically, Mrs. Vogel belonged to Susan, but Jess, being on-call, had inherited the woman. After doing a delivery, Jess was running late making rounds and was tardy discharging the new mother. She'd better haul ass to the woman's room. Before she even introduced herself and explained why she was running behind, Jess caught an earful of rage because of things beyond her control. She couldn't believe the words coming out of Mrs. Vogel's mouth.

"I paid big bucks for this goddamn fancy hospital

room because it had a hotel-like atmosphere. But the so-called gourmet dinner served last night sucked. The filet mignon was cold, and when I sent it back, that Mexican orderly got uppity." Mrs. Vogel's no-longer-pregnant belly's loose skin wiggled under her t-shirt as she wagged her finger at Jess.

Her husband, Mr. Vogel, sitting in a chair across from the bed, said, "Now, honey, my lamb chops tasted delicious."

Mrs. Vogel, ignoring her husband, continued her tirade. "And you're late. I should have been released an hour and a half ago."

With a deep breath, Jess shoved down her impulse to beat the woman with her own chart. "Ma'am, I'm sure the hospital can come to some sort of understanding about the cold meal—"

"You're damn right they will. I paid an extra for this room, and it wasn't worth it. Cold food. The wine was some cheap-ass shit sold at a state store for a buck a bottle."

"Ma'am—"

"Where's Dr. Clarke? She should be here, not you. I expected a real doctor, not some Black want-to-be."

"I'm Dr. Clarke's partner and a real physician. In fact, I scored the highest in the nation on my board exams."

"Then go back to whatever nation you came from. I'm an American, goddamn it. I deserve high-quality care, and I didn't get it."

Inhale. Hold. Exhale. Despite the breathing exercise, Jess's temper got the best of her. She burst out, "You stupid bitch. You have no idea how fortunate you are to deliver your baby in a hospital. In Africa, I delivered babies in mud huts."

Mrs. Vogel was shocked into silence but only momentarily. "I want Dr. Clarke."

"You have three choices, Mrs. Vogel. One, you can leave against medical advice—and you would be responsible for your entire bill. Two, you can wait for Dr. Clarke to discharge you tomorrow—and you, not your insurance, would be responsible for the costs of the extra day. Three, I can discharge you."

The next day at their office, Susan called Jess into her office. "I know people elsewhere in the world have little to no health care, but Memorial is committed to providing service above and beyond that of our competitors. So am I. Calling a patient a 'stupid bitch' doesn't deliver on that promise."

"I'm sorry, Susan." Jess looked down to hide her eye-roll. "I'll admit to being tired and cranky, but Mrs. Vogel was a stupid bitch. Whining about her cold steak."

"You should have talked to the kitchen and gotten the facts."

Susan's remark pissed Jess off—her friend/boss apparently thought Jess incapable of performing due diligence. "I did speak to the kitchen. And to the orderly who delivered the meal. He said when he lifted the cloches from the Vogels' meals, steam rose from the food. Their plates were licked clean when he picked up their trays. Insurance doesn't cover her fancy room, so she's trying to weasel out of paying the extra money." Jess sucked in a harsh breath. "She's a racist, too."

"You're being overly-sensitive."

Jess scrunched her eyebrows to emphasize her glare at Susan. "First, she complained about the Hispanic hospital orderly, then she told me she wanted 'a real doctor, not some Black want-to-be.' She also told me to go back where I came from."

"Don't play the race card, Jess. We can't turn down patients because of their beliefs. Don't get snippy again. Our livelihood depends on making mothers happy."

"You're not a Black woman, Susan. You have no fucking idea what it's like, as a well-educated professional woman, to put up with remarks like that. If I told a patient to go back where they came from, we'd have lawsuit on our hands."

"Just watch your tongue, Jess. And your temper."

"Susan, how can you say that? We've been friends—"

"This has nothing to do with friendship, Jess. This is business."

The incident reverberated through Jess's mind for days. Partly because her best friend hadn't backed her up. Partly because Jess was tired of catering to women who thought they were entitled to … well, everything. Partly because she was tired of being treated badly because she was Black. But largely because she felt guilty for not providing health care to people who needed it the most. She was practicing medicine in the wrong country. Somehow Africa had gotten into her blood—or maybe it'd been there all along. She couldn't shake the sensation that she belonged there, not here.

****

Philadelphia, August 1996

Though Jess wanted to serve the underserved in Africa, she didn't want to get caught in the crossfires of another military action. Still suffering with PTSD symptoms, she conceded working in a war environment would be a bad idea. Seeking some way to go back, Jess called PARFA's New York offices. Apparently, after the

Rwanda fiasco, that particular medical aid association ceased to exist. Just as well. She'd never been thrilled with their ineptness in building her clinic.

Fortunately, other international aid societies existed, and once she called around, all were eager to talk to her, including Doctors Without Borders.

She consulted the atlas at the library. The continent of Africa held fifty-some-odd countries, and many were currently or recently involved in some sort of conflict. That eliminated many of the most-needy African areas. Mercifully, the Hannish Island hostilities between Eritrea and Yemen lasted only three days. Uganda, Angola, Algeria, Sierra Leone, Somalia, Liberia were all embroiled in civil wars. Sudan had the honor of enduring its second civil war. Mali and Niger finished their mutual Azawad insurgency. Mali wound down its own civil war around the time Jess came home from Rwanda. Zaire finished its civil war in 1994 when Rwanda's started. Burundi, like its neighbor Rwanda, fought a never-ending Hutu versus Tutsi conflict.

Jess shook her head. What the fuck was wrong with people?

Prompted by memories of Benaco, she studied Tanzania. Despite the country's impotent policing of refugee camps, Tanzania appeared to be stable—and peaceful—largely due to President Nyerere. At independence from Britain in 1961, he constructed a national identity for its citizens, resulting in more political stability than its surrounding neighbors. From nowhere, a memory popped into her head, something Michel told her before they started their road trip through Rwanda. *"The United Nations has established the International Criminal Tribunal for Rwanda. They'll be conducting genocide trials in*

Arusha." The ICTR was in Arusha. If she worked there, she'd be close enough to harass UN officials into finding Furaha and Gatera.

Those factors pushed Jess to seek employment there. Her excitement and sense of renewed purpose grew as she waited for the hospitals' responses. Several weeks later, Mount Meru Hospital in Arusha requested a phone interview.

Jess looked up the hospital's details so she could discuss them sensibly with the hospital administrators. Mount Meru dated from when Tanzania had been a German colony and was initially established as a camp for treating World War I casualties. When the camp erected the first building in 1926, it evolved into a hospital.

When accepted at Mount Meru Hospital, Jess negotiated to work three weeks on, one off, so she had time to search for war criminals. She'd be paid at the monthly rate of a local physician, which translated to roughly what she made in the States in one day. If she lived off the local economy rather than as an extravagant ex-patriate, her savings could fund her planned travels for research.

Frustrated by the UN's bureaucracy and the lack of progress the ICTR was making on prosecuting war criminals, Jess had appointed herself an investigator—an amateur sleuth—to take up the slack. She transcribed the stories she'd collected in Rwanda, plus ones described by Anne-Marie and other connections Jess had forged. She forwarded them to the ICTR. Her efforts were ignored, despite the fact that the UN lacked the resources to find all the war criminals. Though the ICTR arrested and scheduled some perpetrators for trial, others had sought refuge around the world. Jess was outraged that the maximum sentence the ICTR imposed was life imprisonment. After everything Furaha and Gatera had done, they deserved slow painful deaths via the same tortures they'd imposed on their victims.

In her spare time, Jess continued her search for *génocidaires*, taking care to conceal her obsession from her family. Her parents couldn't comprehend what drove her to such lengths. If she wanted those monsters prosecuted, she needed to find them herself.

With the world's population standing at 6.1 billion, the odds of finding the two men were statistically slim. She couldn't live with herself, though, if she gave up. At the same time, she couldn't continue like this. Not physically. Not emotionally. Not financially.

She booted up her computer. The screen wavered as she blinked away her tears. With a wet snort, she wiped her eyes and nose with her shirt sleeve, then watched the snot sink into the cuff of her shirt. Gross. And unhygienic.

Opening a new document, Jess typed her current bank balance at the top, projected how much more she could save while working for Susan, subtracted conservative estimates for travel expenses to Africa, hotels, credit cards payments, then divided by twelve. Ouch. The negative number made her wince.

After readjusting her figures, she divided by twelve, then by nine, then by six, before concluding if she lived like a pauper until she got her board results, she could fund seven to eight months of research abroad. With a deep sigh, Jess decided to finish her contract with Susan and, as soon as she passed her oral boards, move to Arusha. Travel to African nations would be cheaper and simpler from there.

With her new self-imposed clock ticking, Jess turned

back to her Rwanda data and lost herself in the horror of butchered bodies, eyewitness accounts, and death statistics, seeking the men who had murdered her children and destroyed her life.

Chapter Forty-Eight

Michel

Arusha, Tanzania, February 26, 1997

In his new position as counsel for the ICTR, Michel opened a fat manila envelope addressed to his predecessor. He set everything else aside while he read the cover letter, offering him "the enclosed documentation of Rwandan atrocities." At the bottom of the page, a familiar name, *Jessica E. Hemings, M.D.*, stared up at him. *Merde*. He never expected to hear from her again. He'd refrained from writing her at her parents—the only address he had—because she'd been so adamant about them resuming their former lives. He thought about her, though. A lot.

Though Manon had erased his tape, she couldn't erase his memories. Like any good reporter, Michel kept duplicates tapes in a safe deposit box. He'd promised his wife his fidelity, so he left them in Paris when they moved to Arusha. Unlike her first pregnancy where her hormones sent her libido into high gear, with the second, Manon's interest in sex decreased in inverse proportion to her belly size. Despite his assurances to his wife, Jessica became the major source of his fantasies. Even now, thoughts of her brought an uncomfortable tightness in his slacks.

With a shake of his head, Michel suppressed his longing and brought himself back to the present. He dictated an appropriate business letter.

Dear Dr. Hemings,

Thank you for your contributions to the International Criminal Tribunal for Rwanda.

The United Nations appreciates your concerns; however, we strongly feel that civilians should allow professionals to handle war criminals.

Sincerely,
Michel P. Fournier, Esq.

When his secretary, Lizette, brought the letter for his signature, Michel reread it. He sounded cold and distant, but he couldn't reveal personal feelings on ICTR stationery. After all he and Jess had been through, he couldn't send her such a cold, formal letter. He pulled a pad of yellow paper from his desk, scribbled a note, and tucked it inside the envelope. Then he sealed it himself to keep the message from prying eyes.

Chapter Forty-Nine

Jessica

Philadelphia, March 21, 1997

Jess checked her mail, tossed the junk, and kept the only legitimate envelope, the one with the UN-blue ICTR logo. She dropped on the sofa, plopped her feet on the coffee table, and ripped open the letter. Just what she'd expected—another form letter dismissing the work she'd done. Shit. Shit. Shit. Then the signature caught her eye. *Michel P. Fournier, Esq.* An attorney. It had to be the same Michel—her Michel. After all the horrors they'd survived—not to mention that last night of unbelievable sex—she rated only four frigid lines. An aggravated breath escaped her lungs.

She replaced the letter in the envelope and found a note tucked inside.

> *Ma petite caille, my little quail,*
>
> *I was so happy to hear from you. I think of you often—always with a mélange of pleasure and sadness. I hope you've been able to return to your former life. Mon Dieu. I have tried but cannot. You, I think, are the only one who understands this.*
>
> *Based on my articles for Global News Syndicate and my law degree, the UN offered me a*

position. I work for the prosecuting branch of the ICTR, responsible for investigating and prosecuting génocidaires.

Manon and I moved to Arusha. She is happy I am lawyering at last but is not thrilled to be in Africa, especially with our second child on the way.

I can't say I am shocked at the information you forwarded to the ICTR. You have continued your search for the ghosts of your Rwandan past. I know you will disregard my warnings, but I repeat what I said "on the record"—please leave the investigation of war criminals to professionals. Recent reports show both Hutu and Tutsi operatives are dispatching those who might incriminate them. I would hate for you, ma chérie, to be among those harmed or killed.

Avec beaucoup d'amour,
Michel

Jess was somehow not surprised Michel too had been unable to let go of their Rwandan adventures. She still had mixed feelings about him, unsure if she loved him or was simply experiencing emotions engendered because he was the only person who understood her. She wondered how he'd handle her move to Arusha. After several days' vacillation, she decided to accept Mount Meru Hospital's offer of employment but not tell Michel. They'd be unlikely to run into each other in a city with a population of 120,000. Jess didn't want to impact their marriage, especially since he and Manon were expecting again.

****

Philadelphia, March 30, 1997

After seeing Tom multiple times at her parents' Sunday dinners, Jess grew accustomed to being around him again. Fortunately, between their individual on-call schedules, she ran into him only once or twice a month. Even that familiarity, unfortunately, bred acceptance rather than contempt. She entered her concerns in her computer journal.

> *Despite my efforts to keep Tom at a distance, I slip too easily into patterns formed during nine years of togetherness. Tonight, he put his hand on the small of my back. I'm such a sucker for that gentle pressure and can't help but remember how we once moved in the same direction.*
>
> *I was astounded when he asked me out—yet again. In a weak moment, I agreed. I've put him off for over two years. By now he should realize I'm not interested romantically, but I hope we might become friends.*

Friday night, Tom picked her up at the carriage house and drove downtown. As they passed through familiar streets, Jess recognized the area. "Isn't your condo around here?"

"Yeah. Right on Rittenhouse Square. After the divorce, I bought a studio as an investment, thinking I'd live there awhile and eventually rent it out. I never moved. It's too convenient. Besides I'm rarely home, so

I might as well stay." He shrugged. "I can walk to Angel of Mercy. Saves time. Gas. Money. I get some exercise. Do you mind walking across the Square?"

"Of course not."

"Thanks. We'll avoid parking hassles. I doubt we'll find a spot any closer than the one in my building anyway." He pulled into his parking place. "Do you want to see my place before dinner?"

She shook her head. It was definitely not a good idea to go to this apartment.

Tom didn't seem to take offense but escorted her across Rittenhouse Square to a la-di-da restaurant. Jess surveyed the subdued elegance and totaled the potential check in her mind. Tom must think he was getting lucky tonight.

He put his hand on the small of her back again and steered her to their table.

She shook her head, reminding herself she was in control. Nothing would happen unless she placed herself in a vulnerable situation.

Dinner went well until he reached for her hand. With a sincere expression, he said, "Jess, I still love you. I've never stopped loving you."

She withdrew her hand. Her voice was harsher than she'd intended. "The woman you loved doesn't exist anymore."

"What do you mean? You're right here."

Staring at the starched white linen tablecloth, she searched for words. Her throat constricted. Her words, trapped inside, escaped with difficulty. "When I first got to Rwanda, I was still in love with you. I encountered so many things I thought you'd be interested in. Every night I wrote you a letter—"

"I never got them. I swear I didn't hear a word from you—"

"I didn't send them." Her breath hissed between her lips. "The next morning, I tore them up. I realized if you'd been really interested, you'd have been with me. And you weren't." So much had happened since the death of their relationship, she no longer had the energy to despise him. She also didn't want to guilt-trip him. "At this point, I'm grateful we learned that our paths lead in different directions before we married and had children." A tiny shrug accompanied her remarks. "Had we stayed together, things could have been more complicated."

Tom expelled a breath. "Jess, I regret the past, but I can't undo it. I wish you'd given me a chance to explain before you took off."

Her nonchalance evaporated. "Explain what? Why you accepted a fellowship without telling me? Why you fucked another woman in our bed? Why you married her on the day we'd chosen for our wedding?" Jess gulped her wine. "From my perspective, there wasn't much to explain."

Tom's tone became defensive. "Kimberley and her mother chose the date. I didn't have any choice."

Jess remained silent.

Tom's Adam's apple bobbled several times. "Marrying her seemed like the right thing to do at the time."

"The fact that she's the daughter of Philadelphia's top cardiologist had nothing to do with your actions?"

"Look, I was still reeling from your disappearance when she announced she was pregnant."

Jess sat bolt upright. "You have a child? And you didn't tell me?"

His voice carried his regret. "Kim lost the baby right

after our honeymoon." He gazed at Jess intently. "The whole thing was a huge fucking mistake. Every day I think back on how I got the fellowship I wanted but lost the woman who would have made it worthwhile." He refilled their glasses and took several sips of wine. "That's long past. I'm sure we've both had lovers over the past few years?"

The question mark at the end of his comment told Jess he was fishing for information, maybe to relieve his own guilt. She fought down the pain tightening her features. One rape. One unattainable lover. She wasn't prepared to tell Tom about either, so she dipped her chin once.

Tom flinched. "So here we are. What do we do now?"

"Be friends?"

His face twisted in a grimace, and his words came grudgingly. "Not exactly what I'd hoped for."

Before she could ask what he'd wished for, unbidden, their waiter brought a single chocolate mousse, two spoons, and a bottle of champagne which he poured into tall flutes. Sweet. Romantic. Obviously pre-arranged. Such lovey-dovey acts wouldn't get Tom what he wanted, though. She lifted a brow. "Champagne?"

"I'd hoped we'd celebrate getting back together."

In a firm voice, she replied, "That's not going to happen."

"Napoleon once said, 'In victory, you deserve champagne. In defeat, you need it.'" He lifted his glass and saluted her. "As far as I'm concerned, this a temporary defeat."

"It's the best you're going to get." Jess peered intently at him. "I'm still too ... scarred, I guess ... from what happened. I haven't made the shift to"—she gestured at their table and at the restaurant in general—"being where people enjoy such prosperity and appreciate it so little." She closed her eyes. "In Rwanda, you can really see the stars, sense the immenseness of the universe. At night there's a silence you never experience in Philadelphia." She paused. "What was that poem we read in our American Poetry class? The one about fog and little cat feet?"

"Carl Sandburg?"

"Yeah. The mists undulated as silently as cat feet through the valleys between these incredible green hills." Nostalgia laced her voice. "The landscape seduced me. The people seduced me. Sometimes I miss all that and think of going back. Then I remember everything else, and I get …"

"Get what?"

She shook her head. "Nothing." She'd almost blurted out that she got all panicky, but she didn't want Tom to think she was crazy.

The silence between them grew long and awkward. Absently, Jess stuck a spoon in the mousse and began eating.

Tom tilted his head back and guzzled his champagne. "So, what are your plans for the future?"

"I got my exam date." She gulped. "I hope I'm ready."

"You'll pass with flying colors."

"Knock on wood." She tapped the table. "I no longer care if I get the top score—I just want the test to be over."

"After the boards, what?"

"I'll work with Susan 'til I get the results. After that,

I'll decide whether to practice with her or go out on my own ...." Jess wasn't sure why, but she decided not to tell him about her real plans.

To get out of the restaurant before she told him about moving to Arusha, she polished off the mousse single-handedly, then her champagne. At some point, she and Tom split the last of the bottle. The conversation dwindled. She shrugged. "Why are we torturing each other? I should get going."

"I'll drive you home."

"Don't bother. I'll catch a cab."

"I insist."

Jess, as they walked toward Rittenhouse Square, hoped the crisp fall air would counteract the wine she drank. She wasn't drunk-drunk, just a little woozy. When she stepped off a curb, her heel caught in a drainage grate, and she pitched forward.

Tom swept her up as she tumbled to the pavement.

His lips were entirely too close to hers when he picked her up. She kissed him. She hadn't planned the action. She only wanted to thank him for rescuing her. When his lips crushed hers, she didn't break away. They raced to his apartment, stopping every few feet to kiss. Sexual desire, the longing for intimacy, maybe even a scintilla of their old love rushed through her. She knew better but couldn't disconnect.

Inside his apartment, Tom pressed her against the door the second it closed, unbuttoning her blouse and sliding it off her right shoulder.

That action snapped her out of her lust-driven haze. Jess recoiled. No! He'd see her scars. See how Gatera had marked her. She wasn't ready for explanations. She jerked away. "I better go, Tom."

She flew out his door to the elevator. Inside, she frantically pushed the close-door button. The elevator door shut in his face. In that tiny sanctuary, she rebuttoned her blouse.

On the first floor, as the elevator door opened, footsteps sounded on the stairs.

She dashed across the lobby but not fast enough.

Tom grabbed her shoulder as she ran past the doorman. "Jess, what's wrong?"

"Nothing. I forgot I have an early surgery in the morning."

"I'll drive you home."

She shook her head. "Thanks. I can take a taxi."

"No. I'll take you home."

They drove in silence. Quiet and withdrawn, Tom focused on the road.

Silently Jess ranted at herself. Familiarity had loosened her resolve not to get involved with Tom. She was still drawn to him. Besides plain old sex appeal, he represented safety, comfort, maybe children. Despite their history, they'd had a good run together. With effort, they might even recapture what they'd lost. She wanted to be loved, wanted to be touched, but didn't want to use him to banish her needs. Two years post-Rwanda, her emotions remained too fractured. She was incapable of sustaining a healthy relationship. There wasn't much point in getting involved for a few months anyway. She renewed her focus on finding Gatera and Furaha.

****

Philadelphia, June 8, 1997

Jess attended her usual Sunday dinner with her parents—and Tom. Her mother asked if Jess had received her scores.

She nodded.

"Well?" her father said. "Are you going to keep us in suspense?"

"I passed."

Tom raised his glass to toast her. "Have you decided whether to practice with Susan or go out on your own?"

Hesitant to announce her decision, Jess examined each face around the table, watching their reactions. "I gave Susan notice the first of May. In August, I'm moving to—"

Red-hot anger stained Tom's face. "Christ!" He slammed his glass on the table hard enough to slosh wine onto her mother's starched tablecloth. "You're going back, aren't you?" He stormed out, slamming the door behind him.

Jess's announcement pissed off everyone in her immediate world. Her parents pressured her to remain in the States.

Tom called multiple times, begging her not to go. "Whatever happened to you in Rwanda, you're not over it. Going back won't be good for you. Stay here. Let your folks—and me—take care of you."

"I have to go back."

"Look, Jess, I don't know what's going on, but looking at gory photographs and reliving the genocide isn't good for you."

She ignored his statement. "Philadelphia doesn't seem like home. I don't want to be here anymore."

After that last phone call, she didn't have to deal with Tom again. He'd been invited to the annual Endicott-Hemings Fourth of July barbeque but didn't show up. Just as well. Even without his presence, Jess's tension level reached the toxic level, and she drank too much and left as soon as dinner was over.

Part III

Rwanda and Tanzania

Chapter Fifty

Jessica

Philadelphia, July 13, 1997

Babies dropped like dominos while Jess was on call, falling at 12:02, 2:25, 3:57, and at 6:43. She finished the last one in time to make rounds and head to the office to work beside a grumpy Susan. Though they'd been friends for a quarter of a century, things hadn't been right between them since Jess's run-in with the bitchy Mrs. Vogel. Despite the tension, when Jess gave her notice, Susan took the news hard. She and Kevin were trying to get pregnant, and Jess's departure would make it difficult for Susan to juggle a practice and a pregnancy.

Jess spent her evenings packing up the carriage house. She took consolation in knowing her countdown was nearly over, with her last day, July eighteenth, circled in red on her calendar. She allowed herself a week to rest and visit her family and a week acclimating in Arusha before starting her new job on August fourth.

In the middle of the night, her phone rang, jolting her from bed. Sleepy and confused, she grabbed the receiver before remembering she wasn't on call. Caller ID showed an unknown number. Anxiety zapped through her. "Hello?"

Static sizzled in her ear.

"Hello? Hello?" Her voice echoed through the line.

After a long delay, a metallic voice grated her eardrum. "*Docteur* Hemings?"

"Yes?"

"*Je suis un ami ….*"

Somehow the caller disguised his voice with an electronic gadget that made him sound like a robot. Jess had seen such devices used to protect people on the witness stand in TV courtroom dramas. The cold tone sent a chill rattling up her spine, despite the caller's pronouncement of himself as a "friend." Her home phone was unlisted. Other than the hospital, few people had her number. She hesitated then replied, "*Oui?*"

"*J'ai une information particulière à vous communiquer.*"

To gain time to think, Jess feigned lack of comprehension. "*Je ne comprends pas. Repetez, s'il vous plaît?*" What information could this stranger have?

"*J'ai des informations …*" the voice repeated, louder—as if Jess's hearing rather than her comprehension was in question—in the pedantic tone Europeans used solely to communicate with stupid Americans, "*… concernant Cyprien …*"

Jess let out an explosive breath. "*Oui?*" For the next several minutes, she listened carefully.

The disguised voice continued in French, "Do not contact the authorities. Or the ICTR. Come as soon as possible. Call me tomorrow at this same time with your itinerary."

"I'm on call at the hospital. I might not be available."

"I'll give you a fifteen-minute window. Should you call before or after, I won't accept the call. Write down this number."

Unable to find a piece of paper, with shaking fingers, Jess jotted the number on the palm of her hand. She repeated it to him.

"*C'est exact.*"

The mystery call ended abruptly. The line went dead. No farewell. Nothing beyond a click followed by static on the line.

Too shocked to hang up, Jess stared at the phone. On occasion, she got anonymous phone calls or letters related to her research on the genocide. She passed them to the ICTR. After investigation, most were discounted as hoaxes set up by people seeking financial reward or revenge. This caller, claiming to speak on behalf of a former member of the Rwandan government now in self-imposed exile, had agreed to meet with her and provide information regarding Cyprien Gatera—if she went to Belgium.

Instinct told her this call was genuine. In fact, the hairs on the back of her neck still stood at attention. The man recited details only someone present when her children were killed could know, the particulars of which made her heart jackhammer in her chest, stirring memories so frightening she nearly wet herself. The electronic voice-altering machine made everything seem rather espionage-ish but also made the call more believable. If her contacts needed such posturing, their information might truly lead her to Gatera.

She didn't want to go to Europe, and a last-minute ticket to Brussels would be expensive. As a former colony, Rwanda had ties to Belgium, and a man who'd found refuge there would be reluctant to leave. Despite her misgivings, this was her only substantive lead. She didn't have much choice. Though the United Nations had offered a reward of five million U.S. dollars for information leading to the arrest of "persons indicted by the

International Criminal Tribunal for Rwanda for serious violations of international humanitarian law," the monster who murdered her children had never been found. Of course, she wasn't tracking down Gatera for the reward—she wanted justice.

If she called back, maybe a secretary would answer and provide Jess with a company name or another clue to the caller's identity. With a trembling hand, Jess pressed redial.

An automated voice announced in French, "*Le numéro que vous demandez est hors de service actuellement.*"

How could the line not be in service? She had spoken to someone there only seconds ago. She tried again. Same results. With an irritated jab of her finger, she disconnected and studied the number her mysterious caller had given her. Definitely not an American code. Somewhere in Europe, she guessed. She dug out the phone book and transferred the phone number from her palm to the first page, just in case she smeared the scribble on her hand. Then she looked up foreign area codes. Not Zaire. Not Paris. 32-2 was Brussels. She glanced at the clock radio while rubbing the back of her neck. Three a.m. here. Nine a.m. in Belgium. People there would be starting their work day.

The second must have been a different number as she didn't get an *out of service* recording. She let the phone ring thirty times before hanging up. Immediately she dialed back. Another thirty rings. No answer. Her caller meant it when he told her to call only at the specified time.

Jess's agitation grew. Her heart rate accelerated to warp speed. Her respiratory rate skyrocketed.

Recognizing the signs of an impending panic attack, she wrapped her arms around herself, focusing on the texture of her soft cotton nightgown beneath her fingers in an attempt to calm herself. She had no reason to hyperventilate and pass out. She was safe in her own home. Not Rwanda. Not Benaco. Inhale. Hold. Exhale. She forced her breathing into the oft-practiced pattern. As she centered herself, the sense of immediate danger passed, but she remained hyper-vigilant. Every time she dozed off, the screams of her babies awakened her. Once those grew silent, her own shrieks echoed through her apartment.

****

The next morning at the office, Jess performed two Pap smears before taking a moment to call the Belgian Embassy in Washington DC. After learning she didn't need a visa, she booked a room and rescheduled her flight to Tanzania. She'd take British Air from Philadelphia to Brussels with a twenty-four-hour layover to meet her mysterious man before continuing to Arusha. The price of this last-minute ticket change threw a staggering blow to her wallet.

At the end of the day, Susan signed her patients over to Jess and went home. When on call, Jess slept on the OB ward. It was easier than running back and forth from home, though home was only minutes away. The precaution kept her off the streets at night. This nice safe neighborhood bore no resemblance to the Rwandan forest, yet she got the jitters walking alone between home and hospital.

On the obstetrical ward, only one patient waited to deliver, and her cervix was barely dilated. In theory, she wouldn't deliver for hours. Jess crossed her fingers, hoping the baby held its arrival until she made the call.

She set an alarm for 2:45 a.m. then lay down in the call room. Too antsy to sleep, she constantly checked the time.

At three on the dot, Jess dialed the mystery number. After a split second of silence, a static-filled echo-y connection came through. Someone picked up on the first ring. After a long pause, the creepy metallic voice said, "*Bonjour*, *Docteur* Hemings."

Jess shivered. "I'll arrive on July twenty-first."

"*Très bien*. That particular flight arrives at 8:55 a.m. if I recall correctly." He gave her a third number and advised her to call by noon the day of her arrival. "*N'oublie pas*. Don't forget—if you're late, I won't take the call."

****

Brussels, July 20, 1997

With her laptop open on the tray-table, Jess looked out the porthole of British Air Boeing 747. The sudden change in plans meant she'd needed to concoct a whopping lie to tell her parents. They still went into a tizzy. She'd packed in a rush, thrown her belongings into her parents' attic, and spent her last two nights with them, trying to assuage her own guilt.

She turned her attention back to her computer and typed in her journal.

> *I'm edgy about meeting this unknown man. I pray I'm not following a will-o'wisp. I've sworn to quit searching for Gatera when my savings run out, but with luck, this trip to Belgium might end this phase of my life.*

She rubbed that spot on her neck. Her fingers felt damp. She looked at her hand. Her nails were stained pink. Blood. She wrinkled her nose in disgust. Her incessant scratching was unhygienic, but the mysterious phone call had shifted her anxiety into high gear. She pulled a small bottle of hand sanitizer from her purse, squirted a bit onto her hands, and smeared some on her neck. To restrain herself, she sat on her hands. Five minutes later she was digging at her neck again.

The *thwap thwap thwap* of tires slapping the tarmac announced her arrival. She glanced at her watch and set it to Brussels time. The plane had touched down ten minutes late. Mr. Mystery Caller had put her in a time crunch by demanding she call by noon.

Customs was a royal pain in the ass, but Jess brought it on herself. Over the past several weeks, she'd called every physician and drug company representative she knew, scrounging donations of surgical equipment and drugs to haul to Mount Meru Hospital. Her two large checked suitcases contained these medications and supplies, so she spent an inordinate two hours getting through customs, the officials fondling every bottle and asking about its use.

Her ordeal over, she stashed her bags in a locker in the departures area before dashing to the airport basement to catch a train. She kept glancing at her timepiece. Though her hotel, the Hilton Brussels Grand Palace, was conveniently located on Carrefour de l'Europe only steps from the Gare Centrale train station, by the time she signed in, she'd be pushing the deadline.

As she reached the gray arched windows marking the entrance to the hotel, she checked her watch. Twenty-six minutes to spare. She exhaled, relieved she was going to make it.

In front of the building, a massive SUV perched like an ominous vulture. Curious, she slowed and glanced inside. The darkly-tinted windows revealed nothing. She hoped it didn't belong to some obnoxious wealthy tourist who'd demand too much time from the reception desk and slow Jess's check-in. She didn't want to make this call from a public phone.

Resuming her rapid pace, she flew past the behemoth and entered the lobby. Its marble floors and ornate moldings contrasted with stark ultra-modern furnishings. A quick inspection showed several people scattered through the lobby, reading newspapers and chatting, plus a couple of men in dark suits leaning against one wall. Fortunately, no one waited at the reception desk.

When Jess gave her name, an overly-cheerful receptionist welcomed her. "*Docteur* Hemings, we've been expecting you. *Un moment, s'il vous plaît.*" She peered around Jess and beckoned to someone.

Jess assumed Ms. Perky was motioning to a bellhop, so when someone took her carry-on, she released it. But when a hand clamped on her right shoulder, she jumped at the unexpected touch. She whirled and found herself trapped between the reception counter and the two men in suits. Her gaze flipped between them. Identical dark suits. Identical white shirts. The only differences were the colors of their ties and their complexions. Suit Number One, a Nordic blond with eyes as blue as Tom's, faced her. Suit Number Two, gypsy dark, scanned the hotel lobby. Both stood a foot taller than she and had with an authority inherent not merely in their size, but in their occupation. She knew a cop when she saw one.

Chapter Fifty-One

Jessica

Brussels, July 21, 1997

Anxiously, Jess stared at Suit Number One.

"*Docteur* Hemings?" A light whiff of minty mouthwash accompanied his voice as it crossed the space between them.

Jess swallowed. "Yes?"

"Finish checking in, please. Then come with us."

"Why? Who are you?" These guys made her nervous. She snuck a glance at her timepiece, hoping they didn't keep her from making her call. Had they been sent by her contact? Her anxiety increased, and her heart rate raced. "What do you want? I only arrived—"

"We are aware of that, *Docteur*." His tone was crisp.

"I haven't been in the country long enough to get in trouble. I'm on a tight schedule. I don't have time—"

Suit Number One peered over Jess's head and spoke to the receptionist. "Put her in the suite we arranged."

Jess shook her head vehemently. "No. I can't afford a suite. I want the room I reserved." She jabbed the counter with her finger. "Your cheapest room."

"Don't worry about the price. Finish checking in." His clenched jaw gave him a pugnacious appearance.

"I demand to speak with the American Embassy."

"That won't be necessary." Suit Number One placed a hefty arm around her shoulders. He hissed in her ear as he spun her to face the reception counter. "Please cooperate—it's for your own good. I'll explain once we're in a more secure environment."

"M-m-ore secure environment?" Her blood pressure soared until her pulse echoed in her ears. What was with the cloak-and-dagger stuff? She took a deep breath to squelch the oncoming panic attack. Inhale. Hold. Exhale. She opened her mouth—

He held up a hand to silence her. "Save your questions. I'll explain in a few minutes."

Jess looked him up and down. "Who the hell are you guys?"

He fished in his coat pocket for an official-looking identification card which he waved under her nose. As he wiggled it, a holographic image wobbled back at her. The card sure appeared bona fide.

She weighed her options. At this point, to avoid getting deeper in trouble, she'd better comply. As soon as she could, she'd call the American Embassy and get things straightened out.

Reluctantly she completed the check-in process. She couldn't figure out how, but she'd gotten herself into a tight spot she didn't know how to wiggle out of. Hell, she didn't know what the situation was. Maybe these guys thought she was a drug runner. She was a licensed physician, though, and the medications in bags she'd left in the airport locker were legit.

Maybe she could make a run for it and lose herself in the crowds at the train station.

Suit Number One must have sensed her intent. His arm tightened around her shoulders. Between their bodies, a hard lump jabbed her upper arm. Realizing what it was, she gulped. A holstered gun.

The second she scribbled her signature on the hotel

forms and laid down the pen, Suit Number One firmly grasped her elbow and guided her toward the elevator where Suit Number Two held the doors open.

The doors swished closed. Jess placed her hands on her hips and glared at the strangers. "Okay, what's going on? I demand answers." She stamped her foot for emphasis, the dull thud echoing through the hollow elevator shaft. "I'm an American citizen. I have rights. You can't manhandle me—"

Suit Number One sighed. "Our apologies, *Docteur* Hemings. Please be patient a few more minutes."

"You don't understand." She peeked at her watch. "I need to call someone within the next twelve minutes. It's urgent."

The blond clenched his jaw several times, peered heavenward, then leaned toward her. In a barely audible whisper, he said, "I'm Lucas Mertens." He nodded at his dark companion. "That fellow is Milo Bisset. We work for the Close Protection Services, part of the *Veiligheid van de Staat* or VSSE, the Belgian agency in charge of federal intelligence and security. Rather like your CIA but on a smaller scale. Along with national security, the VSSE is responsible for protecting VIPs." Mertens's English, with a classy British accent, was flawless.

"I'm not a—" Her voice came out in an excited squeak.

He held up a finger to shush her then pressed the button for the ninth floor.

Jess checked her watch. Ten minutes to go.

The elevator buttons lit up. The agents remained silent.

Her anxiety rose faster than the elevator. She peeked at her wristwatch. Nine minutes.

When the elevator opened, Bisset glanced again toward both ends of the corridor before motioning Jess off the elevator. The three walked toward a room. Bisset keyed the lock, opened the door, and gestured Jess and Mertens inside.

Inside, Jess mentally ran through her limited options for escape. She glanced back toward the door. Before it, solid as a boulder, stood Bisset. She'd never budge him. With a quick spin, she dashed to the window, glanced down, then slumped. From nine floors up, she'd never survive the fall.

Mertens eased between her and the glass. "Stay away from the windows, *Docteur* Hemings." He pulled the drapes. The view of Flemish buildings with decorative gables and mansard roofs vanished.

She studied her timepiece again. Six minutes until the appointed phone call.

Opening drawers, lifting the phone, looking behind picture frames, and under sofa cushions, Mertens methodically moved around the room. He entered the bedroom area and, judging from the sounds, searched the closet, the dresser drawers, and even peeked behind the shower curtain.

Five minutes. Anxiously Jess jiggled on her feet.

After Mertens returned, Bisset spoke for the first time. His English, like Mertens's, was excellent. "I'm sure you know a fair number of Rwandans sought asylum in this country, both after their independence in 1962 and again after the genocide in 1994. To assist the ICTR, we monitor them fairly closely."

"So?"

"Your name pops up from time to time because of your"—he managed a wry smile— "research."

"Why all the James Bond stuff?"

"We've intercepted several recent communiqués from the Rwandan Embassy that indicate a person or persons there may constitute a threat to your personal safety."

"Me? Seriously?"

"Yes, your life may be in jeopardy."

Jess glanced at her wristwatch for the umpteenth time. Four minutes.

"That's the tenth time you've looked at your chronometer—"

"You're counting?"

"Just observant. Why are you monitoring the time so closely?"

"I told you. I have to telephone someone within the next"—reflexively she glanced at her watch—"three minutes. It's urgent."

"What's so vital about this call?"

Jess stared at the two men, still uncertain why they had accosted her. "Let me see your IDs again. Both of you." She held out her hand.

With obvious reluctance, they handed over their wallets.

Jess turned her attention to their drivers' licenses and VSSE identification cards and inspected them closely, running a finger over each hologram. They looked real, but how would she know a counterfeit from a real one? Holograms were supposedly more difficult to forge, but for the right price, she was sure someone somewhere could accomplish it. With a *humph*, she returned their documents then spoke to Mertens at a rapid clip. "You guys know who I am. I suppose you're who you say you are." She began pacing. "I need to make this phone call, but I was warned not to contact the authorities."

Mertens held up a hand to interrupt her. "What are you talking about? Who warned you?"

Rapidly Jess ran through the history of her mysterious contact. "I have to call this guy." She tapped her wristwatch with her fingernail and gasped as the second-hand tripped past the appointed time. "Like ten seconds ago."

After a glance at Mertens, Bisset spoke. "Go ahead. Use the room phone. Put him on speaker so we can hear, but don't reveal our presence. Keep him on the line as long as possible. This phone is tapped—"

Jess glanced up in alarm. "Why?"

"The VSSE's primary objective is collecting and analyzing any intelligence that might prevent threats against the security of the state or international relations—"

"I'm not a threat to anyone."

"—and the protection of certain people—like you."

"You're protecting me?" Jess's laugh bordered on hysteria.

"*Exactement.*"

From across the room, Mertens added, "Don't agree to meet this guy anywhere that isn't in broad daylight in a public place. You don't want to get killed in a dark alley somewhere."

Jess pinched the bridge of her nose to forestall a headache, then dialed the mysterious number. This time, the connection was instant, but again a long pause before the mechanical voice answered in French. "*Bonjour, Docteur* Hemings. You're two minutes late."

"Not according to my watch." Nerves made Jess's voice jagged. She could barely pull enough French from her memory banks to converse with him. "Who are you?"

"*Je suis désolé*. Sorry, but to assure my safety, I can't identify myself."

To keep him on the line, Jess peppered the man with questions. "Where are you?"

"Nor can I reveal my location."

"Do I know you?"

"We met in Kigali."

"How did you get my home phone number?"

"We have ways of obtaining information. You made it easy, having demonstrated remarkably little discretion in your activities."

Uh oh. Jess had thought she was being surreptitious. "Why exactly are you calling me?"

His laugh was harsh, bitter, forced. Through the voice-changing apparatus, his cackle reminded Jess of a horror movie sound effect. "I have information for you. To be delivered in person. I'll come to your room."

Bisset caught her eye and shook his head.

Jess nodded her understanding. "Customs took me forever. I just arrived at Gare Central. If we get this meeting over with quickly, I can fly out tonight and not bother checking into a hotel."

Her caller sounded irritated. "*Trés bien*." He paused. "Le Institut royal des Sciences naturelles de Belgique. Rue Vautier 29. In the dinosaur hall. *À une heure pile. Etre à l'heure c'est déjà en retard.*"

Jess blinked. Mentally she translated his axiom. At one o'clock on the dot. He really wanted her to be on time. "How will I know you?"

"Don't worry, *Docteur*. I'll recognize you." He hung up abruptly.

Jess's hands were shaking so badly that, when she

placed the handset on the cradle, she missed. The phone clattered to the floor. She picked the receiver up then turned to the two intelligence agents. "Well?"

"Not bad for an amateur." Mertens gave a slight chuckle. "Unfortunately, we still don't know if he's planning on killing you—"

Jess gasped.

"—or simply providing information. Since he's meeting you in a public place, though, he's unlikely to try anything funny."

"You've got to be kidding. I've been doing this for three years. I've never been threatened before. Never felt like I was in danger."

"Really?" Bisset snorted. "You're far too trusting. What makes you think you're qualified to investigate something like this? An untrained civilian shouldn't be engaged in espionage."

"It's not espionage. It's research."

"What's espionage if not sophisticated research?" Mertens laughed as he shook his head. "If the Museum is halfway, I bet he's calling from the Rwandan Embassy. It's nearly noon. He's obsessed with time, so we'd better be there early."

"We?" Jess asked.

In response, Mertens nodded at Bisset who opened the door and glanced up and down the corridor. "Clear."

The two men, repeating the stealthy maneuvers they'd used earlier, escorted her to the entrance. Mingling with several people who were exiting the hotel, they led her to the SUV still parked before the hotel.

While Bisset climbed behind the wheel, Mertens put Jess in the back seat.

Once Mertens closed the vehicle's doors, Bisset

continued, "We hadn't planned on getting involved. We were supposed to deliver the message, not interfere. However, we can't permit you to handle this alone. *Laquelle on nous aurait blâmés quoi que nous ayons fait.*"

Jess grinned. "Damned if you do, damned if you don't, huh?"

"*Exactement.* If you get killed on our watch, Mertens and I will be in what you Americans call *deep shit*. We don't have a plan. We're going to fly with this."

"You mean *wing it*?" Jess asked.

"Yes. Wing it." He grinned at the American slang. "We don't have time to return to the office and wire you with a microphone. Pay attention to every detail, even if it doesn't seem important. You'll hear his real voice this time. Listen to his accent. Remember what he says, every word, every inflection of his voice. Try to identify where he's from. Memorize his facial expression, body language. Any trifle may help identify him."

They drove in silence for several minutes.

Jess peered out the windows of the vehicle, trying to figure out where she was. "Your tour of Brussels really sucks."

"*Vous en avez exactement pour votre argent.* You get what you pay for." Bisset laughed. "I'll drop Mertens off several blocks from the museum and you a bit later."

Shortly, Mertens slipped from the vehicle and eased into the crowd exiting the Metro stop.

"You ready, *Docteur* Hemings?" Bisset said a few minutes later.

She took a deep breath. "I guess. Nervous, though."

"That's understandable. We're currently on the Chausée de Wavre. When I tell you, get out and walk that way"—Bisset pointed to the east—"You'll pass

Rue Godecharle and Rue Wiertz. Turn left on Rue Vautier. The museum is on the right. A big dinosaur sits out front."

"Left. Rue Vautier. Big dino. Got it."

"Take your time walking to the Museum. You've got twenty minutes to cover a few blocks. Stroll around. Act like a tourist. Mertens will be within a few meters of you at all times. Whatever you do, don't call attention to him by looking for him. He'll mix with the pedestrians but keep track of you. You focus on the person you're meeting. I'll park at the Museum and meet you in the dinosaur hall. You might not be aware of me, but like Mertens, I'll be there. Any questions?"

Jess shook her head. She had a million questions, but none could be answered in the next ten seconds.

"The 95 bus just pulled over. A bunch of people are getting off. Hop out. Blend in with them."

Jess climbed out and inserted herself into the crowd of passengers and headed in the direction Bisset had indicated. With its mix of the archetypal Flemish decorative gables and mansard roofs and more modern though outdated architecture, this definitely wasn't the most scenic part of Brussels. The streets were paved, but the sidewalks were cobblestoned. The group that had gotten off the bus dispersed over the next block or so, several disappearing into the Victory Apartments. She stopped and peeked in a shop window to see if she was being followed. Didn't spies do that? As far as she could tell, she was alone. She couldn't find Mertens and wasn't sure if that fact reassured or scared her.

She passed a red brick church, then Rue Wiertz to her left. Rue Vautier should be next. When she got to the street, no pedestrian crosswalk was painted on the macadam, and the previous one was half a block behind her. All she needed was to be arrested for jaywalking. She looked around. When she didn't see a *gendarme*, she jogged across the street.

On her right, half a block down, she found the dinosaur Bisset had described. She purchased her ticket, glancing at her timepiece as she waited for her change. Twelve minutes to go. She entered the museum. Though tempted to search for Mertens, she reminded herself that he was a professional.

A group of schoolchildren, eight-year-old wiggle-worms, were gathered at the entrance receiving instructions on how to behave while touring the museum.

Jess sidled up to them, hoping in her jeans and sweater set to pass for a chaperoning mother. Holy shit! If she were assassinated here, innocent people—children—might be injured.

In her haste to get away from the kids, she backed up without looking. As she did, someone slammed into her hard. She lost her balance and staggered.

A firm grip on her elbow caught her before she fell.

Slightly alarmed, Jess gazed into a pair of startlingly blue eyes.

Mertens winked. "*Excusez-moi, madame*. Are you all right?"

To hide her relief, Jess forced her face into a bland expression and nodded. "*Je vais bien, merci*."

He released her arm and strode off, his nose buried in a museum map. Okay, she wasn't as alone as she feared.

Jess let the children move ahead before turning in the opposite direction. She feigned absorption in a display of insects until a covert peek at her watch told her it was time to head to the dinosaur hall.

Chapter Fifty-Two

Jessica

Brussels, July 21, 1997

In the dinosaur hall, Jess studied every face, but none seemed familiar. Then, though dinos weren't exactly her thing, she read the Royal Institute of Natural Sciences guidebook to distract herself, lifting her head often to anxiously scan the exhibit's patrons.

She pushed up the sleeves on her cardigan to discreetly keep an eye on the time. Two minutes after one. Once more she checked out the people visiting the exhibit. Damn. Another bunch of kids was coming in. She started to walk through the hall again, then decided she'd be easier to spot if she stayed in one place. When a nearby bench emptied, she made her way there, sat, placed her purse beside her on the seat, and waited for something to happen.

Another secretive glance at her wristwatch. Despite his rush-rush attitude on the phone, her mystery man was ten minutes late.

Jess tapped her foot as she waited on the bench. She dug in her bag for her hand sanitzer, squirted it on her palms, then rubbed it in while wondering what would happen if her contact didn't show. She wouldn't have to worry about being killed, but she'd never get the information she'd traveled four thousand miles to obtain.

Someone settled beside her.

Jess looked to her right. A woman in a black burqa

gave a single nod.

Unable to see beyond the grid covering the woman's face, Jess replied with an uneasy smile. She returned the hand sanitizer to her purse.

The woman placed something between their feet.

Jess glanced down. It was a large paper bag from the museum shop.

A trace of the woman's cologne drifted between them. The scent, heavily laden with sandalwood and patchouli, was oddly familiar. Jess couldn't figure out where she'd encountered it. She considered moving. She wasn't prejudiced, but she feared the woman's presence might discourage the mysterious contact. Paralyzed with indecision, Jess remained in place. After several moments, the woman stood and walked away, her tread heavy in orthopedic-appearing shoes.

Relieved, Jess scooted to the middle of the bench to discourage anyone else from sitting beside her. As she shifted, her foot hit something. She looked down. The woman had left her bag behind. Jess shouted, "*Madame! Vous avez oublié votre sac.*"

The woman kept walking.

Jess stood and reached for the sack, planning to chase the woman.

An arm encircled Jess's waist, sweeping her off her feet, jerking her away from the bag. "Don't touch it!"

Her fingers closed on air.

Mertens whirled her behind him, placing himself between her and the paper bag. He called to Bissett, some twenty feet away. "Go after that woman. The one in the burqa. I'll evacuate the hall and call the bomb squad."

Someone overheard and screamed in panic. "Bomb!"

Like lightening, the word flashed around the hall.

"*Une bombe! C'est un explosif!*"

"It's a bomb."

"*Het is een bom!*"

People raced toward the exits, thrusting others out of the way, mowing them down.

Mertens released Jess and shoved her toward an exit. "Get out of here." He gave a loud whistle to get peoples' attention then shouted in English, Dutch, and French. "Everyone, remain calm and listen. *Alstublieft calm blijven en luisteren! S'il vous plait, que tout le monde se calme et m'écoute.* Women and children first. *Vrouwen en kinderen eerst.*" He directed the school children and their teachers to an exit. "*Docteur* Hemings. Go with the kids. Get them—and yourself—out of here."

Jess moved toward the children, ready to guide them outside.

In the background, a car backfired, startling Jess into stillness. A second later, she realized the noise hadn't come from a car. She was inside a large building whose thick walls blocked outside noises.

Another sharp bang. Shit! Now she recognized the sound. One she'd heard too often in Rwanda and Benaco. Automatic weapons fire. Her heart stopped.

The noises pinged off the walls and marble floor. She couldn't tell how many shots had been fired.

Zing! An angry high-pitched whine buzzed past her ear.

Mertens shouted at Jess. "That bullet was meant for you. Get down!"

Two boys near her stopped short. One cried, "*Een pistool. Die heeft een pistool!*" In a quivering voice, the other said, "*Quelqu'un braque un pistolet.*"

Jess bent to take their hands.

Something flew over her head and pinged off the wall. Wood crackled as it splintered.

Mertens yelled, "Damn it! Get down!"

Jess flung herself over the two boys, pinning them to the floor. For several minutes, she lay there with their little bodies quivering beneath her. Nothing happened. No more bullets zipped overhead.

The kids whimpered.

Jess counted to one hundred.

Nothing.

With undue caution, she raised her head and peered around.

Mertens was all the way across the room, simultaneously talking on the phone and helping museum guards direct people toward exits.

Jess caught his eye. With a motion, she indicated she was taking the boys outside.

He nodded.

She shooed the youngsters toward the door. "Hold each other's hands. Remain calm, but hurry. Go to the parking lot." She put her hands on their shoulders and curled her body over theirs. "Stay low," she whispered. "I'm behind you."

Once they'd crept from the dinosaur hall, she grabbed their hands and, half-dragging them, ran outdoors.

Museum employees guided people away from the building toward the parking lot. There, teachers tried to count their charges, an impossible task with the children milling uncertainly about.

Jess yelled at a teacher. "Put the children between the vehicles. They'll have some protection from shrapnel if a bomb explodes."

Struggling to remain calm herself, she tugged her own charges to the far end of the parking lot near Rue Vautier, quickly shoved them between two cars, then squeezed in with them. She sat with her legs crossed, pressed their heads in her lap, and curled her torso over them.

The sirens of emergency vehicles reverberated between the museum's hard walls and the cars.

Audible over the klaxons, Jess's heart pounded in her ears. *Lub dub lub dub.* Her body shook. Her third panic attack in eight days. She'd controlled the first two, but this one seemed beyond her. Despite her rapid respirations, she couldn't get enough air into her lungs. Her hands went numb. Her lips tingled. She was going into respiratory alkalosis. If she kept this up, she'd faint. She had to protect her children. With both hands cupped over her mouth, she rebreathed the stale air—in out in out in out—until the tingling stopped.

Time disappeared. She became unaware of the emergency vehicles. The police and firemen. The mayhem surrounding her. Conscious only of two little hearts thumping against her thighs, she had no idea how much time passed.

A hand touched her shoulder.

She lurched in fear.

"*Docteur* Hemings?"

The sound of her name penetrated her haze. A shadow passed over her eyes. She looked up. Above her a huge man stood, silhouetted by the late afternoon sun, his features unidentifiable.

She tightened her grip on the boys and hunkered more closely over them, waiting for the wail of the machete as it sliced downward.

A gentle hand lifted her chin. "*Docteur* Hemings, are you all right?"

Jess blinked. Long seconds passed before she recognized him. Mertens. Her body sagged. Unable to form words, she nodded.

He helped the boys up.

Jess stood on her own. Swayed. Her knees buckled.

Mertens caught her before she fell and set her on the hood of a car, lifting her feet above her head, and resting them across the windshield.

Jess couldn't control her shaking. *Rat-tat-tat.* The heels of her shoes rattled against the car roof.

"*Vous êtes hors de danger maintenant.* You're safe now." Mertens stroked her curls with one hand. With the other hand, he directed the two boys to the area where their teachers and other students in their field trip had gathered.

After giving her a few minutes to recover, he said. "Come with me. Someone's been shot."

Chapter Fifty-Three

Tom

Philadelphia, July 21, 1997

The fierce *beep* of Tom's pager shattered the soft chatter of his team and the violins in Vivaldi's *Four Seasons* playing in the background. "Damn it." In sterile gloves, he couldn't return the call, so he ignored it. Seconds later the beeper sounded again.

"Will you get that, Amy?"

"Sure." The circulating nurse, Amy, wiggled her hand beneath his surgical gown, pulled his pager from its holster, and dialed the number. "Dr. Powell, someone named Jake Brennan is calling."

"Tell him I'll check with him later."

"He says it's urgent." Amy slid the beeper back into place at Tom's waist, following her action with a little pat on his ass.

He grinned. A cute little redhead in her late twenties, Amy had the hots for him. If he could catch her eye, maybe he retained enough charm to entice Jess back into his life. "I'll call him as soon as I'm through here."

Tom lost focus thinking about Jess. Fortunately, he could do a cardiac cath in his sleep. His own heart was still reeling from the night he'd taken her to dinner. They'd been so close to rekindling their love, but something had spooked her. That night, he'd planned to tell her everything. How he'd been pissed that she had skipped the Angel of Mercy Spring Gala where residents were honored and fellowships handed out. She'd gone to Chicago to accept her own award at the OB-GYN national convention. A big deal to her—and rightly so. That didn't keep Tom's feelings from being hurt. Of course—he banged his head against a mental brick wall—if she'd *known* about the fellowship, she might have shown up. He hadn't told her, though, knowing she'd believe he'd abandoned their dream. He'd meant to tell her—eventually—then suddenly it was too late, and the snowball of his life began rolling toward Hell.

The night of the gala, he drank more than he'd ever drunk in his life. So much, in fact, Dr. Clooney made his daughter, Kimberley, drive Tom home. One thing led to another. He didn't even remember making love—scratch that, having sex—with her, but the bedsheets were spotted with the evidence. The next morning, he nearly choked on the engagement ring Jess had left in his coffee cup. His heart plummeted to the floor as he realized she'd found him in bed with another woman.

He was still reeling from losing Jess when Kimberley turned up pregnant. He'd married her. Partly out of guilt. Partly because he deemed marriage the right thing to do. Mostly because he was lost. Lost because Jess had left him.

In a daze of regret, Tom finished another cardiac catheterization then made rounds. His day over at last, he strode to his car to head home. As he unlocked his Beamer, his phone rang. He glanced at the caller ID. Jake Brennan again. Christ, Tom had forgotten all about him.

Jake, his voice gruff and hostile, said, "Doc, I told your nurse this was important. I didn't expect you to take forever to return my call."

"Killer day." Tom started his car and pulled out of

his parking place, his phone crunched between shoulder and ear. "What's up?"

"Got a call from a buddy at the Police Department. Someone broke into Dr. Hemings's house."

"What?" Tom rearranged his shoulder to push the phone closer to his ear.

"Someone burglarized Dr. Hemings's apartment. They were looking for something and wanted it real bad. Trashed her place completely."

"Holy shit."

"I pulled her phone logs. I told you she was a spook or something. We might need to add international drug dealer to our list. Someone called her at three in the morning on Thursday. She immediately rescheduled her trip to Tanzania and went by way of Brussels rather than Amsterdam. Any idea why?"

"No clue. I'll meet you at her place."

Tom and Jake knocked on Susan's door.

When no one answered right away, Tom knocked louder.

Her husband Kevin appeared, dressed in holey jeans and an old t-shirt spattered with pale green paint. "Tom, what brings you to this neighborhood?"

"Susan around? I need to talk to you guys about Jess."

"Come in." Kevin motioned Tom and Jake inside.

"Who is it, Kevin?" Susan's voice called from upstairs.

"Tom Powell and a friend of his."

"Oh?" Susan's voice held a note of surprise. "Let me cover the paint rollers with plastic wrap, then I'll be right down."

Kevin ushered them to the parlor. "Take a seat.

Drink?"

Susan breezed through the door. "Hi, Tom. What are you doing here?"

"I heard about the break-in. I got worried ... wanted to be sure everything was okay."

She shuddered. "We're rather concerned, too. Thank goodness, we have a burglar alarm. I kept telling Jess she needed one, too. A woman living alone can't be too careful these days."

That's why I—we—are here." Tom introduced Jake.

Kevin said, "We didn't realize anything had happened until we showed the carriage house to a potential new tenant and discovered the place had been trashed.

Jake asked, "Any idea who broke in? Why? What they were looking for?"

"None." Susan shrugged. "Thank goodness, she was at her parents' in Gladwyne." Her eyes widened. "She might have been raped. Or killed."

"Jess changed her plans at the last minute. She's in Belgium."

"She didn't tell me." Susan glanced at Tom, a bewildered expression on her face. "How do you know, Tom? I thought you two weren't speaking."

"Yeah. She's been so different since she came home from Rwanda. I just wanted some answers, some way to get through to her ...." Tom squirmed. "Jake's a PI I hired to—"

"Thomas Powell! You're investigating Jess like a common criminal? You little piece of pond scum."

"I just want her back, Susan."

"So all's fair—"

"Sort of." Tom's ears burnt with heat. Ashamed, he slumped into his seat. "I only hired Jake because she wouldn't talk to me."

"That's no excuse."

"I know." He sighed. "She needs help. Even you need to admit that. She's been home two years and still looks like she'll shatter any minute. I keep thinking what happened was my fault. I want to help her, even if she thinks she doesn't need my help. Even if she doesn't want it. I owe it to her."

Jake broke in. "Susan, any idea why Dr. Hemings is going to Tanzania?"

"To work in some hospital. Why?"

"Not to cast aspersions on her character, but any chance she could be involved in anything illegal? Like running drugs?"

"Jess? Never! She's as anti-drug as you can get. Also, my office and the hospital have mandatory random drug testing. She's always been negative."

"What about her Rwanda days?" Jake thrummed his fingers on the end table. "Anything illegal back then?"

"Like Tom said, Jess hasn't been too forthcoming about what happened in Rwanda or Tanzania. Her children died there. She worked with Doctors Without Borders in a refugee camp. That's literally all I know." Susan glanced at Tom. "She's so distant. She doesn't confide in me like she did when we were kids. We had a stupid argument, which didn't help the situation, and things have been sour between us since. Now I can't confide in her either." She reached for Kevin's hand. "We just learned we're expecting a baby—"

"Congratulations." Tom smiled at the couple. Their news explained the splatters of gender-neutral green paint on their clothing. "I'm happy for you. I bet Jess was thrilled."

"We haven't told her yet." Kevin squeezed Susan's hand. "We're afraid to—"

"—because of her children." Susan finished.

"Jess isn't that petty. I'm sure she'd understand."

Jake broke in. "Have you guys done anything to Dr. Hemings's place since she moved out?"

"It's still a mess." Kevin shook his head. "We wanted to finish the baby's room before we tackled the carriage house." He rolled his eyes. "For the second time."

"Would you mind if Jake and I take a look?"

Susan said, "Jess cleared out her personal effects, but she still wouldn't like anyone poking around in her private life—especially you, Tom."

"Come on. It's for her own good." Tom jerked a thumb toward Jake. "He thinks she's involved with some international spy ring or something."

"Jess a spy? You're kidding!"

"I wish I was."

"We have a spare key." Susan stood but didn't retrieve the key. She seemed to be debating with herself. After several false starts, she said, "I'll get it."

When she returned, Kevin took the key. "I'll walk them over. I don't want you and the baby anywhere near danger."

The three men hiked across the yard. The carriage house loomed ahead. Somehow, this perfectly genteel neighborhood felt sinister in the gloomy night.

"Jess would freak out over this." Tom broke the eerie silence. "Susan's right. It's a good thing she's abroad right now."

"Maybe not." Jake's voice held an element of doom.

"What do you mean?"

"You'll see soon enough. The PD warned me about

what we'd find." Jake donned latex gloves, opened the door, lifted the yellow CRIME SCENE DO NOT CROSS tape, and motioned Tom and Kevin inside. "Don't touch anything." He flipped the light switch.

Shocked by what he saw, Tom's heart dropped like an elevator in free-fall. Involuntarily he stepped backwards. "Fuck!"

Kevin put a hand on Tom's shoulder. "We just had the place redone. Jess was our first tenant. She left the apartment spotless. We're grateful she wasn't hurt …."

After his initial shock, Tom slowly peered around. Smashed glass was strewn everywhere. Every picture was off the wall, torn from its frame. Every couch cushion had been slit open and its stuffing removed. Every drawer turned upside down. Obscenities and giant penises were spray-painted in red on the wainscoting. Streaks dripped like blood from the words *Tutsi Whore*.

Chapter Fifty-Four

Jessica

Brussels, July 21, 1997

Jess followed Mertens into the museum. At the far end of the dinosaur hall, the woman in the burqa sprawled face down on the floor, arms and legs splayed in random directions. Beneath her head, blood crawled across the marble floor.

A policeman stood above the body, snapping photos.

"We wonder if you can identify—"

Jess knelt, worming her hand through the voluminous folds of cloth to find the carotid artery. "No pulse." She paused. "Did you guys shoot—"

"No, not us. Someone we haven't identified yet." Mertens placed a hand on Jess's shoulder. "We're going to flip her over so you can visualize her face."

"His face."

"Smart woman. I didn't want to prejudice your ID"—Mertens' grip tightened—"but you figured things out."

"Scratchy facial hair. Men's shoes and slacks. She's definitely a he."

Two policemen turned the body over.

"You ready?" Bisset said.

"Give me a second." Jess closed her eyes, took a deep breath, and mentally stiffened her backbone. She opened her eyes and nodded.

A policeman wiggled the burqa up to reveal the

facial features.

Though slack with death, the face seemed familiar. On the upper lip was a scar from a bad harelip reconstruction. The scar and a whiff of the corpse's cologne sparked her memory. Alarmed, she gasped and retreated a step. "He is—was—Sylvestre Furaha. The liaison between the Rwandan government and PARFA, the agency I volunteered with."

Mertens said, "Was he your contact here?"

"Him? He wouldn't lift a finger to help me."

"Why?"

Jess hesitated. "We never got along very well." She backed up, leaned against the wall, and let herself slide to the floor.

"*Docteur* Hemings?"

She wrapped her arms around her legs. "I'm all right. Just tired. I haven't slept well in days, and now this …"

Bisset pressed her head between her knees. "Don't pass out on us." A few minutes later, he helped her up. "We'll take you to your hotel. Let you get some sleep. By the way, our supervisor wants to debrief you tomorrow."

At the Hilton, Jess jumped out the minute their Hummer stopped moving. "Thanks for the lift."

Mertens took her arm before she could dash off. "We're coming with you."

From the driver's seat, Bisset fished in the rear of the vehicle and handed a briefcase to Mertens. "I'll park and catch up with you in a minute."

Upstairs with Mertens, Jess threw her purse, then herself onto the sofa. Within seconds she was rubbing the back of her neck. Actually, more like digging at the skin. With a growl of disgust at her lack of hygiene, she removed her hand. Hours had passed since she'd thought about washing her hands or using hand sanitizer. She glanced at her wristwatch. Nearly eight o'clock. Her last shower had been Sunday morning, Philadelphia time, thirty-plus hours before. No wonder she sensed germs crawling over her filthy body. She needed to get rid of her bodyguards so she could clean up.

Mertens made her nervous with his methodical sweep of the room, checking closets, drawers, cushions, looking for bugs, hidden cameras, and other potential hazards.

Bisset, carrying two overnight bags, let himself in.

She glanced between the two men and their baggage. "Surely you're not spending the night?"

"We'll stand guard while you sleep."

"I don't need a babysitter."

Mertens added, "If Furaha was your contact, whoever shot him may come after you."

"I won't be able to sleep with you here. I need privacy."

"That's why we got a suite." Mertens grinned. "You take the bed. We'll share the sofa."

"Your day's been rather stressful, *Docteur* Hemings. Do you need something to help you sleep?" From the briefcase, Bisset removed a small zippered pouch which he opened to reveal multiple syringes and small bottles of medication.

"What have you got in there?" She yanked the case from his hand and inspected vial after vial. Ketamine induced a trance-like state. Morphine, an opioid pain medication. Diazepam, an anti-anxiety medication and sedative. Sodium amytal, a sedative also used as a truth serum. Scopalamine treated motion sickness, but long ago, had been used as a somewhat unreliable truth serum. Vercuronium was a paralytic agent. She shivered in disgust. "You're a walking pharmacy. Are you planning to dope me up before interrogating me?"

"The boss will debrief you in the morning. Without drugs." Bisset smiled. "After your flight and the circumstances at the museum, you must be exhausted. I simply thought you might need a good night's sleep."

Jess studied the collection of drugs again. A little diazepam was tempting. Just to take the edge off her shot-to-hell-by-the-day's-events nerves. She hadn't slept worth a darn since that first strange phone call, and today's events guaranteed an insomniac state.

After a long moment, she sighed and closed the case. "I'll take my sedative from the mini-bar." She crossed the room and withdrew a bottle of orange juice and a miniature vodka. With a wave of her hand, she disappeared into the bathroom and filled the tub with hot water and enough bubbles to cover her breasts.

****

A sound awakened Jess. Repeated at fairly regular intervals, it sounded like snoring. In her dream, she'd been cuddled with Tom, post-lovemaking, enjoying the mingling of their body heat, the dampness where their bodies had joined. Tom didn't snore unless he was exhausted. She reached for the opposite side of the bed. He wasn't there.

After several blinks, she became more alert. The dream-Tom faded, but the soft, regular sound continued. Beneath the snoring lay a second sound, the nearly-inaudible murmur of voices. A slash of flickering blue light from a television peeped through her cracked door, barely illuminating her surroundings. She glanced at her wrist. Her watch was gone, and she was on the wrong side of the bed.

Several seconds passed while she processed her environment. Memories tumbled into her mind. Hotel. Brussels. Mertens. Bisset. Recalling Furaha, she shivered violently. She remembered going to the bathroom, pouring the vodka into the orange juice, getting into the tub, but nothing after that. She'd slept extraordinarily well for the first time since she could remember.

She stretched, the sheets clinging to her naked body. Something tugged at her upper arm. When she touched the spot, she found a slick plastic bandage on her deltoid and a tender area beneath. Someone had given her an intramuscular injection. Had those secret agents doped her without her knowledge? Scowling, she reviewed the medications she'd seen in Bisset's briefcase. Scopalamine induced short-term amnesia but left people hungover. Instead she felt rested and infinitely calmer. Diazepam maybe?

She wondered if the two men were still around.

The bed creaked as she stood. Before she could throw on a robe, the door flew open and crashed into the wall. A man appeared, silhouetted against the light, a gun in his extended arms.

Chapter Fifty-Five

Jessica

Brussels, July 21, 1997

At the sudden appearance of an armed man, Jess screeched in alarm.

"*Docteur* Hemings?" He flipped on the light.

Jess was momentarily blinded by the sudden change of illumination. Seconds passed before she recognized Bisset. She sank to the bed and slipped into the robe. "You scared the shit out of me!"

He lowered the firearm. "You all right?"

She nodded. "I will be when my pulse drops to normal."

Mertens, also sporting a pistol, appeared behind Bisset.

"Good morning." Jess said dryly. "What time is it? I can't find my watch."

"Six a.m." Bisset crossed the room, picked up something from the bedside table, and handed it to her. "Your watch."

"Have you been awake this whole time?"

"We've been taking two-hour shifts."

"Did you drug me?"

Bisset's expression remained neutral. "Why?"

"I don't remember anything after I got in the tub." She stared at him a moment. "What on earth happened to your eye?"

His mouth twitched in a grin. "You slugged me."

"I'd never do anything so … so … violent."

"Mertens and I heard screams coming from the bathroom. We broke down the door, thinking you'd been attacked. But you'd fallen asleep in the tub. You were having a hell of a nightmare, thrashing, water flying everywhere. We removed you from the tub because we were afraid you'd injure yourself or drown—"

Jess glanced at the door. Wood hung in splinters from the frame. They really had crashed through the door. Something else occurred to her. "Oh, God, you saw me naked!" She yanked her robe more tightly over her chest.

Bisset blushed. "You fought like you were trying to escape something—or someone. Your fist inadvertently contacted my eye. You didn't realize what you were doing. You were so agitated, I gave you two milligrams of Valium—"

"Without my consent?"

"You were under duress. You needed it."

****

After breakfast, Bisset and Mertens drove Jess to the VSSE headquarters. In a cushy office on the top floor, they introduced her to their supervisor, Hugo Lambert.

Lambert withdrew two plastic animals from a museum bag. "I believe these are a *Tyrannosaurus rex* and a *Spinosaurus aegyptiacus*." With one in each hand, he crashed them against each other amidst fierce growls in a mock battle. He glanced up, his face twisted in a sardonic grin. "Congratulations, gentlemen. You saved Belgium from plastic dinosaurs."

"No bomb?" Mertens's expression revealed both his chagrin and astonishment.

"*Qu'on n'est jamais trop prudent*. It was a credible

threat. Better safe than sorry." Lambert looked up. "We have the security tapes from the museum. Would you mind reviewing them with us, *Docteur* Hemings, to see if you recognize the shooter?"

Jess nodded.

The four of them faced a monitor while Bisset fast-forwarded the tape in such rapid increments Jess felt nauseated. A man clothed in baggy dark pants and a hooded sweatshirt appeared several times. Bissett stopped the video randomly to see if Jess recognized the suspect. The unknown man dragged his right foot in a pronounced limp. Except for the chin, his hood obscured his face. All Jess could tell from the grainy black-and-white security footage was that the man had dark skin and a double chin.

The woman in the burqa approached him.

The sweatshirted man pulled a pistol and fired several rounds in rapid succession. Once the burqa-ed woman hit the floor, he fired another shot point-blank into her—his—head, then strode rapidly toward the exit of the dinosaur hall.

"I don't recognize him." Jess shook her head. "I don't know anyone with a limp."

The tape played further. The man picked up speed as he approached the stairwell, breaking into a run.

"Stop!" Jess blurted. "Rewind a bit."

Bisset complied.

"Watch. His limp is fake. It's not consistent from stride to stride." She pointed to the screen. "See. Right there. Where he's running away?"

"You're right. You're certain you don't recognize him?"

"There's no clear shot of his face. The sweatshirt

and baggy pants disguise the true shape of his body, but he appears to be rather broadly built. The only thing I can determine conclusively is that his limp is fake."

"Very well, *Docteur* Hemings." Lambert assessed Jess over steepled fingers. "Perhaps you would be good enough to explain how you know Mr. Furaha, the man who was killed yesterday."

"He was the first person I met when I arrived in Kigali in 1991. He served as liaison between the Rwandan government and the aid agency I worked for." Jess's voice dwindled as her memory followed well-worn trails.

Lambert's voice jerked her back to the present.

"Sorry. I missed your question." She shook her head. "Mr. Lambert, I warned you about Furaha and Gatera in December of 1994, and you didn't take me seriously back then."

He looked down and drummed his fingers on his desk. When he raised his eyes, he wore an abashed look on his face. "I apologize; however, no one in the world took the genocide seriously. Now, back to the current situation. Why didn't you get along with Furaha?"

"Personality conflicts, I suppose. I'm a little uptight—"

Mertens snorted.

She shot a fierce glare at him. "—and Furaha has—had—a rather laissez-faire attitude. He was the nephew of Dr. Cyprien Gatera, my medical supervisor and a Hutu radical. I didn't get along well with Gatera, either."

"Why not?"

Jess's lips tightened in a grim smile. "After several Tutsi women perished under his care, I investigated and concluded he intentionally allowed them to die. After I confronted him, he banished me to the boondocks of

Rwanda."

At her pause, Lambert nudged with "What then?"

"His nephew, Furaha, was supposed to help me establish an obstetrical clinic not far from the Tanzania border. He bought a beat-up old Land Rover and leased a small house for me as well as a building for my clinic. My home was livable, the best in the village, but the clinic needed a new roof and major repairs. A generator for power. A reliable water supply. An autoclave. Furniture. A toilet."

Astonishment flew over Lambert's face. "You were expected to run a health center under such primitive conditions?"

"No kidding," Jess acknowledged. "Weeks passed. Nothing was done. Things often seemed to move backwards. Construction materials arrived one day and vanished the next." She grimaced at the memory. "By then, medical supplies were being delivered. I had no place to store them except my three-room house. Furaha hinted he could make my problems go away, assuring me things would work more smoothly if I donated a third of the medications and supplies to him. I figured he'd sell them on the black market. When I refused, work stopped completely on the clinic, and my stock of medicines disappeared the next day, stolen from my house while I was work."

"Unbelievable." said Lambert. "Do you think he was the man who called you?"

Jess gave a vehement shake of her head. "I doubt it." She paused, tasting the bitterness of her antipathy. "Whoever called used a voice-changing machine, so I was unable to identify him. I can't imagine Furaha would help me. He'd have to butt heads with Gatera, the titular head of their family. I doubt Furaha has—had—the gumption to do that." A memory jolted her brain like a lightning flash. When she'd stumbled with fatigue while treating Gatera's soldiers, Furaha had taken her elbow and asked if she was all right. Perhaps he had been more sympathetic than she realized.

"Any significance to the dinosaurs Furaha left at your feet?"

She gave a bewildered shake of her head. "None that I know of."

"Did he speak to you? Have any other contact besides abandoning the bag?"

Jess shook her head. "I smiled at him. That's it." She stopped abruptly at the memory of Furaha with a bullet hole between his eyes.

"Why was he camouflaged as an Islamic woman?"

"I don't know. There aren't many Muslims in Rwanda, maybe five percent of the population." Jess shrugged. "It's a perfect disguise. No one would suspect a Catholic male would disguise himself in an Islamic woman's garment."

"Why might such a man be assassinated? By whom?"

"Perhaps members of the Rwandan Patriotic Front killed him because he was a *génocidaire*? Or some Tutsi seeking revenge?"

Lambert leaned forward and looked directly at Jess. "Or a Hutu who feared Furaha was about to pass information to someone connected with the ICTR?"

Jess squirmed under Lambert's scrutiny. "I'm not with the ICTR."

"We know." He chuckled. "You're a Baker Street irregular. You do the research and feed the information to your friend, Michel Fournier, at the ICTR. Correct?"

"Not exactly. I didn't know Michel's whereabouts until I got a letter from the ICTR in which he said he worked there." She reached back to rub that spot on her neck, caught herself, and jerked her hand down.

"What we don't understand is how an American woman got caught up in this. Why do you persist in this crazy search"—Lambert glanced at an open folder on his desk, then studied her from beneath raised eyebrows—"at significant personal costs, both financial and emotional?"

Jess stood and moved to the window. For a long moment, she stared out the window at the peaceful streets of Brussels, steeling herself for the onslaught of emotional overload. Then she began pacing, head down, watching her feet crush the tweed carpet. If she even looked at the men around her, she'd break down.

She turned back toward the window, staring outside again. "I was in my clinic delivering a baby when Gatera and Furaha burst in. Their men, FAR soldiers, dragged my patients out back, slaughtered them, and discarded the bodies in a drainage ditch. Then they forced me and my staff to treat their wounded."

Lambert's face twisted into an expression of outrage. "Then what?"

"I managed to escape." Recalling the specks of blood, brain matter, and curls from her babies' heads imbedded in the wall of her office, she shivered. She couldn't talk about that, so she told of crossing the Rusumo Bridge into Tanzania and working with Doctors without Borders. "When MSF pulled out in November, though, I stayed behind. I'd met someone—"

"Fournier?"

Jess lifted an eyebrow. "Yes. Mr. Fournier, a journalist, was doing interviews and collecting data on the genocide. He wanted to show the effects of the war."

"And you're the Dr. X Fournier wrote about."

Jess nodded. These guys seemed to know everything about her. Did they know she'd slept with Michel? "I joined Michel because, in Rwanda, traditionally older female relatives teach young girls about sexuality. I hoped women would be more willing to talk to another woman about … sensitive subjects."

"Like rape? HIV?"

"Yes." Jess looked down. Her knuckles were white with strain. "You have to realize that the Hutu used rape as an act of war. They literally released men from HIV hospitals, drugged them with *khat*—"

"What's that?"

"A leaf that, when chewed, causes an amphetamine-like excitement. Anyway, the Hutu used these men as deadly weapons. They armed them with machetes and turned them loose to kill and rape—and spread HIV, another way of killing Tutsis." She closed her eyes, blocking memories.

"How horrible."

"You can't imagine. In those days, I swear it was more dangerous to be a woman in Rwanda than to be a soldier. FAR soldiers were indoctrinated to believe Tutsi women were a fifth column bent on destroying Hutus." Jess's breath snagged in her tight throat. "Believe me, rape is a form of torture. It not only destroys a woman, it destroys a community. Rape is a slow method of killing, but it's still murder."

"What did you and Fournier do?"

"We interviewed survivors. I provided medical

exams when needed to verify people's stories of torture—and to help where I could. I'd seen so much ... I suppose it was a vain hope, but I thought if I helped document the horrors, such depravity might never happen again."

Lambert questioned her for hours. His tone remained friendly, but from his repeated questioning on the same subject from different tacks, she knew she was being skillfully interrogated, her story being probed for inconsistencies or outright lies. He was almost as good at digging out facts as Michel.

"And Furaha? Can you tell us more about him? You have no idea who his killer is?"

"I've told you all I know. I'd heard he was in Zaire—"

"But you didn't get any hits on your research there, and your friend Anne-Marie Bwakira hasn't turned up anything either."

"Correct." Jeez, where did these guys get their information? "In Rwanda, neither faction trusts people who stayed rather than fled. Either side might want him dead."

"Furaha's a bit player, but we've had our eyes on Gatera for some time. We suspected he participated in the genocide, and your story confirms that. He's slippery as an eel, though. The VSSE can't pin him down. However, that doesn't mean you should continue your search."

"I'd hoped that this new connection would lead me to Gatera. Furaha—if he was my contact—was my last hope."

"I recommend that you cease this *volunteer work*, as you call it, for the ICTR. You've done a tremendous job, but, frankly, at this point your life is at risk, and you're not trained in the techniques you need to survive. Gatera has access to Rwandan military intelligence. The French supported the Hutu both during the genocide and afterward with Operation Turquoise, so he may also be getting information from French intelligence."

Lambert stood and extended his hand. "We'll provide protection as long as you are in Belgium, but we cannot extend that protection beyond our borders. Bisset and Mertens will guard you until you resume your journey to Tanzania."

Chapter Fifty-Six

Jessica

Brussels, July 21, 1997

Accompanied by Mertens and Bisset, Jess returned to her hotel where she rescheduled her flight. After talking with the airline, she called Mount Meru Hospital, explaining that, due to unforeseen circumstances, she wouldn't arrive until the twenty-third.

She turned to Bisset. "The croissants you fed me for breakfast are long gone. Is starving a prisoner part of your interrogation process?" She whirled and headed toward the door. "I'm going downstairs for dinner."

"We all should eat." He stopped her by grabbing her shoulder. "Room service is our best option. You've already been shot at once."

"Not to mention nearly blown up by toy dinosaurs." She couldn't resist teasing Bisset. His thunderous look said her attempt at humor wasn't appreciated.

Room service wheeled in a cart laden with food. Though she'd been hungry earlier, when dinner arrived, she picked at her food. Everything that had happened, including seeing Furaha's dead body, stirred up memories she'd suppressed.

"I thought you were starving." Bisset leaned back in his chair and propped his feet on the coffee table. "You didn't eat enough to keep a quail alive."

A rather piquant thought of Michel whizzed through her mind at the mention of *quail*. "Not as hungry as I thought." Jess wrinkled her nose. "I found the past two days rather nerve-wracking."

"The tale you told Lambert earlier doesn't explain why you started tracking down war criminals. What's the real story?"

She shivered in revulsion. "You don't want to know."

"Try us."

Jess hesitated. She'd left Rwanda two and a half years ago but still had trouble talking about her experiences. Susan had received a highly-expurgated version of reality. Her parents and Tom even less. The only one she'd told the whole story to was Michel. Between the middle-of-the-night phone call and what happened at the museum, memories clamored for release.

She stood, moved to the window, staring beyond the closed drapes, scratching her neck.

Seconds later she jumped when someone lifted her fingers and wiped them with something cool and damp. She angled her face to check who it was. Mertens.

"Blood's dripping down your blouse." He placed a damp washcloth on her neck and put her hand on top. "You need to stop this."

"Bad habit."

"It's a stress response."

"I'm a physician. I know that." Her voice held a trace of irritation. "I can't help it."

"Why do you persist in such difficult work if you react like this?"

Jess removed the cloth from her neck. For a long time, she stared in silence at the scarlet stain on the brilliant white. She finally spoke, her voice was tiny, a whimper in her own ears. "I think about it all the time. About surviving. About being alive. Life itself, not death, is an accident of fate."

Mertens placed a hand on her shoulder. "*Docteur* Hemings … Jessica … sometimes strangers are easier to talk to." His voice sounded almost tender.

Overcome by his concern, Jess nearly broke into tears. He was right. She'd never lay eyes on these men again, would never again be subjected to their speculative stares about what a monster she'd become in Rwanda. With a sigh, she began. "During the genocide, people expected to die, each hoping not to die cruelly, but expecting death nonetheless. Resignation to death became the norm.

"The delicacy of surgery didn't prepare me for the butchery, the sheer number of whacks needed to dismember a person with a machete. For those doing the hacking, killing was hard work. Sweat poured from Hutu faces as they chopped fellow humans into bits. The slow killing was worse. The *Interahamwe* sliced their victims' tendons so they couldn't run away, then amputated one limb at a time to prolong their targets' agony. If people were willing to pay or barter, they could plead for a swift end by a bullet rather than be tortured or hacked to death with a machete."

She started to pace, her feet keeping time with her words. "I didn't realize my driver, Jean-Baptiste, had stockpiled cheap local beer for weeks. Once we realized how bad things were, he loaded the Land Rover with the alcohol, thinking we might bribe the soldiers at checkpoints with it. To our misfortune, Gatera and Furaha commandeered my clinic before we could leave."

Jess paced faster. The washcloth fell to the floor unheeded. Her fingernails dug deeper into her neck. "Gatera forced me to watch as he killed my children."

A shudder crawled up her entire body. "He laughed the whole time, saying 'Two fewer little cockroaches.'" She paused, holding her breath, before releasing the words in a rush. "After my babies were gone, something inside me snapped. I was going to die. I knew it. Accepted it. My demise would be cruel. Gatera would ensure that. So when my chance came to escape, I abandoned my staff, my friends, everything. I tucked my tail between my legs and ran."

Mertens patted her shoulder with a gentle hand. "You did what you had to."

"Every day I ask myself why I survived. Sheer luck? If so, I swear the people who died were luckier …." After a lengthy silence, she continued, "Now I hunt for Gatera." She swallowed. "I owe something to my sons, to all those people I didn't stop to help, to all those bodies by the roadside I didn't—couldn't—try to save." She couldn't mention the little boy she'd killed with her own hands. A sob gurgled from her throat. Oh God, she was blubbering in front of these men. "I have to atone somehow."

Bisset gathered her in his arms and rocked her.

When her tears dwindled, Mertens said, "You're going to continue this insane search, aren't you?"

Jess sniffled. "I've given myself six months. If I haven't found them by then, I'll stop. I'll have no more resources—financial or emotional—to continue."

Mertens clapped her on the shoulder. "Then we have less than twenty-four hours to teach you everything you need to be a spy."

Chapter Fifty-Seven

Jessica

En route to Rwanda, July 22, 1997

Jess was relieved when Mertens and Bisset accompanied her through the Brussels airport and waited with her until she got on the plane to Amsterdam. They assured her their constant surveillance revealed nothing.

On boarding the plane, Jess was both relieved and concerned at being out of their care. No one occupied the seat next to her. Exhausted from the bomb scare and from her crash course in staying alive, she was grateful she wouldn't be required to chitchat. She started to rub her neck, stopped herself in mid action, and dug in the bottom of her purse for her hand sanitizer. Something white lay beneath the bottle. A bolt of unease shot through her. She removed a piece of paper tightly folded into a one-inch square. With trembling hands, she opened it. Beneath a logo for a hotel in Kigali, one she'd never stayed in, she found the words *Return to Rwanda. Find Jean-Baptiste, he has a package for you* printed in block letters.

The woman in the burqa—rather, Furaha—must have placed it there while they sat on the museum bench; however, his motive for passing on the message remained unclear. Had someone killed him to prevent the exchange of this note?

Profound religious and political differences existed between Furaha and Jean-Baptiste. She considered

Jean-Baptiste a deeply religious man and a moderate Hutu. Furaha, on the other hand, was an opportunist, plain and simple. He used his relationship with Gatera and other Hutu radicals in his attempt to rise through the political system, improve his personal status, and increase his wealth. With Tutsis out of power, Hutus like himself filled the void. What would prompt him to help her? She hoped she wasn't being lured into a trap.

She drew comfort in that Jean-Baptiste had survived, but to find him she must to return to a place she'd thought she'd left behind. A good friend, he'd be willing to help her now. She'd seen her home and clinic in Kirehe. Nothing of value had remained in either location. She couldn't image what he had unearthed from those ruins. Whatever it was must be important for him to entrust Furaha with a message.

Jess thought back to the museum's security video. When she'd last seen him, Gatera had been stocky enough to be the guy in the video, but without seeing the face, she couldn't be certain. Lambert had said that Gatera had access to military-grade intelligence. So, he might have learned of her arrangement to meet someone and killed the contact to prevent the exchange of information. Her heart thumped harder as she realized Gatera might know her destination.

With her anxiety growing by the minute, she tossed vague theories around until her plane landed at Schiphol. For the third time in a week, she changed her ticket, this time to fly to Rwanda. The tally of last-minute changes was devastating to her funds.

She caught the 8:35 flight with minutes to spare. She'd get a short-term visa at Kigali International Airport. Once settled in her seat, she opened her laptop to add a few words to her journal. With trembling fingers, she typed: *Someone tried to kill me yesterday ....*

After completing her entry, she closed her computer. Thoughts of Furaha carried her back to Rwanda. Should the lead to Jean-Baptiste not work out, she'd query her former neighbors and friends. Much like Lambert at the VSSE had delved repeatedly into her story, she'd dig for information that might lead to Gatera. Somehow, she'd nail the bastard. Not for revenge, she kept telling herself. For justice. For revenge, too. Hell, yeah.

****

Kigali, Rwanda, July 22, 1997

Jess's flight landed in Kigali without incident. She figured anyone who might have followed her from Belgium would assume a *muzungu* would stay at a major hotel like Mille Collines or the Diplomates. Mertens and Bisset had warned her to stay as far off the bad guys' radar as possible. She didn't know who—or where—the bad guys were. In hopes of remaining invisible, she chose a small hostel near the Kigali Airport.

Once there, Jess dropped her baggage on the floor and didn't bother washing the travel dirt off. She was hungry, and the restaurant would close in half an hour. But before she went to dinner, she removed clear plastic tape from her computer bag and placed an inch between the sill and the sash of the window. If anyone came in through the window, the tape would be disturbed.

After she arranged her belongings in her suitcase and memorized their positions, she slid the zipper until precisely six teeth remained between the sliders. Anyone who searched her belongings would be unlikely to return the zipper to that identical spot.

As she left, she closed the door on the *Do Not Disturb*

sign, trapping it inside the jamb, so she could tell if anyone entered. She stood for a moment outside her room. She didn't get that hair-raising sense that something was amiss, but the techniques Mertens and Bisset taught her increased her wariness rather than making her feel safer.

Downstairs, as she passed the reception desk, she asked, "May I borrow your phone book?"

The receptionist hesitated, acting like the local phone book was a first edition of the Gutenberg Bible.

"I'll be within your range of vision." She poked her chin toward the restaurant. "I'll return it in a few minutes."

Jess sat in one of the ubiquitous cheap plastic chairs and ordered. While waiting for her food, she scribbled a list of names of people she needed to find, then looked each up in the phone book. She ran her index finger down the page of Fs several times looking for Sylvestre Furaha then the Gs for Cyprien Gatera. Not surprisingly, no listing existed for either.

Jess couldn't even track down their relatives. In her first few weeks in Rwanda, she'd learned there was no way to figure out family connections based on names. Most people had a Kinyarwanda name, a family name from the father's side, and a religious name. On occasion, a person kept all three names, but more commonly, people chose two to use as their "official" name. The lack of consistent surnames even within a family presented obvious problems for understanding familial relationships and for finding relatives for reunification post-genocide. Or searching for a criminal.

In Africa, where street addresses didn't exist, birth certificates often weren't filled out, and officials were easily bribed, changing one's identity was simple.

Furaha and Gatera might have established new identities with forged papers and emigrated. Jess checked page after page of the phone book. Other friends and acquaintances from the relief agency weren't listed either. Jess growled. She foresaw a lot of door-to-door canvassing in her future.

The waiter delivered goat brochettes and plantains.

She chewed and considered her options. Hiring a car and driver to be at her disposal was tempting and would be a tremendous timesaver. But that would make her more of a *muzungu* than she already was and would prevent people from opening up when she questioned them. Also, she would draw attention to herself, the last thing she wanted to do.

Once she arrived in Kirehe, her first priority would be to reestablish contact with people. In late 1994, when she'd returned with Michel immediately after the conflict, half the population was either internally or externally displaced—or dead. With the country's infrastructure devastated, tracking down people proved impossible. The existence of a phone book indicated the country was returning to some degree of normalcy.

She dropped the phone book off at the reception desk and returned to her room. All the little devices, her telltales, remained undisturbed. So far no one appeared to have tracked her to Rwanda.

****

Rusumo Falls, July 23, 1997

The next morning, she took a *twegerane*, an eighteen-passenger Toyota mini-bus, from Kigali to Rusumo Falls. No one seemed to have followed her from the hostel. The bus wasn't full, so she waited an hour for the conductor to decide sufficient people had boarded to warrant taking off. She cautiously studied her fellow passengers. No one who boarded showed signs of being overly interested in her. Mosquitoes buzzed in and out of the mini-bus. She slapped one in mid-bite, then pulled insect repellent from her backpack, squirted some on her hands, and rubbed it on her face, body, and clothes. Then, for good measure, she gave her hands a squirt of sanitizer.

The RN3 highway was in surprisingly good condition. Jess scrunched her eyes shut. Her fingers closed into tight fists. She'd traveled this road many times before but didn't want to think about the last time.

Miles passed as did hours, the bus schedule determined by the driver's whim. He stopped for passengers who hailed the vehicle from random points on the roadside and halted just as arbitrarily for people to disembark. Should the bus grow too empty to be profitable, he pulled before the Rwandan equivalent of a convenience store and parked until his vehicle filled. Without complaint at the delays, travelers took advantage of the time to stretch their legs, buy a cold drink, use the toilet, or chat.

Jess pretended to sleep. She didn't dare talk to anyone—she didn't trust her long-unused Kinyarwanda.

A man in his mid-twenties sat beside her. He smiled but didn't make eye contact. Jammed between him and the frame of the bus, she had long since melted from the sun pouring through the window. She'd forgotten the cardinal rule of bus travel in Africa: always sit on the shady side of the bus. At least she'd obeyed rule number two and kept her luggage with her.

Once the van was back in motion, she drifted for real into a half-conscious doze. Her head sank to her chest.

She snapped awake with a sudden jolt when she bounced in her seat. Milliseconds later, she realized the bus had hit a massive pothole at a high enough speed that she'd been momentarily airborne.

Something slapped her lap. She glanced down. A brown arm stretched across her thighs. She knocked it away. The young man had taken advantage of her inattention to delve into her knapsack. He gave a better-luck-next-time shrug in response to her irate glare.

The bus took seven hours to travel a distance of just under a hundred miles. Jess arrived at Rusumo Falls during one of those sunsets the tropics were famous for, where the sky turned flame-red as the sun vanished almost instantly. She disembarked. Because of its elevation, Rwanda got cool after dark, so she slipped on a light sweater before walking to the Motel Amarembo. Not a great place to stay, but hotels here in the boonies were few and far between. Once she'd had friends who'd have welcomed her into their homes, but she no longer knew if they were still alive.

Chapter Fifty-Eight

Jessica

Rusumo Falls, July 23, 1997

The thunder of the Rusumo Falls, combined with the rumble of passing trucks, made the floor and walls of Jess's room vibrate—at least that's what she attributed her nausea to. She felt *mzunguzungu*—like she was drunk or her equilibrium was off. Hoping to settle her stomach, she decided to eat a light dinner. On leaving her room, she repeated the protocol Bisset and Mertens taught her, placing telltales at the window, the door, and her suitcase.

Again, she asked for a phone book, the few pages of which she studied as she ate vegetables and drank mango juice. A glass of the freshly-squeezed juice had been one of her favorite things about living in Rwanda and always seemed the height of luxury.

Health care, when Jess had first arrived, was non-existent across much of the country. The only hospitals had been in Kigali or Butare with a rare health clinic in the boonies where she worked. The genocide must have devastated the already-fragile system. Two years later, with repairs barely underway, she was certain Kirehe hadn't recovered.

She returned the book to the reception desk. "Did the health clinic reopen?"

The male receptionist nodded.

"Is it in the same place?"

"No. It shifted to near the Kirehe market on the highway."

Jess returned to her room and tried to sleep but tossed and turned. With time, her tiredness overcame the constant noise, and she fell into a sleep disturbed by dreams as turbulent as the waters of the Kagera.

In the wee hours, a strange sound jarred her from slumber.

Snick-snick-snick. The handle of her door jiggled. In the streak of yellow light beneath the door, shadows of feet danced back and forth. *Snick-snick-snick.* Someone was trying to open her door.

Her heart pounded a staccato tattoo in her ears. Jess eased out of bed and fished in her purse, searching for the closest things she had to weapons. Bisset had assured her the sturdy stainless-steel pen in her purse was strong enough to put out an eye. Petite, she didn't stand a chance of hitting someone in the face, so he'd advised her to hold the pen in an underhanded grip, duck, and aim for the groin. He informed her a pen to the balls would incapacitate any man on the spot.

She tiptoed across the room and grabbed her perfume from her suitcase. A spray in the face might blind an attacker long enough for her to stab him.

At the door, as ready as she would ever be for an attack, she waited for it to spring open.

A woman's giddy giggle.

A drunken male's unintelligible reply.

The feet moved on.

Jess flopped on the bed in relief. She'd just arrived, and Rwanda was already unnerving her. Maybe it was just the memories. Maybe she wasn't quite the spook she thought she'd become—despite the help of Mertens and

Bisset. Maybe it was plain old fear.

The next morning, Jess planned to knock on doors and search for old friends. Still overly-anxious from the night before, she left her telltales which she now termed the Mertens-Bisset protocol.

After breakfast, carrying only her backpack, she headed to the main road. The Kagera River's surging waters were a local tourist attraction, but Jess couldn't bring herself to walk the short distance to the Rusumo Falls Bridge.

Despite the already-warm morning, chills trickled down Jess's spine. Back in 1994, as she crossed the bridge into Tanzania, she'd made the mistake of looking over its side at the waterfall. A dark blob tumbled over the precipice. Every minute or two, another would spill into the churning waters below. Jess had nearly fainted when she realized those shapeless masses were bloated corpses.

Shaking off her dire thoughts, she caught a minibus, another "stopping taxi" that halted anywhere passengers needed a pick-up or drop-off.

"Where to?" the driver asked.

"The Kirehe market on the Kibungo-Rusumo highway." The best place to start looking for Yvette, her former nurse, would be where they both once worked.

Fortunately, the mini-bus was quite full, and Jess didn't wait long before it pulled onto the highway. She gave a casual-appearing look around, memorizing the people surrounding her. No one paid any attention to her. Several stops later, the bus let her out. Everyone who was on the bus when she boarded had already exited, so she didn't believe anyone followed her.

Jess hiked the hundred yards to the health care

center. At the front desk, she spoke to the receptionist. "*Mwaramutse*. I'm Dr. Jessica Hemings."

"Good morning, *Docteur*. I am Evaline. How may I assist you?"

"I worked at the clinic in Kirihe a few years ago." Jess hesitated to ask if Evaline knew if Yvette was still alive, so she phrased her question more delicately. "Back then, my nurse was Yvette Safi. I wonder if you might know of her?"

"I'm sorry, but no. Let me introduce you to our new doctor. Perhaps he knows her."

Chapter Fifty-Nine

Jessica

Kirehe, July 24, 1997

Jess gaped as she followed the receptionist down a hallway. This clinic was much larger than her little dump had been—and much better equipped.

Evaline said, "This wing houses a pharmacy, our surgical suite, and *Docteur* Muzehe's office." She pointed to her left. "That wing has eight beds for general patients and four for labor and delivery."

Painted on the frosted glass of the most distant door were the words *Dr. Théophile Muzehe, Directeur de l'Hôpital*. Though it was open, Evaline knocked.

"*Oui?*" A trim man raised his head.

"Sorry to disturb you, *Docteur* Muzehe, but *Docteur* Hemings has a few questions for you."

"*Certainement.*" He smiled and motioned the women into his office.

After introductions, Evaline returned to her duties.

With a glance at Jess, Dr. Muzehe plugged two immersion water-heating coils into a wall outlet and dropped them into pots. "Would you like some tea?"

"*Yego, nyabuneka.*" Jess was relieved she was remembering some Kinyarwanda, even though "yes, thank you" was pretty basic.

Tea, the traditional Rwandan beverage of welcome, marked every social occasion. Dr. Muzehe heated the water and brought fresh milk to a boil, whipped the milk slowly into the tea, and topped the mixture with a sprinkle of ginger. He talked as he performed the ritual. "So, you're the inimitable *Docteur* Jess? I've heard a lot about you. Your patients still judge me against your high standards."

Flattered, Jess smiled at the younger man. "Thanks. I did the best I could under difficult circumstances." She took a sip of tea and exhaled in wonder. It tasted better than any American tea. With a lift of her shoulders, she continued, "Despite the frustrations, I loved it here. I only left because of the unrest."

"I missed all that, thank goodness. I was in France, finishing my training. I returned a year after the conflict." He opened a tin of British biscuits and offered her one.

Jess accepted a cookie, then glanced around. "This building is wonderful. You've done a great job."

Muzehe smiled. "Your old clinic was a burnt-out shell. Anything not stolen was torched. I had to *recommencer depuis le début*, start from the beginning. All new equipment, new everything. Fortunately, the very countries that ignored the genocide now feel guilty enough to pour foreign aid into Rwanda. By no means have we recovered, but we are making progress."

"I almost envy you. The aid society I worked for was so underfunded, my place initially didn't have the basics like running water, electricity, an autoclave, a roof—"

"You're legendary around here. My patients tell me you helped renovate the clinic and designed the biggest loo in the area."

Jess laughed. "After graduating from medical school, I never dreamed I'd need construction skills."

"What have you been doing since?"

"After the conflict, I worked at Benaco."

He raised his eyebrows. *"C'est impossible à faire.* An impossible job."

She looked down, silent a moment. Tough didn't begin to describe either her work at the clinic or her responsibilities at Benaco. "I wonder if you could help me?"

Muzehe arched a brow.

"My staff have vanished. Do you have any idea where they might have gone?" Jess swallowed. "Or if they're still alive."

"Many people disappeared. Others assumed new names …"

"How about my medical records? When the … conflict … started, I left in a hurry. I couldn't carry out documents I needed." She paused before telling a white lie. "I'd like to complete articles I was writing on maternal-fetal mortality, but I need to review my statistics."

Muzehe shrugged apologetically. "Ashes. Even now, records throughout the country remain in disarray. Most pre-conflict papers have disappeared."

That was what Jess feared. Computers and electronic back-up systems hadn't existed in Rwanda in 1994. Everything had been hand-written or typed on old-fashioned paper with carbon duplicates. In the immediate aftermath of the conflict, no one could find copies of her sons' adoption paperwork that she left with the authorities. Her babies' identities vanished. Not only had their bodies disappeared, but she also had no proof of their existence, a fate her children shared with thousands of others.

She sighed. "My old patients? How many remain? Especially the Tutsis?"

"Few Tutsis remain. Unless they were lucky enough to make it into exile, I estimate some ninety percent were killed. This is a topic we rarely speak of in public. I can't specifically say I treated any of your Tutsi patients. Rwanda is trying to recover from the genocide, and it's considered bad form these days to ask someone's ethnicity." He nodded absently, stared into the distance, then spoke through tight lips. "Of course, in private, all the old prejudices remain."

"I understand. It was a bad time for Rwanda." What an understatement. Words couldn't begin to detail the horrors. She paused for a long time, then set down her teacup. "Thanks for your help."

"Another cup for the road?"

"No, thank you. You've been too kind. I won't take any more of your time. Should you think of anything, please give me a call or an e-mail." She handed him her business card.

"*Murgire amaharo*, go in peace, *Docteur*."

After saying goodbye to Evaline, Jess backtracked to the village where she'd lived. As she walked, a man approached her, a hoe over his shoulder.

Through lowered lids, he gave her a quick look, then turned his gaze straight ahead.

He didn't greet her. Not only that, he averted his face and passed her without another glance. His demeanor struck Jess as odd. Rwandans in rural areas greeted literally everyone they met with complex salutations, while folks in big cities like Kigali generally acknowledged only people they knew.

With a stocky body and a broad nose, he looked Hutu. Had he been a *génocidaire*? Had his hoe been his weapon? Or had he used a machete? Or a club?

My God. Killers walked the streets of Rwanda. Jess's pulse throbbed loudly in her ears.

She continued walking, suddenly realizing the perpetrators, doomed to face their guilt and their accusers on a daily basis, must live the same uncomfortable lives as their victims. She gave herself a mental shake, unable to believe she, who was struggling to bring Gatera to justice, felt an iota of empathy for such monsters. The new Rwandan government urged its citizens to reconcile, but she wasn't obliged to conform to those dictates.

Half an hour later, she came to her old village. Some buildings had been rebuilt. Others, presumably those in which all the former inhabitants had been killed, remained in shambles. Jess's former abode was among the latter. She'd worked hard to make her first residence without Tom or her parents into a real home for herself and her children. When she lived there, a tiny yard surrounded the bilious-yellow stuccoed house. Jess hand-carried every stone that outlined the two patches of grass and planted the flowers that delineated the foundation. A swept red dirt path led to the door. In the back, bananas, avocados, and passion fruit grew with abandon. She'd never forget her pride at picking her first homegrown banana, its flavor so intense it seemed artificial.

Justine's house next door looked bad too. Apparently unoccupied, Dorcas's was in worse shape. The roof and one wall, in poor repair back then, had collapsed. The dirt path, no longer swept daily to keep down snakes and weeds, was overgrown.

Dorcas had lived there with her two children while her husband, Furaha, lived in Kigali. The women never grew close, largely because Furaha moved his wife out of their house so he could rent it to Jess. His callousness toward his wife's feelings led to Dorcas's hatred of Jess, and Radio Mille Collines fanned that hostility.

Jess truly didn't believe Dorcas had anything to do with Furaha and the *Interahamwe*. Nevertheless, the best way to trace his movements, and possibly those of Gatera after the genocide, would be to question her regarding her husband. Jess wasn't sure if Dorcas knew of her husband's death yet, but Jess didn't want to be the one to break the news. Judging from the condition of their house, though, the family had moved on.

Between Jess's old house and Justine's sat a battered Land Rover. Jess wasn't certain if it was hers, but the parts that hadn't rusted were the same faded olive hers had been. The license plate number seemed somewhat familiar. How had the vehicle survived the war and its aftereffects?

Jess returned her attention to her former home, wondering who lived there now. Could—or would—they help her?

Most folks would be unlikely to give her a straight answer regarding Gatera's whereabouts. They'd give her a response, one they thought she wanted to hear, but one that might not be completely true. Partly due to the Rwandan sense of privacy. Partly due to the desire to please her. Partly because dissembling had become an art form in Rwanda.

She couldn't blame them. Those who provided evidence against war criminals feared reprisals. Though the UN did its best to protect them, witnesses in the Arusha trials took a calculated risk in testifying against their neighbors—with the added challenge of returning to Rwanda to live near the person they had testified against.

In the right front window, a tattered curtain moved, bringing Jess back to the moment. She saw a face but couldn't make out the features. She waved hello.

Immediately the fabric dropped.

She waved with more force to be sure they saw her motion, then waited. Whoever had been at the window didn't come greet her. Again, the off-kilter behavior struck her. In the old Rwanda, the inhabitants would have rushed out to catch up on the latest gossip.

Jess stood in the road, wondering if she should knock.

"*Docteur* Jess?"

A voice from her left interrupted her thoughts.

"*Oui?*" Jess pivoted to see who had spoken.

"*Bonjour.* Is it truly you?" A mother, with two youngsters beside her, greeted Jess.

Jess stared at the woman. After a moment, she identified her as a former patient. "*Muraho*, Keza. It's been too long." Jess gave the woman a hug. She looked down at the children and blinked. "Are these the babies I delivered? I can't believe it. They've gotten so big!" She managed a bright smile though her heart ached that these two had survived, but her own hadn't.

Keza's laughter rang out. She reached over her shoulder and patted a little head. "Yes, plus one."

Drawn to Keza's merriment, more people arrived. Recognizing Jess, they greeted her warmly. They swept her to a house at the center of the village. In the past, when Jess had been a guest in a Rwandan home, the hosts had never greeted her with empty hands. That custom remained the same. From nowhere, fruit, a sorghum-based porridge called *igikoma*, and other delicacies appeared—as well as the traditional Rwandan tea. *Mandazi*, the local version of doughnuts, accompanied the beverage. Word spread that *Docteur* Jess had returned, and folks appeared, each carrying a perfect fruit or other small token of welcome.

A man murmured "*Muraho*" as he extended a handful of baby bananas toward her.

As she reached for them, she recognized the man. Snippets of memories tumbled into place. The last time she'd seen him, he'd worn a blood-stained *dashiki* and had just murdered one of her patients.

Chapter Sixty

Jessica

Kirehe, July 24, 1997

Jess's stomach lurched toward her throat. Never a turn-the-other-cheek personality, her desire to accept the man's hospitality warred with thoughts he'd killed someone. In the dense air, she smelled her own sweat. People pressed so tightly around her she could neither gracefully retreat nor avoid greeting him. With great effort, she fought the urge to break through the surrounding crowd and run away. She dared not be impolite, dared not refuse his gift, so she hid her horror. Inhale. Hold. Exhale. Though her hands trembled, she accepted his gift, determined to dispose of the fruit as soon as she left.

The Rwandan custom of lengthy questioning about one's family seemed to have changed after the genocide. Though her old friends and neighbors asked about Jess's parents, they avoided mentioning her children, and they replied to her questions about certain people with flat expressions accompanied by a scant lift of shoulders to indicate "Who knows?" or perhaps "Don't ask, won't tell."

Her soul clenched as she realized how many friends—from both sides of the conflict—were missing. She looked around. The genocide had left the population mostly Hutu, nearly seventy percent female, with few older people, and vast numbers of orphans. She didn't know how, but somehow these people had moved beyond the conflict. She knew better than to remind them of the past.

After visiting for a while, Jess felt more at home speaking Kinyarwanda. Her efforts still brought good-natured chuckles, but for the most part she made herself understood. When she didn't, a code-switch to French or Swahili communicated what she needed to.

She checked her watch. Nearly four. The sun would go down around six. Tropical sunsets tended to be swift, and she was reluctant to be out after dark without an escort. She made her excuses, said *mwirirweho,* then began the hike back to the Kibungo-Rusumo highway.

As she passed her old home for the second time, she decided to knock. Maybe whoever had moved in could give her information about Dorcas. Perhaps they could pass on the news that Furaha had been killed. Jess didn't relish having to tell Dorcas the news.

At first Jess knocked gingerly. "*Mwiriwe*? *Bonsoir*?"

Shuffling sounds. No one answered.

She knocked more forcefully. "*Mwiriwe*?" Still no response. For a moment, Jess stood there. Then she left the handful of bananas on the bottom rail of the door, and, after a shrug, continued toward the bus stop.

Only a handful of people passed her, yet the hairs on the back of her neck prickled. She heard nothing but bird calls and insect buzzes with the occasional rumble of a distant motor, but an increasing sense she was under surveillance permeated her being. Maybe seeing the ex-*génocidaire* had stirred up her emotions and made her paranoid. She bent over, pretending something was in her shoe, and took a moment to look around. Nothing unusual.

She continued along the road, increasing her pace slightly. She mustered all the restraint she had to keep from breaking into a jog. At a small open-air market, she slowed and peered around as if she was searching for something in particular.

In the near distance, a man with mirrored sunglasses and Western clothing walked toward her. Since she'd already seen one *genocidaire*, instinct forced her into taut alertness. Discreetly, she kept an eye on him, her tension rising the closer he came.

When he drew within ten yards of Jess, he turned and greeted a woman and stair-step children.

Jess let out a slow sigh of relief. A man meeting his family was unlikely to be trailing her. She huffed at her own paranoia. Since that fateful day she'd been condemned to survive, she'd hated the sensation of vulnerability. She'd learned to defend herself emotionally and physically against ever being in that position again.

Again, her gaze wandered over the market. The sounds of the market had changed since her first trip to Rwanda. Men were nearly wholly absent. Now soprano voices hawked fruits and vegetables without the deeper male undertones. Children sported shorts and t-shirts, rejects from American thrift stores imported and sold in Rwandan second-hand shops. Women wore vibrant native fabrics wrapped around their waists and twisted about their heads. No one looked out of place or suspicious.

Jess continued to the bus stop, but her concern persisted. Pausing before a tiny store, while appearing to window shop, she used the reflection in the window to observe the dirt road behind her. Again, nothing seemed amiss. She walked on, but her sense of impending doom intensified.

A rattling of trash cans startled her as she passed an

alleyway.

Jess jumped, then squinted into the shadows, her body tense, ready for fight or flight. The high contrast between the gloom of the alley and the bright equatorial sunlight kept her from seeing worth a darn. A scrawny dog zipped from between the two buildings and onto the street.

She hissed in relief but turned to move on, still sensing something odd.

A high-pitched "*Psst!*" sounded from the darkness.

She stopped. Her heart pounded.

A whisper escaped the poorly illuminated passage. "Don't be frightened, *Docteur* Jess."

She turned and peered into the alley, allowing her eyes to adjust.

A boy stood in the gloom, dressed in a well-worn t-shirt, tattered shorts, and plastic sandals.

"Who are you?" Her shoulders slumped. A boy would be unlikely to be a potential killer—then she remembered the boy-soldiers of the genocide.

"*Je suis un ami.*"

A friend. The repetition of Furaha's words in his mysterious call made Jess uneasy. "How do you know who I am? Why are you hiding?"

The youngster didn't step out of the alley but scanned the street beyond the gloom hiding him.

Against her will, her gaze followed his. She didn't see anything untoward.

Apparently, the lad didn't either. He motioned her closer and, as he shook her hand, pressed something into her palm. His voice remained low. "Go to this shop. Buy something, anything. Someone wishes to meet you there."

"Who?"

Without answering, the boy vanished into the murky passageway.

Jess shifted her watch on her wrist while she took an unobtrusive glance at the piece of paper he'd slipped into her palm. With a quick frown, she set off in search of the store.

Chapter Sixty-One

Jessica

Kirehe, July 24, 1997

Jess entered the shop to a lilting "*Karibu kiriya,* welcome, customer" from the shopkeeper's voice.

"*Mwiriwe.*" Jess spent a few minutes looking around the shop. The encounter with the unknown lad had made her uneasy, so she occasionally checked the window to see if anyone had followed her.

"We keep special items in the next room. Perhaps you would like to see them?" The shopkeeper took Jess by the arm and, pulling aside a curtain, shoved her into a small dark room.

Wondering if she was being led to her death, Jess struggled to free herself from the woman's grasp.

"It's all right, *Docteur* Jess. Don't worry. *C'est moi.*"

The voice was familiar but so laden with sorrow Jess couldn't immediately place it. A man stepped forward, barely illuminated by the light from the other room. As her eyes became accustomed to the poor light, she recognized the face that went with the voice and swallowed her gasp. Jean-Baptiste, her former translator and driver, had aged dramatically. His eyes had turned into pools of infinite sorrow. His hair was white as the starched shirt that reached nearly to his knees. A crocheted cap covered the top of his head.

A staunch Catholic, Jean-Baptiste now wore clothing that marked him as a Muslim, a member of Rwanda's largest non-Christian minority religion. Many Christian pastors had granted Tutsis refuge in churches, then permitted Hutu death squads to massacre those who sought asylum. In the midst of the conflict, Muslims sheltered both Tutsi and the moderate Hutu who didn't participate in the genocide. Knowing Jean-Baptiste to be a righteous man, she'd bet he'd been unable to remain faithful to a religion that had actively participated in the mass killing.

Jean-Baptiste continued, "Don't return to your old house. Furaha's wife, Dorcas, got tired of Zaire and came back. She's living there. She even drives your Land Rover."

His news explained why no one had answered her knock. Jess couldn't blame Dorcas for reclaiming what rightfully belonged to her.

Jean-Baptiste continued, "Furaha was afraid to return permanently, so he snuck back from Zaire every few months for conjugal visits. Finally, he went to Europe."

Clearly, Jean-Baptiste hadn't heard about Furaha's death. "I'm afraid I have bad news. Furaha was killed in Brussels."

Beneath his ebony skin, Jean-Baptiste's face blanched. "How? What happened?"

"He was shot."

"*Mon Dieu*. Who shot him?"

She shrugged. "The Belgian VSSE is working on that. Why did you choose him to contact me? I thought he was all about Hutu power."

"He is—was—already in Europe. Allah be praised, Furaha realized what terrible things the government and the *Interahamwe* were doing, so he changed sides. In the end, both factions wanted him dead. For his own safety, he went into exile." Jean-Baptiste's face crinkled with worry. "He was only supposed to tell you I had some things for you."

"I didn't know." Jess's hand flew to her mouth in dismay. "I thought he was just a low-grade bureaucrat moving up the hierarchy. Then he arrived with Gatera at the clinic, carrying a gun and acting aggressively."

"Gatera was his uncle, the head of his family, and a powerful man. Furaha had to obey him." Jean-Baptiste gave a wan smile. "Jess, you're not safe here. Strong undercurrents of hatred still swirl through the country. FAR soldiers are hiding in neighboring countries. It's absurd, but not everyone wants our nation to heal."

She grimaced. "Any idea where Gatera is now?"

"No. He was so furious that you escaped he beat the guards nearly to death. He's looking for you. Don't forget, he's ex-military with access to military intelligence. Word travels quickly here. Everyone knows you've arrived and are investigating for the Arusha trials. Gatera will do anything to keep from going to prison—even kill. Your life is in danger."

Jess shivered. "What about the rest of the clinic staff? Didi, Elise, Yvette?"

Jean-Baptiste's fingers twisted around themselves like a nest of serpents. "Gatera forced us to help with the wounded during the day. I took photographs with your camera when I could. In the evenings, he turned the women over to his soldiers to use as they wished. When he was ready to move on, he lined us up and shot us. By the grace of Allah, I was only wounded. I played dead until they left. I'm so sorry for what happened. To our nurses. To you. To your children—"

"Don't blame yourself." She placed a hand on Jean-Baptiste's arm to calm him. "The entire country was out of control. There was nothing either of us could have done."

"*Haba na haba, hujaza kibaba.* Small things, when combined, make up big things." He shrugged. "Had we all resisted, perhaps we might have stopped the conflict."

"It's hard to resist machetes." Jess pinched her lips together to seal in her sorrow. "We'd both be dead."

The silence between them lengthened as they relived memories neither wished to remember—and couldn't bear sharing.

"We couldn't have predicted what would happen." Jess's voice strained with emotion. "Between true friends, all can be forgiven."

"Every day … every day … every single day I wonder if death wouldn't have been easier."

His words so nearly mirrored Jess's own thoughts, she was astounded. A whimper made its way through her throat. "Me, too."

Jean-Baptiste gave her a long, searching assessment. "It's been three years. You haven't regained your smile."

She searched his face. "You haven't either. It's so hard."

"My child, an old proverb says you can outdistance that which is running after you, but not what is running inside you. Give up the past."

"I can't. Not yet."

"Find a man who can understand what you've been through. Have babies. Start a new life. Before it's too late."

"I will. Someday." Only one man could comprehend what she'd been through, and he was married.

Jean-Baptiste gave a final pat to her hand, embraced her, and said, "The shopkeeper has a package for you.

Follow the instructions." He turned toward the rear of the store and walked away.

After he disappeared into the shadows, Jess returned to the front room of the shop, reflecting on the changes in Jean-Baptiste. He too had lost his smile. Sadness had redefined his face, erasing his laugh lines and sculpting deep grooves around his mouth and eyes. When they first met, he had been upbeat, never a worrier, convinced God would provide for him and his family. His cheerful whistle of popular tunes, his endless string of Rwandan and Swahili proverbs—one for every occasion—and his jolly laugh had filled her clinic.

Jess had met so many people like Jean-Baptiste after the conflict. In flat emotionless voices, they recited how they'd lost every member of their family. She'd expected them to break down, to cry, to wail, to scream in grief, yet they spoke matter-of-factly, the only way, she supposed, they could cope—by distancing themselves from what occurred. She had her own method of coping—compartmentalizing—by trapping her memories into the ultimate circle of her subconscious hell.

While waiting for the shopkeeper to connect with her, Jess looked through souvenirs, but decided not to buy anything bulky since Jean-Baptiste had given her impression she was in danger and might need to move quickly. Fabrics would fit the bill. Longer lengths of fabric were designed to be fashioned into an *umushanana*, the traditional floor-length skirt with a sash draped over one shoulder, worn over a tank top or bustier. Smaller rectangles, large enough to use as a sarong, were called *kanga*. Some of these had *jina*, proverbs or political slogans along with fanciful patterns. Jess didn't feel like walking around announcing *Today is a good day for a happy wedding*; *I thought of you as gold, but you are such a pain*; or *Vote for His Excellency*. Instead she chose *kikoi*, lengths of cloth with dazzling geometric designs without the slogans.

"*Vous avez fait des choix très agréable, madame.* Some of our most beautiful fabrics." The shopkeeper folded the lengths of cloth, wrapped them in newspaper, tied the package with twine, and handed it to Jess. "Are you having a good visit?"

"*Oui, merci*. Rwanda is a beautiful country." And a land where blood and decaying bodies fertilized the soil. Jess kept her mouth shut as she took the parcel. It was larger and weighed more than she'd expected. The shopkeeper had slipped something inside, and Jess hadn't noticed. She didn't dare peek, not where others might see her.

In the doorway, Jess studied both ends of the street before stepping outside. Again no one looked suspicious. Carrying her package and trying to keep her face calm, she walked along a narrow path, a shortcut toward the main road. On her way, she passed a shop with hand-painted sign reading *farumasi*. On second thought, the little pharmacy would have items to use if she needed to disguise herself. She backtracked and purchased shoe polish and scissors.

At the main road, she caught a taxi back to the Motel Amarembo. Safely in her room, she ripped open the bundle from the souvenir shop. Wrapped in the fabric she found a Leica camera, her passport, the carbon copies of the adoption paperwork, and her sons' incomplete birth certificates. She stared at those. Her fingers stroked the footprints memorialized in black ink, remembering holding those tiny feet in the palm of one hand. The whorls and ridges of the prints shifted as tears obscured her vision. Reluctantly, she set the papers aside, returning her focus to the contents of the package.

The dent in the front corner of the camera proved it was a long-lost friend. Since college, the Leica had documented her life. The last time Jess had seen it, Jean-Baptiste had been taking pictures of her, the boys, the clinic, and her staff, recording what were supposed to be her final memories of Rwanda.

There was also a piece of dark fabric she hadn't purchased. She shook it out. A burqa. How odd. Most Rwandan Muslim women wore only the hijab, the headscarfy thing covering their heads and chests. A woman in a full burqa was rare.

As she shook the garment, a piece of paper fluttered to the floor. When she retrieved it, she found a note written on the back of her receipt: *Truck delivering goods to the Amarembo tonight at 7. Will smuggle you to safety in Tanzania. Wear this.*

Chapter Sixty-Two

Jessica

Rusumo Falls, July 24, 1997

Jess started to shake, nearly dropping Jean-Baptiste's note. Such intrigue meant, after searching for two years, she must finally be getting close to Gatera—rather, according to Jean-Baptiste, Gatera was getting close to her. As a novice investigator, she frequently blundered her way through interviews, not knowing the right questions to ask or how to probe indirectly. Later, as her research skills grew more skillful and her bullshit meter more astute, the quality of the intelligence she collected improved exponentially. Though she hadn't found Gatera, Jess garnered information about other criminals she turned over to the ICTR—and which Michel and his predecessor had warned her to stop collecting.

Jess thought she'd been cautious. Until the incident at the Brussels museum, she'd never felt threatened. Now someone might be tracking her.

No matter the personal risk, she had to keep searching. If Gatera hid for a few more years, the genocide trials would be over. The search for criminals would fade away. He would escape imprisonment. She would have failed.

She laid her clothing on her bed and reviewed her potential disguises. The burqa. A few American clothes. Once she got over the border into Tanzania, she would wear the *kikoi*, either as a head covering or wrapped around her hips like a skirt. By switching pieces of cloth, she would vary her outfits. Mertens and Bisset said a surveillance team watching from a distance memorized blocks of color to easily keep track of their prey. Thus, someone looking for a bright yellow turban might be fooled if she switched to a blue one

She tried on the heavy burqa. Outdoors during the day, she'd be miserably hot, but the attire solved a major problem with disguising herself. Most of her coffee-and-cream skin would be covered by the garment. She only needed to worry about her hands and around her eyes. The hardest part would be keeping her mouth shut so her accent wouldn't betray her. Maybe she should feign an illness. Nothing like a hacking cough to discourage a close inspection. She pulled off the burqa and threw it on her bed.

A knock on her door sent her pulse into overdrive. She searched for a place to hide the papers and camera. In desperation, she shoved them between the bed and the wall.

A second, louder, more impatient knock. She took a deep breath to compose herself. Surely someone coming to kill her wouldn't have knocked a first time, much less a second. Most likely someone innocuous, like a maid with more towels, waited behind the door.

Jess placed one eye against the little peephole. Her jaw slammed to her chest when she recognized the person on the other side. What the hell was he doing here? She jerked the door open and peered both ways down the hallway to see if anyone else was present. Empty. She grabbed his hand and yanked him into her room.

"What's going on?" His deep voice boomed through the little room.

Violently, she waved a finger before her mouth to shush Tom Powell.

He dropped his voice to a whisper. "Jess, you're in trouble. Your life may be in danger."

"You can't know that."

"Someone broke into your place at Susan's."

"No!" Shocked, she backed up until her legs touched the bed. This had to be a coincidence. A Philadelphia break-in couldn't possibly be tied to Gatera and Rwanda. She took a deep breath to calm herself and managed a flippant little shrug. "I got burgled. Shit happens in Philadelphia."

Tom raised an eyebrow. "This burglar spray-painted *Tutsi whore* on your wall."

She wobbled. Gatera had called her that as he'd raped her. "Where'd you get your information? How'd you find me?"

"I hired a private detective—"

"You had me investigated?"

"I wouldn't have, except you wouldn't talk to me." He reached for her.

With a sidestep, she dodged his hand. "Don't talk. Just listen. I need your help."

"After all this time?" He snorted. "What happened to Little Miss Independent?"

"Will you help me?" Her voice became snippy. "Or not?"

"Slow down. What exactly do you want me to do?"

"Deliver a package. Please?"

"I came halfway around the world to help you. To take you home where you'll be safe. Not be your errand boy. I'm not agreeing to anything until you explain yourself."

"It's best you remain in the dark. Just in case." She strode around at top speed.

"In case what?" He grabbed her arm, forcing her to stop pacing and look at him. "Are you in trouble?"

"No … maybe … yes." Her words bubbled out faster than she could organize her thoughts. "Act like we've never met. Fly to Arusha tomorrow morning." She broke free, wiggled her hand behind the bed, and pulled out her Leica and her papers. "Deliver these for me." She held them toward him.

He raised a hand to demur.

She spun on her heel, tossed the papers and camera on her bed, and resumed her marching, her hand digging at her neck.

With one hand, he grabbed her again and turned her around. With the other, he lifted her hair off her neck. "Christ, what the hell are you doing to yourself? Your skin looks like shit. You've scratched your neck into a nasty open wound that's going to get infected."

She pulled away again. "I know. It'll go away—eventually."

"Not without scarring and hyperpigmentation." He held her shoulders and shook her slightly. "Jess, give up whatever you think you're doing here. Come home with me."

She gave a vehement shake of her head.

"You're out of your depth." He pulled his phone from its holster on his belt and thrust it toward her. "Call the police."

"Your cell won't work here. Besides, I don't think Rwandan police can be trusted."

"Christ, you're paranoid."

With a huff, she pivoted. "I don't have time to

explain. Will you deliver this or not?"

"What about you?"

"I'll act as a decoy. Whoever's after me will chase me and leave you alone."

"What exactly am I transporting?"

"I'm not sure what's on the camera. The rest is my old passport and ... uh ... some official paperwork. Can't you take my word that this is important?"

"Nothing's as important as your life."

"Some things *are* more important than a single life. This is one of them."

He pulled her close, pressing her forehead against his chest, kissing the top of her head. "Not to me."

With her nose pressed against his chest, his scent jolted through her. How easy it would be to—no, she couldn't give in to those feelings. In self-defense, she pulled free. She appraised him with a long gaze. "If you ever l-l—" Her vocal cords seemed paralyzed, the word *loved* trapped in her throat like a fishbone.

"If I ever what?"

"If you ever c-cared—if I ever meant anything to you—" She moved across the room. He'd let her down in the past. How could she could trust him now? With a dismissive shake of her head, she said, "Never mind."

"Jess, I still care for you. I've told you over and over I've never stopped loving—"

She raised one eyebrow in a doubting quirk.

He flinched. "I'll prove it. What do you want me to do? I'll do anything—"

Hell. She had no choice. She had to trust him. "Take this to the ICTR."

"What's that?"

"The United Nations International Criminal Tribunal

for Rwanda. The genocide trials in Arusha." She dumped everything from her backpack, found a piece of paper, scribbled a note, and handed it to him.

With quick motions, she shoved her camera and papers back into her satchel. At the last second, she added her laptop. "Give these to Michel Fournier. No one else." She handed her backpack to Tom. "Tell Michel I'll travel overland by an indirect route. If I'm not in Arusha within a week, he'll know something happened and will know what to do with this evidence."

"I'll do this, Jess, but you have to do something for me."

She chewed on a hangnail as she backed away. "What?"

"When this is all over, promise you'll talk to me, really talk. We were good together. You're smart enough to realize that. Tell me what keeps us apart."

She hesitated.

"Please, Jess? After that"—he swallowed—"I'll leave you alone. If that's what you really want. I promise."

The catch in his voice tore at her. With a savage motion, she ripped off the cuticle with her teeth. "Okay."

"You'll tell me everything? Cross your heart and hope to die?"

She placed one hand behind her and crossed her fingers. "Yes."

He started to leave but turned back, tossing the backpack on her bed.

Before she could dodge him, he tilted her face toward his, pressed his lips against hers. She tried to escape his hold, but he wrapped one arm around her waist, pulling her closer. No! She didn't want to return the kiss, but her lips betrayed her.

He picked her up.

In a reflex reaction to her feet dangling in midair, she flung her arms around his neck. In a split second, he trapped her between his body and the door. The hardness between his thighs pressed into her groin, the doorknob in the crack of her rear end. Her cheeks tingled from the scratching of his scruff. His lips were hot, damp. His tongue delightful. That little moan had to have come from him, not her.

Long minutes later, Jess remembered she was on a tight schedule and pulled her arms from his neck. She slid to the floor, her knees locked to keep them from buckling. "That wasn't fair."

He chuckled and gave her a peck on her forehead. "The spark's still there, Jessica. You're just afraid—"

"I'm not afraid of anything." She shook her head, retrieved the knapsack from the bed, and shoved it into his hands. "That fire died out long ago." With a rapid pivot, she opened the door and scanned both ways down the hall. "The hallway's clear. Remember, deliver this to Michel Fournier at the ICTR. It may help him charge men with war crimes." With a shove, she propelled him from the room, closed and locked the door.

He was gone. Jess leaned against the wood and slid to the floor with relief. Her chafed lips and taut nipples told her in she'd enjoyed his kisses. How could the physical attraction remain so strong? For ages, she'd suppressed her feelings for him. At first, pure anger fired her. Then the aftermath of the genocide filled every waking moment, and her relationship with Tom Powell retreated into the deepest recesses of her heart.

Back in Philadelphia, she'd done her best to keep

him away. Her jumbled feelings—love, hate, anger, desire, even envy for the way his life had turned out compared to hers—resurfaced. Knowing he'd divorced that woman and was free again—Jess stopped those thoughts immediately. Here and now, she didn't have time to imagine a future with him.

She had no idea why Tom followed her to Rwanda. She couldn't decide whether to be angry or grateful. His unexpected arrival had solved a major problem. Unfortunately, that solution presented her with another dilemma. She made a rash promise she might be unable to keep, especially if it meant opening up about Rwanda. He'd broken every pledge to her, so she'd have no qualms about breaking her word. She consoled herself with thinking he wouldn't want to know anyway. Her past was too horrible for a nice young American cardiologist to handle.

She glanced at her watch. 6:05. Talking with him put her behind schedule. She needed to ready herself. In Tanzania, women often shaved their heads, so she would be less conspicuous without her corkscrews. With the scissors she bought at the *farumasi*, she snipped her hair close to the scalp, watching the curlicues bounce into the sink, then shaved her head with the razor she used on her legs. When she was done, she hardly recognized herself. Carefully, she placed all the hair in a plastic bag to discard elsewhere. If Gatera was truly hunting her, he mustn't become aware she'd changed her hair.

She improvised a hobo pack by wrapping two bottles of water—all she had—plus insect repellent, a pair of flip-flops, and her chopped-off locks in a *kikoi*. Her sneakers would brand her as a foreigner, but she had no idea where she would be going and might need more foot support than plastic sandals provided. The rest of her belongings she'd abandon. Funny how that occurred every time she was in Rwanda.

After dumping her cosmetics from a zip-lock plastic bag, Jess stashed most of her money, credit cards, and passport in it, securing them inside a second baggie, then a third, which she safety-pinned inside her bra. Next, she pulled on a dark t-shirt and jeans. She put the rest of her cash and her only weapon—the stainless-steel pen—in her pants pockets, then wrapped a *kikoi* about her waist. With a glance in the mirror, she realized she appeared slightly pregnant. She folded another around her pelvis to increase the effect. July was winter here, and nights could get chilly at high altitudes even in equatorial Rwanda, with temperatures down to the mid-fifties. She pulled a sweatshirt over the added bulk. Now she looked quite plump. Last, she picked up the brown shoe polish and carefully stained her hands and face.

The second she pulled the burqa over her head, an immediate loss of identity stabbed her. The woman looking back at her through the webbing at the eyes was alien. Jess forced herself to shift gears and become a shapeless shadow. She must be cautious getting out of the hotel and into the truck Jean-Baptiste said would come for her. Hopefully, he'd provide falsified papers for her. She didn't think it would matter if the face matched her own. Border guards would be unlikely to lift the burqa to inspect her more closely, especially if they thought she was pregnant.

Once Jean-Baptiste's contact spirited her out of Rusumo, Jess still had to get to Arusha. She'd escaped Rwanda once but had been lost amidst hundreds of thousands of refugees. In Tanzania she'd be considered a *mzungu*—her lighter skin and blue-green eyes making her an oddity—therefore easier to follow. Thanks to Tom, if she was caught, Michel would receive whatever—if anything—was on her camera and the photographs and other genocide data she'd stored on her computer.

Chapter Sixty-Three

Tom

Rusumo Falls, July 24, 1997

Tom returned to his room carrying Jess's things, grateful Jake Brennan had tracked her credit card transactions and discovered she was staying at the primitive-by-American-standards Motel Amarembo, the only hotel for miles. He shivered in revulsion thinking of the musty showers. No phones thus no wake-up calls. His room lacked a mirror, though one hung in Jess's room. He hesitated to lie on the bed, being pretty sure bedbugs existed in the tropics.

Like a caged beast, he paced his eight- by ten-foot room. He expected, if not a joyful reunion with Jess, at least some gratitude for his traveling halfway around the world to rescue her. She never let him explain his plans to become her white knight. Instead, she conned him into being her errand boy. He started to say no, but as soon as he pulled her close, he was lost. With the first deep breath, the smell of her hair filled him, reeled him in. How could the scent of a woman hold such power to evoke the past? By the time their lips met, he'd have done anything to relieve the strain on her face, to make her feel better, to heal the God-awful patch on the back of her neck, to win back her love.

Jess's refusal to confide in him hurt. But she seemed frantic, and he'd never known her to be the panicky sort. Damn it. He'd follow her instructions and see what happened. He hoped he didn't live to regret it—and prayed she faced less danger less than he feared.

Fuck! With an abrupt change of mind, Tom realized he couldn't leave her to fend for herself. He returned to her room. Light crept beneath her door. She must still be there. After multiple knocks, she didn't answer.

Someone down the hall opened their door and peered out. "Keep the noise down, will you?"

Some tourist like himself, a blond dude with a German-sounding accent. Damn it. Tom had called attention to himself and thus to Jess. She'd left her room. He tried the restaurant then looked around outside. Nothing. Once again, she vanished without a trace. Once again, he was too late.

Angry at himself for not forcing the issue earlier, he returned to his room, threw himself on his bed, and reviewed her papers. First, he studied at her old passport. They'd gone to the photography studio together for their official photos. She seemed so young in the picture, with none of the stress currently in her face. Then he turned his attention to the documents. They were printed in French with the blanks filled in by a typewriter. With his weak language skills, he couldn't translate them but thought the words *Certificat de Naissance* meant birth certificate. The inked imprint of tiny feet on the reverse confirmed that notion. The twins she tried to adopt. The children that should have been theirs.

He didn't bother with her computer but turned the camera over and over in his hands. An old Leica MP-4 with a dent in the bottom left. That dimple proved it was Jess's, the camera she used it for every photograph she made while they were a couple. She kept the camera in pristine condition, except for the divot. On a hike in the hills near Conshohocken, she slipped on scree and tumbled down a hillside. She'd been more worried about the camera than about the road rash on her forearms. Now grime covered the Leica, its lens cap was missing, and the lens coated with dust and grease. The film counter showed thirty-three of the thirty-six frames had been exposed.

Tom wondered if the images were black-and-white. Jess had always been a black-and-white kind of girl, preferring the subtlety of images without color, the graininess of Kodak Tri-X film, and the documentary styles of the old WPA photographers like Dorothea Lange and Russell Lee. What images had she captured that would be worth her life? If these things were so important that she would die for them, he'd get them to Arusha if it killed him.

Chapter Sixty-Four

Jessica

Rusumo Falls, July 24, 1997

A few minutes before seven, weighed down by the burqa, Jess eased toward the hotel's kitchen. The shoe polish made her face damp and waxy. Her scalp prickled from being shaved. Her nerves jangled with anticipation. The night was quite dark, excellent for sneaking about. The moon wouldn't rise until the wee hours. She only had to contend with the lights from curtained hotel rooms, a lone streetlight in the parking lot, and a few cooking fires dotting the hillside behind the motel.

Outside, she looked back toward her room, the fourth one from the end. She'd left the light on, hoping people would think she remained inside.

A shadow of herself in the burqa, Jess slipped through areas of darkness between bushes against the side of the motel. She wished she had better vision. The mesh across her eyes limited her field of view and gave her claustrophobia. Crouched beside several rubbish bins, she paused, her thoughts buzzing as loudly as the flies. She hoped Jean-Baptiste came. How could she trust a stranger?

Thirty feet away, an Isuzu refrigerator truck with its motor running was parked near the back door of the kitchen. A narrow trapezoid of yellow light spilled from the kitchen door. From her current spot, Jess couldn't visualize the truck's cargo area, only its left side painted with the words *Agahozo Restaurant Supply Company, Dar Es Salaam.* The burqa made sense if she was being taken to Dar. A sultan had built the city in 1865, and a large Muslim population still inhabited the city.

Two stocky adolescents unloaded crates of plantains, carrots, potatoes, sacks of rice, and boxes of liquor and beer.

Her gaze followed their every trip back and forth, fearful they'd signal her and she'd miss it.

Their task apparently complete, they disappeared into the motel.

She waited an eternity, though in reality only a few minutes passed.

At last, two older men stepped into the night, silhouetted by the illumination from the kitchen, one of them a stocky older man with snow-white hair.

With a silent breath of relief, she recognized Jean-Baptiste.

The second man counted a number of bills and handed them to Jean-Baptiste. After recounting the money, he stuck it in his pants pocket. They shook hands. Then, like the youngsters, the second man disappeared into the motel, closing the door behind him. The vast darkness of the African night sucked up the beams from the single light bulb illuminating the parking lot.

Jean-Baptiste headed toward the truck.

Deciding not to wait for his signal, Jess started to step out from her hiding place and join him.

The hairs on her neck prickled.

She froze.

Something was wrong. She didn't know what. The sense persisted, intensified. She wanted to scratch her neck but was afraid to move.

She looked around, but nothing seemed amiss.

Jean-Baptiste reached to close the rear doors of the truck.

She opened her mouth—

Before she could speak, a horizontal streak of silver slashed across the truck's dark interior.

Instantly, she stifled her words.

Jean-Baptiste gave a strangled cry of alarm.

A grunt.

A gurgle.

He reached for his neck. Staggered backward. Collapsed to the ground.

Jess swallowed a scream. The doctor inside her wanted to rush to help her friend. She suppressed the urge. Logic told her he wouldn't survive having his throat cut.

Someone dressed in black, his face obscured by a baseball cap, leapt from the truck bed. With two powerful strokes of his machete, he severed Jean-Baptiste's head. "You're a traitor to the Hutu cause."

He had the same thickset body she'd seen on the tape in the VSSE office. The voice, too squeaky for the massive body, struck terror in her heart. Gatera!

The world spun around Jess. She pressed herself against the wall to keep from falling. Forced herself to remain utterly still. Swallowed the vomit that crept up her esophagus. Once again, the bastard had murdered someone she cared for. Once again, if she took time to mourn, he would capture her. Once again, she knew he'd kill her. She worried less about death than what he'd do to her beforehand. He'd ensure her demise came slowly.

Gatera searched Jean-Baptiste's pockets, removed the money and the car keys. Leaving his victim on the ground, he ran toward the motel.

She withdrew into the darkness.

In seconds, he would reach her room. Another minute to enter through the window. Only an instant to realize she wasn't there and to start hunting her.

Returning to the hotel was impossible. She couldn't trust the personnel. The two young men must have been Gatera's accomplices and had known he'd concealed himself in the truck.

Jess reviewed possible places to hide. With a parking lot to the east and the RN3 to the south, she had few choices. A four-foot stone wall supported a drop-off to the highway. The best place to conceal herself was in the trees on the opposite side of the road. At least on the macadam of the parking lot and road, she wouldn't leave a trail.

Jess edged around the motel's landscaping and slipped into the night, grateful for the dark burqa, though it limited her motion and vision. A pay phone on the motel wall caught her attention when she reached the stone wall. Though tempted, she couldn't take the time to call Michel. She'd have to rely on Tom to deliver her message.

She came to the wall, dark stone joined by white cement, mimicking a giraffe's spots. She considered jumping from the top, but the slap of her feet against the asphalt might alert Gatera to her presence, so she sat on the wall and slithered down.

Across the deserted road she flew, then slipped from tree to tree until she could no longer see the motel when she looked back through the brush. Then, listening acutely, she squatted in the undergrowth to catch her breath.

With few street lights illuminating roads, night-time

driving was dangerous. Unlike in the United States, the constant din of vehicles didn't exist in Rwanda, so sounds carried long distances. Someone's laugh interlaced with a radio program lilted through the air. Insects chirped near her. The faint swish of the wind penetrated the burqa. Nothing else.

Jess turned to face the road and waited, afraid to move, afraid not to.

Something that sounded like a small engine purred to her left not twenty feet away. She jumped, then compelled herself to remain still and calm. A *twowoooot twowooot* followed. Relieved, she allowed her shoulders to droop. An owl, not a vehicle.

Above her on the RN3, feet slammed the pavement, immediately followed by an *oomph*. Gatera must have jumped the wall. A few seconds of silence. Then his feet pounded the asphalt, going to toward the Tanzanian border.

Jess inched southward, keeping her head below the level of the surrounding bushes.

After several minutes, the rhythmic beat of footsteps announced his return.

Beneath a bush, she stopped dead, fairly certain he couldn't identify her in the dark burqa.

The stomp of feet ebbed toward the west. He must have jogged to the Rwandan checkpoint. The immigration office closed at five, so he wouldn't take long to realize she wasn't there.

She moved a few yards further south. With her eyes covered by the mesh, her visual field was limited, even once her eyes grew accustomed to the inky night. The land here dropped steeply to the flood plain of the river. She feared she'd stumble on the unfamiliar terrain and announce her location. With a sprained ankle, she'd be an easier target. When she thought Gatera was out of earshot, she continued toward the south, hunching beneath undergrowth as she moved.

Moments later, a heavy tread, accompanied by raspy breathing, grew steadily louder. Gatera huffed and puffed, then his noises faded.

After several minutes, the screech of wheels on tarmac rose behind her.

Jess hazarded a backwards glance.

The Agahozo Restaurant Supply truck careened from the parking lot. Gatera slammed on the brakes at the edge of the road and left the engine running and the vehicle lights shining into the trees, aimed almost directly at Jess.

The brightness haloed through the holes in the grill of her burqa.

Aided by headlights, he headed toward her.

She sucked in a harsh breath and sank deeper into the shadows.

Stones rattled down the slope, one landing by her foot, as he grew nearer.

Audible over the engine's chug, the rhythmic swish of branches grew closer. That metallic *zing* meant he was beating the bushes with his machete.

She was afraid to look, certain the movement of turning her head would reveal her presence. Silently she inhaled. Inhale. Hold. Exhale. She prayed he wouldn't find her.

His breathing grew nearer, harsh and irregular with his exertion. The slash of his machete grew so close she feared she'd lose an ear. She was glad she'd been so preoccupied shaving her head and dressing that she hadn't thought to spray herself with insect repellent. In the fresh night air, he'd smell the DEET. Fortunately, the burqa covered enough of her to serve as mosquito netting. Again, she inhaled. Held it. Held it. Held it. She didn't want him to hear her breathing. At last Gatera's footsteps moved away. The swish of the machete stopped.

Jess exhaled with a silent *whoosh*.

More stones skittered downhill as he climbed to the main road.

She couldn't be certain he'd gone. He could linger on the road, hoping she'd reveal her position. Prepared to wait him out, she remained in place. Her anxiety drove her to scratch her neck to relieve her tension. It took every ounce of restraint to not reach for her neck. Inhale. Hold. Exhale. She calmed herself and took mental stock of her situation.

Tomorrow she could cross the river to the Tanzanian border control station. She already had a multi-entry volunteer visa, so getting into the country wouldn't be difficult. Unfortunately, she foresaw multiple potential problems.

First, the Tanzanian border control only functioned during business hours, so all international traffic had halted until eight tomorrow morning, which meant she must remain concealed through the night, then cross the border without being noticed. Last time, one woman among a quarter of a million people, she had "disappeared" with no trouble. This time wouldn't be so easy.

Second, Gatera expected her to cross the border, so she needed an alternative path. Any other route meant an illegal crossing and required more time.

Third, additional time required nutrition, and she had no food. Like before, she could scavenge from the fruit orchards that dotted the landscape, but that meant stealing from people who needed the income from their harvest.

Last, and most important, she had only two liters of potable water. Though the Kagera was nearby, she wasn't sure she could make herself drink from it—not without remembering the bodies tumbling in it back in 1994.

Jess gave into the urge to scratch and reached for her neck. She gave a quiet snort. One advantage to the burqa—she couldn't get to that irritated patch of skin.

As long as she kept the river on her left and moved downhill, she'd be heading south. Somewhere, not far from the falls, the Ruvubu River met the Kagera in a Y-intersection. If she followed the Kagera south, she'd be in the boonies of Burundi—albeit illegally. No major cities for miles. If she crossed the Kagera, she'd be in Tanzania—again illegally. Twenty-five kilometers southwest of Rusumo, Tanzania, lay the hamlet of Ngara and the Benaco refugee camp. Friends at the Anglican Diocese and Murgwanza Hospital and people she'd met at Benaco would understand her dilemma and help her. Alternatively, she might catch a bus to Arusha. She had to face it: with limited supplies and Gatera hunting her, an illegal crossing into Tanzania was her best option, even with limited supplies.

The only plus to her situation was that, unlike the last time she crossed into Tanzania, she wouldn't have to deal with the persistent heavy rains of the *masika*, the long rainy season. Now, with the days slightly overcast, the temperature would rise to the high eighties, hot but not unbearable for hiking. July was historically the driest month which meant the water levels of the rivers would be low. If she couldn't find someone to ferry her over the river, she should be able to swim. She'd deal with the authorities once she got where she was going.

At last, Gatera revved the truck engine.

Over the motor's sputter, Gatera's cry echoed across the valley. "Tutsi whore. I'll get you sooner or later."

Chapter Sixty-Five

Tom

Rusumo Falls, July 25, 1997

The next morning, Motel Amarembo's roosters served as Tom's alarm. He couldn't believe he was in such a rustic area. Recalling his disgust at the shower, he skipped it in favor of a sponge bath. He stepped from his room and heard birds chattering nearby. *Go-away-go-away-go-away.* He looked over the RN3 highway toward the south. The early morning light elongated the shadows of the trees across the road. A light fog hovered over a gorgeous landscape. In the distance, a river glittered. He turned. Behind him rose the famous thousand hills of Rwanda.

With his little pocket camera dangling from his neck, Tom walked east the quarter mile to the Rusumo Falls Bridge. Had Jess had escaped that way the first time? How would she get out now? So many questions. The answers would have to wait until she got to Arusha. He clenched his fists. If she made it there.

A policeman offered to take a photo of Tom before the falls, and he agreed. After looking at the waterfall—not as impressive as Niagara Falls—he hiked back to the Rwandan border crossing and hired a taxi to drive him to Kigali.

Five hours later, he entered the departures hall at Kigali International Airport and changed his ticket. Jess was right. His cell phone didn't work here, and its one-hour battery had died long ago. Savagely, he twirled the dial on the payphone. Accustomed to instant access and pushbuttons, he hardly remembered how to dial a rotary phone.

He called his office collect and explained the situation to his partner. "I don't know when I'll be back, Charlie. At least a week."

"What do you mean? You said you'd only be out a few days."

"Things got real complicated real fast. I'll tell you everything when I return. I'll call as soon as I know something definite." He hung up before Charlie could protest further. Tom hadn't taken a single vacation day since he and Charles Fincher opened their practice, yet his partner gave him grief about taking a fucking week off.

Tom glanced at his watch. One p.m. With hours to kill, he faced a long afternoon of boredom. The only flight available from Kigali to Arusha had been a multi-city monstrosity leaving at seven p.m. with an eight-hour layover in Nairobi, then a three-hour layover in Dar Es Salaam before arriving in Arusha. For a guy who'd never been out of the States, he was certainly getting around.

He decided to call this Fournier guy and give him a heads-up. Otherwise, Tom's delivery would have to wait over the weekend.

Tom spoke to a woman with a British-sounding accent and was transferred to Fournier's office.

After a brief time, the phone clicked. "Fournier *ici*."

"Uh ... *bonjour*." Tom dragged the French word from his memory banks. "I'm Dr. Thomas Powell. I have a message for Michel Fournier."

"*Oui?* I'm Fournier."

Mercifully, Fournier switched to English. A grateful Tom exhaled. "I have a package for you from Jess ... Dr. Jessica Hemings. I'm to deliver it to you personally."

"Where are you?"

"Kigali. The only flight I could get out arrives at Kilimanjaro Airport tomorrow morning."

"*Merde.* Tomorrow is Saturday. We're closed." Fournier paused. "Doesn't matter. Come directly from the airport to my office at the ICTR. Stop at the security desk at the main entrance of the ICTR. Present your passport to get an official visitor's pass. A guard will escort you to my office."

Tom boarded the flight to Nairobi while thinking that before he'd found Jess again, he'd been ensconced in his practice, doing the same safe things day after day, week after week, conforming to Newton's first law of physics: an object at rest tends to stay at rest, unless acted upon by an unbalanced force. That force was his desperate need to warn Jess of the danger she faced. Now, the same force shifted him to Arusha. This might be what he'd been looking for, the new Event A that would lead to Event B and propel Jess back into his life permanently.

On his flight to Arusha, he reminded himself that Regina, Jess's mother, had reassured him Jess's situation wasn't his fault. But, in reality, it was. The thought tormented him that, if years ago, he hadn't backed out of their trip, if he hadn't sold his soul for money, if he'd just kept his prick in his pants, she would be safe. She'd still be his.

Chapter Sixty-Six

Jessica

Rusumo Falls, July 25, 1997

A shriek from somewhere nearby echoed in Jess's ears. She jerked awake and found herself engulfed in a suffocating cocoon of darkness. She couldn't see clearly. Overnight she'd gone nearly blind. After calming down and checking her mental status, she determined, as usual, she'd been the screamer. Her fingers plucked at what felt like a mesh covering her eyes. Shit. She remembered where she was. And that she was disguised in a burqa. No wonder she couldn't see worth a darn.

Still hidden beneath a bunch of low shrubs, she remained motionless, listening intently. Only the whisper of the wind and bird calls. No nearby human sounds.

She rose and peered around. No evidence of anyone close at hand—yet. She peeled off the burqa. Her vision cleared. A combination of fear layered on chilly air made her shiver. The burqa hadn't been quite enough to keep her warm through the night. When the temperature dropped to the mid-fifties, the chill had seeped through the fabric. Her upper body, covered by a t-shirt, sweatshirt, and burqa, had been somewhat comfortable, but her legs and feet became downright icy. She peeled off the sweatshirt, too, knowing once she got moving she'd warm right up.

She opened the *kitinge*, and her water bottles leered up at her. Her tongue desert-dry, she looked at them with longing. It'd be easy to polish one off. She restrained herself and took two sips. In a few hours, when she really needed fluids, she'd treat herself to more. To her left, the sun brightened in the eastern sky. Roosters crowed in the distance. The scent of breakfast cooking at the motel drifted down the hill toward her. With no food since the *mandazi* and tea the afternoon before, her stomach grumbled in response.

She pivoted to survey the road. Traffic, mostly big cargo trucks, was building, waiting to cross into Tanzania. Gatera's truck was gone, and no one appeared to be standing at the side of the road searching for her. He wouldn't give up, but she prayed he'd assume she would return to Kigali or cross the Rusumo Falls Bridge into Tanzania. Surely, he'd never dream she'd sneak across the river illegally.

Above her a bird called, telling her what to do. *Go-away—go-away—go-away*. She decided to take his advice.

She gave herself a quick spritz of insect repellent before rolling the bottle, the burqa, and her sweatshirt tightly in her hobo pack. In the bright new day, her dark clothing stood out against the red volcanic dirt and green underbrush. To camouflage herself, she patted handfuls of red dust on her t-shirt and jeans.

With mountains behind her and the river below, she stood at an altitude somewhere in the middle. During the rainy season, the land mass formed a peninsula, shaped somewhat like the state of Florida, which extended into the flood plain. Jess was on the eastern side of the panhandle. She would be safer on the western side, out of view of anyone at the motel, so she zigzagged across the upper portion of the peninsula, following an erratic path in hopes anyone who saw her would think he imagined the movement.

People arrived to work their fields. She skirted them, not wanting to interact with anyone who might later identify her. In one field, someone had left a hoe propped along a terrace wall. With both hands, Jess gripped it. Designed to turn over the hard, red soil, Rwandan hoes were heavy. At first, she swung the implement tentatively, then with abandon, getting a sense of its heft. The hand-carved wooden handle was burnished, worn smooth from wear, and its metal blade was honed to a sharp edge. The hoe was so well-balanced it was a work of art. She gave a fierce nod. The tool would function as both weapon and walking stick. Jess appropriated it but left some Rwandan francs under a stone to compensate its owner.

Gradually she worked her way to the southern the tip of the peninsula from which she had a great vantage point. She looked north, back toward Rusumo. Beyond the falls, the hills of the ravine were too steep to climb. Below the falls, rapids ran about eight hundred yards, the water too rough for a safe crossing. Looking south at the juncture of the two rivers, the wild currents of the brown Ruvubu swirled into the greener Kagera. That didn't look like a safe crossing either. The only viable point seemed to be dead ahead. The ground dropped hundreds of feet to a narrow strip of swamp. From there, a stony beach led to the narrowest part of the Kagera. The distance totaled only a few thousand feet, but a third of that was rough terrain.

By the time Jess reached the flood plain, her thighs and knees ached from the descent. Her butt felt bruised from when she'd slipped and skidded several yards on her rear end. She was in pretty good shape, but the last time she'd climbed mountains had been during her first escape. She was definitely using muscles she hadn't used since.

On flat ground at last, Jess started across the mosquito-filled swamp. During Rwanda's two rainy seasons, the papyrus marshlands flooded, but the big rains had ended. The area was fairly dry, though shallow water still filled some depressions, leaving reservoirs for mosquitos to breed in. She swatted insects by the thousands. In mid-slap she stopped, realizing she'd stupidly left her malaria pills, as well as her antibiotics, antidiarrheals, and hand sanitizer, in her motel room. Gatera had rattled her to the point her brain wasn't functioning.

At times she plunged knee-deep into brown goo. The sensation of the viscous mud oozing between her toes grossed her out as much as the sucking sound her feet made as she extracted them. Her mouth grimaced in disgust. There was no point in stopping. She sloughed on.

Herons, ibises, egrets, spoonbills, and occasional turtles kept her company as she crossed the flood plain. Several feet ahead, a large snake slithered across her path. It lacked the triangular head of a venomous snake, but she gave the reptile plenty of time to disappear into the undergrowth, then—just in case—moved several yards in the opposite direction before hiking on.

At last she came to the stony beach she'd identified from above. There was little cover beyond the typical brush and low trees of the savannah, so she shifted from shrub to shrub, concealing herself a few minutes under each before dashing to the next. Someone using binoculars might be able to see her from the motel, but she doubted they could recognize her.

Jess followed the edge of the water to the narrowest point of the Kagera. Tanzania lay dead ahead. Once she crossed the river and another thousand feet of swamp, she would reach the Rusumo-Ngara road.

She studied the surrounding area with care. Not another soul to be seen on either bank except a fisherman in a boat way upriver, twirling a net over the water.

A few crocodiles basked in the sun in the far distance. When she'd lived in the area before, most crocodile-related deaths occurred near the national parks where the reptiles were protected. According to local folklore, they wouldn't attack unless their prey came within three meters. These crocs—at least the ones she could see—were much farther away than that. Hopefully, today wouldn't be the day she'd test that theory. And hippos, another deadly animal, were rare around here. One less thing to worry about—she hoped.

She untied her hobo pack, gave her face, neck, and arms another spritz of DEET, then rewrapped the pack and tied it to her shoulders. Before entering the river, she paused, thinking of the bacterial load in droplets of gutter water she'd inspected under the microscope in medical school. Gross. She tightened the knot in her hobo pack and strengthened her resolve.

One last peek confirmed the crocodiles remained in place.

Jess stepped into the river. Before placing each foot, she gauged the depth of the water with the hoe, a third purpose she hadn't thought of when she appropriated it. She was capable of swimming the distance if needed—surely all those years of swim meets hadn't been wasted—she just didn't want any surprises.

Cautiously she inched her way forward. Soon the water crept past her ankles. Then her knees. Then her thighs. A quarter of the way across, she sank precipitously to her waist. She tucked her hoe between her knees and tied her hobo pack to the top of her head, knotting it under her chin.

Something brushed her thigh while she was standing in this awkward position. Surprised, she squawked. A sideways glance at the crocodiles showed they hadn't budged. She inspected the water around her, but the murky water limited her vision. She gripped her hoe with both hands in case she needed to bash a crocodile in the head. Just as she lifted her foot to continue walking, a hard whack caught her behind the knees.

She pitched backwards into the water.

Her hoe flew from her grasp.

She barely had time to seal her lips before water closed over her head.

Chapter Sixty-Seven

Tom

Arusha, Tanzania, July 26, 1997

Tom arrived at Kilimanjaro Airport on Saturday morning. Taxi drivers mobbed him, vying for his business.

"*Jambo, bwana!*" A wiry young man with a wild array of dreadlocks preempted everyone else by grabbing Tom's suitcase and leading him to a beat-up taxi.

Bwana? Tom had thought that was a made-up word from old Saturday morning Tarzan movies.

The driver, who introduced himself as Mposi, tossed Tom's luggage in the trunk, put him in the back seat, and cranked up the radio volume, bobbing his head in time to a Bob Marley reggae. Over the music he shouted, "You come for safari?"

"No ... business trip." Tom hadn't thought far enough ahead to have concocted a lie.

"*Wapi?* Where to?"

"Take me to the ICTR."

Forty minutes later, Tom, with Jess's knapsack in hand, stood before the tall, blue metal fence enclosing a building, staring at the white sign with the blue UN laurel wreath and a silhouette of the scales of justice. He'd never dreamed he'd be standing where he was. He paid the driver and said, "Wait for me, please."

Tom handed his passport to a sentry in a blue uniform that matched the UN logo. "I have an appointment with Michel Fournier."

The guard glanced at Tom's backpack. "I need to inspect your satchel too." After he rifled through Tom's things, the guard dialed a phone.

Soon a trim woman in a business suit stepped toward the sentry box. "Mr. Powell?" She spoke with a clipped British accent.

"Yes."

"Come with me." She nodded to the guard who handed Tom a visitor's pass. "I'm Lizette Cheyo, Mr. Fournier's secretary." Her heels clicking on the concrete, she led Tom toward Fournier's office where she knocked on a half-open inner door.

"*Entrez, s'il vous plaît.*"

"Mr. Powell to see you, sir." She gestured Tom in.

At Tom's introduction, a lanky man uncoiled from behind a desk. The guy stood several inches taller than Tom, making him at least six-three. He appeared to be in his mid-forties with prematurely grizzled strands running through the hair at his temples and his neat goatee.

Tom rubbed his face with his hand, conscious of his scruff and wishing he'd checked into a hotel and cleaned up before coming here. Generally, he groomed to fulfill his patients' expectations of a top cardiologist, but he thought Jess's safety merited coming straight to the ICTR. Fournier's innate lean elegance made Tom feel grungy. After living in airports for thirty hours and having had only a sponge bath over twenty-four hours before, he *was* grungy.

"*Merci*, Lizette." Fournier's mouth quirked in an odd smile. He stretched a hand toward Tom. "Nice to meet you, Dr. Powell. Michel Fournier, at your service."

They exchanged handshakes.

"Take a seat." Fournier gestured toward a seat then accordioned himself into his chair. He raked a glance over Tom before nodding at him over steepled fingers. "Dr. Thomas Powell. I never would have predicted you might come to Tanzania."

Completely at a disadvantage, Tom remained quiet. He had no idea how Fournier knew who he was or why.

Fournier grinned. "From Jessica's description, I'd expected the Devil Incarnate."

Tom raised a questioning eyebrow. "What does that mean?"

With a shrug, Fournier said, "You are better acquainted with Jessica than I. For her, everything must be black or white. One is either a saint or a sinner."

No one called her *Jessica*—ever. This guy not only called her that but pronounced it *Zhesseeca*. Hell, somehow her name sounded sexy in Fournier's French accent. It grated Tom's nerves. And that she'd confided in Fournier nettled Tom further. How much had she told the Frenchman about their breakup?

Fournier leaned back in his chair. "So, what is she up to? What is this package you have for me?"

After a moment's debate, Tom began. "I'm not sure what's going on, but Jess is in danger."

Fournier sat up abruptly, concern on his face. "Why do you think that?"

"Someone broke into her house in Philadelphia."

"So?"

"The burglar wrote *Tutsi whore* on her wall."

"*Mon Dieu!*"

Tom stood and paced. "She was supposed to start a job here at Mount Meru Hospital on August fourth." Tom was pleased to see surprise flit across Fournier's face. Apparently, Jess hadn't confided everything to the guy. "I was afraid she didn't realize what was going on, so I hired a private detective to find her. I followed her to Brussels, then to Rwanda, to warn her. Finally, I caught up with her in Rusumo Falls. She asked me to deliver this to you." He handed Jess's backpack to Fournier.

Fournier dumped its contents unceremoniously on his desk, peered at the camera, the computer, the paperwork, and read the note. He glanced up. "Where's Jessica now?"

"I'm not sure." Tom gave an exasperated shrug. "She insisted we travel separately—"

"*Cette femme est un imbécile.*" Fournier smacked himself in the middle of the forehead with his fist.

Tom understood the word *imbécile* and nodded in agreement.

Fournier picked up his phone. "Lizette, please call Kilimanjaro Airport and check whether *Docteur* Jessica Hemings flew in from Kigali."

Minutes later, Lizette responded on the intercom. "Dr. Hemings deplaned in Amsterdam, but her baggage came on through. It's at the airport now. She took a flight from Amsterdam to Kigali but didn't catch her connection to Arusha."

Fournier shook his head. "Advise baggage claim someone from here will fetch her luggage." He returned his attention to Tom. "When did you see her last?"

"Monday night."

Clearly perturbed, Fournier closed his eyes and sighed deeply. "I warned her to let the UN do its job, that she was getting too close to Gatera, and it might be the death of her."

"Who's this Gatera?"

"She didn't tell you?"

Tom glanced down, hesitant to reveal how little he knew about Jess's life since they'd split up.

"He was the only other OB-GYN in Rwanda—and Jessica's *némésis*. He hated her."

"Why?"

"Several reasons. She was a better physician. She was part White. Mostly because he was convinced she had underlying Tutsi blood." Fournier exhaled slowly. "After the war, he disappeared. She searched for him as we travelled from Benaco to Kigali. I did my best to discourage her, but she showed his photograph to everyone she met. In November of '94, the UN established the ICTR to deal with Rwandan war criminals. I urged her to let us find him. You know Jessica. Patience is not"—he paused a moment—"one of her, I think you Americans would say, long suits?"

"She's nothing if not hard-headed." Tom nodded. "Why's she looking for him?"

Fournier gave Tom a long appraising look. "She hasn't told you any of this?"

Tom shook his head.

"Then I can't betray her confidence."

His reply left Tom more worried than he'd been before he arrived.

Fournier paused while he punched a button on his intercom. "Lizette, please find me a map of Tanzania."

Minutes later she entered and handed him a road map.

"Thanks." He placed Jess's camera and papers on a nearby chair, unfolded the map, and spread it across his desk. "It's nine hundred kilometers from Rusumo to Arusha. A petite woman all alone. Bad roads. Bad transportation. Bandits. Wild animals. With Gatera on her tail."

"She said if she wasn't here within a week, you'd realize something happened and would know what to do with this"—he waved his hand at her belongings spread over Fournier's desk—"stuff."

"*Merde.*" Fournier shook his head then snorted as he studied a calendar on the opposite wall. "Depending on her route, a week is optimistic. *Shiftas*—bandits—abound. It's dangerous to travel at night—I speak from experience—and even more dangerous for a woman alone. Jessica is aware of this. For her to choose an overland route, she must believe she has no other option."

He returned his attention to the map. "This is where you left her at Rusumo Falls." He tapped his finger at the western border of Tanzania. "The most direct overland route to Arusha is following the B3 to the B143 then the A23. Knowing Jessica, if you were carrying her satchel by air, she would take the most circuitous overland route to throw off anyone following her. The more indirect routes"—he traced highway lines with his finger—"would be north to Mwanza or south to Dodoma on some of the worst roads you've ever seen. Either of those could take her upwards of a week, barring complications like bus breakdowns—or worse. In either city, she could catch a train to Dar Es Salaam, then another here. The trains only run twice a week, and it's a two-to three-day trip."

"She seemed rather jumpy when she gave me the camera."

"I'd be jumpy, too, knowing Gatera was after me. The man has no conscience. The only saving grace is that she's crossed Tanzania alone before. It took her eight days in 1994." Fournier gave an exasperated huff. "There's no point in searching for one woman wandering in 250,000 square kilometers of savannah, much of which has no infrastructure and is all-too-easy to get lost in. It'd be like looking for *une aiguille dans une botte de foin*, a needle in a haystack. All we can do is wait and pray she shows up. But if we can't find her, it's likely Gatera can't either. He may have the benefit of military intelligence, but even they can't find someone in the wilds of the Serengeti."

Lizette carried in a tray with a French press coffee pot, two cups, and a plate of several things that looked like muffins. She poured for the two men.

Fournier pointed to the sweets. "Those are *vitumbua*, the Tanzanian equivalent of your American doughnuts. Delicious. Perfectly safe to eat." He popped one in his mouth, following it with a sip of coffee.

She headed for the door.

Fournier called after her, "*Merci*, Lizette. Please call Dr. George Ndassa at the Murgwanza Hospital in Ngara, Reverend Joseph Bakari at the Anglican Diocese, and *Médecins Sans Frontières* at Benaco. See if *Docteur* Chuck Bernard is still there. If not, talk to whoever's taken over for him."

A minute later Lizette spoke over the intercom. "Mr. Fournier, Dr. Ndassa is at a medical conference in Dar. None of his staff has seen her. I'll try the Reverend next."

Tom glanced at Fournier. "What do we do now?"

"We wait." Fournier strummed his fingers on his desk while he waited for the call to go through. "Jessica and I worked together at Benaco. We have friends there who wouldn't hesitate to help her. If we're lucky, she's contacted them."

Chapter Sixty-Eight

Jessica

Rusumo Falls, July 25, 1997

Unexpectedly finding herself beneath the surface of the water, Jess thrashed around. Disoriented in the murk, she couldn't tell down from up. Amorphous shadows, too small to be whatever had sideswiped her, zoomed in and out. Water soaked the parcel she'd tied to her head. The bundle containing the heavy burqa and sweat shirt slipped backwards, weighing her down, wrapping itself around her neck, strangling her.

She struggled with the knot. Too wet. Couldn't get it untied.

Running out of air.

Panicking.

Fighting the urge to inhale underwater, she tried to pull the bundle over her head, but it hung up on her chin. At last, she tightened her jaw against her neck, slid the fabric over the back of her head and released it.

It dropped.

What an idiot. It dropped. Heavy things *sank*.

With a massive effort, she kicked as hard as she could, moving in the opposite direction. Coughing and spitting, she broke the surface and treaded water. No blood. No pain. She hadn't been bitten by anything. She looked around. Ten feet away something long and brown bobbed up and down.

A crocodile!

It rolled in the water, revealing a slim branch with wilted leaves. A downed tree had side-swiped her.

The gritty silt in her mouth reminded her amoebae and bacteria were invading her body. She spit up as much as she could to lessen the blow to her immune system.

She took a minute to catch her breath, but with the extra weight of her soggy sneakers and the *kikoi* wrapped around her waist, her legs soon grew tired of treading water. She couldn't afford to kick off the shoes. No telling what lay at the bottom of the river that might damage her feet.

A backward glance showed a quarter of the river lay behind her. The Tanzanian border lay not far ahead, a few laps in an Olympic-sized pool. Without her fatigue and the extra weight, she could have done it easily.

Jess stretched out and began swimming. Half-way. Three quarters. Not much further. She would make it.

With the next downstroke, her fingers touched something squishy. With the next, solid ground met her fingers. She stood and, barely able to lift her feet from the water, staggered the last few feet to dry land, her feet squelching in her sodden sneakers. Over the past few years, she'd kept up her jogging but hadn't done much upper body work. The last time she'd swum competitively had been in high school. Her arms and shoulders burned. She knelt and blew her nose to rid it of silt, then forced herself to throw up, though emptying her stomach was pointless. First, bacteria had already slithered down her esophagus. Second, unless she found another source of fluids soon, she'd have to drink from the river. Her bottled water, essential for her survival, now lay at the bottom of the Kagera.

After her near-drowning, Jess crawled beneath some

brush. She shook her watch and, amazed the second hand still circled the dial, gave herself ten minutes to rest.

Rusumo Falls was a mile away as the crow flies, but with the indirect route she'd taken, dodging from hiding place to hiding place, bypassing fields, scrabbling down the steep grade, trudging through the swamp, and nearly drowning to boot, the distance seemed light years further.

She'd crossed the border not far from the Falls and border control, but she hoped Gatera wouldn't realize she aimed for the southern end of Rusumo, Tanzania.

Jess forced herself to get up and move. She trekked through the papyrus swamplands. Soon the sun moved straight overhead. Sweat poured off her body, re-saturating her clothing. The sun burned her freshly shaved scalp. Frogs and turtles scurried out of her way. But, to her relief, no hippos, crocodiles, or big snakes. The humidity along the river became unbearable. Her dunk in the water had washed off her insect repellant, leaving her vulnerable to mosquitoes' aerial assaults.

With every step, mud oozed between her toes. She should clean the gunk off, but if she removed her shoes, she'd be reluctant to put the disgusting things back on. And her flip-flops, like her hoe, burqa, sweatshirt, water, and insect repellant lay at the bottom of the river. At least she didn't have to find a secure place to dispose of her curls—the Kagera had swallowed them.

At the top of a little rise, trees planted in three straight lines indicated an orchard, but no one was working there. She estimated a distance of only a few hundred yards until she hit the dirt road.

She patted her boobs and pockets. Thank goodness for bras and tight jeans. Her money and her ballpoint pen remained in place.

As she progressed, lilting songs, bits of conversation, and flashes of color carried through the foliage, alerting Jess the road lay ahead. She halted before she broke through the trees and peered through the greenery. People crowded the road. Unlike much of the Western world, foot-power was the primary means of transportation around here. When the current throng thinned, she slipped out of the trees and turned to her left. The ferry lay not far ahead. Hot, sticky, and dying of thirst, she hoped to get something to drink.

A woman called "*Jambo*" in greeting as she passed Jess.

"*Sijambo*."

The woman pushed a bicycle so loaded with bananas that, rather than riding, she walked and pushed the bike. This unusual method of cargo transportation, a common sight in Rwanda and Tanzania, always amazed Jess.

The bananas gleamed in the daylight, ripe, aromatic, and as golden as sunshine. Unable to resist, Jess bought a dozen. Heavy physical exertion on top of twenty-four hours without food had left her famished, and she hadn't had a decent banana since she'd left Africa. Picked long before they ripened, the ones in the States tasted flat. Around a mouthful she asked, "*Kituo cha basi kiko wapi*? Where's the bus station?"

The woman pointed across the river.

They walked to the ford together, making small talk along the way.

When they arrived, Jess glanced around. Too tiny to be called a village, this place consisted of the ferry, a dock, and a shack that served as the ferry office. There were no places to stay. No banks. No telephones. No border control.

The ferry lay on the opposite bank. Jess called over the river, but the ferryman wouldn't operate just for her. Though she had enough cash to bribe him to make a special trip, the action would call undue attention to herself. After her prior near-drowning, she wouldn't risk wading the Ruvubu, which was wider than the Kagera and with stronger currents.

In the office, Jess bought a pair of plastic sandals to replace her flip-flops, bottles of Kilimanjaro water, and an orange Fanta. The water tasted divine. From her first sip when she arrived at Benaco, she'd been convinced water from Kili's glaciers was the best in the world. Another private joy: Tanzanian Fanta. Despite its dull yellow color, the beverage tasted of real oranges, unlike the American version in which a neon-orange advertised its artificial flavor. The soda was warm but fizzy and sweet, and combined with a few more bananas, restored her.

Her immediate thirst sated, Jess took off her shoes and washed them in the muddy river water. She dipped her feet, wrinkled like prunes, in the dirty water and rinsed them. After cleansing her sneakers as much as possible, she removed the *kikoi* remaining around her waist and tied her shoes inside. She slipped into her new sandals.

Then, with nothing else to do, she chatted with the locals who were also waiting, though more patiently. She asked about the bus schedule.

One said, "The westbound bus should have arrived yesterday but didn't. Might come today, might not." He shrugged, his attitude revealing complacency regarding the vagary of bus schedules.

Another added, "*Bibi*, once you cross the river, the

eastbound bus comes on Tuesdays and Saturdays. It will carry you to Rusumo then eastward."

Jess wrinkled her nose. She definitely didn't want to head toward Rusumo. She'd go to Ngara instead.

The long overdue westbound bus arrived and was ferried over the Ruvubu. Immediately, people wended their way out, stretching cramped legs. Many relieved themselves at the latrine, another long-drop loo, surrounded by a privacy curtain made of repurposed blue UNHCR tent material. Jess looked at the river, back at the loo, and cringed. The latrine was located too close to a major source of drinking water, and she'd been dunked in water not far from here. Gross.

The sun moved lower in the western sky. Outside of big cities, Tanzanian roads were risky to drive at night, so the bus system shut down completely until sunrise.

Jess sighed. She wasn't going anywhere until morning. She gathered her belongings and approached the office to buy a ticket to Ngara. "*Ninataka kununua tiketi ya hadi Ngara.*"

The bus was a seriously over-crowded mini-van, but she'd be warm and sheltered inside. She was about to climb aboard when a white truck screeched to a halt on the opposite side of the river and parked in front of the ferry office. She couldn't read the words painted on the vehicle, but she recognized the logo. Agahozo Restaurant Supply. The driver jumped out. With a squeaky shout, he demanded the ferry return immediately and carry him over.

Chapter Sixty-Nine

Michel

Arusha, July 26, 1997

Michel forced himself to remain calm as Lizette telephoned his contacts in Ngara. Though Jessica had navigated across Tanzania once, as a woman traveling alone, she remained at high risk for misadventure.

Lizette passed on negative results. "No one has seen Dr. Hemings. They'll call right away if she shows up."

"Please call the Rwandan and Tanzanian Border Controls at Rusumo. Check if *Docteur* Hemings went in or out of either country since Saturday. And alert the police on both sides to be on the lookout for her."

Lizette reported all replies were negative. Jessica had indeed vanished.

Tom stood and paced. "I should go search for her."

"You'd embark on a fool's errand, Dr. Powell—"

"Call me Tom."

"You're not acquainted with the land, the language, or the people. At this point, she might be in Uganda, Burundi, Rwanda, Tanzania—or on another continent entirely." Fournier tried to reassure both Tom and himself. "She's a capable, resourceful woman. She'll get here. She managed a similar trek before."

"What do you mean?"

Michel wondered if Jessica had confided in anyone besides himself. "She hasn't told you?"

Tom shook his head. "All I know is that Jess escaped

from Rwanda and worked at Benaco."

"Those are the basics." Fournier snorted. "Highly expurgated, though. Jessica lost everything when she left Rwanda. She entered Tanzania illegally. She had a difficult time getting a new passport. Your country requires rather extensive documentation: passport photos, driver's license, birth certificate, travel itinerary. None of which, as a refugee, she had."

"I never guessed things were that bad."

Michel's face twisted in an ironic grimace. "I'm sure a White woman wouldn't have faced the same difficulties, but a Black woman claiming to be an American at the height of an international Black refugee crisis caused by a genocide the world refused to acknowledge—impossible. Even with her upper-crust Katherine Hepburn accent." Fournier opened the laptop and stared pensively at it. "She must have thought she was in serious danger if she gave you her computer."

"She kept some gruesome pictures on it."

"I bet she stores her genocide data on it. Perhaps even a clue to Gatera's whereabouts." Michel booted up the laptop. "*Merde*. It's password-protected. I'll have our tech guys get in."

"Try *Mutter Museum*."

Surprised, Fournier glanced up.

"My private investigator hacked Jess's e-mails. With luck, she used the same password for her notebook." Tom moved to stand behind Fournier.

"Private investigator? You were investigating Jessica?"

"I had a PI research why her apartment was broken into and by whom. Someone was tapping her phone and hacking her emails, so Jake figured she was either a spy or a terrorist."

Michel blinked in astonishment. "Jessica? She's not the type."

"Anyway, according to him, someone is tracking her moves. They want something she has and want it real bad. I thought I should warn her, so with Jake's help, I tracked her to Rusumo where she gave me this stuff."

Michel wondered why Tom hadn't told him those details the second he walked in—his information changed everything. But Michel only said, "*Très bien.*" He typed in *Mutter Museum*, and up popped Jess's files. "As intelligent as Jessica is, sometimes she's quite stupid."

Tom said, "Yeah."

Michel talked as he scrutinized the computer's desktop. "I don't understand how she's accumulated all this data." He shook his head as he scanned her files. Ntarama Church, Rusumo, Nyanza. Even Sylvestra Gacumbitsi, the mayor of Rusumo who refused to let refugees cross into Tanzania. "I always thought she was out of her league and discouraged her investigations." He tapped the computer screen. "This is interesting. A file is labelled *Reverse Genocide*. Another *Operation Turquoise*"—he looked at Tom—"that was the French effort to establish a 'safe zone' in southwest Rwanda. *Mon Dieu*. All this information, and no encryption. She left everything out in the open." He clicked on *Operation Turquoise*. *Merde*, she had more information on the French involvement in the genocide than he'd gathered in months of research. Maybe he should give her his Albert Londres Prize for journalism. He wouldn't have won it without her anyway.

He clicked on *Journal,* then the most recent entry.

July 22, 1997, Brussels.

Someone tried to kill me yesterday. A bullet literally zinged past my ear. I haven't been so frightened since Rwanda ….

"Fuck!" Michel blew out the expletive with a harsh breath then glanced at Tom. "Pardon my French."

Tom chuckled. "I've used the word a time or two."

Michel scanned the screen. "Things are worse than I thought. Someone tried to kill Jessica in Brussels."

"Fuck!" Tom moved around the desk to read over Michel's shoulder as Michel surveyed the next entry.

July 24, 1997, Kirehe.

I found J-B who gave me my old camera, my passport, and the birth certificates I forged for my children. While being held captive by Gatera, J-B secretly took photographs with my camera.

For some reason, Furaha changed sides during the conflict, which may explain why he tried to help me—and why someone killed him in Brussels.

I need to get this stuff to the ICTR. To Michel. Maybe it contains something that will be useful against Gatera.

With a bitter expression, Tom said, "So that's where I came into the picture—Jessica's delivery boy." He gulped. "I told her nothing was as important as her life, and she said some things were more important than a single life."

"I truly believe Jessica would sacrifice herself to bring down a mass murderer, especially this one." Michel pressed the intercom. "*Merde*. It'll take days to wade through all these files."

Lizette appeared, and he handed her the laptop. "Drop everything else and go through this. Start with Dr. Hemings' most recent documents for anything on Sylvestre Furaha or Cyprien Gatera."

Lizette left to begin her new assignment.

Fournier picked up the camera, turning it over and over in his hands. "Thirty-three frames exposed. Did she tell you what was on here?"

Tom shook his head. "She wasn't sure."

Michel jabbed his intercom. "Lizette, please call the Evidence section. I need someone to come in today."

"On a weekend?"

"*Absolument*." Michel turned to Tom. "According to Jessica's journal, Jean-Baptiste took pictures. If she sent the camera along with her documents, she must think something useful is on it. Something supporting her claim that Gatera killed her children."

Tom dropped into a chair. "Her children? I knew they were dead but not murdered?"

"She really kept you in the dark, didn't she?" Michel arched an eyebrow. "Look, Tom, it's Jessica's decision to tell you her story—or not."

Tom dropped his elbows to his knees and buried his face in his hands. "You're that journalist, aren't you? Just tell me—was she Dr. X?"

Michel hesitated. Then decided one word wouldn't hurt. He grimaced and forced out, "*Oui*."

"Fuck! I knew it." Tom slumped. "I couldn't bear knowing she'd endured so much."

Michel glanced at Tom. The other man sounded near tears.

"So when she denied being Dr. X, I believed her."

"Let's take this to the Evidence Support Section." Michel clapped a hand on Tom's back. "If they can't process the film, they can recommend someone who can do so quickly and discreetly."

Chapter Seventy

Jessica

Rusumo Falls, July 25, 1997

Agahozo Restaurant Supply. Jess's heart raced at the sight of the white truck. Her stealthy maneuvers hadn't fooled Gatera. With access to sophisticated intelligence, he would have known within minutes that she hadn't left Rwanda via the Rusumo Falls Bridge. He would search the bus, the office, probably even the toilet looking for her.

Another panic attack began bubbling up, but rather than spazzing out in public, she reined in her emotions. For a minute, she mingled with a group of bus passengers coalesced around the loo before easing away, heading back into the swamp, her heart sinking lower than her feet did into the muck. The ferry would take several minutes to cross the river and several more to return with his vehicle. She had ten or fifteen minutes in which to get lost.

Half an hour later, the sun highlighted a pillar of red dust caused by the truck barreling down the Rusumo-Ngara dirt road. The bus, rather than stop somewhere in open country, would have stayed put. A sigh of relief whooshed from her. Gatera had moved on.

Jess moved back to the road, walking along its verge until the sun sank beneath the horizon. Time to find shelter. She shinnied up the tallest tree she could find, wedged herself into a crook, and tied herself in place with a *kikoi*.

She ate a banana but held off drinking water—nothing like having to pee in the middle of the night from a treetop. She'd learned that on her first escape from Gatera.

The breeze through the trees shushed a lullaby, but she had a hard time getting to sleep. She estimated the temperature to be in the low sixties, but in her damp clothes, it seemed colder. Shivering, she huddled into a ball. Somehow, she dozed off.

Gwok, gwok, gwonk-gwokwokwok.

The deep, irregularly-spaced grunts infiltrated Jess's disturbing dreams. She snapped awake, recognizing a leopard's cough. Her first instinct was to untie herself and move higher, but her intellect told her any branch stout enough to hold her would support a big cat too. It'd be smarter to remain in place rather than move around and draw its attention. The same logic convinced her the risk of encountering wild animals was low. When Benaco and the other camps had been established, the refugees hunted the local wildlife to supplement their diet. Animal populations dropped. With no small mammals for prey, large predators moved on. The ecosystem would take decades to recover.

Minutes later, the sound repeated from high above her. Those thin upper branches wouldn't support a leopard. She couldn't remember the name of the owl, but its cry sounded like a leopard. She drifted off again.

When she awakened, the sky was just lightening. The glow-in-the-dark hands of her watch read five a.m. From a neighboring tree, eyes gleamed at her. Big round eyes. Bushbabies, not predators.

At full light, Jess dropped from the tree and drank a quarter of a water bottle and ate a banana as she walked, prepared to dive into the brush if a vehicle approached.

She should arrive in Ngara before dark. Hopefully, Gatera would have already passed through.

An hour later, her head began to ache. Soon she felt nauseated. She convinced herself the upset stomach stemmed from the headache. Audible grumbles erupted from her abdomen. Though she'd eaten several bananas, she hadn't consumed nearly enough calories in the past forty-eight hours. Minutes later she dashed into the bushes and emptied her bowels. Not a good sign. She'd expected at least a forty-eight-hour incubation period from the bacteria she picked up during her swim. Instead, she'd sickened in less than twenty-four.

Though she passed an occasional farm, Jess kept going, hoping the watery stools would stop. After all, she'd consumed the banana part of the bananas, rice, applesauce, and toast anti-diarrhea BRAT diet.

The loose bowels grew constant, to the point she couldn't walk ten feet before another bout. Unable to go anywhere without one end or the other spewing fluids, she hid in a clump of brush. She removed her jeans and underwear and wrapped a *kikoi* around herself so she could relieve herself without struggling with clothing. Eventually, the vomiting slowed to dry heaves, but the diarrhea persisted. She wiped her bottom with dried grasses and leaves so often her rear end turned raw.

Her bottled water was gone, so she couldn't replace her lost fluids. In hindsight, she should have bought more, but she thought she'd be on a bus heading to her destination. Now on a part of the road with few settlements, she had no choice but to move on, though her pace slowed. At this point, the nearest water, whether surface or bottled, was at the ferry, and she didn't have the strength to backtrack. She'd expected the aches in her over-used knees and ankles, but not the total body pain she was experiencing nor the severe headache. Jesus, it even hurt to move her eyes.

Maybe she was in sickle crisis. The sickle trait, inherited from her mother, provided some protection from malaria, but increased her risk of complications with dehydration. Under stress, her red blood cells formed the abnormal sickle shape and blocked small blood vessels, causing bone, muscle, and abdominal pain. The symptoms should clear once she was rehydrated.

Then she remembered swatting that daylight mosquito in Kigali. Damn! This wasn't just sickle. Grimly, she diagnosed herself with dengue or "breakbone" fever, a mosquito-borne viral illness that wouldn't kill you but would make you wish you were dead.

Jess forced herself to keep going, refusing to slide into delirium and death, though it would be an easy way to die. Far better than being hacked to bits. If she died, Tom would deliver her message to Michel, who would recognize the significance of her papers, and perhaps, something on her camera would bring Gatera to justice.

His recent actions proved he had no remorse about what he'd done. He'd killed Jean-Baptiste, a moderate Hutu. Gatera—and all *génocidaires*—needed to be punished. She recalled the RTML broadcast which urged the Hutu soldiers and the *Interahamwe* to return to places where they'd already killed, saying, "You have missed some enemies. You must go back and finish them off. The graves are not yet full!"

Jess wanted Gatera to squirm on the witness stand. She wanted to watch the expression on his face when he was sentenced to life imprisonment. She wanted to see him hauled away in chains. To do that, she had to survive.

Hours later she lay on the ground, too ill to move, too weak to swat away mosquitoes, her tongue too dry to moisten her cracked lips. Chills racked her body. Her teeth clattered against each other. She had never been so sick in her life.

Holding on to a tree branch, she weakly pulled herself up, then staggered down the road, no longer sure where she was going or why. Sometimes she thought she was home in Philadelphia and, at others, in Rwanda.

She kept her gaze on the ground, afraid to look up, afraid her distinctive eyes would give her away. Thousands of people swirled around her, all waiting to cross into Tanzania. The smells of shit and body odor burrowed into her nostrils and stayed there.

With no food or water beyond what she stole, Jess monitored every mouthful.

She attached herself to a family, helping the mother with her little ones, trying to appear part of a group rather than a lone woman. The next day, she assisted an elderly woman, filling a daughter's role. Every day she shifted her location within the mass of people.

Everyone held transistor radios to their ears. God only knows where the refugees found batteries. Daily the Hutu-controlled Mille Collines radio station spouted propaganda. Faster than the rampant diseases spread, chattered rumors claimed Tutsi cockroaches had reinvaded. In retaliation for the genocide, they'd kill all Hutus in a reverse genocide. The crowd at the border swelled as panicked Hutus joined refugees already there.

At last, after two weeks, the border gate opened. Hidden among those seeking asylum, a relieved Jess crossed into Tanzania. She'd escaped Gatera.

Groggily, Jess pushed herself into a sitting position. Her head still pounded, but she pried her eyes open and looked around. She was alone in the middle of a road. What happened to the refugees who'd been with her? How had she slept through the din of 250,000 people marching past her? Gradually, she regained her orientation to time and place. She must be sicker than she thought if she'd been hallucinating, if she'd become so confused she'd relived the mass exodus into Tanzania.

Jess had escaped Gatera once, but if she didn't get moving, he'd catch her this time. She stood and forced herself to push on. Within minutes, she was hot, so hot, but so cold her teeth chattered. The world wobbled. Trees jumped around. Clouds swirled. Her feet weren't where they ought to be, wouldn't follow her command. She stumbled, falling hard. Unable to summon the strength to move, she sat there, drifting in and out of awareness. Her mouth and lips were dry as dust. Water! Water shimmered in the road ahead. Waves bobbed, breaking up the reflection of the sky. She crawled a few feet toward the tantalizing wetness.

Puzzled, she stopped. Her elongated shadow stretched ahead. It was nearly sunset. The sun was behind her. Somehow, she was certain she should have been walking west, toward the sun.

She looked back.

Footprints wandered erratically over the road as far as she could see. Surely, she hadn't made them.

In a moment of semi-lucidity, she realized she was wandering like a *mzungu*. Worse, she had no idea how long she'd been heading in the wrong direction or how long she'd been sitting in the middle of the road.

A *thrum* filled her ears, growing louder, penetrating

her daze. The sound came from behind. She turned to investigate. A red cloud billowed in the distance, coming rapidly toward her.

The drone became the chug of an engine. A white vehicle flashed in and out of the obscuring mantle of dust.

A white truck. Jess needed to hide but couldn't remember why. She tried to stand but collapsed in the middle of the road.

Chapter Seventy-One

Michel

Arusha, July 26, 1997

In the Evidence Support Section, Michel introduced Tom then handed Jessica's camera to the technician.

The tech studied the camera. "It hasn't been well cared for. It's really dirty." He wrinkled his nose. "Thus, the film inside may have suffered from heat and humidity. Any latent images on the film may have degenerated."

Tom asked, "What's a latent image?"

The tech grinned but didn't seem to mind coaching an uninformed novice. "When someone takes a picture, the film is exposed to light, and a reverse image is made on the film, but it remains unstable until the film is processed."

"Do you think anything's there?" Fournier asked.

"A lot depends on the type of film and its storage conditions. Some black-and-white films, if stored in cool, dry conditions, have good retention of latent images and can last for years with little deterioration. Unprocessed images on color films, particularly those that rely on dyes, degrade at a more rapid rate." The tech rewound the film, opened the camera, and grinned. "Tri-X. We're in luck. This particular emulsion has a reputation for excellent stability. Film exposed over twenty years ago has been processed with only slight fog on the printed images. So, it's possible something might be hiding here. Give me a few days to develop the film and print any photos."

"Can you do it sooner?" Michel's brow furrowed. "It's urgent."

"Everything at ICTR is urgent. For you, Michel, tomorrow afternoon."

"Thanks."

Tom and Fournier walked back to Fournier's office.

Michel stretched his neck to work out some stiffness. "How long will you be in Tanzania, Dr.—Tom?"

"I took a week off. I didn't expect Jess to disappear. I'd like to remain here until she shows up, but I can't stay forever. I left my partner running our practice alone."

"What hotel are you in?"

"I don't have a reservation anywhere. Shit, the taxi driver is still waiting for me." Tom gave an exasperated huff. "Any recommendations?"

"Go to the Arusha Hotel. It's within walking distance of my office. I'll give them a call to squeeze you in. If I learn anything about Jessica, I'll get in touch with you. In the meantime, if you want to visit some sights but stick close to town, you can tour the Arusha National Park. It's less an hour away on the side of Mount Meru." Fournier pointed at the blue mountain behind them. "The park doesn't hold the variety or quantity seen on the Serengeti but is worth the trip."

"Thanks, I'd rather stick around in case we hear some thing about Jess." Tom turned to Fournier. "You sure we shouldn't be looking for her? I feel useless just hanging about. I ought to be doing something, anything."

"Me too. But the police are aware Jessica's missing. They have a better chance of finding her than we do."

Chapter Seventy-Two

Tom

Arusha, July 27, 1997

Tom paid his patient driver, arranged to be picked up again the following day, then settled into the Arusha Hotel. The building was a bit old-fashioned, but light years above Motel Amarembo. The concierge informed him a bank, the post office, and Town Grocers were located nearby. With only eighty-six rooms, the Arusha was small enough to be inviting. Most rooms had those French balconies, no more than a footprint wide, and Tom could gaze out on the city.

After indulging in a late breakfast, Tom met his driver, then killed time until his appointment with Fournier by letting Mposi show him tourist attractions like the Uhuru Monument to African brotherhood.

Amazed at the lack of infrastructure in Arusha, Tom couldn't believe women carried jugs of water on their heads—or that they scooped run-off from rains out of open trenches along the road, water contaminated with petrochemical byproducts from vehicles and asphalt, human and animal excrement, decaying vegetable matter, not to mention mosquito larvae and millions of microbes. The thought of putting such filth into his body repelled him. Never again would he take tap water for granted.

His driver insisted they visit a jewelry store to shop for tanzanite. "Best place to buy in all world. Only found in the Merelani Hills"—he pointed to the north—"between Arusha and Mount Kilimanjaro."

"No, thanks."

"You're a rich man with plenty of pretty women. Buy something nice for them."

Not in the mood for gemstone shopping, Tom balked. "No. No pretty women for me."

"Just look then."

Hell. The dude probably got a kick-back for dragging in customers. As poor as people here seemed to be, the driver might need the income, so Tom, with plenty of time remaining before he met Fournier, visited the store. Tom found the stones both beautiful and reasonable compared to the States. He bought a pendant and earring set for his sister-in-law and one for Regina. A gorgeous blue-green "peacock" emerald-cut stone surrounded by diamonds caught his eye. He bought the ring because the central stone reminded him of Jess's eyes. Though their relationship remained strained, in Rusumo, she'd returned his kiss with true passion. He remembered when he'd knelt before her and presented her with her first engagement ring. This would be her next ring, replacing the unimpressive one he'd bought on his resident's salary, the one she'd returned to him. Not that he was hoping or anything.

After the clerk wrapped Tom's purchases, he returned to his cab.

"Now, take me to the ICTR, please."

Chapter Seventy-Three

Michel

Arusha, July 27, 1997

Jessica's computer sat on Michel's desk. He was going through her files hoping for some insight into what had carried her into harm's way. Whoever had written *Tutsi whore* on her wall was a Hutu—and likely her arch enemy.

A male voice sounded from the reception area of his office. "Hi, Lizette."

Michel lifted his head.

Tom Powell, brandishing a visitor's pass, strode into Fournier's inner sanctum, left the door open, and dropped into a chair. "Any news?"

Michel shook his head. "Nothing."

The phone rang in the outer office. Lizette answered, her voice rising with excitement. She stuck her head into Michel's office. "A man just pulled in at the front gate. He has a woman in the back of his truck. He said she told him to bring her here dead or alive—and he thinks she's nearly dead."

Tom glanced at Michel. "Fuck. That truck pulled up as I came in."

Michel gritted his teeth. When his jaw popped, he forced himself to relax. "It's got to be Jessica."

"Damn well better be." Tom was on his feet and heading to the door.

Following him, Michel said, "Lizette, call the AICC

hospital. Get a bed and a physician for her."

"Shall I call an ambulance?"

Michel shook his head. "We can carry her there faster than an ambulance can get here." He turned to Tom. "The Arusha International Conference Center maintains a thirty-two-bed hospital for VIPs and visitors on Old Moshi Road, not far from your hotel. It's one of the most modern in the area. If someone is hunting Jessica, the hospital is small enough we can keep track of who's coming and going. Plus, since it's almost next door, we can assign a UN security guard to protect her."

Chapter Seventy-Four

Tom

Arusha, July 27, 1997

Tom gave Lizette his hotel key with instructions to pick up his physician's bag after she contacted the hospital, then he and Michel dashed to the front gate to verify the unconscious woman was Jess.

A white truck, with *Bonite Bottlers Ltd—Distributors of Soft Drinks and Kilimanjaro Water* painted on the side, was parked at the front entrance while the sentry engaged in an argument with the driver.

"Where's the woman?" Michel demanded of the ICTR guard.

"Still in the truck." He gestured toward the open back doors of the truck. "The driver wanted to dump her on the ground, but I wouldn't let him."

Tom peeked in. After his eyes adjusted to the light, he stared for several seconds before recognizing the thin bald person. "It's her." Christ, she looked so scrawny she must weigh less than a hundred pounds. Blotches in multiple shades of brown decorated her face and arms. Countless insect bites speckled her skin. Her lips bled from deep cracks. Stubble had replaced her mind-of-their-own curls. What the hell had happened to her since Monday night?

Tom leaped into the back of the truck. Heat from her skin scalded his fingers when he palpated her pulse. Without glancing at his watch, he knew her heart rate galloped along at 120 beats per minute, twice her normal rate, but nice and regular, consistent with fever and dehydration rather than a cardiac abnormality. He continued his evaluation, planning to lay his head on her chest to listen to her heart. He steeled himself before putting his ear against the filthy-beyond-belief t-shirt she wore. Below, she wore a sarong-sort-of-thing that was coated with feces. Over the traffic noise he was unable to pick up any new heart murmurs. She moaned in pain as he touched her belly and extremities. "She's really sick, Michel. We need to get her to a hospital stat."

Michel turned to the driver. "Where'd you pick her up?"

"In the middle of the Rusumo-Ngara road." He waved his hands wildly, apparently totally exasperated. "I wanted to take her to the hospital in Ngara, but she said to bring her here, dead or alive, to someone named Fournier."

"I'm Fournier," Michel said. "So, she was talking then?"

The driver nodded. "Saying lots of crazy things about people wanting to kill her."

From inside the truck, Tom asked, "Has she had anything to eat or drink?"

"Three bottles of Stoney Tangawizi."

Tom shot a questioning look toward Michel who replied, "Ginger beer."

"He gave a sick woman beer?"

"It's not real beer, more like a strong ginger ale."

The driver withdrew a bottle from the back of his truck and handed it to Tom.

Tom glanced at the contents—*carbonated water, cane sugar, ginger root, natural flavours, citric acid, yeast, preservatives, ascorbic acid*—and the *330 ml* on the label. A good choice. Even sick, she thought like a doctor. The ginger would have helped with nausea, plus three bottles totaled about a liter. "At least she got some fluids."

Lizette came up awkwardly jogging in her heels. "Mr. Fournier, the AICC hospital has no beds. They're full of British tourists who got sick on safari."

"Damn." Michel looked at Tom. "The closest hospital is Mount Meru." He addressed the driver. "You need to drive us there."

"I'll be late getting back to—"

"It's right across the street."

Tom remained in the back of the truck with Jessica while Michel jumped in the front seat.

The driver masterfully dodged garishly painted, overburdened trucks and jam-packed mini-vans called *dala-dalas* to cross East African Community Boulevard.

Over the engine noise, Tom hollered to Michel. "Is Mount Meru any good?"

"It's been around since World War I and, as a secondary referral center, is one of the better hospitals in the area."

The truck pulled up in front of the hospital.

Tom hopped out and thrust a handful of bills at the driver. "Thanks." He and Michel carried Jess into the Emergency Room.

At the front desk, Tom rushed through Jess's paper work, anxious to return to her side.

Minutes later, Lizette walked in.

Tom took his doctor's bag from her. "Thanks. I appreciate your help." He then introduced himself to the physician, a lanky man in dark slacks and a starched lab coat. "I'm an interventional cardiologist from Philadelphia."

"Dr. Gerard Mbatia." He shook Tom's hand. "Do you have a volunteer permit? Or license to practice in Tanzania?"

"No."

"Then you're strictly an observer."

"She's my fiancée."

Tom caught Michel's look of surprise.

Dr. Mbatia raised an eyebrow. "All the more reason to let someone objective handle her. After all, a physician who treats himself or his family …"

Tom finished the old axiom "… is a fool."

"You have things under control, Tom, so I'll head back to the office." Michel waved as he took off.

Dr. Mbatia said, "Her temperature is 40.5° Celsius."

Tom converted the temperature to Fahrenheit and whistled. "Almost 105? Way too high for an adult."

"I'll admit her to our ICU where we can keep a closer eye on her."

Nurses, with Tom and Mbatia beside them, rolled Jess's gurney to the intensive care unit. They passed several small buildings with open porches, each housing a particular medical specialty.

Mount Meru Hospital didn't impress Tom one bit. The ICU was as basic as it could get. No walls of electronic equipment. Not even curtains between patients. A nurse sat at a small table. No heat. No air conditioning. Rusty oxygen concentrators. The entire ward shared one blood pressure cuff. Small plastic baskets housed the few available supplies in an all-but-bare supply storage area. Worse, patient charts weren't well-organized. Some didn't even have room numbers. Papers were scattered everywhere. God, it would be so easy to confuse patient paperwork. The place was a set-up for malpractice.

Mbatia drew her blood. Holding several tubes in his hand, he said, "I'm going to the lab. You coming?"

Tom followed the other doctor and watched him prepare a microscope slide. "By the way, she has sickle trait."

Mbatia lifted his head from the microscope. "I don't see any ring forms, trophozoites, or schizonts, the usual signs of malaria, but we need to draw blood every eight hours for a day or two to be certain. A third of her red blood cells are sickled. I'd say she's in sickle crisis from being dehydrated."

Tom peered through the microscope. It'd been so long since he'd had basic hematology, he wasn't certain what he was looking for. "I thought sickle protected people from malaria—"

"Not a hundred percent, especially with only the trait. The sickle crisis should resolve with fluids." Dr. Mbatia continued talking as he and Tom walked back to the ICU. "We presume anyone who comes with a high fever has malaria and treat them prophylactically with chloroquine and primaquine."

"Without testing?" Tom was astonished.

"Here, malaria is so common we're right half the time." Dr. Mbatia gave a harsh laugh. "She'll get fluids as fast as we can pump them into her. If her pain doesn't resolve with rehydration and we don't find malaria, we need to assume something else is going on, maybe dengue fever. We'll draw blood and urine cultures too."

Tom pushed aside a rolling screen that separated Jessica from the rest of the intensive care unit.

Two nurses shooed the physicians out. "Come back

when we've finished our assessment."

While Tom and Mbatia waited outside the rolling privacy screen, Tom indicated the only other patient in the ICU, a young man with visibly distended jugular veins. "What about him?"

"Congestive heart failure from chronic rheumatic fever."

Tom whistled. The disease, caused by untreated strep throat, was so rare in the United States he'd never seen a case. In his mind, he visualized the chart in his medical texts listing the Jones criteria for the diagnosis and heard the associated heart murmur, a high-pitched apical holosystolic murmur radiating to the armpit. He opened his doctor's bag, removed his stethoscope, and strode across the room.

Dr. Mbatia followed. "We never have enough antibiotics to treat most cases of strep, especially out in the bush."

"Penicillin won't relieve his symptoms." Tom listened to the young man's heart. "He needs a valve replacement."

Mbatia shook his head. "That won't happen here. All we can do is make him comfortable until his heart gives out."

Tom sighed, knowing that in the States the young man's faulty valve could be repaired. At least Tom could give some short-term help. He withdrew all the appropriate cardiac medications from his bag and set them on the nurses' desk. Jess wouldn't need them, but the man in the other bed would. "I'll send more when I get back to the States. My office gets more samples than we can use."

The nurses smiled as they exited Jess's makeshift cubicle. "We're finished. You can enter now."

Tom rushed in and patted Jess's cheek. "Babe? Can you hear me?"

Her eyelashes fluttered. The cracks in her lips deepened in a puny smile. "Tommy? You're finally home from the hospital?"

He choked at the weakness of her voice—and her impaired mental status. "How are you feeling?"

"Tired."

"Go back to sleep then, sweetheart."

"Night. Love you." Her eyes closed, but she left her hand in his.

Tom stroked her sweaty forehead then her rounded skull. Its stubble rasped his palm. A memory flashed through his mind—his fingers playing with her curls, pulling her near, only to find that her ringlets had imprisoned him and he couldn't let go if he tried. "Love you, too, babe."

Christ, she looked like hell. The *I love you* told him she wasn't oriented, but he'd take her words—and the fact that she'd left her hand in his—as signs she still had feelings for him.

Reluctantly he released her hand and removed the blood pressure cuff and pulse oximeter from his bag. Not that he didn't trust the nurses at Mount Meru, but he preferred obtaining his own vital signs. Jess's blood pressure was low and her pulse high, both consistent with dehydration. Her oxygen level was normal. Through his stethoscope, her heart and lungs sounded normal. Despite her belly pain, her liver and spleen were normal in size. Beyond that he was clueless. He hadn't practiced medicine, other than his usual subspecialty, in ages. He knew nothing about tropical medicine. Maybe he should have come to Africa with Jess back then. Maybe he depended too heavily on modern imaging and testing rather than clinical acumen. He'd need to rely on Dr. Mbatia who'd seen it all.

Chapter Seventy-Five

Tom

Arusha, July 27, 1997

Once Tom got Jess settled into Mount Meru, he called Fournier. "Is this the best you guys can do for a hospital?"

Fournier laughed. "Welcome to the Third World, Dr. Powell. I'll be over there in a bit. I'm working late tonight."

True to his word, Fournier arrived within the hour and handed Tom two plastic bags.

"What's this?"

"Take-out and bottled water for you. Broth for her if she wakes up. Soap. Washcloths. My spare shirt from the office for her. She'll need clean clothes until we pick up her suitcases at the airport."

"Thanks." Tom grinned. A real practical guy. No wonder Jess liked him.

Concern on his face, Fournier glanced at Jess. "How's she doing?"

"She's quite ill but stable. Agitated. To keep those insect bites from becoming infected from her constant scratching, we might need to restrain her. We're waiting on labs to come back, but her primary problem is severe dehydration."

Fournier pursed his lips. "I'll find someone to stay with her."

"Why?"

"Things are a little different here. Families do most of the routine patient care themselves. Mount Meru doesn't have a canteen—a hospital cafeteria—so families must provide food for patients and themselves."

"I can do that."

Fournier raised a doubtful eyebrow. "How long can you stay?"

Tom clenched his jaw. "Not more than another few days."

"Then I definitely need to find someone to care for Jessica."

Tom scowled. There was that *Zhesseeca* again. "I should take her back to the States. She'd get better care there."

"I'm not sure she'd be comfortable with you making those decisions for her." Fournier stroked his goatee. "An air evacuation is a lot of trouble for dehydration, isn't it?"

Tom shrugged. He didn't like the idea of leaving Jess here, but Fournier was right.

"Someone will need to sit with her if she isn't discharged before you leave, and she may need care afterwards." Fournier *tsk*ed. "I'd take her home with me—"

Tom bristled.

Fournier held up a calming hand. "—except she and my wife ... they would be *comme l'huile et l'eau*, like oil and water." He nodded toward the main door into the ward. "Come with me. I'll introduce you to Jessica's guard."

"Guard?"

"We must assume Gatera is after Jessica, so she warrants the same protection the ICTR provides other witnesses. I'll station a man at the front door of the ward to check the identity of everyone entering, but I doubt Gatera tracked the Bonite truck here."

Tom shook his head. "I'll talk to Dr. Mbatia. We can place her in isolation."

"Good idea. I'll go talk to the hospital administrators and get a private nurse, if one's available." Fournier strode off.

After he left, Tom realized for the first time in his medical career, he literally had to care for a patient rather than delegate tasks. The nurses had removed most of Jess's foul clothing and covered her with a sheet. He commandeered more rolling screens and positioned them around Jess to hide her from view. She was still sedated, so it'd be a good time to examine her thoroughly—and bathe her. He crinkled his nose. If she woke up smelling this bad, she'd be mortified.

A nurse brought Tom a basin filled with tepid water and a bar of yellow soap. "Be sure she doesn't drink the water. It's all right to bathe in, but *wazungu*—foreigners—usually get sick if they drink it."

"I'll be staying with her. Can you please find me a chair?"

"Yes, *bwana*."

That word again. Tom shook his head. He'd been certain Hollywood had made it up.

The nurse dragged in a plastic Coca-Cola chair.

Tom shook his head. Those uncomfortable seats seemed to be everywhere here. With a damp cloth and Fournier's Kilimanjaro bottled water, Tom wiped Jess's mouth and teeth. Her tongue reached eagerly for the dampness. He dripped a few drops into her mouth, not enough to choke her, just enough to moisten her mouth. Then he switched to the local water in the basin and scrubbed the brown stain off her face, forearms, and hands. Thick and waxy, the stuff was hard to remove. He sniffed the washcloth, trying to figure out what the substance was, but Jess reeked so badly he couldn't pick out a scent beyond shit and body odor.

Tom cleaned each extremity, Jess's current appearance warring with memories of making love to her. His fingers found her body strange yet familiar. He couldn't yet bring himself to look beneath the sheet at her breasts and mons.

When he could no longer put it off, Tom lifted the drape. A tiny bra covered her breasts. A safety pin held a plastic bag to the bra. He'd check its contents later.

He removed the brassiere and immediately jerked down the cloth.

He slammed his eyelids closed in denial. He couldn't have seen—

A hand clasped his shoulder.

Tom jumped.

Fournier's voice sounded in Tom's ear. "I should have warned you."

Tom lifted the drape again and couldn't tear his gaze from the scars on Jess's left breast. Someone's initials. Carved into her delicate flesh, *cGa*. A monogram that marked her as someone's property. His voice shook. "How'd you know?"

Fournier paused for a long time. "I saw it while we were traveling together." He shook his head. "She doesn't know I know."

"These cuts are incredibly precise. A surgeon did this. A monster."

"Cyprien Gatera is a monster. But that"—Fournier indicated the scars on Jess's breast—is nothing compared to what Jessica and I witnessed during the genocide." His laugh was harsh. "She never told me everything that happened. She was always more concerned about finding Gatera because he murdered her children. But I suspect he raped her, perhaps repeatedly, and marked her to be his sex slave."

"Fuck."

"Exactly." Michel handed Tom Jess's luggage.

With an absent "Thanks," Tom took the suitcase.

Fournier leaned something against the wall. "I have Lizette calling around to borrow a wheelchair. This is a Maasai walking stick." He waved it in the air. "She can use it for support once she's up and about. I'll check on you tomorrow, Tom." Fournier left.

Tom continued Jess's sponge bath. His mind was elsewhere as he washed her body. He couldn't imagine Jess willingly allowing herself to be scarified. She'd been under duress when Gatera cut her, but once back in the States, why hadn't she had the scars surgically excised? Tom would have recommended a plastic surgeon. And if Fournier had seen Jess's breasts, what else had he seen?

Tom removed the plastic bag safety-pinned to her bra. Inside he found her damp passport, credit cards, and a hodgepodge of currencies: American dollars, Belgian francs, Rwandan francs, Tanzanian shillings. He set everything aside and dug into the food Fournier had brought and polished off a bottle of Kilimanjaro water. Maybe he was just thirsty, but it was the best water he'd ever tasted. Way better than Philadelphia municipal water.

Tom mulled over Jess's situation while he chewed. Her babies. Her rape. Those hideous scars. His stomach turned over, and he set the food aside. Fournier had heard Jess's story. Why had she trusted Fournier with her story and not her parents. Or himself? And when had Fournier seen those scars?

Chapter Seventy-Six

Jessica

Mount Meru Hospital, Arusha, July 31, 1997

Blinkety-blinkety-blink. A light flashed above Jess. Seconds later she realized her fluttering eyelids were causing the strobe effect. Her eyes finally stayed open long enough to recognize fluorescent fixtures.

A voice to her left said, "How're you feeling, babe?"

Weird. The voice sounded like Tom. But he was back in Philadelphia. Jess moaned as she turned her head. Tom *was* here. But how? Why? "Where am I?"

"Arusha. Mount Meru Hospital."

She raised her head and, with a whimper, dropped back onto the pillow. "How'd I get here?"

"You don't remember?"

"No ..." Fragments of memories swirled around, like randomly-shuffled playing cards, slowly aligning themselves into cogent patterns. Gatera. River. Jean-Baptiste. Burqa. White truck. "Yeah—sort of." She stared at him. "What are you doing here? Why aren't you in Philadelphia?"

"I took some vacation days." He took her hand. "I couldn't go home with you so sick."

"How long have I been here?"

"Three days."

"What's the date?"

"July thirty-first."

"I'm supposed to start work—"

"Babe, I took care of that. They're aware you're here and that you'll be starting late."

Her passport. Birth certificates. "The camera?" She struggled to sit up. "What happened—did you deliver—"

"Take it easy." Tom gently pressed her back into the bed. "I carried your package to Fournier, just like you told me."

"Any film in the camera?" Panic tinged her voice.

"Yes. We took it to be developed." He knew she'd demand to see the images right away, so he lied, "But the photos aren't ready yet."

"I need to talk to Michel."

"He'll be here later. He's been to visit you twice a day since we brought you here."

"I'm so tired, Tommy. And every bone in my body aches. I diagnosed myself with dengue fever." Triumph on her face, she added in a weak voice, "But I killed that damned mosquito."

"Go back to sleep, babe. I'll wake you when Michel comes."

Chapter Seventy-Seven

Michel

Arusha, July 31, 1997

Just after dark, Michel raced across East African Community Boulevard from the ICTR campus to Mount Meru Hospital. He'd been surprised Tom volunteered to stay with Jessica. Even more astonished to learn he and Jessica were engaged. She didn't have a ring on her finger, but perhaps it had been stolen on her journey. Despite the fact that Michel rather liked Tom, an unwarranted jealousy surged through Michel.

When he reached Jessica's bedside, he nodded at his new friend. "She awake yet?"

"She regained consciousness for a few minutes. Long enough to ask about the camera."

Michel blew out a harsh breath. "The photos are damning. There's enough evidence on them to convict Gatera. The minute Jessica is able, I'll get her statement corroborating the images." He shook his head. "Brutal stuff. She doesn't need to deal with them now."

She stirred. Her gaze bypassed Tom. "Michel?"

"*Oui*, I'm here, *ma chérie*."

"The camera? Were there photos of my babies?"

Michel clenched and unclenched his jaw several times. He stalled for time. "How are you feeling?"

"Were there photos of my babies?"

"*Oui*, but—" Michel glanced at Tom, hoping for support.

With a nod, Tom added his opinion. "Babe, wait until you're stronger."

"I want to see them. Now."

Merde. Michel had known she'd be obsessed with seeing the photographs. "When you're better …"

"Do you have them with you?" Jessica struggled to sit but sagged back onto her pillow.

"No. I left them at the office. Once you're feeling better, I'll bring them."

"Go get them."

Michel shook his head.

"P-p-lease." Her voice snagged in her throat. "Don't deny me this."

Michel sighed. "Are you sure?"

"Yes." Her faint voice held certainty.

Michel dashed back across the street to his office. Once inside, he leafed through the eight-by-tens. In the first, taken by someone else, Jessica, with a child on each hip, stood before a rustic building. She looked not only happy but content. Above her head, a sign read *Clinique Mère-Enfant*. The next shots showed Jessica inside her clinic with all her employees, all carefully posed and smiling.

Then the photos changed dramatically. Crooked, sometimes out of focus, sometimes not centered, with the point of view from waist height rather than from eye level, they appeared to have been taken by a photographer who wasn't looking through the viewfinder. These must be the ones Jean-Baptiste took surreptitiously.

Michel's hands shook. He'd taken—and seen—literally thousands of genocide photos, but these were different. They involved a woman he loved. He'd already tortured himself by studying them countless times. Bile rose up his throat every time. He closed his eyes while looking at the last few. One showed Jessica pinned on a desk by two men with Gatera between her legs. Another revealed blood stains on the wall behind Jessica. Michel recognized the room where her babies had been killed. No wonder her face appeared frozen and wooden, her eyes dead.

He shook his head. Enough! He grabbed a large manila envelope and a portable tape recorder from his desk. To protect Jessica, he wanted to censor the images, but she would immediately sense images were missing. So, he shoved them all into the envelope.

He returned to Jessica's bedside, he asked, "Are you certain?"

"Positive." She slammed a clenched fist against the mattress.

Unwillingly, Michel withdrew the images. "Jessica, let's do this later. Looking at them will be too difficult—"

"No. I've waited long enough!"

Michel started to replace the photographs in the envelope, making one last effort to dissuade her. "Trust me, you don't want to deal with these images right now. You need to be stronger."

"Now."

"*D'accord.*" He gave an exasperated *tsk*. "I'm going to record you, if you don't mind."

"Fine. Documentation of Gatera's crimes is important." She looked at the first photo and smiled, a lovely expression Michel didn't think he'd ever seen, one that softened her face, almost erasing her illness.

"Jean-Baptiste took this one of me and the boys in front of the clinic." Her voice cracked. "We had packed to leave. Oh, my God. This is the last ph-ph-photograph—"

She ran her fingers over her children's faces. A sob strangled her words.

Michel removed the photo from her hand. "I told you, Jessica. These can wait 'til you're better."

He didn't know how Jessica found the strength, but somehow, she snatched the entire stack from his fingers. With the first, she said, "That's Jean-Baptiste and Yvette, my driver and my nurse." Vehemently she muttered, "Gatera. That son of a bitch." She flipped to the next and screamed.

The photographs fluttered to the floor.

Chapter Seventy-Eight

Tom

Arusha, Mount Meru Hospital, July 31, 1997

The wails of a wounded animal filled the hospital ward. Jess's scream ripped into Tom's heart. He moved toward her. Damn. Too late.

That damned Frenchman, Fournier, gathered the anguished Jessica in his arms, placing gentle kisses on her neck, her head, her shoulders, anywhere his lips could reach. "*Ma caille*, I know it's hard. Don't review them now. Later you can identify the man who killed your children. Once Gatera goes to trial, you'll never have to look at them again."

Tom stared at Fournier and Jess. Fuck. It had it never occurred to him, but they had been lovers. That explained Fournier's familiarity, his protectiveness. And maybe Jess's reluctance to get involved with Tom again. Not to mention why Fournier had stated Jess and his wife were like oil and water.

Tom, while still processing this revelation, picked up the scattered images and flipped through them, wondering what had prompted Jess's reaction.

His stomach contents rose in rebellion and raced up his throat as he studied the photos. Unlike the carefully-composed images found in all the *Time* and *Newsweek* articles he'd read, these—with their odd angles, unexpected points of view, and unusual framing—were much more immediate. The fact that his Jess—he shivered in revulsion. The first image showed men dragging a woman out a door. In the next, they'd shot her. Two toddlers, mouths open, skulls crushed. Nurses being gang-raped. A pile of bodies baking in the sun. Horror after horror. Then Jess being raped. Looking at them, Tom had never in his life felt so impotent. Things had happened to her he couldn't have prevented. And the images! No wonder Gatera was after Jess. Any jury viewing these photographs would find him guilty. Whoever Jess had met in Rwanda, whoever had given her the camera, had risked his life three times over, by taking the photos, by keeping them hidden, and by returning them to her. Jess had been right. The images *were* worth more than one person's life. He laid the photos on the bed.

Slowly Jess's sobs abated. "Let's get started."

Fournier, still with one arm supporting Jessica, asked, "Are you sure you're up to this?"

Her faint but firm voice answered, "One hundred percent."

Fournier shot Tom a doubting glance. With his other hand, he picked up the images. "All right, Jessica, tell me about the photos."

"Okay." She took a deep breath. "Let's do it."

With his arm still around her, Fournier held a photograph before her.

With her index finger, she tapped on the image. "That's Cyprien Gatera. He murdered my children."

After she reviewed all the photos, Fournier said, "I'll type up your official statement. When you feel better, you can sign it. In the meantime, a guard will protect you from Gatera." He patted Jess's hand. "Get some rest."

She nodded then appeared to study him. "You look good, Michel. This is new." She stroked his goatee. "It becomes you."

The gesture, so simple, yet so intimate, sent ice-pick stabs of jealousy through Tom.

"Thanks." Fournier winked. "I grew it for you, *ma chérie*." He bent and gave her a swift kiss. "I'll see you tomorrow." He strode out of the ICU.

"Goodbye." Tom wanted to add *good riddance*, but he'd actually come to like Fournier, and the man certainly had Jess's best interests at heart.

The second Fournier left, Jess collapsed on her pillow. "I'm exhausted."

"You did too much, babe." Tom took her hand. "Get a bit of shut-eye. I'll be right here."

In seconds, Jess was asleep, a slight snore revealing the extent of her fatigue. When she and Tom had lived together, she only snored when she came off one of those thirty-six-hour days their residency program was famous for. Even in her sleep, she was digging at the insect bites covering her arms and legs. Afraid her entire body would soon look as bad as that patch of skin on her neck, Tom unwillingly asked for restraints, and the nurses brought strips of soft cloth to bind her to the bed frame.

The private nurse Fournier hired replaced Tom for a three-to-eleven shift. With her babysitting Jess, Tom returned to the hotel to freshen up, eat some real food, and sleep in a real bed. Dozing in the red plastic chair provided by the ICU didn't cut it. The weather was warm and humid. The hospital had no central air, so the plastic seat made his butt sweat.

When Tom returned to Mount Meru Hospital, he chatted with the ICTR guard posted outside the ICU. Nothing had happened in Tom's absence, and the last person to enter the ward had been a doctor a few minutes before.

Tom thanked the guard and stepped inside. Oddly, the partitions that separated Jess from other patients had been pulled completely around her, hiding her from view of the nurses' desk. He'd wanted the screens to protect her from Gatera's eyes, not to prevent nurses from observing her. He strode across the room. To be sure Jess wasn't on the bedpan, he peeked through the crack between the two dividers.

The private nurse was sprawled in the plastic chair, her head down. Damn, she was supposed to watch Jess, not sleep. A sound caught his attention. He pushed the screens further apart and turned his gaze toward the noise.

Jess's arms and feet, bound by the restraints, thrashed futilely against her bedding.

A stocky man, clad in a white lab coat, stood at the head of her bed, pressing a pillow onto her face.

Tom thrust the screens apart, sending them crashing to the floor.

The doctor jumped at the sound.

Tom rushed toward Jess's bed, grabbed the man's shoulders, and flung him away. "What the hell are you doing?"

With a wild swing of his arm, the man struck Tom in the jaw, whirled, and fled.

Tom's head bounced off the wall hard enough to make him stagger. Dazed, he shook his head. He started to run after the assailant but halted to be sure Jess was still alive. "Stop him!" he yelled at the ICU nurse.

He turned to Jess. The pillow shook with her efforts to remove it from her face.

Tom lifted the pillow and shook her. "Are you all

right?"

Too short of breath to talk, Jess nodded, then pointed her chin toward her private-duty nurse.

Tom turned. Still sprawled in her chair, the nurse's head drooped on her ample chest. The woman hadn't moved since he'd first seen her.

Reluctantly Tom left Jess's side. His heart thudded as he felt for the woman's pulse. Nothing. He lifted her head. A thin red line encircled her neck.

He turned toward Jess. "She's dead."

She struggled to her head. "My God, she's been garroted." Even those few words made her gasp for air.

"How do you know?"

"In Rwanda and Benaco, I often had to determine causes of death." She stopped to cough. "Unfortunately, garroting was fairly common." Her face contorted as she started crying. "He's murdered again, and he's getting away!"

"You sure you're okay?"

"Shook up but fine." Jess coughed again then tried to lift her hands. "Why the hell am I tied up?"

"You were scratching your mosquito bites."

"If I hadn't been restrained, I might have resisted him. Untie me now! Then call the cops."

Boy, was she pissed.

Tom unwrapped her wrists and ankles, then strode to the nurses' desk. "How do I call the police?"

After reporting the homicide at Mount Meru Hospital, Tom called Fournier. The Frenchman's "*Allô?*" sounded sleepy.

"Hey, Michel. Tom. There's been an incident at Mount Meru. You better come—"

"Is Jessica all right?"

"Yes." Tom ran a hand through his hair. "There's been a murder. Her nurse. And Jess's bad guy tried to suffocate her."

"*Mon Dieu*. I'll be there shortly."

The police beat Fournier by a few minutes. Seated at the nurses' station, they began their interrogations with the ICTR guard. Ashamed of his failure, he kept repeating, "But he wore a Mount Meru lab coat. I thought he was a real doctor. He even sounded like one."

The detective asked, "What do you mean?"

"He used big words. He sounded educated."

The cops worked their way through Jess, the nurse at the desk, the patient with rheumatic heart disease, then they questioned Tom.

He described the man he'd found holding a pillow over Jess's face. "He was about five-nine, 200 pounds, real stocky build." He stroked his jaw. "And strong enough to nearly knock my block off."

Jess added, "He's Cyprien Alphonse Gatera. He committed crimes against humanity in Rwanda in 1994."

The detective said, "Did you see his face? Can you identify him with certainty?"

"No," Jess reluctantly conceded. "I was asleep until he covered my face with the pillow. By the time I could breathe, he was gone."

"Without your visual identification, we can't be certain Gatera is our suspect."

In an irritated voice, Jess said, "Who else would it be?"

After their interviews, the police placed the garrote into a plastic bag, collected other evidence, and dusted for fingerprints.

Fournier asked the lead detective, "Can we get

Docteur Hemings out of here? I'm afraid Gatera will try again."

"Certainly. But make sure we can reach all of you."

Fournier let out a deep sigh. "Jessica, I can get you into an ICTR safe house tomorrow. We need to keep you hidden for the remainder of the night." He stroked his beard in thought. "I'll take you to my house—"

Wildly Jess shook her head. "No. Definitely not. I refuse to endanger your family. Can't you think of anywhere else?"

Tom scratched his head. "I could take her to my hotel."

"*Très bien*, Tom. The Arusha is small enough we can cover the exits with UN soldiers. Tomorrow we can move her to the safe house—"

Jess interrupted him. "Don't I have any say in this?"

Christ. What was she thinking? Tom's "No!" came out harsher than he intended. Her near-suffocation had apparently distressed him more than it had her.

Fournier, in a much calmer voice said, "I agree with Tom. The hotel is the best solution for now. Tomorrow we can move you to a safe house and keep you hidden until we track down Gatera."

Chapter Seventy-Nine

Jessica

Arusha, August 1, 1997

When the police finished, Jess, Tom, and Michel prepared to leave the hospital. Tom asked her if she could walk out of the hospital.

Jess snorted. "Definitely." She stood but wobbled dangerously. "Okay, I might need a little help."

Tom laughed. "As long as I've known you, you've never admitted you needed help."

He took one arm and Michel the other. They supported her from the hospital to Michel's car. The ICTR body guard followed closely behind them, carrying her suitcase and walking stick, and took the front seat with Michel.

At the hotel, Jess and Tom waited in the vehicle while Michel and the guard checked Tom's room for hazards. When they returned, the men helped Jess from the taxi, up to Tom's room, and started to deposit her on the bed.

"I'm tired of lying down." Jess pointed to the sofa. "Put me there."

Once Jess was settled, Michel looked around the room. "Nice suite. At least you're on the fourth floor, Tom. Unless Gatera is a mountaineer, he's unlikely to attack from that direction. I'll have men circling the hotel perimeter as well as a guard outside your door. Tomorrow I'll get approval for a safe house."

Jess scowled. "How long will I need to be there? I'm supposed to start at the hospital on August fourth. They found a home for me, but I need to shop for household goods before I start work."

Michel replied, "You'll be taking your life in your hands until we capture Gatera."

Jess's shoulders sagged. Michel was right. She'd been running, trying to escape Gatera for days. And, tonight, he'd come incredibly close to killing her. The sense of suffocation, of her lungs screaming for air, her heart thumping out of her chest, overwhelmed her. Inhale. Hold. Exhale. Only Tom's interference had saved her.

Tom. She'd done her best to evade him, too, but he persisted. He even came to Africa—much too late as far as she was concerned—and envisioned himself as her savior. During her last few months in Philadelphia, she'd learned it was too easy to give in to him, too easy to slip back into patterns developed in their years together, too easy to fall into what-might-turn-back-into-love with him. That kiss in the Amarembo Motel proved she wasn't immune to his charms.

Having both Tom and Michel around stirred up feelings she was unable to handle, but she had to deal with Gatera before she could sort out the men in her life.

"Jessica?" Michel's voice broke into her thoughts.

She shook herself. "Yes?"

"Any questions?"

"No."

"Do you agree to remain within this suite, stay off the balcony, and not to answer the door or the phone?"

She glanced around. The furnishings were standard hotel issue except for the African baskets and photographs of Kilimanjaro nailed to the walls. Nothing at all to keep her mind off Gatera. Her reply was sullen. "Okay, I'll follow orders, but Gatera should be the prisoner, not me."

"I agree, but until he's caught, you need to be invisible." Michel pecked Jess on the cheek.

For a moment, he held her so tightly her achy bones protested, but his embrace reassured her. She nuzzled into his chest.

Michel continued, "*Ma chérie*, I'll get you back to your normal life as soon as possible. Sometime tomorrow, I'll move you into a safe house." He reached for the doorknob. "Keep the door locked. No one in except me and your guard."

"Yes, sir." Jess saluted him.

After he left, she looked at Tom. "I don't have to stay with you. I could get another room."

Tom laughed. "Dream on. Michel set this one up. He says there's not another room in Arusha. With the influx of diplomatic and UN personnel, the city can't provide enough housing, so the hotels have to pick up the overflow." He rubbed the stubble on her head. "You're stuck with me, babe."

"I'm not your babe anymore."

"That's not what you said in the hospital." He gave that cocky grin she knew so well. "You called me *Tommy*, even said you loved me."

Jess shot him a don't-go-there-if-you-know-what's-good-for-you look. "That was delirium on my part and wishful thinking on yours." She sighed. "I don't mean to seem ungrateful. Really, I don't. I never thanked you, but I appreciate you delivering my camera and computer to Michel."

Tom didn't answer immediately. When he did, his voice was hoarse. "Until I saw those ... those photographs, I didn't believe that what you asked me to deliver was more important than your life. Now I understand. That guy's a monster. Putting him away would be worth any cost—almost." Tom dropped to the couch and ran a hand through his hair. "He came so close—if I'd been a minute later, I'd have lost you forever."

She leaned over and pecked him on the cheek. "I owe you another thanks for saving my life tonight." Of course, if Tom hadn't restrained her, she might have fought off Gatera. She lifted a weak arm and dropped it. Realistically, in her current condition, she couldn't fight off anyone. But why make Tom feel any guiltier than he already felt?

He pulled back and changed the subject. "What's going on between you and Fournier?"

Jess's eyebrows shot skyward. "Nothing. Why?"

"It's obvious. You're lovers."

She shook her head. "We're friends."

Tom snorted. "Don't lie, Jess."

"It's none of your business." She blew out a huff of air while deciding whether or not to tell Tom the truth. "Okay. We were lovers—for all of a week. In Rwanda. What happened between us, I guess, was ... dictated by circumstance. Day after day, we faced rotting corpses, people scarred inside and out from the trauma of the genocide, orphans, widows, amputees. And death. Death. Death. When confronted with that many atrocities, you become numb. Your humanity slips away a little more with each passing moment." Her voice dropped to a whisper. "Michel and I slept together more to prove we were still alive than from love or even desire. To prove we could still feel something—anything—good. Afterwards he went home to his pregnant wife—" Sorrow crept into her voice. She shoved it down. "—and I returned to Philadelphia."

Tom persisted in excavating her old wounds. "Did you come here because of him?"

"I didn't realize he was here until after I accepted the Mount Meru job. Why all the fucking questions?" Jess raised her voice and threw in a hefty dose of aggravation.

Tom blinked at Jess's profanity but had the decency to look chagrined. "Jeez, I'm sorry. I wondered if he … if he was the reason you won't get back together with me."

Jess slid away from him on the sofa. "Can we deal with our excess baggage another time?"

"Sorry. You're exhausted from what happened tonight. You take the bed, and I'll sleep on the sofa."

"I'll take the couch if you'll let me clean up first."

"Need any help?"

She shook her head. "Dream on, dude."

"While you're in the shower, I'll watch a little TV. Call me if you need anything."

Jess stood, but her knees quivered. She hadn't felt so weak since she crossed the Rusumo Falls Bridge. She decided to give the Maasai walking stick a try. A beautiful piece of wood wrapped with beads and leather strips, it was taller than she was. Leaning on it, she made her way to the bathroom, a tiled room with a glassed-in shower complete with a teak stool. Luxurious linens. And a real sit-down toilet—not the squat kind.

She rested the walking stick on the wall by the shower door and turned on the water to warm while she brushed her teeth. In the shower, she sat on the stool and let the water stream over her body. Her muscles loosened, and aches eased from her joints. She shifted on the stool so water would hit her back. She should relinquish the bathroom to Tom but couldn't resist staying longer.

Her stomach grumbled with hunger, proof positive she was recovering from her illness. She knew exactly what she wanted—a banana milkshake. The only other time she'd been in Arusha, Michel had ordered one for her. After weeks of bad food at Benaco, the shake was extraordinary, its intense banana-flavor a perfect complement to the ice cream. She'd liked it so much she'd inhaled a second.

The lights flickered, then went out. Damn. The infrastructure in Africa sucked, failing frequently, usually without warning. Hotels normally didn't rely on the grid but maintained their own generators. She wondered why they'd failed. Without their grumble and the hum of fluorescent lights, the place grew eerily silent. The only noise was the rushing of the shower,

The bathroom lacked windows, so the darkness was preternatural. She'd stayed in so long her skin was prune-y and her muscles felt like soggy pasta. After fumbling for the faucet, she turned the water off. She stood, but her spaghetti-legs swayed. Afraid she'd fall, she called for Tom.

No answer.

Maybe he couldn't hear her with the bathroom door closed. She raised her voice. "Tom?"

A faint garbled sound answered her. Tom was snoring. She couldn't blame him for conking out—he'd cared for her for several days.

In the blackness, though, ordinary sounds grew ominous.

Two pops in quick succession. A moment later, another. Transformers popping? She stepped out of the shower, her knees still weak, and slid her fingers against the wall until she touched a towel.

Before she could pull it off the rack, the door creaked open, and the tile floor clicked with the impact of someone's shoes. "Tom?"

The quality of the air shifted, and a draft chilled the water droplets on her skin. Instinct made her reach for the walking stick. "Tom?"

A harsh laugh. Not Tom's.

"I knew I'd find you eventually, Tutsi whore."

Jess swallowed the shocked breath she'd been about to expel. Her wobbly knees vanished, strengthened by a rush of adrenaline.

Not wanting to give away her position, she didn't reply. She reviewed her options. Her only weapons were the walking stick and her ability to outwit him. Stealthily she brought the walking stick to her side. It should be at least as hard on his balls as a stainless-steel pen—and with a greater range.

"You're trapped, *Docteur* Hemings." His voice resonated against the tiles of the bathroom, making it hard to determine his exact location.

Jess visualized the bathroom's layout. She'd heard no more footsteps, so Gatera hadn't come farther into the room. If he fired, he'd aim for her chest. She refused to give him a target, so she squatted. With the advantage of being barefoot, she silently slipped to the far right until her fingers touched another wall.

Gatera stayed put.

So did Jess. She'd wait him out. She had far more patience than he did.

Minutes stretched into eternity. Her bent knees started to give out.

He moved. "Where are you hiding?"

Her ears picked up the faint brush of his clothes as he palmed his way across the bathroom wall. As he passed, the air stirred, hitting her damp skin. Her nostrils caught a whiff of the cigars he favored. She visualized roughly where he was. This was her chance. She duck-walked out of the bathroom. Once she passed through the door, she stretched the walking stick across the opening.

"Your guard is dead. *Docteur* Powell is dead. You're next."

Jess wracked her brain. Tom couldn't be dead. Shit! Those *pops* been Gatera's gun with a silencer.

An "*Oooph*!" was accompanied by the sounds of someone struggling to regain their footing.

Jess smiled. Gatera had tripped over the toilet. He'd nearly finished searching the bathroom and would move into the bedroom.

"Where are you, whore?" His voice grew closer.

She tensed and pressed the walking stick firmly against the opposite wall at ankle height.

Gatera passed through the door and tripped over her staff. The air *whooshed* from his lungs as he landed belly-down on the carpet. He growled his anger. "You bitch!"

She whacked her stick against where she thought his head should be.

The lights blinked off and on as the generators tried to restart. A low-wattage emergency light came on.

Eight feet ahead, Gatera's weapon glinted against the brown carpet.

Jess leaped on his back, flattening him to the carpet,

as she lunged for it. She grasped the pistol just as his hand grabbed her ankle.

She yanked free, stood, and turned, aiming the weapon at him with a shaking hand. Beyond point and pull the trigger, she had no idea how to use a pistol. Guns had safeties. She knew that but wasn't sure where the safety was located or how to release it. Gatera had fired earlier, so presumably he had already done that.

The generators grumbled to life.

The lights turned back on.

He rose slowly to his feet. His eyes raked her naked body, focusing on her left breast. "I was afraid you'd had those scars removed." He laughed. "Even if you had, you'd still be marked. You'd still have a souvenir of our special time together." He walked toward her, his hand out, ready to rip the weapon from her grasp.

She stepped backward with every step he took forward. "They're evidence. I'll have them removed once you're convicted."

"You would still know I was the cause." His smile personified evil. He took another step forward. "You won't fire. You don't have the guts."

"Watch me." She glanced at her trembling hand then pulled the trigger.

Not aiming.

Simply firing.

The sound filled her skull before pinging off the walls.

Her hand jerked from the kickback. She placed her left hand under her right to steady the firearm, then fired and fired and fired until Gatera sank to the floor.

Stunned, Jess stared at her shaking hand, not truly believing she'd pulled the trigger.

"*Docteur* Hemings—Jessica—please."

She looked down.

Gatera lay sprawled on the floor. A red flower bloomed on his right shoulder. He held his left hand against his left groin, but blood spurted between his fingers.

"Femoral artery." He gasped. "Do something."

Chapter Eighty

Jessica

Arusha, August 1, 1997

Seconds ticked by in a bizarre combination of painstaking slowness and ominous speed. If Jess did nothing, Gatera would be dead within 120 seconds.

"Plea—" His voice was weak. He was rapidly losing consciousness and his ability to apply sufficient pressure to stop his bleeding.

Jess wanted him dead. Wanted revenge for her sons. Wanted revenge for all the heartache he'd caused her. Wanted revenge for every Rwandan he'd killed.

"Fuck!" She couldn't allow life to drain from another human. Besides, she'd rather Gatera lived. She wanted to watch his face when he received a life sentence. When he realized his connections and wealth couldn't save him. When he realized his future lay in a crappy Third-World prison.

She laid the gun on the bed, knelt beside him, removed his hand, the hand that had slaughtered her babies, and with a shudder, placed her own hands against his groin, her fingers too near the penis that had violated her. Bone crunched as she applied pressure. She smiled grimly. Her bullet had shattered his proximal femur. Hip pain would be his constant companion for the rest of his life, a reminder of her revenge.

Afraid to remove her gaze from his bleeding groin, she cried out "Tom? Someone? Help. Help!" over and over, hoping Gatera lied, hoping he really hadn't killed Tom.

No answer. Only the whisper of the television.

In the distance, the faint wail of a siren. Was it real, or was it the TV? Hopefully the police and an ambulance were on their way.

Minutes later, a commotion rose behind her. Voices shouting. A loud crash. The splintering cracks of wood giving way.

Someone said, "Check out that guy."

"No pulse."

"Move him out of the way so we can get in."

Please, let *that guy* not be Tom.

Judging from the voices, several men entered the suite.

A familiar voice said, "Put him on the bed until the EMTs get here."

"Michel," she called. "Help! I need a stretcher in here."

"Jessica? Are you all right?"

"I'm fine." She didn't turn her head to answer. "How's Tom? Gatera said he killed him."

"The police are checking him out now."

An unfamiliar voice said, "He's alive but has a head injury and a wound on his left arm. An ambulance is on its way."

"The guard? Is he okay?" She turned to see Michel's face.

"Dead." Michel shook his head, his face tightening to contain his emotions. "He was a good man."

"We need two ambulances. Have someone call another. And find Tom's doctor bag and bring it to me." Tom always carried latex gloves and a liter of lactated

Ringer's solution for emergencies.

Michel rummaged through Tom's belongings until he found the valise. He brought it to Jess.

She gave him instructions. "Put on gloves, then place your hands just above mine. When I remove mine, immediately apply heavy pressure. Don't let up for any reason. I'm going to start an IV."

"You're trying to save this asshole's life?"

"Yeah." She rolled her eyes at the incongruity of her own actions. "Go figure."

They switched hands.

Jess wiped her bloody hands on Gatera's pants before she fished through Tom's bag. She gloved up while reviewing Gatera's ABC's—airway, breathing, circulation. He still had a pulse—barely. He was breathing—barely. What little blood he had left was circulating—barely. His wound was in the groin—no way to apply a tourniquet. He needed to be evacuated to a surgical center stat for stabilization before being air-evacuated to a hospital in Nairobi.

A policeman entered the room.

Jess commandeered him. "Take this"—she handed him the IV bag—"hold it high and squeeze it. He needs fluids as fast as possible."

The cop's gaze raked her.

Oh, God. She was naked. She pulled one of Tom's shirts from the closet and put it on, only taking time to close a couple of buttons.

With a deep breath, Jess grabbed Tom's bag and switched to clean gloves before checking him. He was unconscious, but his pulse was steady and his breathing normal. He had a whopping goose egg on his right temple. She lifted each eyelid and, with a small flashlight, checked his pupils. They were equal. He needed a CT scan, though, to rule out a temporal fracture. With cast scissors, she cut the sleeve off his wounded arm. Just a graze. Nothing that would affect his career. Relieved, she sighed.

Next she evaluated the guard. Definitely dead.

Ambulances arrived, and emergency medical technicians replaced Michel at Gatera's groin and carried Tom and Gatera away.

She tugged at Michel's arm. "Take me to the hospital. I need to see if Tom's okay."

Michel gently took her shoulder. "Jessica, you need to clean up and get dressed."

She looked down. Blood was everywhere. On Tom's shirt. On her hands, arms, abdomen, thighs. On the floor. Her adrenaline high fizzled out. She staggered as she fought for consciousness.

Michel caught her and deposited her on the bed. He slapped her cheeks twice. "Jessica, come back."

Angrily she shook her head. "Stop that. I'm all right. I just ran out of steam. Put pillows under my feet." With a start, she realized she'd touched Gatera's blood with bare hands. She moaned. "God, I need to be checked for HIV."

Michel gave a small laugh. "Even about to faint, you think like a *docteur*."

The policeman standing near her said, "Doctor Hemings, I need to ask you some questions."

"Surely she can have a moment to recover from her ordeal? She needs to shower and dress."

The policeman shook his head. "First, we need to test her hands for gunshot residue."

Michel threw an irritated glance at the man. "Do so quickly."

Chapter Eighty-One

Tom

Arusha, August 3, 1997

Tom and Jess sat across from each other in the restaurant at the Novatel. Michel had found them rooms in the hotel where the UN housed its staff. He also provided bodyguards until the police completed their investigation. In fact, their bored-looking guardians sat a table away.

The knot on Tom's head had all but disappeared, leaving behind a violet bruise. His arm remained in a sling which now he only wore for the sympathy factor. Otherwise he'd recovered. He continued telling Jess what had happened. "I heard pops outside the door. They sounded like firecrackers, so I went to investigate. When I peeked out, Gatera fired through the door, catching me in the arm. He shoved his way in and cold-cocked me with his pistol."

Jess patted his hand. "I'm sorry you got dragged into this mess."

"Don't worry, babe."

"I'm not your babe anymore, remember?"

"Not yet." Tom studied Jess's stubbled head. Without competition from her wild hair, the bony structures underlying her eyebrows and cheeks were architectural wonders. "Thanks for taking care of me, babe."

"You're hopeless." She shook her head, but grinned, then bent her head and slurped her second banana milkshake. For some reason, she seemed obsessed with them.

He grew thoughtful as he took her hand. "Remember our last night in Napa? The hot tub. The stars. The whole night was magical." He pulled the tanzanite ring from his pocket and slipped it on her finger. "We can recapture those feelings. It's not too late. Come home with me. Marry me."

She looked down at the ring, spun it around on her finger, then licked her lips nervously. "It's beautiful, Tom." With a twist, she removed it and returned it. "I can't." She shook her head. "You were my once-in-a-lifetime love. I believed we might have what my parents have. That color didn't matter. That we might live happily ever after. But—"

"We still can."

"No." She shook her head. "You chose a different path and lacked the courtesy to tell me."

"I wanted to tell you. I wanted the fellowship so badly, but applying for it meant hurting you. I put off telling you, hoping to find a way—but every way I thought of would hurt you. And I didn't want to—"

"Bullshit. You chose a different life. You chose to lie by omission. You chose to be unfaithful." She snorted and turned away.

He couldn't see her tears, but he heard them.

"You chose a White woman."

"Jess—"

"Damn you, Tom. She was blonde, busty, beautiful, tall—everything I'm not." She faced him, her eyes glaring behind the sheen of tears.

He couldn't believe she'd said those words. Didn't Jess realize *she* was everything he wanted? He rubbed his face, talking through his hands. "I can't explain what happened with Kimberley. I was drunk. Drunker than I've ever been in my life. I made a stupid mistake." He shook his head then admitted the truth. "I was mad at you because you weren't with me to celebrate the most important day of my life. Can't you forgive me? I still love you. I've never stopped loving you."

She shook her head. "The naive young woman you loved no longer exists."

"Damn, you're as hard-headed as ever. Everything has to be black and white. You leave no margin for error." He blew out an exasperated breath. "Jesus Christ, you're angry all the time. Every time we're together, you start an argument. Get some help. See a shrink or something."

She waved her hand before her face as if her motion would ward off the upcoming disagreement. "Let's agree to disagree."

Tom got the message. Instead of forcing the issue, he touched her hand. "In Rusumo, you promised to tell me everything."

"I've gone back and forth trying on whether or not to keep that promise. You're not the problem. I am. I'm not the woman you think you love. And I'll never be her again." Jess told him everything. "I suffer from PTSD. Almost every night I wake up screaming. I rarely get through a day without a panic attack." When she spoke, pain tinged her voice. "With time, your mind doesn't erase traumas. They become clearer. You remember everything as precisely as a photograph. The accumulated spirits of everyone you watched die, of everyone you didn't help, of everyone you killed haunt you—"

Shocked at the *you killed*, Tom looked at her. She

wasn't sitting at the table with him. She was somewhere else completely.

She seemed unaware of his gaze as she continued. "Their eyes—sad, bewildered, innocent, angry, insane, dull, blank—pop into your mind when you least expect them. Especially the children's eyes. You relive those traumatic episodes time and time again." She closed her eyes. "Some days you wake up with the scenes in your head and go to bed with them still playing, like an endless-play loop you can't escape."

"Back home you could get some help." His voice rose with his desperate plea.

"Working with Susan, I learned I didn't belong in the States anymore. I really want to be here—and you don't. Even way back then, you didn't want to be here but loved me too much to admit it. Tom, we weren't meant to be together. Let's admit it and move on."

Tom remained silent. What could he say? He'd seen enough in his few days in Africa to empathize with the natives, their poverty, their lack of access to First-World amenities, but he'd hate the limitations of living here. From big items like the erratic power and water supply to little things like not being able to sing in the shower for fear of getting contaminated water in his mouth. Not to mention the inability to practice the type of medicine he trained for years to provide.

Across the table sat the woman he'd once loved with all his heart. Once … once … once. His brain registered the word within seconds of his thought. "Once" meant "no longer." After being in love with Jess since attending Swarthmore, in an instant, he realized he didn't love her anymore. He'd pursued her all these months thinking she truly hadn't changed, not underneath. She'd lost a little weight, seemed somewhat subdued, but if they resumed their relationship, she'd bounce back. With his love, she'd recover. The scars on her chest. He'd have those removed. It wasn't that he couldn't—or wouldn't—love her with them, but they were an outward sign of her damaged interior. If she got rid of them, he'd bet her emotional state would improve.

He shook his head, trying to ward off visions of Jess with a gun. The Jess he'd known—the anti-violence, anti-gun, anti-war, pro-choice woman—would never have pulled the trigger. Tom slid the ring into his pocket. Thank goodness she had more sense than he did. He couldn't bear to hurt her again.

"Tom?"

With a start, he realized he'd gotten bogged down in his thoughts. Her voice brought him back to the moment.

"Tom, tell me you understand. Please?"

"I do, Jess." And, somehow, he did.

Chapter Eighty-Two

Michel

Arusha, February 14, 1998

Six months later, as Michel wound down his morning duties, his intercom beeped. Lizette said, "Sir, Dr. Hemings is here."

Jessica was a bit early for their weekly lunch. "I'll be right out." He put his computer to sleep then opened the door.

She walked toward him, wiggling a paper bag in the air. "Our lunch."

Her watery blue-green eyes signaled something was disturbing her. With Jessica, he always hesitated to pry, but she seemed extraordinarily sad. He guided her inside his office. "Let's eat in here."

Without a word, she hunched over his desk and began removing their take-out.

After closing the door, he bent, gave her a quick peck on the cheek, then rested his hand on her shoulder. His thumb grazed her neck, stroking her hard, tight muscles. He winced on seeing the most accurate predictor of her emotional state—that patch of skin on her neck. "You're not yourself today, *ma caille*. What's going on?"

She tilted her head and rubbed her cheek against his hand. "My sons would have been five today."

At her sniffle, he pulled her into a hug. He wasn't sure whether to be relieved or worried that her shoulders shook, but she didn't cry.

Instead, out of the blue, she jerked from his embrace. "Does Manon know about us? Have you told her I'm here?"

Somehow, in the past months, while they struggled to keep their own emotions at bay, they'd acted like his wife and her fiancé didn't exist. Michel blew out a long breath. "She knows. She understands what happened between us—I think. She forgave me—I think. When you arrived in Arusha, I told her I needed to meet with you because you're a witness for the ICTR. That we're not sleeping together. No *chimie*—no chemistry—exists between us and never has."

He didn't tell her Manon moved into the guest bedroom when he told her and had only recently returned to his bed.

Jessica nodded.

No freer than he'd been when he and Jessica first met, Michel understood they couldn't make a relationship work—too much shared trauma both united and separated them. Besides, Manon still gave him a joy he'd never known, and that *soupçon* of friction when she got pissed off gave an exciting edge to their relationship. And, *mon Dieu,* their make-up sex—*c'est magnifique.* "What about you and Tom? Are you still engaged?"

"Engaged? Not in years. If he told you that, it was his wishful thinking. He asked again just before he went back to the States. I turned him down.

"He's out completely of the picture?" At her nod, Michel asked, "So what are your plans?"

Jessica gave him a cockeyed glance from still-sad eyes. "Keep working, of course."

"I thought you might take some time off."

"What for?"

"Jessica, you don't want to hear this, but you need a *psychiatre*. You suffer from PTSD. It's time to get some help."

"I know what the problem is," she all but snarled. "The nearest shrink is in Nairobi, which isn't terribly convenient."

Michel didn't think he'd ever heard her so angry. He pulled out his wallet. "This is my psychiatrist's name. Call him. It's short-term therapy. Only three months. *Docteur* Apollinaire helped me a lot. He saved me. Which saved my marriage. You can stay in our apartment in Paris."

"I doubt therapy will help until Gatera is tried and sentenced." She shook her head fiercely. "I need to know he's been punished. I need the closure."

Michel dropped the subject but noticed she put the card in her pocket. Pursuing the topic might cost him her friendship. He blew out a long, resigned breath. "*Très bien*. I'll be here for you when your traumas catch up to you."

Chapter Eighty-Three

Michel

Arusha, September 1998

Michel and several other lawyers working for the ICTR registry formed one of three teams assigned to a particular Trial Chamber and were responsible for its smooth functioning. They passed an indictment with a precise description of Gatera's crimes and a statement of the facts regarding those crimes to a Trial Judge for review and confirmation. Charges included Genocide, Complicity in Genocide, Incitement to Commit Genocide, and Crimes Against Humanity. Witnesses were not named but identified with a letter of the alphabet. Ironically, Jessica—Dr. X—became Victim X.

Though Gatera had been flown to a hospital in Nairobi, once the injured man was coherent and legally competent to stand trial, Michel and his team drew up an arrest warrant and began work on Gatera's prosecution.

Over a year later, when Gatera recovered from his wounds and completed physical therapy, he was returned to Arusha to await trial. As expected, he pleaded not guilty.

Michel had warned Jessica, "You know it may be years before Gatera's case comes before the Tribunal."

"I've waited this long. I can wait longer."

****

Arusha, March 2000

Nearly two years later, Michel walked into the courtroom, paused, and glanced around, taking in the familiar carpet, light reddish-brown furniture, the mural on the wall, and the woman—Jessica—sitting across the room from his own seat at the prosecutors' desk.

Even before Gatera's trial date had been set, Jessica haunted the ICTR courtroom every minute she could escape from work. She worked the overnight shift then endured the hearings until court was dismissed. Michel wasn't sure when—or if—she slept. She'd gained some weight but not enough. Her hair had grown out, but she wore it trimmed in a short cap rather than the long, tousled curls he found so beguiling. The ugly patch of skin on her neck waxed and waned depending on her state of mind.

At last, Gatera came before the Tribunal. Michel was shocked at how the man had changed. His hair was grizzled. His face wrinkled. He leaned heavily on a cane with a large brass knob and walked with a slow, painful-appearing gait.

"Jessica," Michel told her just before the trial started, "I can't prep you for testimony because—"

"Because we were lovers?"

He nodded. "I'll have Chincia Achike prime you. She's a good lawyer." He referred Jess to the section of the Registry providing support for witnesses ranging from expert psychological support to witness protection, hoping she would get the emotional help she needed.

The trial dragged on for weeks. In random moments, Michel watched Jessica. For Gatera's trial, she had taken a leave of absence from Mount Meru Hospital and had become as much a feature in court as the UN flag and the banner reading *International Criminal Tribunal for Rwanda*. Even after all this time, the testimony and evidence stirred Michel's emotions. For her, the emotional pain must be exponentially greater, yet her face remained stoic. He knew how strongly she'd built the compartments that contained the traumas she'd endured. Still, she remained obsessed with punishing the *génocidaire*.

Gatera's neighbors, hospital personnel, other physicians, and run-of-the-mill Rwandans testified against him. Despite being hidden behind screens with their voices mechanically distorted, they sounded uncertain and nervous. Like many of the ICTR's witnesses, they feared reprisals. Gatera, if he didn't go to prison, would be *persona non grata* everywhere else in the world, and he'd be forced to return to Rwanda. Potentially, they could be living next door to the man they were accusing and might encounter him in the hospital, on the golf course, or at the Mille Collines swimming pool. But spunky Jessica *wanted* Gatera to know she was testifying against him.

So far, she'd handled her testimony with aplomb, despite the defense attorneys' distorted account of her relationship with Gatera. The monster claimed that *she* had neglected the Tutsi patients who'd died. She then seduced him to impede his report to CHUK's board. Despite her attempts to compromise him, Gatera informed on her, and in retaliation, she'd accused him—a model citizen and caring, capable physician—of being a *génocidaire*.

Today Jessica, outwardly calm, sat in the witness box not twenty feet from the man who'd raped her, killed her children, killed her patients, killed her friends and employees. She wore an outfit Michel hadn't seen before, a slim skirt with a blouse that crisscrossed her breasts and tied at her waist. In her only outward sign of nervousness, she fiddled with the ties on her blouse. The strange half-smile she displayed worried him.

The judge said, "You may step down now, Dr. Hemings."

"I have evidence that hasn't been presented yet."

The judge looked puzzled, glanced at the prosecution.

Michel shrugged.

The judge returned his gaze to Jessica. "Please explain."

"I need to show you." Jess tugged at the ribbons at her waist.

Fuck! Instantly Michel understood what Jess planned. He rose, reached to stop her—too late.

Her blouse fell open. As bare-breasted as a Greek statue, she revealed the scars on her chest.

The entire courtroom gasped.

Michel glanced at his fellow lawyers. From the expressions on their faces, they hadn't expected her action either.

Chapter Eighty-Four

Jessica

Arusha, March 2000

Jess sat in the courtroom awaiting Gatera's arrival for his sentencing. Thanks to her, he was no longer the robust man who organized mass killings. His squeaky high voice remained, yet his massive body had shrunk. Heavily leaning on his cane, he limped into the courtroom.

Her lips twisted into a grim smile. His lameness wasn't his only souvenir of their battle in the hotel. He held his atrophied right arm against his side, his hand curved into a claw. Not only had she shattered his left hip, she'd destroyed the nerves feeding into his right arm. She was grateful that, if he evaded prison, he'd never practice medicine again. As she remembered the Tutsi women he allowed to die from neglect and the mothers and babies—her own included—he'd killed in her clinic, she tightened her jaw. The bastard deserved whatever punishment the ICTR handed down. It didn't matter whether the ICTR gave him twenty years or life, he would die long before his release.

Seeking sympathy, he played his infirmity for all it was worth. Once seated, he rested his cane between his knees and caressed its large brass knob.

Jess shivered while staring at his walking stick. It reminded her of the *nta mpongano y'umwanzi*, the clubs studded with nails the *Interahamwe* used to kill their victims. She was certain he chose it to intimidate the witnesses against him. She had done her best to ensure that the *no mercy to the enemy* applied to him.

With his defense attorneys at his side, Gatera stood for sentencing.

"Life imprisonment."

Though supported by his cane, Gatera staggered. The lawyer to his left grabbed him and propped him up.

As UN soldiers escorted him from the courtroom, he turned to Jess. "You still bear my scars."

"I'm free." She couldn't help giving a smile of resolute satisfaction. "And you're far more scarred than I am."

A soldier jerked Gatera to move him along. The door closed behind Gatera, locking him into his new life.

Jess exited the courtroom. Sorrow, relief, pain, grief, all circled her heart, everything but the joy she'd expected. Suddenly weak-kneed, she dropped onto a nearby bench and started her breathing exercises. Maybe revenge was best not served at all. Inhale. Exhale. She took another breath. Inhale. Exhale. No *hold*. She smiled. Without the weight of the *génocidaire* on her shoulders, she could finally breathe.

On the way home, she stopped at the grocery store and picked up several cardboard boxes.

Seated at her desk, she placed document after document in the cartons, ridding herself of all the research she'd collected. She copied her genocide computer files to micro-floppy discs and tucked them in a manila envelope. The worst—or perhaps the best—part about letting go would be saying goodbye to the ghosts of her children, so Jess saved the photographs for last.

In the end, she kept the last "happy" picture of

herself with the two boys. She prayed she'd never again gaze at Jean-Baptiste's pictures of the havoc Gatera had wreaked upon her clinic, the mothers and children massacred at her clinic. With a resolute sigh, she put those photos in the box. Michel would pick up everything the next day, preserving her paperwork for Gatera's inevitable appeals.

Jess studied her empty file cabinet and empty desk. Instead of loss, a little green shoot of hope unfurled in her heart. Because Gatera found her before she found him, she still had most of the money she'd worked so hard to save. She could afford a vacation.

The next morning, Michel came by in a UN vehicle. She helped him carry her boxes outside.

"On one hand, I wish you'd warned me beforehand about that little stunt you pulled." He shoved the last carton in the trunk. "On the other, Gatera's lawyers told me your revelation cinched the case against him."

"I'm glad. He deserves to spend the rest of his life in prison." She handed over the envelope filled with floppy discs. "I've extended my leave of absence for a few months."

"Why?"

"I decided to take your advice." She flapped a business card in his face. "I'm going to Paris."

Michel grabbed her and whirled her around half-a-dozen times. "You can stay in our apartment."

She grimaced. "That's probably not a good idea. I'll find somewhere else to stay—for the sake of your marriage—but I wanted you to know I was leaving. And why."

"You won't regret it, *ma caille*. *Docteur* Apollinaire is exceptional." Michel drove away, calling "*Au revoir*" out the window as he waved farewell.

Jess returned to her desk and, after unbuttoning the top two buttons of her blouse, slipped her hand in her bra, her fingers running over the scars, feeling the smooth, raised skin and the sharp tingle of damaged nerves. She'd run from Tom. She'd run from Gatera—twice. She'd denied herself pleasure, even love, for the sake of revenge.

This time she was running *toward* something—Paris and her sanity. She'd get fat on French bread and butter, buy all the fancy underwear she wanted, take a sexy French lover, and—she studied the postcards she'd bought in Paris—visit the Louvre, the Eiffel Tower, the Dôme des Invalides, all the dreams she'd relinquished.

She flipped the business card Michel had given her end over end, over and over, her eyes following its circular course. The revolutions of the card between her fingers slowed, then stopped. Before she changed her mind, she emailed Ambrose Apollinaire, Psychiatre to let him know of her arrival.

Glossary

FAR — *Forces Armées Rwandaises, the Hutu military*

GNS — *Global News Syndicate, a fictitious news agency similar to Associated Press*

ICRC — *International Committee of the Red Cross*

ICTR — *International Criminal Tribunal for Rwanda*

MRND — *National Republican Movement for Democracy and Development, the governing party of Rwanda*

MSF — *Médecins Sans Frontières, Doctors Without Borders*

NGO — *Non-governmental organization*

PARFA — *Physicians Aid and Relief for Africa, a fictitious foreign aid NGO*

RPF — *Rwandan Patriotic Front or Front Patriotique Rwandais, the Tutsi military*

RTML — *Radio Télévision Libre des Mille Collines, a hate radio station*

UNAMIR — *United Nations Assistance Mission for Rwanda*

If you're interested in reading more about Rwanda, genocide, or Africa in general:

Fiction:
1994 A Novel of Rwanda by L.K. Branson
In the Shadow of 10,000 Hills by Jennifer Haupt
Say You're One of Them by Uwem Akpan
A Sunday at the Pool in Kigali by Gil Courtemanche

Nonfiction:
A People Betrayed: The Role of the West in Rwanda's Genocide by L.R. Melvern

Africa: A History by Alvin M. Josephy

An Ordinary Man: An Autobiography by Paul Rusesabagina

As We Forgive: Stories of Reconciliation from Rwanda by Catherine Claire Larson

Human Death in Rwanda: Deaths by Firearm in Rwanda, Massacres in Rwanda, People Executed by Rwanda, Rwandan Genocide by Books LLC

Journalism's Roving Eye: A History of American Foreign Reporting by John Maxwell Hamilton

Land of a Thousand Hills: My Life in Rwanda by Rosamond Halsey Carr and Ann Howard Halsey

Life Laid Bare: The Survivors in Rwanda Speak Jean Hatzfeld and Linda Coverdale

Machete Season: The Killers in Rwanda Speak by Jean Hatzfeld and Susan Sontag

Manners in Rwanda: Basic Knowledge on Rwandan Culture, Customs, and Kinyarwanda Language (Multilingual Edition) by Joy Nzamwita Uwanziga

The Media and the Rwanda Genocide, edited by Allan Thompson, with a statement by Kofi Annan,

International Development Research Centre.

The Men Who Killed me: Rwandan Survivors of Sexual Violence edited by Anne-Marie de Brouwer and Sandra Ka Hon Chu

Military-Civilian Interactions: Humanitarian Crises and the Responsibility to Protect, Second edition by Thomas G Weiss

Mountains Beyond Mountains: The Quest of Dr. Paul Farmer, a Man Who Would Cure the World by Tracy Kidder

My War Gone By, I Miss It So by Anthony Loyd

Newsweek, April 18, 1994, "Suicide: Why Do People Kill Themselves?", article on Rwanda

On A Hill Far Away by C. Albert Snyder

Shake Hands with the Devil: The Failure of Humanity in Rwanda by Roméo Dallaire

Strength in What Remains by Tracy Kidder

Time Magazine April 18, 1994, Vol. 143 No. 16, "Is It All Over for Smokers? The Battle Against Tobacco is Turning into a Rout." Article: 'Descent into Mayhem (Central Africa): Tribal slaughter erupts in Rwanda, trapping foreigners and forcing the U.S. to send troops to the region'

Time Magazine May 16, 1994 "There are no devils left in Hell," the missionary said. "They are all in Rwanda." Article: 'Why? The Killing Fields of Rwanda'

We Wish to Inform You That Tomorrow We Will Be Killed with Our Families: Stories From Rwanda by Philip Gourevitch

Map of Jessica's Escape through Rwanda and Tanzania

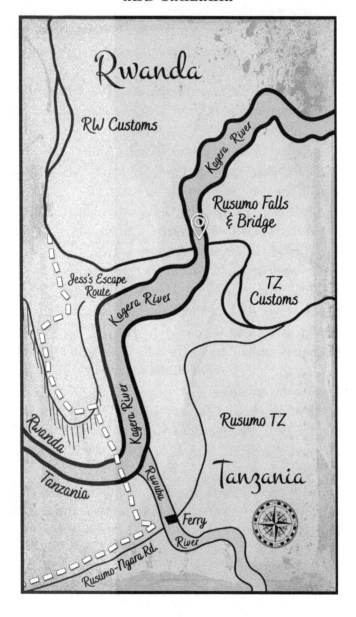

If you're interested in other maps of the region:
http://www.nationsonline.org/oneworld/map/rwanda_map2.htm
https://www.nationsonline.org/oneworld/tanzania.htm

Book Club Questions for

Hunting the Devil

1. What did *Hunting the Devil* teach you about Rwanda?

2. How does the enmity between Jessica and Gatera mirror the tumultuous history of Rwanda?

3. Each character represents a different type of reaction to the genocide. Discuss these reactions and why each character was best-suited to demonstrate that reaction.

4. Who suffers the most in this story? Why?

5. Jessica's obsession with punishing Gatera borders on vigilante-ism. Is her behavior justified? Why or why not?

6. Would the story have ended differently if Tom hadn't been unfaithful? How about Michel? How does their infidelity differ?

7. How do you think the characters fare after the story ends? Do you think healing is possible for such scarred people?

8. Which leg in the love triangle between Jessica-Michel-Tom would most likely to succeed in the future? Or are all doomed to failure?

9. *What are the odds Jess will have a happily-ever-after? Would you read a sequel in which that happened?*

10. *Did the book change your feelings on racial discrimination? Why or Why not?*

11. *How is sexual violence used in the book? Did the book change your attitudes toward the current #MeToo movement?*

12. *Could this novel be made into a movie? If so, who would you cast in the lead roles?*

13. *What is your favorite quote from the novel? Why?*

14. *What do you think of how the story ends? Is justice served?*

15. *The novel includes many universal themes, including, but not limited to, the importance of friendship, the nature of family, redemption, the nature of justice. Which theme affected you the most while reading? Which theme now stands out to you after discussing this novel with others?*

16. *Were you surprised to learn about the racial tension between the Tutsis and Hutus in Rwanda? Can you think of any culture in the world without a history of oppression? Why do you think minority groups are so often oppressed?*

Author Bio

Suanne Schafer was born in West Texas at the height of the Cold War. Now a retired family-practice physician whose only child has fledged the nest, her world travels and pioneer ancestors fuel her imagination and her writing. Originally, she'd planned to pen romances, but either as a consequence of a series of failed relationships or a genetic distrust of happily-ever-after, her heroines are strong women who battle tough environments and intersect with men who might—or might not—love them.

CPSIA information can be obtained
at www.ICGtesting.com
Printed in the USA
BVHW032020300919
559818BV00001B/9/P